The Mad

and Slaves of the Laughing Death

THE SPIDER®

TWO CLASSIC ADVENTURES OF

by Norvell W. Page
writing as Grant Stockbridge

plus a new historical essay
by Will Murray

SANCTUM BOOKS

This Sanctum Books edition is an unabridged republication of the text and illustrations of two stories from *The Spider* magazine, as originally published by Popular Publications, Inc., N.Y.: *The Mad Horde* from the May 1934 issue, and *Slaves of the Laughing Death* from the March 1940 issue. These stories are works of their time. Consequently, the text is reprinted intact in its original historical form, including occasional out-of-date ethnic and cultural stereotyping. Typographical errors have been tacitly corrected in this edition.

International Standard Book Number: 978-1-60877-206-3

First printing: May 2016

Series editor/publisher: Anthony Tollin
anthonytollin@shadowsanctum.com

Consulting editor: Will Murray

Copy editor: Joseph Wrzos

Proofreader: Carl Gafford

OCR text reconstruction: Rich Harvey

Cover restoration: Michael Piper

The editors gratefully acknowledge the contributions of John Locke, Chris Kalb (www.spiderreturns.com) and Bill Thom (www.pulpcomingattractions.com).

Published by Sanctum Books
P.O. Box 761474, San Antonio, TX 78245-1474

THE MASTER OF MEN!

SPIDER®

Volume 9

Thrilling Tales and Features

THE MAD HORDE
by Norvell W. Page (writing as "Grant Stockbridge") 4

THE WEB by Will Murray 68

SLAVES OF THE LAUGHING DEATH
by Norvell W. Page (writing as "Grant Stockbridge") ... 72

Cover art by Raphael DeSoto

Back cover art by Raphael DeSoto
and John Newton Howitt

Interior illustrations by J.T. Fleming-Gould

ABOVE THE LAW ... SWORN ENEMY OF THE UNDERWORLD ... HATED BY BOTH ...

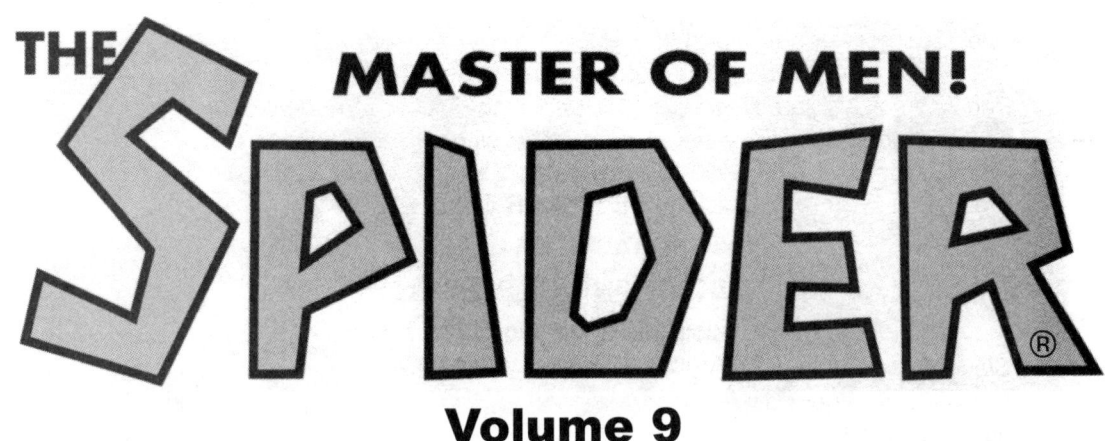

The Mad Horde

By Grant Stockbridge

CHAPTER ONE
The Maniac Kills

THE shortwave radio beneath the dash of Richard Wentworth's roadster whistled in thin crescendo, and a voice rasped out: "Scout car 2103, go to 567 Crossroads Street. An insane man is in the house. Scout car 2103, go to..."

The dispatcher's voice broke its stereotyped sing-song and grew clipped and hurried.

"… an insane man in the house. WGPK, Cologne Police, Dispatcher Frederick. *Hurry! He's killing someone!"*

Wentworth felt the horror that caught at the throat of that dispatcher, used as he was to the chronicle of a hundred crimes a night. A maniac, killing someone— A tingle ran down Wentworth's spine. He peered out beneath the pale brows that were part of his disguise and spotted a street sign, white letters showing against an enameled blue field: *Crossroads Street.*

"Stop the car," Wentworth ordered, and Ram Singh, his Hindu servant, swerved to the curb, the powerful motor soundless beneath its sleek, streamlined hood. The night was a smother of darkness upon a suburban street of homes whose windows were yellow oblongs. It was June, but there was no softness in the air. There was heat, sultry as the breath of Hell, and on the far horizon sheets of lightning shimmered.

Wentworth listened and felt coldness run like poison through his veins—felt his scalp tingle beneath the close clasp of the blond wig that concealed his own crisp black locks. To any man it

Wolves—dogs—cats—vampire bats—all victims of hydrophobia—spreading death-dealing havoc.

Never before in history had anything quite so horrible as the Mad Horde been loosed upon a terrified humanity! In rural towns and through the thronging streets of great cities the death-bringers stalked, spreading the slow madness of which they themselves must soon die! The SPIDER, dismayed and horrified as never before in his long career, is forced at last into risking the life of the girl he loves—so that a million others may live!

would have been horrible, that cracked hoarse and high-pitched bark and the yammering, senseless howls that followed.

They died out as if the throat that sent them shivering into the night had strangled over the cry and choked it off slowly. The sound itself was terrifying. But to Wentworth it spelt a far more fearful menace. For that cry, blood-chilling and full of an eerie threat, was the howl of a dog gone mad. And Wentworth, driving disguised through an Ohio town, knew that somewhere in this vicinity was a man who had recently purchased five thousand dogs!

"Wait and watch," Wentworth told Ram Singh and sprang to the pavement, his hand sliding to the flat automatic beneath his arm. He waited for the dog to cry again. It did not howl, but another sound tore the night apart—sent Wentworth sprinting down the pavement toward a house whose windows blazed light. That sound, rising high and shrill in the evening silence, tightened Wentworth's heart with dread. It was the cry of a woman in mortal terror, screaming hoarse words of frenzied, pleading protest.

"Do-on't! 0-o-o-o-h—God!"

Then silence. Silence in which the swift thudding of Wentworth's feet was like the heartbeats of time. He cut across grass, took four steps to the porch of the house in a single bound, crashed his elbow through the glass panel of the door. Broken fragments glistened on the floor, fragments that contained numbers in gilt and black. 567.

Go to 567 Crossroads Street, an insane man in the house—

That hurried radio message echoed in Wentworth's ears as he reached through the broken glass, unlatched the door and flung inside. A moment before terror had screamed in the house; now it was still, as still as death. In the hall a lamp with a red shade gave dim light. Beyond a partly closed door, white brilliance blazed. Then Wentworth heard it, a snorting sound that was half like the short bark of a dog, half like a human being breathing.

The partly opened door moved slowly, and a man with massive shoulders, with a drooping shaggy head, was silhouetted against the light. In his right hand he held a hatchet that was smeared with blood.

The man's chest labored. From his mouth issued the snorting half-bark that was like a worried dog. As he gazed at Wentworth, his jaws began to champ, to snap together like a slavering wolf's. White foam flecked his lips. Wentworth knew those dread symptoms. *The man had hydrophobia!* One scratch from his teeth meant death! The man raised the hatchet with its bloody bit, charged.

WENTWORTH slid aside like a shadow before an advancing lamp. As the madman blundered past, slashing violently downward with the hatchet, Wentworth slipped a blackjack from his pocket and struck accurately behind the ear. The madman fell, his body twitching horribly. His jaws snapping.

Wentworth darted beyond him into the room of brilliant light. It was a shambles. Two children, a boy of ten, a girl a few years younger, lay upon the floor, their skulls crushed. No life there. But the woman, her forehead gashed, her golden hair streaked with blood, still breathed.

Snatching out a first aid kit, Wentworth dropped to his knees beside her. A hypodermic needle shot in its stimulant. His hands moved skillfully as a surgeon's. Bent over its task, his face was keen, the gray-blue eyes alert.

Despite the disguise, the pale brows above his eyes, the straw-yellow hair that bristled upward with Teutonic brusqueness, the square-built forehead and jaw which Wentworth's makeup genius had contrived, the vital strength of the man was apparent. Calm behind those wide-spaced eyes was such a brain as is given mankind only once in a generation, the brain that made him a Master of Men, that inspired the genius-directed Crusades of justice, that had created the *Spider*.

To his ears as he worked came the whining crescendo of a police siren. He worked on, trying to bring one instant of consciousness to this dying woman, one instant of intelligence during which she might give him some clue to the cause of her husband's hydrophobia. The man Wentworth hunted might well be behind it.

He bent lower over the woman as the first fluttering sigh of returning consciousness stirred her breasts, tautened them against the thin cheapness of her calico house dress. Wentworth waved smelling salts beneath her nose. Footsteps pounded on the porch. The woman jerked as the salts knifed into her nostrils. Her eyes flew open.

"Quickly," said Wentworth, "was your husband ever bitten by a dog or a cat?"

The woman's eyes clouded with pain.

"No!" she gasped. "Have you called in a strange doctor?"

Wentworth saw in the woman's eyes that he had guessed the truth. But the footsteps now were in the hall.

"Quick! His name!" he ordered.

The woman's lips opened, sound began.

"Hands up, you!" a voice ground out behind Wentworth.

He jerked his head about, eyes blazing. Two police stood with leveled guns.

"Shut up!" Wentworth ordered. He whirled back to the woman, bent close. His hand shot to her throat. There was no pulse. He worked frantically for a few moments, then straightened slowly. The woman was dead. If those police had delayed a half second longer—Wentworth got to his feet, turned toward the men.

"Did you put handcuffs on him?" he demanded. "He'll be coming around in a few seconds, and—"

The guns thrust their muzzles toward him. "Hands up!" one of the police ordered again. The muscles knotted along the ridge of his heavy, outthrust jaw.

Wentworth's blue-gray eyes were like flame. "Fool!" he spat out. "I'm the doctor. Put handcuffs on that man in the hall!"

"There ain't no man in the hall," said the cop stolidly. He swallowed heavily. His face was pale and his eyes shuddered away from the three who were horribly dead upon the floor. "And you're coming along with us! We found the hatchet you used."

"Is he gone?" Wentworth's tones were excited. "Good Lord, officer, that man has rabies, hydrophobia. He's crazy. He'll go around killing every living thing he meets. Don't you understand?"

THE men still stared at him stolidly, the guns unwavering in their hands.

"Get around behind him, Oscar," directed the square-jawed cop. "If he's got a gun, take it."

"You fools!" Wentworth snapped, then caught himself up. There was nothing to be accomplished through argument. Eventually, he would convince them. But meantime, that madman was loose in the city, that mad dog whose howl had shivered through the air was a constant, horrible menace.

Wentworth's lips opened. From them poured a high-toned cracked bark, a series of senseless, choked howls. The square jaw of the cop dropped open. He retreated a step. Wentworth sprang sideways into the path of the one called Oscar. Oscar threw up his gun with a cry of fright. It was wrenched from his grasp almost before it was raised. A thrust on the throat sent him reeling, strangling backward upon his companion.

Wentworth fired upward. The lights went out. Blackness shut down upon those pitiful, hacked bodies, upon two frightened and dazed police. Wentworth went out a window. A flitting shadow plunged toward him. Lightning flamed across the heavens, glinted on the fearsomely bared teeth of the shadow, a dog that sprang without sound, whose least scratch meant death by torture!

Wentworth hurdled the charging beast. As his feet struck the ground, he whirled and fired. The beast fell, writhing. The menace of the mad dog was eliminated. But the madman was free, his brain numbed by the agony of the disease, goaded by its torturing pain to strike at every living thing that crossed his path. Wentworth's lips puckered and he sent a wailing, high-pitched whistle into the night. The answer came from three blocks down the blackened street. Wentworth whirled that way, sprinting.

On all sides excited voices were calling back and forth from the closely clustered homes. The shouts of police were hoarse. Wentworth heard their blundering stumbles in the house. Their white lights stabbed rays about, thrust inquiringly out the window and found the carcass of the mad dog. Wentworth's swift feet left behind the confusion of their search for him. His car whined backward up the street. He sprang to the seat beside Ram Singh.

"A man who left the house just before the police came! Where is he?"

The Hindu's dark face jerked toward Wentworth, his eyes glinting.

"He took a car from the next house, Sahib." His words came in rapid Hindustani. "He drove like a man without his senses toward the highway."

"Follow him," Wentworth ordered, his chest stirring to the rhythm of his swift run. "That man is without his senses. He is mad. God help anyone he meets tonight!"

CHAPTER TWO
Castle of Gloom

THE Hispania's tires moaned as the big car swung from Crossroads Street into the Columbus Road. Ram Singh nailed the accelerator to the floor and presently a spot of red dancing like a firefly showed ahead of them on the highway.

The Hispania droned on. The car ahead became defined in the back glow of its own headlights. It was a small coupe. As Wentworth watched, it yawed widely, sidled almost off the highway, then darted with equal vehemence for the opposite side. It continued to zig-zag like that, though its pace was furious.

"Ease off," Wentworth ordered tensely.

He knew what that erratic driving meant. The madman's paroxysm of insanity had passed. He was in the grip of one of those semi-sane interludes of pain when he was stricken with a partial paralysis, but during which his mind was more nearly normal. The man must have some purpose in driving along this road when he persisted despite the pangs of hydrophobia. Was he intent on vengeance, or—?

The last of Cologne's street lights flickered past. The road swooped up and down over rolling hills like a Coney Island switchback. Woods, as black as the storm clouds piling on the horizon, alternated with the sweeping smooth lawns of rich estates. And ever ahead danced that firefly taillight.

Sultry wind in his face, Wentworth lounged back into the soft depths of the Hispania's cushions, his mind racing like his roadster's flying wheels. What fearful thing was this that threatened, heralded by a mad dog's cracked and senseless howling?

Wentworth had come west to trail a clever and

ruthless criminal named, among other aliases, Douglas Brent. A brief story in *The New York Times* had attracted the ever-alert mind of the *Spider*. It stated that the Associated Societies for Prevention of Cruelty to Animals had protested against the sale of dogs from the pound—where they were supposed to be destroyed painlessly—to scientists who used them for vivisection. The story had stated that in two weeks the New York pound had sold a thousand dogs.

What experiment could require such vast quantities of dogs? Wentworth, investigating, had discovered that during recent months, five thousand dogs had been sold to one man in Cologne, Ohio. A man who gave the name of Douglas Brent. The description of this man—he had been forced to appear personally to arrange the unusual transaction—had sent Wentworth racing to his home, had sped him and Ram Singh westward to Cologne.

For the secret, exhaustive files of the *Spider*, mysterious avenger who devoted his life and vast fortune to checking crime, revealed Douglas Brent as a shrewd and utterly unscrupulous criminal who many times had skated perilously close to the gates of prison, once for a particularly brutal and merciless murder in which an alibi had won him an acquittal. Because his crimes had not menaced the people at large, he never before had warranted the *Spider*'s swift justice. But now, a menace as vast as it was horrible was centering about the sinister figure of this man. How vast, Wentworth still could not fathom, but these things he knew: a dog howled, with hydrophobia gripping its throat. A man, crazy with the disease, had killed his wife and two children, and that man had not been bitten by a rabid animal. He had called in a strange doctor. All these things had happened in a city where a singularly cunning and cruel killer had collected five thousand dogs, the chief breeders of hydrophobia! Was Brent about to loose five thousand mad dogs upon the land to further some criminal plot? Wentworth could scarcely credit it—and yet the *Spider* had fought many fiendish plots that hinged on wholesale murder. And the few facts he had gathered were eloquent of crime and death. That madman ahead might hold the key.

WHILE he thought swiftly over his investigation, Wentworth had never taken his eyes from the taillight of the maniac's car ahead. Now he snapped forward in his seat as that red spot amid the blackness darted to the right, swerved left and bounced into the air with a crash that echoed resoundingly above the increasing mutter of distant thunder.

Ram Singh sent the Hispania lunging forward. The hot push of the wind became a hurricane. Then with dry-skidding tires he snubbed the car to a halt beside the smashed coupé. Wentworth flung from his seat, sprang to the other car's side. It was empty!

A foot on the running board, he vaulted upward and stood on the hood which had been rammed into a wall of gray granite. He could just peer over it into high, close-set trees that stirred restlessly with the breath of the coming storm. Beneath them a shrubbery-dressed lawn rolled gently toward the distant cold lights of a house. Wentworth sent the thin rays of his pocket flash prodding through the darkness. No trace of the mad killer. He sprang to the Hispania.

"There's a house on the hill here. Up to it, quickly!"

Ram Singh whirled the roadster, sent it zooming up to iron gates that were heavily braced between stone pillars. Lights flooded over the car, two gray-clad men, guns at their sides, popped out a wicket in the gate and strode forward arrogantly.

"There's a crazy man climbed over the wall," Wentworth shouted at them. "He's loose in the grounds. Phone the house! Search the grounds!" The men stared at him suspiciously. Wentworth leaped from the car, and one guard retreated a pace, hand on his pistol.

"Move!" Wentworth snapped at them. "I trailed this man all the way from Cologne. He killed his wife and two children there, stole a car—"

"Where's the car now?" the second guard demanded, hand also on his gun.

Wentworth murmured a few words to Ram Singh and walked gesturing toward the two men in gray uniform. The eyes of the two were direct and hard beneath the visors of their caps. Their hands were ready on their guns and seconds were precious. He could not delay to argue.

Without warning, the Hispania's motor roared wide open. The eyes of the guards jerked to the car. Their pistols flashed out.

"Hey!"

One strode toward the Hispania. As the guard passed him, Wentworth hooked out an arm and caught him about the neck. Carrying the man before him, he charged the second guard. As he rushed, he wrenched loose his prisoner's gun and pistol-whipped the wrist of the second. He freed the guard, leveled their own guns at the two.

"Hold them," he called to Ram Singh, saw the Hindu's flat black automatic take command of the situation and darted for the wicket in the gate. He found no phone there, plunged on.

"Help!" a guard bellowed behind him. "Robbers!"

WENTWORTH smiled grimly as he sprinted across rolling green lawns toward the lights on the hill that marked the mansion. Overhead trees tossed in a travail of mounting wind. The heat lightning that had danced upon the horizon had died and a great jagged fork of white fire split the heavens. Thunder clapped on its heels. The shouts of the guards were drowned in the torment of the skies.

Clumps of evergreens and flowering shrubs writhed and bunched like wrestling men. Among them Wentworth's stabbing glances found no trace of the madman. Better to dash to the house and warn the people there. At any second that hulking maniac with his powerful shoulders might crash in.

Blue-white lightning flared again against black clouds, and Wentworth, darting out of clustering woods into the open, saw the house rear before him. Frowning gray walls of granite, with turreted towers loomed like a castle. Nowhere was there any bright light. But dim wraiths of luminance filtered out from windows like arrow slits high in the towers; and through the wide French windows on a raised stone terrace, yellow oblongs of it fell coldly. Wentworth threw a swift glance over the entire front of the wide-flung building. Still no trace of the madman. Wentworth hand-vaulted to the terrace, plunged across it to the French doors and rapped heavily on the panes.

Peering in he could make out people dimly through the curtains, two men seated at ease before a leaping fire upon a stone hearth. At Wentworth's knock, they jerked erect in their chairs, eyes staring toward the door. Lightning flared and thunder made the glass vibrate beneath Wentworth's hands. He knew it outlined him as a black, peering figure. The two snapped to their feet. A gun glinted in the hand of one and they strode toward him.

Wentworth stepped back, thrust the guns he had seized from the guards into his pockets. The door was flung open and the wind rushed in, sending the fire leaping furiously, wrenching at the shade of a floor lamp, snapping curtains on the doors. The man who faced Wentworth, gun in hand, was gray and solid.

"What do you want?" he demanded.

"There's a maniac loose on the grounds," Wentworth told him. "I followed him here from Cologne and he crashed his car and disappeared over the wall."

The man before Wentworth stood unmoving, head thrust slightly forward from squared shoulders. Behind him a taller, slighter man whose head and shoulders drooped, studied Wentworth, too. Abruptly the man with the gun stepped aside.

"Come in where I can see you," he ordered.

Wentworth strode in, closed the door and turned the latch. He threw a quick glance over the room, a huge, high-ceilinged chamber whose stone walls were hung with shields and spears of another age. The place was chill despite the thick rugs upon the floor and the leaping fire. The storm had cut the sultry heat, but this penetrating chill was something inherent in the house, in its huge thick walls of gray stone.

There was no one else in the room, but through arched doors, where roseate light showed black draperies, there came the thin plinking of a piano. Its notes seemed muted by the vast reaches of the house.

Wentworth smiled easily. But there was a taut watchfulness about his eyes. Was the madman bound here for vengeance? Did he blame his tortures on one of these?

"It would be much better," he said calmly to the gray man, "if you called everyone together in one room where the doors could be watched. This man has a homicidal mania, hydrophobia to be precise. He just killed his two children and his wife in Cologne."

"Hydrophobia!" It was a woman's gasp.

WENTWORTH turned his head slowly, stared at that arched doorway where the light was roseate. A woman stood there now, a woman in trailing scarlet silk against a draped arras of black. Her hair was black, too. It made her white skin whiter still. She came forward slowly.

"Did you say hydrophobia?" she asked hesitantly.

The square face of the man before Wentworth became firmer, the jaw line more sharply defined. When he spoke his voice was harsh and unmusical.

"Will you tell me now what all this is about?" he demanded.

Wentworth bowed slightly, "I will," he said, "but I'd do it more willingly if everyone were in this room—out of danger."

"The castle is well guarded," said the man impatiently.

Wentworth smiled. "I'm here."

The man started as if he had not before realized the import of Wentworth's presence unannounced, had not realized that he must have evaded his guards.

"Your guards were as obtuse as yourself," Wentworth said shortly. "I was forced to circumvent them at the gate so as to warn you in time. Are you going to—"

He broke off shortly and shouted, "Help! Help! Police!"

In the room beyond, the music stopped with a discordant crash. Servants popped in at another door, and in the draped archway where the woman in scarlet had stood, a pale girl in blue appeared outlined against the dark clothing of a husky young man whose brown hair straggled an obstinate lock across his forehead.

Wentworth smiled thinly at the man in gray.

"Now that all are safely in this room I feel more comfortable about taking time to talk," he said. "My name is Sven Gustafsson," he went on, giving the name he had assumed for the present investigation. "I was driving through Cologne when I heard a woman scream and immediately after that a mad dog howl. You are familiar with the sound that a mad dog makes?"

He paused, eyeing the five people before him and the two men servants who still stood in the doorway beyond the fireplace. Lightning spewed blue-white flame against the French doors, dimming the lights within. Thunder smacked against the walls. The wind made a low whining, then a shriek in the chimney.

The woman in scarlet moved closer to the gray man with the gun, moved closer to the man with the stooped, thin shoulders. Now that she was near, Wentworth saw that her lips were red as bruised cherries, And there were smudges of shadow about black tragic eyes. Her shoulders, bare and warm despite the chill of the gaunt house, made an exquisite line of her throat. Her bold coloring made the stooped man insignificant until he twisted his face toward the door and the harsh direct rays of the lamplight showed the thin-bridged nose, the puckered firmness of a small mouth. Save for that mouth he was not unhandsome.

"Get on with it," the man with the gun said impatiently. His iron gray hair was as close as a steel cap upon his skull, and his face was gray and bitter.

Wentworth told of breaking into the house in Cologne and following the madman after his escape. He made no mention of the police. The girl in blue came closer now. The broad young man with the recalcitrant hair moved like a part of her, behind her with a hand protectingly upon her rounded shoulder. The girl was pale, her hair like sun-warm straw, yellow and gleaming. She was pale, but her lips were red.

"I followed the car till it crashed against your wall. When I reached it, the man was gone." Wentworth waved a hand. "I came to warn you."

The gray man let his gun hang at his side now. "It's easy enough to find out if you're telling the truth," he said.

"Quite," Wentworth nodded. "You can send some men—I would arm them well if I were you—to look at the wreck of the car. It's about two hundred yards south of the main gate. You can call police and ask them what happened at 567 Crossroads Street in Cologne."

"What's that address?" The words were snapped at him by the gray man.

Wentworth repeated it, and the blue eyes of the man were like chips of frozen sapphire. "That's the address of the captain of my guards," he said slowly. "He has been ill for two days, and—"

The flare of lightning was so startingly brilliant that it stopped his words and pulled all eyes toward the French doors. High and clear, even above the explosive crash of the thunder, the screams of the two women knifed the air. Outside those windows, outlined against the dazzling burst of the lightning, were the hunched shoulders of a man with a massive, sagging head.

"The maniac!" Wentworth barked out, hand flying to his gun.

The doors sagged, burst inward with a blast like a shotgun, and the man reeled in, his mad, wild eyes roving, lips flecked with white. Wind charged in with him so that he seemed a part of the heaven-ripping storm. Tensing his powerful arms, he advanced toward them!

CHAPTER THREE
A Madman's Warning

WENTWORTH walked slowly forward to intercept the man, his gun ready in one hand, blackjack gripped in the other. The gray man's harsh voice rasped out behind him:

"What does this mean, Rusk?"

The maniac's mouth opened, breath barking in his throat. Sounds that were scarcely human came with his harsh breathing, sounds that hinted vaguely at words. Wentworth stood on alert feet just beyond his reach.

"Warn you!" the man's word-sounds phrased. "Warn!"

"Against what?" snapped Wentworth.

"Here, drink this," said a voice at his elbow, and Wentworth heard the gurgle of liquid from a bottle.

"Fool!" Wentworth bit out, whirling. He knocked the bottle across the room,* spun back to the madman called Rusk. The maniac had stiffened, head thrown back in torture. His jaws snapped like a dog's and mangled his tongue.

• It is a peculiarity of the advanced stages of hydrophobia that despite an intense craving for drink, it is impossible for the victim to take any liquid. Even the sound of liquid frequently is enough to bring on the violet paroxysms which precipitate spells of madness and which ultimately kill the person afflicted. The snapping of the jaws is part of this muscular reaction, the hoarse breathing a part of the throat and chest paralysis which also are symptoms of the malady and not, as once was thought, due to a transformation of the human being into something dog-like by the strange and horrible disease. — AUTHOR.

Blood spilled from his mouth corners. He reeled backward, hands clutching at his throat. His dragging feet tripped him and he plunged to the rug, writhing in tortured convulsions.

Behind him, Wentworth heard the terrified cries of the women, the confused voices of the others. He dropped on his knees beside the madman, careful to keep clear of those plague-laden jaws. Rusk's writhings became a violent threshing. He was dying.

Wentworth snatched out the medicine kit he always carried, thrust a morphine filled needle into an arm he managed to pin down for a moment. Gradually the threshing quieted. Wentworth bent over the man.

"That warning," he said clearly. "What was it?"

His eyes, his powerful will commanded the man. The morphine began to take hold. For an instant, the dying man's gaze cleared. His mouth began to work; sounds squeezed out between his hoarse, terrible breathings. "Warn doctor!"

"What doctor?" Wentworth demanded.

The man writhed, eyes clouding with madness.

"What doctor?" Wentworth bored into him with his icy gaze.

The man's convulsions mounted to a climax, so that his body was inhumanly contorted, then broke into sudden limp stillness.

"Brent!" Rusk whispered clearly. "Brent!"

His chin drooped, his head sagged to the side. His hoarse breathing slowed. Wentworth got to his feet, turned from that tormented body to the others in the room. The two women had their faces buried on the chests of two men, the tall young man with the sprawling hair and the stoop-shouldered one whose offer of a drink had precipitated this violent paroxysm which was bringing on the man's death.

The gray man still faced him, narrow eyed, lips folded in upon themselves by their compression. Wentworth's thoughts were whirling. This dying man had cried a warning against a Dr. Brent. And Douglas Brent was the ruthless criminal Wentworth was hunting, fearing that he planned to loose hordes of hydrophobic dogs upon the people of the nation!

With the sound of the dying maniac's hoarse breathing still in his ears, visions of horror arose before Wentworth, visions of the hundreds of thousands that, fleeing before the mad hordes, would be bitten and die in writhing torment.

True, the use of Pasteur injections had cut deaths from this dread ailment to a scant hundred a year in the United States, but for that very reason the danger of this fiendish attack was increased.* Because the disease was comparatively rare and the serum of an intensely perishable nature, few laboratories prepared it and they kept only small quantities. That meant that if this monster loosed his hordes suddenly and over a wide area there would not be enough of the serum in the nation—in the entire world— to save those whose torn flesh would admit the fearful germs of madness and death.

But what could possibly be the purpose of such wholesale destruction? Wentworth could only guess. But this much is apparent: the guard who had died had been struck down for some definite reason—apparently by an injection of the virus by a Dr. Brent. And the victim had apparently believed that the threat affected his master also, affected this gray, challenging man before him.

---

* There are a number of ways of preparing the injections which build up immunity to hydrophobia, but all have as their basis the preparation of a weakened virus which is injected at gradually increasing strength. The usual method is to infect rabbits with the disease by means of injection directly into the brain and bypassing the germs through a series of animals, using virus from the last animal injected each time from the last animal infected, to build up what is known as a "fixed" virus. This virus has a "fixed" incubation period of six to seven days. This process is necessary because of the widely varying incubation period of the "street" virus. After this "fixed" virus is achieved, rabbits are injected with it and allowed to run the full period of the disease up to the test day when they are chloroformed. Their spinal cords then are removed and dried in stopper bottles, in the bottoms of which potash has been placed. Pasteur's method was to start with injecting emulsions of spinal cord which had been thus dried for fourteen days. The second day spinal cord dried thirteen days would be used, and so on until fourteen injections had been made, the last being of cord dried only one day. Fourteen days after the final injections, immunity has been built up. The U.S. Pharmocopeia method is to begin with cord dried eight days. This is the so-called active immunization method and is the basis of almost all anti-rabic injection, though varying methods of weakening the virus are employed, including heat, gastric juice, bile, etc. After the cord has been weakened by the desired number of days drying, it may be kept at this fixed strength by immersion in glycerine. But glycerine will preserve the cord for only 30 days. Then new preparations must be made.

There is another method of injection which was developed by Babes and Lepp, later Tizzoni and Centanni, which is called "passive" immunization. In this method instead of infecting the virus of the disease, the scientists inject a serum from an immunized animal. This method has had some success and has been preferred by some because only two injections a few days apart are necessary and because its preparation may be preserved longer than the perishable Pasteur cords. However, it is the Pasteur method which is now used almost to the exclusion of the other systems of both active and passive immunizations, because this method has had the widest tests and the widest success.

— AUTHOR

SLOWLY the gray man put away his gun. "I thank you, Mr. Gustafsson," he said heavily. "I appreciate the great lengths to which you went to warn me." He ordered a butler to call an ambulance for his guard, sent another to bring Ram Singh to the house. He offered his hand to Wentworth. "My name is Berthold Healy," he said, his voice as harsh and unyielding as the solid palm that met Wentworth's.

When they had left the chamber of horror for the music room beyond, he introduced the others in turn. "My wife," he said, and the woman in scarlet turned a pale face.

"My daughter—"

The girl in blue nodded, still shrinking against the chest of the hulking young giant behind her.

"My daughter's fiancé, Jack Collins." The young giant nodded, his lips set, and the straggling lock of hair sprawled across his forehead. He tossed it back with a jerk of his head.

"And Heinrich Scarlet."

The stooped man came forward and gripped Wentworth's hand strongly, his handsomely strong face apologetic.

"I have to apologize for offering that poor man a drink," he said softly. "I didn't realize... I forgot for the moment... hydrophobia."

Wentworth nodded affably. "Quite all right," he said, "the natural thing to do."

He turned toward Healy.

"May I have a few words in private with you?" he asked.

Healy nodded his compact, gray head, gestured with a restrained arm toward another door which revealed book-lined walls when he touched a light button. Wentworth walked in with him. He heard subdued voices rise behind them.

The young man called Collins drawled to the girl, "Do you feel like playin' any moah, Go'geous? It might take yoah mind off—"

Scarlet offered Mrs. Healy a drink.

Even into the library, the chill dampness of the building penetrated. The flashes of lightning outside the room's single high window were almost continuous now. As Healy waved Wentworth to a seat, an especially violent crash of thunder broke the back of the clouds and sent the rain down in a washing flood across the window. Healy dropped into a lounge chair and was absorbed into the shadows of its wings. Wentworth sat opposite him beside the black hearth and offered his platinum cigarette case, lighted up when Healy refused.

"I want to tell you in advance," Wentworth said, snapping out his lighter, "that it looks very much as if this attack on your guard was actually directed at yourself. The fact that Rusk came here to warn you is pretty evident of that. I hold certain powers from the federal government for investigation and I was on the trail of a man named Brent when I came here. Brent was the name Rusk gasped just before he died. I tell you this because I want to ask certain questions."

WENTWORTH saw the shadows shift in the depths of the chair and knew that Healy had nodded his head.

"What business are you in, Mr. Healy?"

The man rasped his throat harshly. His voice came sharply out of the dark.

"I'm tied up with a number of industries," he said. He jerked to his feet, stood a moment, then started pacing up and down with short, striding legs. "My biggest holdings are in steel. Steel town near here is my biggest plant. Six or seven thousand men and their families live there."

Wentworth's pulse quickened. An attack of rabid dogs against an industrial town could cripple the operation of that factory!

"Have you any other such towns?" Wentworth asked softly.

Healy halted his pounding stride up and down the room, stopped and stared down at Wentworth. His feet were braced, straddling out before the black hearth, his arms locked behind him. With his short, corpulent figure and his large, square-cut head, with its close-cut hair like a steel cap, he might have been Napoleon in modern garb.

"Yes," he said in his unmusical, harsh voice. "I have a number of such towns. The people are happier that way and I have a firmer grasp upon the workers. They are less apt to become disrupted by radicals. I have cotton-mill towns in North Carolina; I have communities of workers on wheat plantations in the west, this steel town, a couple of mines—"

"You are very wealthy, then?" Wentworth asked, the false square brows of Sven Gustafsson frowning.

Healy stood immovably rigid before the hearth. "Not immensely," he said heavily. "My holdings are extensive, but not very rich." He chopped off his sentence. "Would you mind telling me where all this is pointing to?"

Wentworth stood. "Just this," he said. "A man named Brent has bought more than five thousand dogs. If he gave those dogs hydrophobia and releases them on one of your industrial towns, wouldn't you pay handsomely to save the others ?"

Healy's head jerked up. Breath hissed between his teeth. "The damned scoundrel!" he grated out. "Would any man release mad dogs on women and children just for money?"

Wentworth's mouth twisted thinly. "Men have killed before this for money," he said.

"But mad dogs!"

Mad dogs! Distantly as he spoke, through the even wash of the rain, the retreating thunder of the storm, came a cracked, high-pitched bark, a senseless yammering of howls that clenched Wentworth's fists at his sides! The sound jerked Healy about in his tracks—to stare panicked eyes at the black bulb of the single high window. As they stared, distant white lightning burned and something hunched and furry was outlined against the panes!

Healy's hand flew to the gun in his pocket. He sent lead crashing through the window. A cat yowled thinly like a suffering child, and the hunched, furry thing was gone. Healy spun back toward Wentworth. His face was drawn. Excited voices from the next room screamed questions.

"In God's name, what is happening?" Healy demanded of Wentworth.

Wentworth smiled thinly. "Rusk warned you," he said. He spun toward the door. "I'll be back. I want to find that mad dog that howled." He paused a moment. "Do you know a national guard commander near here?"

Healy jerked a nod, frowning. "General Lansing. Brigadier General Francis Lansing at Saginal. He comes here some times."

Wentworth nodded and went out.

THE four in the music room were hurrying toward the library as Wentworth strode out. The women stared with frightened eyes. The two men started forward, then Healy showed in the doorway, and they fell back. Wentworth hurried on, past two men in white who were lifting the still-unconscious madman to a stretcher. He passed out into the high, vaulted hallway where Ram Singh, imperturbable behind folded arms, awaited him.

Out into the sheeting rain, Wentworth strode. The Hispania was not in sight, and he raced to the cover of the bowing trees, Ram Singh at his heels. Once more, reedily through the night, came the insane howling of a dog. But it was no longer a single cry. It had become only one of a muffled chorus of mad yelps. Wentworth reached the wall. Ram Singh crouched, hands linked between bent knees. A quick step, a heave and Wentworth was atop the wall.

Once more the thin, senseless howling, this time almost at hand. No slinking black forms ran blindly along the road; no threatening horde of madness loomed, but the yellowish lights of a large truck sped toward him, the heavy rain like slanting crystal rods across its headlights. It droned past, and abruptly, Wentworth knew why the howls had seemed muffled. They came from inside of that truck. *A load of mad dogs was being transported to be loosed upon an unsuspecting countryside!*

Wentworth sprang down from the wall.

"Quickly, Ram Singh, the car!"

Ram Singh darted away. Wentworth headed for the gate. A rustling sounded above his head, and he flung aside, as a horrid, yowling scream tore downward and claws struck into the shoulder of his coat. Teeth grated as they gnashed in the brim of his hat. It was a cat, and that thin, hoarse cry meant it was mad with the fearful madness of death, *a cat which had hydrophobia!"*

CHAPTER FOUR
Horde of Doom

WENTWORTH knew that if that mad cat's teeth struck into his throat or face, he would have small chance of escaping the horrid death of madness, for the germs attack first the brain, and wounds in the throat and head are nearly always fatal. If he attempted to seize the hydrophobic animal with his hands, he was certain to be lacerated.

He knew these things without conscious thought, and he acted as swiftly as the knowledge flashed across his mind. He flung to the ground, rolling, felt for and found a water puddle, rolled the clawing cat into it.

He heard Ram Singh dart close.

"Stand clear, Ram Singh!" he snapped, but the Hindu ignored the command.

Wentworth felt the cat ripped from his shoulder, heard its body strike suddenly against a tree as it was flung savagely aside. He sprang up, snatched out a small pocket flashlight and turned it upon Ram Singh. A glint from the tree above caught his eye. His automatic leaped to his hand, belched leaden death.

A man's scream began and ended in a choked curse, and a man's body plunged downward and thumped upon the wet ground. He flopped over on his back and Wentworth spotted the bullet hole in his forehead. He paid no further attention to the man, ignored the distant shouts of Healy's guards and made a hurried examination of Ram Singh. The Hindu's right wrist bore the toothmarks of the mad cat!

Wentworth took Ram Singh's keen-edged knife and gashed out the flesh about the wound, then he tugged out his medical kit. At a sign from him, the Hindu bared his abdomen and into the flesh Wentworth shot the contents of a hypodermic syringe.

"Get the car quickly," he told the Hindu and wordlessly his servant turned away.

Wentworth whirled to the body of the man he had slain, stared down at the face by the white light of his hand torch. The face was strange to him, a lowering, dark countenance. Wentworth drew out a cigarette lighter and pressed its base on the brow of the man who had attempted to murder him with a hydrophobic cat.

When he had taken the lighter away, a red spot glowed on the man's forehead, a red spot that had hairy, ugly legs.

It was Wentworth's calling card of death—*the Seal of the Spider!*

He restored the lighter to his pocket, seized the body and with a single heave of his broad shoulders, lifted it at arm's length above his head and tossed it over the wall to the road. That would warn the criminals that justice stalked them! He ran then to the gate of the grounds, found the two guards he had disarmed, waiting there with hard-gripped rifles. When they identified Wentworth, they scowled, but did not bar his way. They had had their orders from Healy.

Headlights flashed down the road, and the Hispania skated to a stop. Wentworth flung in.

"To the left," he ordered. "There's a closed truck we must trail."

The Hispania swished out onto the rain-drenched road, laid its belly to the pavement. In two hundred yards it was doing seventy miles an hour.

Water dripped from Wentworth's clothes and from Ram Singh. Blood dripped, too, from the gash in the Hindu's wrist.

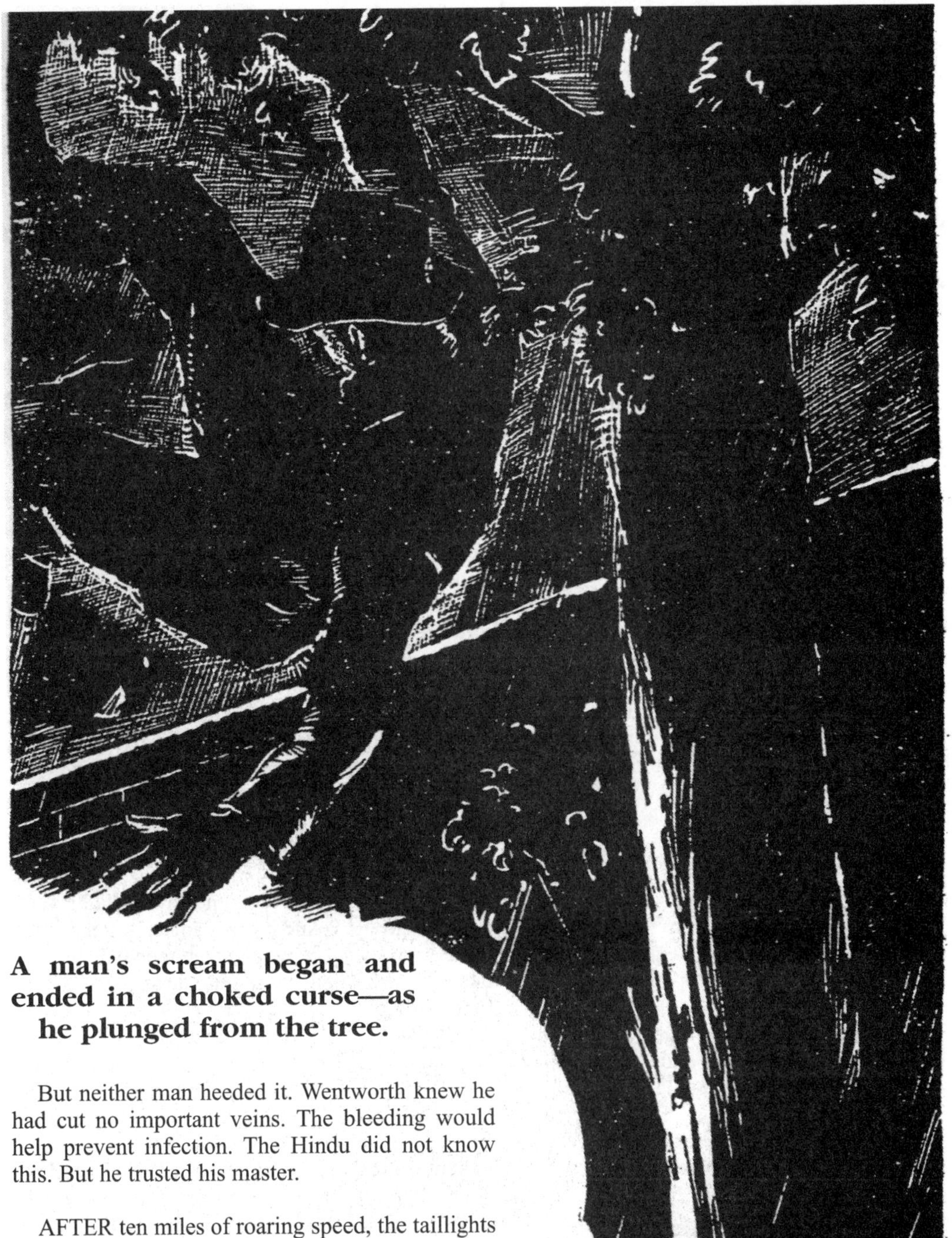

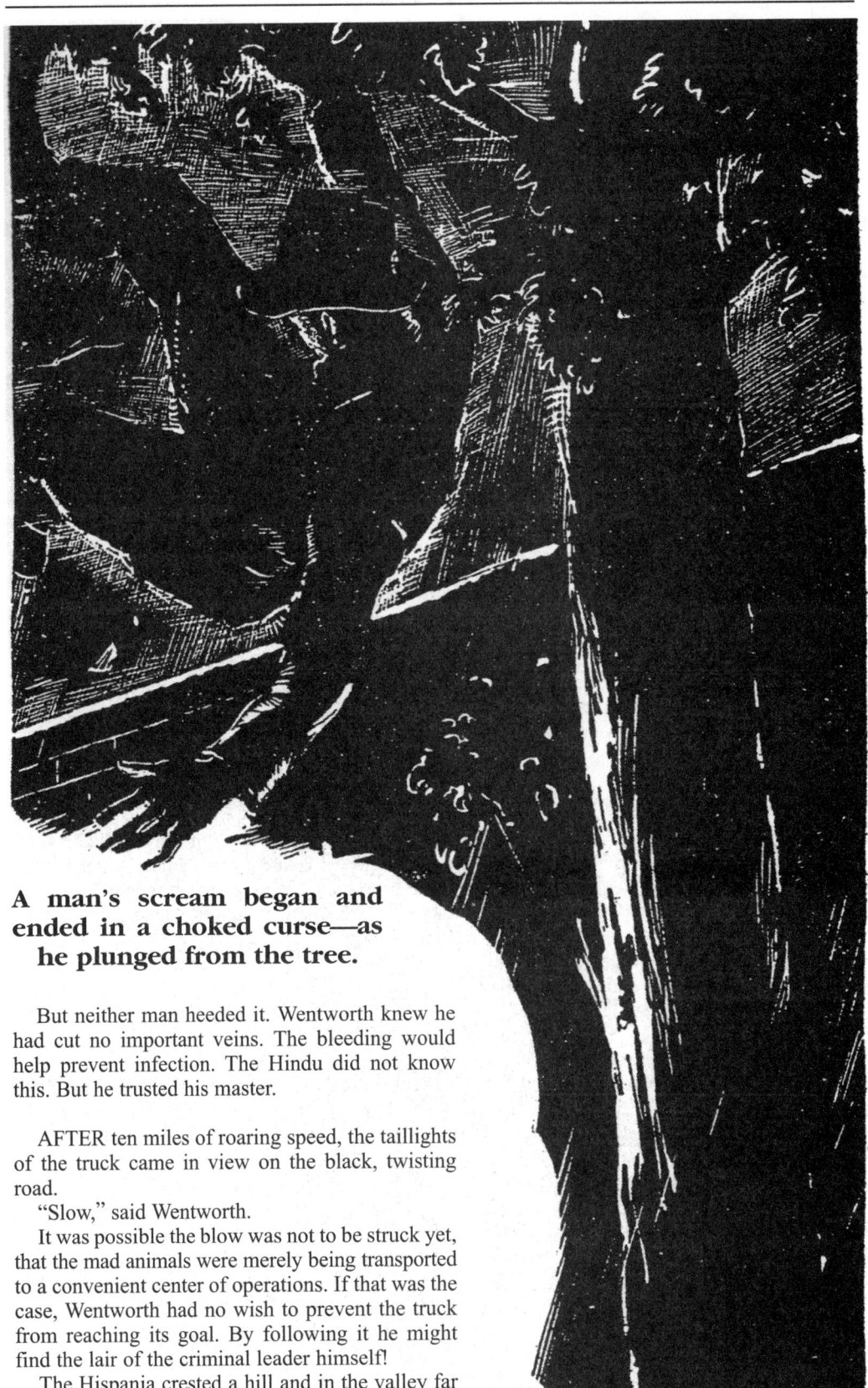

A man's scream began and ended in a choked curse—as he plunged from the tree.

But neither man heeded it. Wentworth knew he had cut no important veins. The bleeding would help prevent infection. The Hindu did not know this. But he trusted his master.

AFTER ten miles of roaring speed, the taillights of the truck came in view on the black, twisting road.

"Slow," said Wentworth.

It was possible the blow was not to be struck yet, that the mad animals were merely being transported to a convenient center of operations. If that was the case, Wentworth had no wish to prevent the truck from reaching its goal. By following it he might find the lair of the criminal leader himself!

The Hispania crested a hill and in the valley far below lights were haloed by dwindling rain, the lights of a town. *Washington Courthouse*, the road signs read. The roadster closed up on the truck. If a man made a move to open it and loose the plague upon the people, Wentworth would shoot him down.

They descended toward the town, jounced over railroad tracks. The truck pushed on. As they turned left into the main street of the village, Wentworth turned to Ram Singh.

"Burn that wound with strong nitric acid or gunpowder," he said. "It will help insure against infection." He drew out his medical kit, put a fresh charge into the hypodermic needle and handed it to Ram Singh. "Tomorrow, inject this into your abdomen as you saw me do.

"Stop at the next corner. Call the surgeon general's office at Washington in my name, and tell them it is imperative that anti-rabic serum be generated at full speed and that large quantities be shipped to Ohio. Tell them that there is going to be an outbreak of hydrophobia here such as the world has never before known!

"Phone General Francis Lansing at Saginal and tell him, for me, that a plague of mad dogs threatens and he is to prepare for a call. Tell him to call Berthold Healy for particulars."

The Hispania slowed, Ram Singh dropped out and Wentworth instantly took up the pursuit behind the wheel. Lucky for Ram Singh, he thought, that setting upon the trail of dogs, Wentworth had thought to supply himself with a dosage of anti-rabic serum,* the passive variety which was rarely used, but which required only two injections. He had carried only that single double dose, but if it saved Ram Singh, he was repaid for the risk he must run from now on, unequipped with a guarantee against the dread hydrophobia.

MILE after mile through the night, the plague-bearing truck droned northward; and ever behind it Wentworth tooled the sleek Hispania. The rain had ceased now. The white of drying cement began to spot the black wetness of the road. Wentworth turned his mind to the man behind this impending horror. Back in Cologne, he must check up on this Dr. Brent whose visit had preceded the death of Healy's guard.

That was a queer thing, that death. Why did the criminals, if they intended to attack one of Healy's industrial towns, begin with the murder of one of Healy's *home* guards? And why were mad cats loosed about the grounds of the estate? Killing the goose even before it laid the first golden egg seemed a trifle absurd.

Abruptly Wentworth straightened behind the sensitive wheel on which his hands rested lightly. The truck was swooping down a long grade, and in the valley below the patterned lights of another, larger town were laid out with geometrical precision. Off to the right there was a glimmer of gray light along the horizon, the first herald of dawn. Its dim radiance faintly illumined a line of fat chimneys, tall along the southern edge of the town. The truck swooped toward it like a diving eagle. The Hispania's motor deepened its roar.

Here, Wentworth realized at once, was an industrial town. He saw that a crossroads signboard flashing past spelled out Eatonville, and he frowned. A steel town, right enough, but not Healy's. Grimly, Wentworth crowded the truck. To loose that captive horde of rabid dogs upon the town, men must open the back of the truck. When they did—

His left hand light upon the wheel, Wentworth dipped into his pockets, drew out the two weapons he had taken from Healy's guards, and laid them upon the seat. He gripped his own automatic in his right hand. The mad race down the grade ended in a dwindling drone of powerful engines. The truck turned right and threaded a way between tall brick buildings protected by fences topped with strands of barbed wire. Guards paced within.

Wentworth frowned again. Of what use would mad dogs be in an attack against such a place? Give the industrialists a few hours notice, and they would have every man, woman and child behind such fences with sharpshooters in impregnable towers ready to fell any mad dog that came near. Mad dogs? Yes, but couldn't hydrophobic cats wriggle through? And if this damnable fiend could use cats and dogs, why not other animals? Why not rats and mice which could filter through a still finer mesh of defensive wire? Why not—

Wentworth cursed and spurted as the truck whirled a corner at high speed and shot eastward. For hours the wailings, and howlings of the mad horde had been silenced. Now the blood-chilling chorus of doom sounded again.

With frantic speed, Wentworth wove in and out among the red-walled factories, shot clear of the tangle and sped among wide-lawned suburban streets. Lights burned in windows now as men prepared to go to the mills. A woman opened a door and stooped for a bottle of milk. The truck spun a corner and sloughed to a stop.

Wentworth flung his Hispania broadside. With grimly watching eyes he crouched forward, two guns ready in his hands. The first man who opened a door—then, without warning, the back of the truck popped open, swinging from hinges at its bottom!

* This was the Centri method described in a previous footnote. —AUTHOR

It dropped to the street, forming a perfect gangway— a gangway for the Mad Horde of doom!

The inside of the truck was a stygian cavern, full of a thousand unseeable horrors. For an instant there was neither sound nor motion. Then a single dog thrust from the blackness into the light. Its lower jaw hung laxly and flecks of white clung viscously to lips and fangs. There was red madness in its eyes.

The bark of Wentworth's gun was swift as thought. The dog sprang vaultingly out into the air and crumpled in the street. As if Wentworth's shot had been a signal, a half dozen more menacing heads thrust into the light. His guns spat again and again, but now there was a stampede of the Mad Horde. Dog after dog he tumbled dead in the street.

But others poured out behind them, reached the ground in a single bound and trotted on stiffly mechanical legs off into the half darkness amid the homes with their unsuspecting victims.

GUNS blazed now from the black interior of the truck. Wentworth crouched behind the bulletproof sides of the roadster, tooled it so the windshield protected him. He fired only at the plague spreaders. The men could wait.

Still they poured from the huge truck, dogs and cats, huge sewer rats, white laboratory rats and mice. Truly a horde of horror. A scratch from the teeth of any one of those beasts, and a man would die in writhing agony. And these animals would attack on sight any living thing they met! Other hundreds of dogs and cats and vermin would become infected and help to pass on the mortal madness. For months, the virus would spread.

Wentworth churned among the mad horde with the heavy wheels of his car. A dog with drooling jaws sprang upward at his leveled gun hand. He jerked down the muzzle, fired directly into that yawning mouth. Its dying body slammed against the side of the car.

A cat hooked its claws over the door, its snarling mouth a red threat of death. Wentworth's lead hurled it to the street. Pale faces showed at the windows of nearby homes now. A man flung wide a door and strode out, a hulking fellow with suspender straps over his chest-bulged red undershirt. A rifle was in his hands.

A half dozen dogs swerved in their soundless fury and hurled at him. Two he shot. A third got past his rifle, and the man struck with his fist. The animal buried his teeth in it. Two more dogs struck him. The man cursed, lashing with his rifle. A dog got past him, and within the house a woman screamed.

All about Wentworth's car lay the carcasses of mad animals, but scores had escaped. The truck, its tail door slowly rising into place again, lurched forward. Not a man had showed himself.

The Hispania surged in its wake, but three blocks farther on Wentworth hurled about a corner, jerked to a halt before a cottage and raced to its door. His frenzied beating brought no response from within. He snatched a lockpick from a compact kit of tools he carried always strapped beneath his arm. In seconds the door yielded and he plunged into the dark hallway, found a phone and called police.

"This is a federal investigator," he spoke with crisp syllables. "A criminal has just turned loose scores of mad dogs, cats and rats upon the city... Yes, hydrophobia... Get every exterminator you can busy eliminating them, and phone Washington for anti-rabic serum. Yes, hydrophobia. I don't know who did it."

He slammed up the receiver and darted to the door. He jerked it open, and a policeman leveled a revolver at him.

"Hands up!" The man ordered. "I saw you break into this house."

"But, officer," Wentworth stepped forward a pace.

"Keep back!"

Wentworth's left hand brushed the revolver's barrel aside. It jerked with the explosion of its discharge, and lead slammed through the door behind him with a crashing of glass. Then the policeman went backward and down from a right to the jaw, and Wentworth was sprinting toward his car.

Police sirens moaned in the distance, crescendoed to a wail as a squad car with a half dozen men clinging to it rounded the corner. Wentworth reached his car, slapped a hand to the door, then snatched it away as a furred fury flung at him from within, a rat with gnashing teeth. Wentworth's gun flew to his hand. A bullet smashed the mad rodent's head, hurled its kicking body to the floor. A jerk at the door, and once more Wentworth halted. The bullet that had wiped out this new menace, a rat undoubtedly planted there by the criminals he pursued, had smashed through the ignition switch of the Hispania! Not a chance to start it.

The squad car skidded to a halt, nose jammed against the Hispania's front bumper. Even if Wentworth had been able to start it, he could not have escaped now. Men spilled from the squad car, riot and machine guns glinting in the double glare of the autos' headlights.

Two men sprang toward Wentworth, sawed-off repeating shotguns leveled.

"One step," the leader spat out. "And you're a dead man!"

One step, yet Wentworth could not wait. While he stood there, a captive of police guns, the murderers who had loosed their fearful hordes upon the city were fleeing. While he attempted to explain, they would put miles between them and the *Spider*. Miles that meant defeat!

Wentworth stepped to the side of his car.

"Halt!" the cop ordered again. "One step, I said, and—" He lifted the gun, his eyes cold behind the wide black muzzle—a muzzle that could blast a hole like a dinner plate in a man's body....

CHAPTER FIVE
The Death's-Head Brand

WENTWORTH had his back to the Hispania. He slid his left hand behind him into the pocket on the door, fingered out two glass tubes that nestled there. Luckily his abandonment of the car could not incriminate Richard Wentworth. The motor numbers had been stripped from it, and the license plates were in the name of Sven Gustafsson. He could leave that all right, if he could escape the police.

He stared into the threatening muzzle of the riot gun while other officers crowded close behind the man who held it. A submachine gun was held low at the hip by a second policeman.

"One step is a mighty small thing to kill a man for," Wentworth said calmly. "Don't you think so?"

He took one step backward.

He saw the policeman's eyes narrow, and he dived behind the car, as the blast of the shotgun ripped open the night. Its buckshot peppered the back of the Hispania but Wentworth's leap had been lightning fast. He rolled toward the far side of the car, tossing the glass tubes at the feet of the police by lobbing them over the Hispania's low top.

The shotgun blasted again. The machine gun stuttered, drumming lead against the armor of the roadster. Thin gray gas spiraled upward from the broken tubes of glass. The man with the riot gun reeled backward, choking. The machine gun stammered its leaden hail again.

"Stop it, you fool," a man gasped. "You'll kill some of us."

Coughing, choking, eyes streaming from the tear gas Wentworth had loosened upon them, the police scattered to escape the fumes. Behind the Hispania, Wentworth sprang toward the squad car. The driver had fled with the rest. Under the *Spider*'s skilled hands, the car leaped backward, checked and, whirling on moaning tires, whizzed up the avenue. Banging guns were as futile as the strangled shouts of the gassed police.

Within three minutes, Wentworth was out of the town, the way cleared by his moaning siren, and was racing southward again, back along the road over which he had trailed the truck of the Mad Horde.

The truck was unburdened now. It would make fast time, but that long grade out of Eatonville would slow it, and—Bellowing into the first gradient on the climb, Wentworth peered ahead through the dawn, red now with the first light of the sun, and saw its rays glint upon a crawling truck near the crest. The squad car roared wide open. It was a third of the way up when the truck dipped from sight at the top. When it crested the rise, the truck was a mile away, rounding a curve like a schooner heeling to the wind.

Wentworth nailed the accelerator to the floor. The speedometer needle wavered at sixty and crept upward as the momentum of the roaring green car mounted. Past sixty-five, and upward. The red truck was swaying wildly. A coupé skittered from its path and poised on the brink of a ravine, toppled slowly. A man leaped out and shook an infuriated fist as the machine rolled downward. The squad car zipped past at seventy, its siren shrieking once.

On a downgrade, the truck held its own, then, braking for a turn, twisted its rear from side to side violently. It swung, half broadside into the curve, flashed out of sight. Moments later, even above the bellow of his own motor, Wentworth heard a rending, fearful crash. He cut the gas, kicked the brake, and went around the curve at fifty. The railing of a bridge was smashed through. The truck lay on its side twenty feet below, its rear out of sight in a narrow, deep creek that streamed muddy clouds over its splintered red fragments. Wentworth, braking savagely, jerked his eyes to the woods that crept close to the road and spotted moving branches.

He threw the squad car to the left of the highway, flung out while it still rolled and readied the woods in a bound. The running footsteps of three men sounded plainly on the rain-softened earth. He dived into the woods, reloading the automatic clenched in his fist. Trees were thick and scrub growth choked the way. Visability was less than fifty feet. The ground became hard, the trail of pounding footsteps dimmer. Wentworth halted, listening, heard a furious threshing through underbrush ahead.

He plunged on, ducking under down swooping limbs, weaving between wrist-thick saplings whose switches slashed his face with a sting like nettles. The growth became thicker, but still the crashing ahead led him on. Beneath his feet, the earth slanted downward. He ran faster, ducking briar vines. The grade grew steeper so that he skidded on his heels to slow his descent. Abruptly, he bent double, dived headlong and hooked an arm about a small tree.

A huge gray beast hurtled over the spot where he had stood. Long white fangs snapping, it whirled with silent fury.

SPINNING about the tree with the momentum of his dive, Wentworth snapped a shot into the animal's head, sent it threshing to the earth. He regained his feet and crouched, steadying himself with a hand lightly against the tree. Ten feet away shrubbery crashed violently and two more of the gray beasts charged with hanging heads and slavering jaws. They were wolves, mad wolves, and upon their foreheads were branded human skulls, the symbol of death!

The evil import of those branded skulls, the proof this attack by mad wolves was a trap of the criminals he trailed, might have unnerved a lesser man, laid him a stunned and helpless victim before the slashing fangs of these savage beasts. But Wentworth's gun hand was steady, his eye as unfailing as ever. Twice his automatic spoke. And a bullet, smashed through the center of each death's-head brand.

Wentworth flung himself aside from the wolves' dying slashes. He screamed horribly with his throat wide open, beat about in the shrubbery with his left arm. But his right hand gripped the gun ready. He kept on screaming, let his cries grow weaker.

The wolves were dead now, lying stretched out stiffly on the earth. But all animal victims of hydrophobia are silent when they attack, silent when they are wounded. Their silence gave no warning to the man who, sneaking through the shrubbery, thrust out to make sure of the victim's death. He stared with mouth agape at Wentworth, straightening from the covert where he crouched.

Wentworth, a grim smile on his mouth, waited until the man's surprise changed to fear, until desperately he jerked up a gun. Then he drilled the man through the heart. He bounded past him and on through the woods. Fifty yards more and he saw sky between the far trunks of trees and seconds later burst out onto another road. But its far curves were empty. A quick search of the earth revealed the footsteps of three men beside the deep tire tracks of a car. His quarry had escaped.

Wentworth sped back to the body of the man he had slain. A swift search of his pockets revealed no clue to his identity, nothing to indicate where headquarters of the gang might be. Wentworth's mouth was straight and hard. The gangsters had spread their havoc, left their death-dealing hordes to kill and had shaken off pursuit. Obviously, this escape passage through the woods had been well planned, the man planted there to cover the retreat after the truck had been wrecked.

Wentworth's hand slid to his cigarette lighter. He stooped over the dead man, over the slain wolves and on the forehead of each, in the midst of the death's-head brand, he imprinted the menacing red seal of the *Spider*.

The Horde Master's men had escaped, but not unscathed. Back there by Healy's home lay the body of one; here was another beside three of their foul servitors, the mad wolves. The Horde Master would know that the *Spider* was on the trail!

The sound of a roaring motor that died into a mutter jerked Wentworth's head about. It came from the direction of the squad car. Police had arrived. Then the *Spider* must be on his way.

AS he strode silently southward through the woodland, Wentworth's hands were deftly at work. The yellow wig was removed with the false blond brows and, dampened with an inflammable fluid from the cigarette lighter, flared into an unrecognizable charred mass beside the *Spider*'s swift path.

First putty, then transfiguring plates of thin, hard rubber came from mouth and nostrils and forehead, and now it was Richard Wentworth himself that stole through the thickets with such soundless efficiency, his lean jaw firm with determination, the gray blue of his eyes cold as ice.

The vital strength of the man was at once apparent, even to a casual glance. Striding along, he skillfully applied black grease paint that gave him a stubble of beard, putty that gave him a broken nose. A scar disfigured an eyebrow. Gone now was Richard Wentworth, wealthy clubman, dabbler in criminology, dilettante of the arts. The man who slouched through the underbrush, his torn coat and mussy trousers burred with woods briars, was a tramp of the road.

The tramp eluded the clumsy police cordons—Wentworth was a trained woodsman; these others were city men—and made his way at last back to Cologne. There, no longer a tramp, but still with his broken-nosed face, he called his fiancée, Nita Van Sloan, on long-distance and asked her to drive West, bringing at least one dose of the anti-rabic serum for herself. She was to try to gain friendly entrance to the Healy home. Among her friends some undoubtedly could give letters of introduction. Wentworth knew that Sven Gustafsson had been revealed as the *Spider*, that his entree at the Castle had been destroyed.

He asked Nita to phone Professor Brownlee and ask him to hasten West, where he was to make every effort to develop some means of killing the Mad Hordes. "I suggest a gas strong enough to kill animals, too weak to affect humans," he said.

Then Wentworth called Washington, got in touch with the surgeon general's office and identified himself.

"It is essential," he told them, "that even more serum than I ordered through Ram Singh be shipped here."

The surgeon general interrupted him. "I have not heard from Ram Singh!"

"You are positive?" Wentworth snapped out the words, hands tense on the phone.

The surgeon general told him the only order for serum had come from Eatonville and that a plane was speeding the equipment there. There could be no doubt about it. Ram Singh had not communicated with Washington!

That could mean only one thing: the faithful Hindu had been prevented by force from fulfilling his task. Either he was a captive of the Horde Master, or he was—dead. Wentworth's mouth shut in a grim line.

"If you want to get more supplies nearer at hand," the surgeon general was saying, "there is a laboratory at Columbus, the Aachen, which has some of the virus on hand."

Wentworth hung up and stood staring at the white wall above the hotel telephone he was using. Ram Singh in the power of the criminals! The thin white scar upon his right temple began to throb, red and angry. If they harmed that faithful fellow—But there were even more serious connotations of his capture. If Brent were alert to the possibilities, he might trace the Hindu through Washington and find that he was attached to Wentworth, learn that Wentworth and the *Spider* were one!

A curse grated between his teeth. It would be fatal now to have the hordes of the criminals loosed upon himself. He must maintain his incognito, continue to battle in secret. He would rescue Ram Singh and smash this gang, but first he must speed to the Aachen laboratory at Columbus. It must throw all its energies into producing the anti-rabic serum. He caught up

the phone again and waited five minutes in grim-faced impatience while the operator tried to raise the laboratory. Finally she reported the line, "Out of order."

Out of order! Wentworth knew what that meant!

"Operator, see that the police are sent to investigate the reason for that wire being out of order. I am positive that criminals are responsible," he snapped. He slammed up the receiver, hurried to the car he had rented since loss of his Hispania and sent it hurtling through the midday traffic to the Cologne airport.

Yes, he knew what that report meant. But God alone knew if he would be in time to avert this new infamy of the Master of the Horde! Not content with striking down thousands with the most dread disease of the ages, Wentworth feared the criminals now were planning to take away the last hope of the doomed wretches they had infected.

The Horde Master was attacking the laboratory that produced the serum!

CHAPTER SIX
Guard the Laboratories

AT THE airport, Wentworth chartered a plane and, springing to the controls himself, sent it skimming from earth, splitting the air toward Columbus. It was eighty miles to the laboratory. Wentworth, straining the motor to the last notch, made it in thirty minutes.

As he swooped above the low-lying laboratory building seeking a landing, he saw men run from it with backward firing guns, saw them leap into a car and race away at top speed. Wentworth threw the plane into a steep bank and whirled in pursuit. Leveling off, he gripped the stick between his knees, jerked two vials from the kit beneath his arm, poured their contents into a silver flask, which he first emptied of the brandy it contained.*

Darting low over the racing car, he hurled the flask accurately into the road. It flashed down past the nose of the car, striking almost beneath the engine. It burst with a flashing roar of sound, a spear-like blossoming of white and red flame. The front of the car was thrust straight up into the air. It plunged in a twisting somersault into the ditch.

Like an echo of that ripping concussion, a cyclonic explosion tore out behind Wentworth. He felt the plane stagger and slide off on the right wing. Desperately, he fought the controls in a maelstrom of freak air currents. One glance backward told him what he had guessed. There had been another, greater explosion than the one caused by the hurling flask. The laboratory had been blown into fragments! Bits of masonry and torn bodies

* I have tried many times to learn the secret of these two fluids which were another of the many inventions which Professor Brownlee contrived for the Spider, for whom he had an undying and unwavering affection. As nearly as I could make out from the somewhat technical analysis that Mr. Wentworth once gave me, the professor had contrived to split trinitrotuolene into two component and harmless parts. This made it possible for the Spider, despite his occasionally strenuous physical encounters, to carry the two vials of liquid in his kit without fear that a chance blow might set them off and blow him to bits. Yet, when the two were mixed, he had at his command one of the most powerful explosives known to man. — AUTHOR

hurtled through the air. Wentworth clenched his teeth, battling the crazy controls. The plane was fluttering within a hundred feet of the earth. He threw the stick forward, jerked the ship into a sharp dive.

Rudder surfaces had been torn, and the ailerons of one wing flapped loosely, but the speed of his dive gave him the beginning of control, and he managed to wheel the ship into a side slip. He wrenched about again and took the ground at eighty miles an hour. Sixty was normal landing speed. The plane struck on the wheels alone, bounced violently.

Off balance with its broken aerolon, it dug a wing into the earth, cartwheeled and buried its engine in the mud. Half dazed, Wentworth freed himself from the belt and struggled clear. Gun in hand, he sped in a stumbling run toward the wreck of the car he had blasted from the road with his improvised bomb. He darted out into the road, then stopped dead in his tracks.

High, leaping flames wrapped the ruin of the car. The black billowing smoke betrayed that the gasoline tank had burst. No clue there. And the laboratory building had been blown to bits! There would be none there.

The fiendish deliberation with which this criminal worked stunned Wentworth afresh. The laboratories could not turn out the serum swiftly enough to save more than a tenth of those he had stricken with his dread plague, but he removed even that possibility. He had destroyed the laboratory which made the serum!

It would be weeks, months before the valuable laboratory equipment, the virus built to "fixed" strength through long intensification in laboratory animals, could be replaced.

Good God! Were they striking at all laboratories? The government must be warned. Guards must be set about them. Otherwise the entire nation would lie helpless before the assault of this ruthless criminal.

Wentworth whirled to race to a phone, a telegraph station, anything to spread the warning. He whirled and froze, hands at his side. Two police had crept upon him while the roar of the flames had hidden the noise of their approach. They stood with leveled pistols. A police car rocketed up the road, stopped with a squealing skid of its tires, and two more men sprang out with drawn guns.

One of the first police began to curse Wentworth with a slow, cold venom.

"You louse!" he snarled. "We saw you in that plane bombing the laboratory! You've killed half a hundred men." He bit out a curse. "Hell, you lousy, murdering—" He aimed his pistol. There was murder in his eyes.

CHAPTER SEVEN
Ambush in the Sky

FOR an instant the life of the policeman leveling his pistol at Wentworth hung in the balance. Through the *Spider*'s mind raced the necessity of his own escape, not for his own sake, but for the humanity he ceaselessly defended. The *Spider* had never killed police in his countless crusades, never intended to. They, like himself, fought for the people. But this gun in a crazed man's hand imperiled the entire crusade. Wentworth was poised for swift action when the policeman's companion struck up his gun hand, sent the lead whistling harmlessly into the air.

"Fool!" he said hoarsely. "You almost killed him!"

"I meant to!" the other raged. "He bombed the laboratory and Sarah—"

Ah, the policeman was motivated by personal vengeance. This was no vast cosmic rage that stirred him to kill in the name of justice. Wentworth, his face very grave, moved toward the four police slowly.

"Listen," he said, wagging his head with a vehemence they would understand. "I didn't have a thing to do with that laboratory. I was in the plane and saw the men in that car over there run out of it shooting back at the laboratory. I dropped a bomb on their auto and spilled it over the ditch. That's all I had to do with it. You can look in the auto and you'll find their guns, and—"

"Stand still," the second policeman ordered.

Wentworth gesticulated with his hands. "I'm telling you the truth. I'm a government agent and I was coming here to warn the laboratory. The same gang that spread hydrophobia in Eatonville bombed this place because it makes the serum that they use to prevent hydrophobia. You can call Washington—"

The policeman who had attempted to kill Wentworth stepped forward and struck at him with his gun. "You louse, you killed Sarah!" His face was white and tightly drawn. Tears ran from his eyes. "You louse!" He struck at Wentworth again and each time his gun swished harmlessly past a ducking head.

Wentworth made no move to strike back at the policeman, made no move to seize the opportunity this man's closeness offered for escape. Wentworth's nimbleness infuriated the policeman. He leveled his pistol again.

"Take this nut away," Wentworth warned, "or I'm going to knock him for a loop."

"Oh, you will, you louse!" The policeman squeezed the trigger again at almost point-blank range. His tightening eyes had betrayed his intention and the lead burned the air past Wentworth's side. He stepped close, his fists battering. The cop went down. Wentworth sprang back, both hands raised.

"I had to do it," he said rapidly. "He was going to kill me."

Two more policemen were coming at him slowly now, their leveled guns ready.

"He ought to," spat one. "Killing his daughter that-a-way." The amiability went from Wentworth's face, left it lean and hard. His eyes had ugly lights in their depths. "Permit me to remind you," he bit out, "that the execution of justice is not in your hands. You are police, hired by the people to arrest suspects, not to lynch them."

The police continued to advance from two sides with their weapons ready. The third officer stood directly in front of Wentworth at a distance, and the other two were careful not to come between him and their quarry. All three were silent.

"I'm warning you once more," Wentworth said deliberately. "I'm a government agent. Take me to your superiors and I'll present my credentials. Touch me at your risk."

"Yeah, you're a government agent," a policeman jeered.

Wentworth smiled into the man's face.

"Incomprehensible as that may seem to you," he said quietly, "that is precisely what I am."

"Then let's see your papers."

Wentworth shook his head slowly. "I present those only to the commissioner himself."

"He's faking," barked the first policeman. "Let's rush him." He raised his gun like a club.

WENTWORTH took a cigarette case from his pocket, tucked a white tube between his lips. He looked upward beneath his brows at the policeman as he lifted flame toward the cigarette.

The cop's lower lip thrust out. He took two strides forward with clubbed gun ready.

Wentworth lifted his head, puffed through the cigarette. No smoke rose from its tip, nothing seemed to happen, but the policeman checked, took another blundering step forward and, a surprised look on his face, crumpled to the earth. There was a tiny drop of blood on his cheek.

The *Spider* bent his head again over the cigarette lighter, ignoring the crumpled policeman, jerked up his head again. Once more he puffed through the cigarette, and this time the sun glinted on a tiny sliver of steel flying through the air, a flying sliver that was too swift for the man at whom it sped to dodge. It caught him beneath the ear and, instantly paralyzed, he too, fell.

Stupidly the third officer had stared while his companions were dropped by the *Spider*'s narcotized darts, blown through a tiny pipette thrust through an ordinary cigarette. The fall of the second officer seemed to snap him from the paralysis of his amazement. He snapped a shot at Wentworth. Crouching forward, he walked in on him, gun belching lead.

The first bullet had sped wide, thanks to Wentworth's split-second reflexes, his ability to dodge like a flick of light. There was no time to insert a third dart in the cigarette undercover of appearing to light it. He snatched out his automatic, and the bullet whanged against the policeman's lead-vomiting revolver.

The man gripped his numbed wrist, stared into Wentworth's set face— and took the third narcotic dart in the throat. The *Spider* raced to the wreck of the automobile he had bombed, seeking some clue to the origin of these men, some way to trace them to their headquarters. Even the license plates of the car were unreadable, melted out of all shape by the blast furnace heat of the gasoline blaze.

Wentworth, his lips twisted thinly, put his ugly, menacing seal upon the paint-stripped and still hot door of the car, then strode off across the fields.

THE horror of the laboratory bombing was all about him. Fragments of masonry and metal were scattered like waste paper over the ground. And there were the dead, men and women and parts of men and women. In the fork of a tree, a girl's nude body was wedged. Her hair was black and stirred faintly in the warm wind. Wentworth strode on, his eyes burning in a dead white face. He could not help the dead, but their dead lips cried aloud for vengeance!

On a parallel highway three-quarters of a mile away, he found a phone in a garage and called Washington, warning the surgeon general to guard other laboratories, advising that they radio a warning to the serum plane and send a convoy of attack ships.

The surgeon general's voice was acid over the wire. "I'm afraid your warning on the laboratories comes too late. Our own here has been blown up. We're checking on others. The plane will be warned."

Wentworth whirled from the phone, paid a garage attendant to race with him to the city where, his disguise altered once more, he was able to rent a plane although narrow-eyed police examined every person intent on leaving the city.

Despite the fierce need for haste, he moved with

deliberate calmness, chatting a moment with the policeman on guard about the horror of the laboratory blast. He climbed leisurely into the cockpit, waved a hand and sent the ship sky-rocketing. He did not spiral for height, but slanted off in a long climb toward Eatonville.

Deliberation dropped from him. He gripped the stick with a rigid hand. His eyes swept the skies feverishly. That planeload of the Pasteur injections spelled life for the hundreds of those the plague had touched in Eatonville. If the criminals managed to strike that down, too, the chances were there would not be a single dose left this side of the Atlantic Ocean!

L'Institut Pasteur, of France, was rushing three thousand sets of injections on the *Atlantica*, he had learned from Washington. Within five days the ship would dock at New York. But it would then be too late to save many of those stricken. And still the *Spider* was without a clue to the fiends behind this fearful plague.

Their purpose was still not clear, though their intention to attack industrial towns had been at once apparent to Wentworth. Thanks to his warning, all such towns now were erecting a mesh of steel fences, setting up powerful floodlights and turning night into day for their expert marksmen. These methods would keep out the dogs and wolves, with the death's head branded upon their foreheads. It might keep out the cats. Exterminators already were combating the horde of rats and mice loosed by the criminals.

These defenses might suffice when they were completed, but those high, strong fences took time. And meanwhile the hordes could range at will among the helpless thousands of the industrial towns, snapping with paws whose slightest scratch meant death to the innocent men and women and children who were the pawns in this hell-bred plot.

Now the patterned streets of Eatonville rose on the horizon, nestling amid the circle of green hills. The ribbon of the road over which Wentworth had roared in pursuit of the fleeing truck was choked with cars. All their hoods pointed away from Eatonville. Wentworth's mouth was a straight, hard line. Panic laughed its shrill senseless laughter in those streets, the laughter that turned men's blood to water. And here panic took the guise of a wolf with a death's-head burned upon its skull, a wolf with foam-flecked, snapping jaws and a cracked crazy howl that was like a maniac laughing.

Wentworth whirled the plane into a steep-climbing spiral, scanning the heavens behind him. Distantly he saw a vague dot that momentarily enlarged. He jerked wide the throttle, hurled the vibrating ship at peak speed toward that spot. Gradually it developed a web-like line to either side. That line thickened into a wing.

Off to the north and to the west, other groups of dots became visible now. Those would be Army warriors sent to protect the serum plane. Wentworth held the stick back. The motor labored, but he gained altitude. There were low-hanging clouds that could hide a squadron of enemy planes. If he could get between those clouds and the serum ship.

What was that?

Tearing from those clouds, splitting the air in an almost vertical dive directly toward the serum ship, Wentworth spotted another ship. He gripped his automatic, the only weapon he carried, and fought to get one more notch on the throttle. Already his craft was traveling at wing-trembling speed. His helpless eyes, watching the tableau ahead, detected a flickering wisp of flame behind the propeller of the down-swooping plane. It had loosed machine guns on the serum ship!

CHAPTER EIGHT
Death in the Skies

THE defenseless serum ship swerved frantically to dodge those death-belching machine guns. It jerked into a side-slip. The diving killer of the skies altered his course and followed inexorably, machine guns still coughing their death message. Through an erratic barrel-roll, a power dive, the plane pursued. No amount of flying skill or daring, it seemed, could save the ambushed serum ship.

The attacking plane was swifter, more dexterous. Easily it followed the writhing, stumbling efforts of the unarmed and heavier serum ship to escape. The end came in the midst of a rudder-kicking, barrel-rolling dive. The tracer bullets smoked home into the cockpit, and the serum plane staggered, zoomed and stood on its tail, pitched off and plunged downward in a screaming tailspin.

Black smoke blossomed as it bored toward the earth; black smoke, then a vicious red fang of flame that turned into a flapping tongue that licked the whole underside of the ship.

Wentworth's lips twisted into a thin, snarling line. The serum plane was doomed, but the ship that had struck it down, if it escaped these onsweeping squadrons, should lead the *Spider*'s fangs to the kill. He wrenched on the stick, sent his plane vaulting into the protecting cloud banks above, himself shrouded in silver mist. Skimming on upward to the sun-drenched tops of the clouds, Wentworth began a slow, wide circling. The pirate craft would undoubtedly seek this protection. Hedge-hopping would be the only other recourse and with those armadas of the air converging, low altitude would be dangerous.

He had scarcely completed a single circle of his grim patrol when the killer vaulted above the cotton-wool cloud tops and, tearing through the crests of those gentle waves, streaked southward, where still thicker bands of mist were piling up. There was a distant dark threat of storm and preliminary lightnings stabbed the murk with flame. Wentworth dived into the clouds and compass-steered southward also.

Now and again, he hurdled upward in a porpoise leap that spotted the ship ahead, and concealed his pursuit again instantly. Of the Army armadas there was no trace. Either they had been shaken off by the swift flight to the clouds or they prowled below, futilely. Once, far off, Wentworth spotted a circling ship, but it was soon left behind by their swift southward rush.

For five minutes now, Wentworth did not spy upon his quarry. Then he eased back on the stick, ripped upward out of the mist and, with a cry in his throat, hurled it back into the obscurity of the clouds again. As he had thrust into view, he had spotted the pirate craft directly overhead. It had dived instantly, twin death flames flickering at the muzzles of its machine guns. And Wentworth's only weapon was an automatic pistol!

Yet Wentworth did not flee the attack. After that single necessary dive, he spun the plane southward once more under the protecting shield of the clouds. He cut his motor and, straining his ears against the drum-deadening beat of the engine, made out the hornet buzz of the other plane slashing through the mists behind him. He gunned the motor, and bucked upward to clear the fouled spark plugs his moment's idling had cost him. Minutes later, the sweet, rhythmic beat once more restored, he thrust into the open again, skimmed the tops of the cloud waves.

For the moment, the upper air was clear, but only for an instant. The pirate plane zipped upward in an Immelman, whirled— and once more its guns coughed. The *Spider*'s lips began to smile, and it was a smile that meant death. All hope was lost now of trailing this ship to the lair of the Horde Master, but the *Spider* would exact vengeance for the wrecking of the serum ship, the doom of the thousands which its fall heralded. With a steady hand he yanked his belts to see that they held securely, then thrust the stick all the way forward. He held it like that, spun downward in that most perilous of all air maneuvers, an outside loop!

INSTEAD of whirling with the bottom of the plane outermost so that the force of the whirl thrust him more deeply into the cockpit, he would somersault with the cockpit outermost, with his body straining to yank free of the restraining belts, with the blood driven to his head by terrific centrifugal force, pounding numbly in his temples. The pirate ship ripped toward him, tracer bullets burning their smoke-streaming path directly overhead.

As Wentworth's ship vanished once more in the cloud bank on a maneuver that the killer could not dream would be attempted, the pirate ship swooped upward again, vaulted into an ordinary loop and swept back, waiting for its victim to show again. That hovering craft was like an eagle with outstretched claws ready to grasp a helpless pigeon, armed only with a feeble beak.

The pirate ship reached the bottom of its loop and Wentworth, head buzzing with the pressure of blood, dangling by the one strap that still held after that death-defying outward loop, swept up on his tail, scant yards away. A kick at the rudder and for a fleeting breath of time, the two ships raced side by side. The startled face of the pirate pilot swung about, mouth agape, an arm flung up unconsciously to shield himself from the leveled gun in the fist of the *Spider*.

Spewing out the entire clip of bullets, Wentworth fanned the cockpit of the other ship with lead. Then he slammed forward the stick, dived into the tops of the clouds and kicked into an Immelmann, sweeping back past the pirate plane on its other flank. In that swift passage, he had flipped out the empty clip of his gun, jammed in another with his right hand. Now, gripping the stick with his knees, he yanked a cartridge into the chamber and was ready.

The two ships zipped past at a combined speed of better than three hundred miles an hour. Wentworth attempted no shot. It would have been futile. He saw the pilot hunched forward in his cockpit, then he had darted past, flung into a vertical bank and was upon the pirate's tail.

The killer was maneuvering weakly. His plane was boring downward toward the clouds with the pilot crouched in his pit. Wentworth knew he had scored a hit. He threw the stick forward, yanked the throttle wide and swept on his prey in a whining power dive. The killer twisted his head about, flung up a hand as Wentworth once more swept past with his automatic blasting, then the clouds swallowed both.

It was like a plunge from a brightly lighted room into midnight. The soft gray billows of the clouds folded about them and Wentworth was alone in a world of swirling silvery mists. He eased the throttle, checking the furious pace of his plunge, and pulled out of the dive just as his plane burst through the lower margin of the clouds into the dull, gray light of a shadowed world.

The pirate ship was below him, its tail whirling

in the fatal nose-down corkscrew of a spin. On and on the pirate ship plunged and Wentworth heard in imagination the banshee-screaming of its taut wires, wailing for the pilot's death. The plane struck nose-on in the edge of a meadow, bounced upward, spattering fragments over the landscape, and collapsed on a crushed side.

After that nothing stirred there, except a flock of crows rising in mucous flight and flapping heavily to nearby dead trees. They peered bright-eyed at the wreck, took to slow wings again as another ship glided to a landing and a man crossed to the wreck, hauled out a dead man and pressed something that glittered to his forehead.

If they flapped near later, scanning that wreckage with their insatiable curiosity, they must have wondered at the sprawling, hairy-legged spot of red upon the forehead of the dead man— *the Spider's warning seal!*

CHAPTER NINE
The Hordes Strike

TAKING off from the meadow where he had sent the Plague Master's aerial killer crashing to his death, Wentworth swept at mounting speed toward Cologne. He had been forced by the pressure of events to turn aside from his quest there for Ram Singh. And every trail he had since followed had ended in death and the seal of the *Spider*. If only he could find some trace of Ram Singh, perhaps rescue his faithful servant, he would have a definite clue to the Plague Master and the whereabouts of his headquarters. In Cologne, too, was the trail of the mysterious Dr. Brent.

Those two slight leads, tracing the movements of two men; one abducted or slain; the other undoubtedly seeking in every way possible to conceal himself, were the only clues Wentworth had. And the land lay helpless beneath the assaults of the Mad Hordes of doom. These were the thoughts that raced through Wentworth's mind as he sped back toward Cologne, weary with the ceaseless battle.

As he flew along, he completed with his deft fingers the hurried disguise he had assumed before renting this plane, the disguise of one Patrick O'Roone, a sandy-haired Irishman with a slightly comic, pug-nosed face. His brows, too, were sandy, and a mustache of the same shade bristled upon his lip. His right eye developed a squint, and a gold crown upon an eye tooth completed the picture of the man who set down the plane upon the flying field at Cologne.

Patrick O'Roone was a jocular, robust man, but there were lines of weariness around his eyes, for whatever Patrick O'Roone had been doing in his imitable Irish way for the last forty-eight hours, his creator, the *Spider*, had been dashing furiously in pursuit of the Horde Master, had battled for his own life and the lives of thousands in the air and on earth and had four times imprinted his dread red seal as a warning to the Underworld.

The Wentworth that was Patrick O'Roone joked with the mechanics at the field, got them to notify the Columbus concern from whom he had chartered the plane that he would be needing it for a few days more and strode with the toe-treading lightness of an athlete to a taxi.

As he was sped through the streets, blossoming with the lights of early dusk, Wentworth saw police stationed in pairs, saw that people moved hurriedly, with eyes fearfully intent upon the shadows. His pug-nosed face remained half humorous, his right eye squinted as in amusement, but his heart began to pound high and thuddingly in his throat in the tempo of anger. He knew what those actions meant. The fate of Eatonville was not enough to cause them. The Horde Master had struck some new blow!

The taxi hit a red traffic light and lounged up to the white stop line at Main Street. Wentworth signaled a newsboy, hoarse from shouting extras, and bought copies of the *Herald* and the *Cologne News-Leader*. He held the *Herald* toward the rays of a streetlight.

23 SERUM LABORATORIES BOMBED

Wentworth caught that headline, saw the word "Healy" in a second streamer, then the taxi inched up on the changing light and, getting the signal, slithered into Main.

The papers must wait. He stuffed them into the wide pocket of his coat. Wentworth would not have done that, but Patrick O'Roone was slightly sloppy as to dress. He halted the taxi at a corner, paid off, and from nearby shops bought a Gladstone bag and some haberdashery. These things were necessary, because police would trace him through the plane wrecked at the laboratory, which they would know had carried the *Spider*.

His purchases were all a part of his new identity.

ANOTHER taxi dropped him beneath the rococo marquis of the Cologne Vanderbilt hotel. He registered again. It would have taken a clever student of handwriting to have detected that the Patrick O'Roone who sprawled big letters along a line was the same man who, a broken-nosed, slightly disreputable figure, had signed earlier this same day in a crabbed, uneducated hand that matched well with his appearance.

Once in his room, Wentworth began a detailed study of the newspapers. The second biggest story, topped only by the laboratory disasters which had killed nearly a thousand persons, was the news that Berthold Healy had narrowly escaped death at the hands of a maniac guard who had already murdered his wife and two children. A small smile twisted Wentworth's mouth. The *Herald* had a nice gift of dramatization. He read on.

In a moment of consciousness, as he was dying, Rusk apparently realized the enormity of his crimes and tried to make amends by whispering the name of the men responsible for them. Police said the name was kept secret, although thorough investigation had revealed no trace of the man named. He was supposed to have been a physician, police reported.

Wentworth squinted the right eye of Patrick O'Roone. Police already had hunted this "Dr. Brent" then—had done that piece of work for the *Spider*. But why had anyone at Healy's done anything so ridiculous as to give that clue to local policemen when Wentworth had identified himself as a federal investigator?

Further reading told him what he had half forgotten. The identity that he had given Healy had been revealed as that of the *Spider*. Small wonder, then, that they had called in police! Still Wentworth skimmed on through the story. Scarlet had done the talking for the household.

There were pictures of Mrs. Healy—her name was Sybil, and the daughter, Doris. Tomorrow, he hoped, Nita Van Sloan would contrive an entrance there, and then he would once more have an inside contact. Meanwhile, this Dr. Brent—

The Horde Master had blasted every laboratory in the country that conceivably could be used for the manufacture of the serum. The government had arranged for shipment of a huge supply, three thousand treatments, by L'Institut Pasteur on the *Atlantica*, the world's fastest steamer. Within five days that would arrive and, the government assured the people, there would then still be ample time to treat those who had been infected by the bites of hydrophobic animals.

Fourteen days to several months, according to the location of the wound, was the incubation period of the disease, and long before the malady could strike, the Pasteur injections would have built up immunity. Thus said the government!

The Eatonville stories stated that twenty persons already had been stricken with hydrophobia, despite cauterizing treatment at the time of the attack. No known form of the disease had ever struck so quickly, doctors stated. They were skeptical, insisting that infection must have taken place some time previously without the knowledge of the victim. But no evidence of such previous infection had been disclosed.

WENTWORTH'S hands, gripping the newspaper, were white with strain. Not only had these fiends loosed a horrible disease upon the country and destroyed all means of combating that ailment, but they had developed a virus which brought on that dread plague within thirty-six hours. Even if the immunizing injections were at hand, they would be useless against this new form of rabies, for immunity was not developed until fourteen days after the injection!

He threw the papers savagely to the floor. Rest was not for the *Spider*, though the gaunt lines of fatigue were beginning to tauten his face and his eyes were sunken with weariness. He must act swiftly.

He strode to the phone, called Adjutant General Lansing and identified himself. He told him that troops undoubtedly would be needed shortly to defend cities against the hordes and made certain suggestions for defense. The general's voice was brisk and agreeable. He thought the suggestions excellent.

Then Wentworth turned to the task of finding Ram Singh. He had been reasonably sure until now that the injection he had given the Hindu would have successfully immunized him to the disease. The news from Eatonville made that doubtful now. Cauterizing within twenty hours after the wound usually prevented rabies, but this new and speedy virus upset all medical information.

He began his search with the hospitals and the morgue, tried police last, but all inquiries were futile. It would be necessary to go to the town of Washington Courthouse, where he had dropped Ram Singh, to trace him.

First, while he was in Cologne, the trail of Dr. Brent must be investigated. Even if the police had worked over the ground, there remained the chance that the *Spider* might succeed where they had failed. And the trail of Dr. Brent would lead as surely to Ram Singh, Wentworth was convinced, as if he followed the Hindu himself.

He tested his automatic, thrust extra clips of bullets into his pockets and strode out of the Cologne-Vanderbilt and along the evening-darkened streets. A taxi took him to Crossroads Street where first the plague had struck.

Wentworth already had ascertained that the shipment of dogs had not been to any specific address, but to the station itself, where it had been called for. There were no more shipments of dogs to be traced. The broadcast alarm which Wentworth had requested through Washington for the man known to New York police under the alias of Douglas Brent had borne no fruit. There had been no trace of the man for months past. Yet Wentworth knew that in some way Healy's guard, Rusk, had run across a doctor named Brent and had had reason to suspect that the doctor was implicated in a plot against Berthold Healy.

No one was alive in the Rusk family to be questioned. Wentworth walked up a white cement path that bisected the neat green lawn of Rusk's next door neighbor. A woman with a child beside her made a porch swing creak rustily. A man had his chair tilted back, his feet upon the railing. Wentworth took off his hat, flashed the broad smile of Patrick O'Roone upon them.

"I'm looking for Dan Rusk who lives around here somewhere," he said. "Can you tell me where to find him?"

The man took a stubby pipe from between his teeth and spat over the railing.

"Yeah," he said.

"Where?"

"In hell!"

Wentworth allowed his smile to grow uncertain. "I'm afraid I don't understand."

"Dan Rusk is dead," the man said, and put his pipe back between his teeth.

Wentworth shook his head heavily, dug out of his pocket a briar pipe. He stuffed it with an emphatic thumb. "Well, that's the way it goes," he said slowly. "We're here today and gone tomorrow."

The man with his feet on the rail watched approvingly as Wentworth lighted up the blackened pipe. He spat again. "You said it," he declared. "Only I wouldn't like to go the way Dan Rusk did."

IT TOOK a half hour of patient roundabout talking, but ultimately Wentworth learned that it had been this man's wife who had given Dr. Brent's name to Dan Rusk's wife when his stomach began to bother him, and she had done it because a friend of hers had told her how this same Dr. Brent had cured her husband's stomach trouble just overnight.

"But how," asked Wentworth, "did you get hold of this Dr. Brent?" He grinned his infectious gold-toothed smile. "I might get a stomach ache some day myself."

The woman got up from the porch swing, went in the house and returned with a slip of paper on which a telephone number had been penciled. "This woman gave me the doctor's phone number," she explained, "just in case we ever had need of him. She was a real nice lady."

Wentworth traced the phone number and found it was located in an office which had been vacated the previous day, although the rent had been paid for an entire month. The superintendent of the building gave dubious assent to a search. The room was bare of letters and file. Apparently, its sole use had been the telephone placed squarely in the center of the desk.

Wentworth lifted the blotter. Under it lay two yellowed newspaper clippings. One concerned hydrophobia and listed all the laboratories that manufactured the serum. The other was a personality sketch of Berthold Healy with a large stipple drawing reproducing perfectly the square-cut heaviness of the face. Patrick O'Roone, watched by the superintendent, squinted his right eye. The name of the paper was the *Eatonville Press*. The story listed all Healy's holdings.

Wentworth made notes of Healy's holdings and left the clippings. He searched vainly for fingerprints and thanked the superintendent. Ten minutes later, he was on the wing with his propeller churning the night air toward Eatonville.

He sent the plane into a slow glide toward the air field on its western flank and the purple glow of its floodlights fanned out across its level green. Wentworth spotted the swiveling wind arrow with its guttering torches, set the plane down and taxied to the hangars. He gave swift directions for disposal of his ship, ordered that it be kept ready for an immediate takeoff and strode toward the two waiting taxis, a hundred yards nearer the administration building.

A sedan spun around a corner of the building, halted before the door. A man climbed out and hurried in. Wentworth saw these things as he paced on toward a taxi, but took no especial notice. From the hangar behind, a man in dungarees ran out calling, "Mr. O'Roone! A message for you, Mr. O'Roone!"

Wentworth did not wait to turn his head. He hurled himself toward the taxis at top speed, high knees flung in a fierce sprint. Out of the corner of his eyes, he saw the sedan dart toward him as the single man who had alighted ran black from the building, pointing toward Wentworth. The sedan's engine whined in second gear, jolting over the rough terrain.

"Taxi," Wentworth shouted. "To me!"

A taxi driver leaned out, saw the sedan's charge and spun his taxi into motion away from Wentworth. The second cab followed suit. Either those two had been bought in by the enemy or they feared to interfere.

Wentworth's lips twisted beneath the sandy brush of his mustache. His swift glance about found no help and no cover. He was in the midst of a wide expanse of open field. The hangars behind? Long before he could dive to their shelter the sedan would have run him down, or the guns of the men would have blasted him into bloody death. The car was between him and the administration building. There was no other cover.

The gears of the charging sedan crashed into high. Straight at him it bored, blazing white headlights shining full upon his racing form. If they were holding their fire, for a moment, it was only to make more sure of his death.

Wentworth's thin grin became a snarl. Death he did not fear. He was prepared always for that eventuality. But his death now would mean triumph for the criminal forces this merciless Dr. Brent commanded. Police had not detected the faint trail which led from a next door neighbor to an empty office.

That empty office had obviously been watched. They'd spotted Patrick O'Roone and sent their killers to wait for him in Eatonville with ready guns!

CHAPTER TEN
A Dying Man Talks

WENTWORTH threw all his superb strength into a headlong sprint. He fairly flew over the earth in a terrific burst of speed. And yet he was racing toward open fields, dashing toward a level stretch of land where he could the more easily be mowed down. In the car the gangsters chuckled. Like everyone else when death threatened, this man had lost his head. The sedan was doing sixty now, plunging like a greyhound, like a sentient beast bent on destruction of its prey. Now it was only a hundred and fifty feet away, now only a hundred. The gangsters braced for the shock of the impact.

In that instant, Wentworth did an amazing thing, a thing no other man would have had the courage to do. In mid-stride, he dug his feet into the earth and spun to face the blazing headlights, then sprinted to meet the onrushing death!

Brakes squealed an instant, and the headlights slowing in their charge as the driver unconsciously stepped on the pedal. Then the motor roared again and the lights plunged forward. Steel glinted in Wentworth's right hand. Fifty feet from those dazzling beacons of death, he halted and fired twice. The lights crashed out. Wentworth hurled himself to one side. He checked dead with sliding feet, then flung flat to the earth, as a whining hail of bullets spewed over his head.

It was over in a split-fraction of a second. Wentworth rolled, threw up his gun and pumped bullets after the sedan as it zipped past. A bullet for the right rear tire, one for the left rear, two to make sure the gas tank was ripped open. He threw another at the right rear tire, snapped out the clip and, reloading, sprinted away from the car whose leaping rear light attested the accuracy of Wentworth's tire shots.

A police roadster flung around the corner of the administration building, missed Wentworth but spotted the erratic taillight and bellowed after it with its siren shrieking.

Wentworth had five one hundred dollar bills in his hand when he plunged through the hangar door.

"Quick!" he shouted. "Whose motorcycle? Five hundred for it!"

A mechanic came toward him on slow feet.

"Quickly, man!" Wentworth shouted. "I'm going to get those damned gangsters if it's the last thing I do."

The mechanic jumped at that, his last doubt vanishing under Wentworth's urgent words. He thrust keys into Wentworth's hands, snatched the money and started fumbling for his registration card. Before he could get his hand into his pocket, Wentworth had whirled the motorcycle, jerked it in gear and was pushing it at a dead run toward the door. Under the powerful urge of his rush, the motor blasted out like a machine gun. He vaulted to the saddle and cometed into the dark with twin headlights blazing.

Above the rattle of his own exhaust, he heard the coughing cackle of a machine gun. The police car's headlights were stationary at the edge of the field, its top down, its two occupants battling. But the flicker of the machine gun's death flame came from the sedan, and the crouching forms of the two policemen stiffened in death. Four men sprang to the police car, their figures black against the fan of the headlights, and the roadster wrenched toward the road.

Wentworth cut his headlights, felt the motorcycle buck like a wild horse between his knees, swerved from the unevenness of the field to the concrete road that bordered it, and roared blindly, in the wake of the fugitive roadster. The Ford beat him to the highway by a hundred yards, screamed its dry skidding tires about the curve and streaked off across the southern boundary of the city, toward that hill road that sloped up from Eatonville.

WENTWORTH leaned into the curve, saw once more the scarlet dance of the machine gun's muzzle flame. He slammed the motorcycle frantically to the left of the highway, succeeded in avoiding the leaden blast which swept back down the road. His lights were off. But it was only a question of minutes before that searching machine gun sprayed its leaden death through the right section of night air and dumped him, riddled and lifeless, into the roadside ditch.

Once more, smiling grimly, Wentworth drew his gun. Picking out the driver's head among those outlined against the reflected glow of the stolen police roadster's headlights, he emptied his automatic with slow-spaced shots.

Frightened shouts zipped back to him on the air, whipped from the mouths of the men in the speeding car.

The machine yawed wildly. Its taillight seemed to spurt backward toward Wentworth as its dwindling speed narrowed the distance. He cut his own pace, reloading. The Ford swerved wildly again, headed

straight across the road. Two tires lifted and it did two barrel rolls and landed upside down, wheels spinning idly in the air.

Wentworth flicked on his two headlights and spilled them over the shambles. Two bodies sprawled in the road. Two others hung from the car. He skidded the motorcycle to a halt, kicked the back-wheel prop down and strode to view the dead. Motors racketed over at the airport. He must make haste. Swiftly he sifted the contents of his victim's pockets without results. Three of the men were dead and upon their foreheads Wentworth affixed his scarlet *Spider* seal. The fourth still breathed hoarsely.

The road behind was alive with lights. Autos raced toward him. He caught the fourth man under the arms, tossed him to his shoulder and ran to his motorcycle. He seated the man with his feet outthrust over the handle bars, his unconscious shoulders sagging against Wentworth's chest, and spurted off up the road while ambulance bells and the wail of police sirens lagged far behind. Across the southern edge of town and up the long grade of the highway the motorcycle shot like a skyrocket. Here the road was empty of traffic—Eatonville was a nearly deserted city since the plague had struck—and, his lights out, he followed the concrete ribbon easily by its white glimmer beneath the stars.

After ten minutes without sign of pursuit, Wentworth switched on his lights and jounced across a roadside ditch into a wood lane. When the thick green growth had hidden him from the highway, he jacked up the rear of the motorcycle again and spilled his captive to the ground beneath its glaring lights. He knelt beside him and explored his injuries with swift, wise fingers. The man's chest was crushed. Death was certain.

Wentworth's face was hard as rock. If he were merciful, he would let this man die in coma. If he were merciful—a short laugh escaped the *Spider*'s lips. The Horde Master had not been merciful!

Wentworth took smelling salts from his emergency first aid kit, shot adrenaline into the crushed chest near the heart.

Groans from the dying criminal, weak groans, then flickering eyelids and consciousness. Wentworth slid into place over his eye-teeth two long glistening fangs of celluloid, stripped off the red mustache and slid on a mask. Thus the underworld knew the *Spider* and feared him. This face, with lips snarling from menacing white fangs, he thrust into the light above the dying man.

The man's death-heavy lids flared wide. A gasp cut into his sobbing breaths. Before that staring face, Wentworth thrust his hand with the ring of the *Spider*, a black ring with a sprawling red spider upon it.

"God!" The man panted. "You!"

The flat laughter of the *Spider* mocked him. "I bring you death," he said coldly. "Torture and death. There is still life in you. I can make you—" Wentworth thrust forward the snarling, masked face with the glistening fangs. "—I can make you suffer!"

"No!" gasped the man. "No!"

Wentworth slid a glittering knife into the narrow cone of light, advanced it toward his prisoner's face. Groans came from the dying man; groans but no words.

"You can save yourself," said Wentworth softly. "A few words from you, and you may die in peace. I have morphine to let you die in peace!"

The man's chest heaved horribly. Blood dribbled from his mouth corner. He tossed his head and groaned. "What—"

"Where are your headquarters?" Wentworth demanded sharply.

The man's head rolled in new agony.

Wentworth slid a hypodermic needle into view. "Peace," he said, "peace in this needle!"

The head became still, the eyes focused on the needle. Gaze unwavering on the syringe, the man began to move his lips. Wentworth bent close, caught numbers and a street.

A hard smile on his mouth, the *Spider* slid home the needle. Almost instantly, the man's lids dropped, his moans lightened.

A twig snapped behind Wentworth. He whirled, hand on gun. The white glare was full on him.

"Hoist them," a man's voice grated from the darkness. "Both hands high, Mr. *Spider*!"

CHAPTER ELEVEN
City of Doom

WENTWORTH curled his lips back from the fangs, his eyes burning through the slits of the black mask.

"Holy mother!" gasped the man in the shadows.

At his first syllable, Wentworth leaped, not toward the voice, but to a tree whose huge gnarled bole thrust into the edge of the headlight glare. The whip-crack of a long-barreled thirty-eight splashed crimson fire into the night. The lead burned across Wentworth's shoulders, made him stumble with the force of its sidewise slap. He spilled behind the protection of the tree, sprang up instantly.

The twin headlights of the motorcycle twisted about, but the hands that maneuvered them remained invisible in the blackness. Wentworth did not fire. That voice had held the accents of authority; that pistol had the ring of a police-positive revolver. The man behind the headlights probably was an officer, and Wentworth did not battle police with deadly lead.

Behind the tree, he dropped some stones into a pocket, then raised on tiptoes, feeling the bark. His fingers found a small knob and wrapped about it. He lifted himself with flexed arms, shot up a hand and found a limb. Still without using his feet, lest the leather rasp on the bark and betray his mode of flight, lest it scar the tree and leave a trail, he drew himself straight upward with bending arms, moved soundlessly among the thick growing limbs.

Below, the man moved the motorcycle, circling the tree. Now Wentworth could see him outlined against the brilliance, see the visored cap and putteed legs that confirmed his guess that the man was of the police. The man stopped the motorcycle and backed away into the night. Seconds later, his hand torch splashed light on the opposite side of the tree.

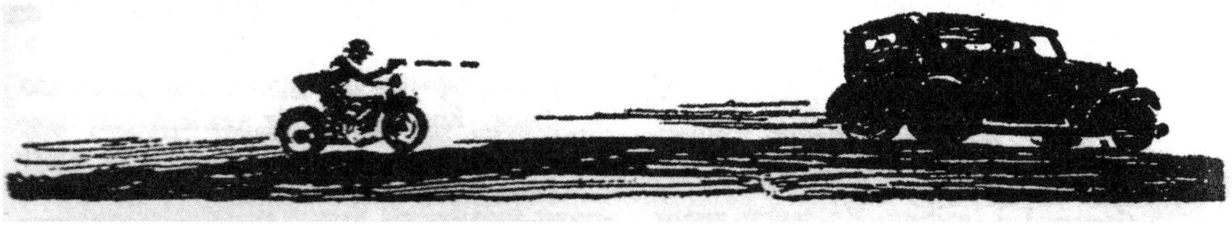

A curse ripped from the man. He fanned the thickly growing shrubbery with his flashlight.

Wentworth tossed one of the stones he had picked up before climbing the tree, flipped it over beyond the edge of the torch's rays. Instantly the policeman whirled that way, his gun spewing lead and flame. He charged toward the sound, yelling, crashing through underbrush. Another stone thrown farther into the darkness lured him on. Wentworth dropped to the ground silently, jabbed his knife into the motorcycle's front tire, and stole away in the opposite direction. Finally he made his circuitous way to the road and found a police motorcycle parked there.

He spun it and, whipping the mask from his face, vaulted to the saddle as the engine roared into action. Within a hundred yards the speedometer needle passed eighty. The wind in Wentworth's nostrils choked him. He leaned far forward. On the long sweep down to Eatonville, the needle wavered past ninety. A touch of the siren scattered traffic, and minutes later Wentworth slowed to a squealing halt around the corner from the Bovita Street address the dying gangster had given him.

He cocked the light gray felt jauntily upon the brushy red hair of Patrick O'Roone and sauntered with a rolling swagger around into Bovita Street. The house was frame and two stories tall and, very much the worse for paint, was squeezed in between a grocery and a shoe repair shop. Bovita for several blocks was spotted with such small stores, and a street car clanged and rattled along a single track down its middle.

Without a moment's hesitation, the swaggering figure that was Wentworth turned into the walk and moved deliberately up the steps. He knew the headquarters of such a gang would be well guarded, that an attempt to enter furtively would be much less likely to succeed than his frontal attack. For a moment before the door he paused, his practiced hand manipulating a lockpick. The bolt slid back silently, the knob and door moved without a sound. Wentworth walked boldly into the darkness, shut the door and stood listening.

FROM the street came the retreating rattle of the street car clattering over poorly laid rails, a swish of released air as it halted, then threshed on. The sound vibrated emptily in the house, vibrated and died. There came then, to Wentworth's ears, the faint rasp of claws on the floor.

Wentworth, cold chills of dread shuddering up his back, threw the minute beam of a small pocket flashlight ahead of him. He flinched back against the door, a cry in his throat. A giant cat was stalking him. It was snarling soundlessly, its white-flecked lips baring needle teeth, its legs crouched for a spring. Its red eyes were wild with the maniacal rage of hydrophobia. And Wentworth dared not use his gun lest the police crash in.

That crouching beast, inching ever closer, with legs tensed to spring, told him the house was empty, that this headquarters had been deserted even as he forced its address from the moaning lips of that dying gangster. Wentworth's hand slid out a blackjack. He saw the cat cease its advance, its tail lashing slowly from side to side. He knew that when that tail stiffened, the cat would leap.

Wentworth sprang first. The cat reared on its hind legs, striking with spread claws. The backjack flicked down, cracked upon the flat, broad head and smashed the cat, kicking to the floor.

Wentworth stepped clear of the threshing death and, guarding the gleam of the flash, swung it over the hall. He found closed doors to his right and bare, steep stairs leading upward on his left. Each of those dilapidated doors might conceal another such skulking killer as this cat, yet the place must be searched. In an abandoned office in Cologne, he had found a clue. Something here might point the way to the next step.

Deliberately Wentworth placed the flash between his teeth, stepped to the first door and flung it wide. Grasping the sill above it he jerked himself from the floor, swung his legs upward as a rush of tiny paws sounded below. Wentworth bent his head forward, and the beam of the light flashed on a dozen rushing gray backs, a charge of mad rats!

Waiting until the last had scampered past him, Wentworth swung forward and sprang into the middle of the room, slapping the door shut. His swift light found the room empty except for the death-stiffened figure of a dog. Not even a large dog. Not even a stick of furniture was in it. A closet was empty, also.

In the next room, Wentworth's swift swung blackjack disposed of a hydrophobic cat, but his search was fruitless.

The second floor, when Wentworth had disposed of two more cats and a dog whose fangs drooled with death-laden foam, revealed a cheaply furnished office, another room where chairs grouped around a cigarette-scarred table that was littered with greasy cards and a third room which held only a mussed bed.

Wentworth frowned and began a more detailed search, wearing gloves of thin gray silk now to guard against leaving fingerprints. In a filthy bathroom he leaned close to inspect the mirror, drew

(Facing:) "Where are your headquarters?" Wentworth demanded sharply.

out a magnifying glass and studied a black, greasy smear upon it. His face tightened with excitement. What he had found on the mirror was greasepaint, such as he himself used in his clever disguises!

Staring at the smear, Wentworth jerked his head about, listening. Stealthy footsteps creaked in the lower hall. The gangsters returning? Wentworth jerked his head in quick negative. The place had been definitely abandoned, or those death traps would not have been set. No, it must be the police. Of course, they had spotted that stolen motorcycle parked around the corner. Someone would have seen a swaggering redhead in a cocky gray hat enter the building.

Wentworth snatched up the body of the dog he had killed, holding it carefully by the leg. There was no danger of infection except from the animal's saliva. He eased up the window, peered out into a small yard behind the house. A man was crouched beside the door, a gun leveled. Wentworth smiled thinly.

He dropped the dog's body on the man's shoulders, felling him, and sprang down lightly as the policeman, yelling lustily with fear of the furry body, wrestled on the ground. As he struggled finally to his feet, Wentworth landed a single well timed right. He eased the policeman to the ground, placed the dog thoughtfully across his chest and loped out of the yard well ahead of the first men answering the policeman's cries.

A crowd was standing in the street, half of them peering toward the alley where the policeman had shouted, where Wentworth lurked.

Wentworth snatched off his hat, threw back his head and ran from the darkness as if desperate with fear.

"Mad dog!" he cried at the top of his lungs. "Mad dog!"

THE crowd scattered like feathers before the wind. Wentworth was only one of a dozen running men and boys.

Within two blocks, he checked his mad dash to a brisk walk. No street car was in sight. No taxi. He headed directly across town for the flying field.

Though it was no more than eight o'clock, the street was virtually deserted. Many people had fled this pest hole, escaping from the scores of mad plague carriers loosed by the Master. Those scores had become hundreds now as rabid beasts infected others. Everywhere walked men with rifles, with pistols slung at their belts. They moved warily and kept a close eye on the shadows.

Wentworth paced beside one.

"Get any tonight?"

The man jerked a single glance at Wentworth.

"Two dogs," he said curtly, as his eye swung back to the darkness. "Two dogs and a cat."

"Mad?" asked Wentworth.

"Probably," the man replied. "Orders are to shoot all animals."

He walked on, and Wentworth kept pace with him past small identical cottages set on rectangular lawns as regularly spaced as squares on a checker board. Here and there were lights, but many houses were dark. As the two men neared a corner cottage, its door flung open and a woman plunged screaming from the porch. A boy of twelve ran behind her, dumb with fright.

A younger woman, apparently a maid, stumbled to the door behind them. Her head seemed heavy. She stepped out on the porch, and the sound of her heavy barking breath reached the two men on the walk fifteen feet away.

"That woman in the door has hydrophobia," Wentworth rasped out.

The mother heard and ran to him.

"Sylvie!" she panted. "Sylvie. My child, my baby!"

"What, ma'am?" asked the rifleman.

"My baby is in the house," the woman gasped out. "Upstairs. That girl—"

As the woman tugged at Wentworth's arm, a child of three in a nightgown toddled into the hallway behind the swaying girl.

The woman screamed. "Sylvie, go back!"

The child jumped out on the porch. "Mummie!" it cried in a shrill treble.

The voice caught the ear of the mad girl. She whirled, and Wentworth now saw the gleam of a knife in her hand. He started forward, as the child caught at her dress, raised her arms to the mad woman.

"Take baby," it said, and the childish treble carried through the night. The mother started to run forward as the knife swept up. Wentworth caught her aside, darted forward. But even as he ran, the guard's rifle spoke. The mad woman jerked to the impact of the bullet, reeled a half pace forward, knocking the baby down. The rifle spoke again and she pitched into the hallway and lay still.

The baby lay staring, a sob beginning in its throat. The mother stumbled up the steps, snatched her child, stood rocking it in her arms, her eyes fixed upon the body of the other woman. Wentworth, eyes hard, turned to the guard. The man's face was white and strained. He drew a hand across his forehead heavily so that it puckered the flesh.

"You don't feel as bad about it as I do," he muttered. "Hell!" The curse was explosive. "What can you do? The hospitals and the asylums are full of them. Every hour they bring in more, and they can't do nothing but let them die."

WENTWORTH looked once at the woman cuddling her child, at the dead woman on the porch.

"Look out!" he cried, and his pistol spoke. Something threshed on the ground beside the porch, writhed out into the light—a mad dog.

Windows showed pale, staring faces. The guard slowly placed a charged cartridge in his rifle. Wentworth left him that way, strode up the street, his heels striking the pavement savagely. Within him, a high, white anger burned. It wiped him clean of the fatigue that had burdened his brain. No death man had ever devised could be harsh enough for the criminal who had loosed this hell upon Earth!

A man walking with heavy slowness along the pavement ahead of him caught his eye. He led a boy by the hand, and he was mumbling to himself.

"I had to do it. I had to kill her, son, You see." His words came to Wentworth, striding past. "Hey, mister," he asked, "where's the police station?"

Wentworth halted, stared at the man. "If you'll go down this street about four blocks, you'll find some police."

The man stared into Wentworth's face. His eyes were wide and without life, as the eyes of a man who had seen untellable horrors might be. "You see, mister," he said, "I had to kill her. She, she—"

Wentworth felt horror writhe like a cold snake within him. What was this man saying?"

"I had to kill her," the voice maundered on. "She went crazy, after the dog bit her. She was going to kill the boy, and—"

"Whom are you talking about?" Wentworth rasped.

"My wife," said the man, "I killed her."

Wentworth's teeth locked together. He whirled and strode away, with the man's mumbling in his ears. A man had killed his wife, driven mad by hydrophobia. A guard shot down a servant girl. The asylums were full, the hospitals jammed and helpless to do anything but wait for death. This rabies that struck with incredible speed, that spread death and crazy fear through this comfortable city of homes, still ran wild in the streets. Every lurking shadow might discharge a new menace, a dog with slashing fangs, a cat whose needle-like teeth—

Wentworth ground out a curse between his locked teeth. The new trail he followed had ended in a smear of greasepaint. Now he must go back to Cologne and Washington Courthouse to seek a new lead to these monsters behind the plague.

Wentworth halted in mid-stride and leaped to the darkness beside an unlighted house as a screaming siren heralded a police car that side-slipped into the street with its engine roaring wide open. It rocketed past, whirled another corner.

Hurrying on, Wentworth heard the crashing of pistols, the racketing of a machine gun. Peering down the street where the police car had spun, he saw a blue-coated figure stretched on the sidewalk before a bank. Floodlights illuminated the scene like daylight. Men fired at the building from behind poles, from behind parked cars.

Wentworth's lips were drawn tight with bitter anger. These criminals were not content to stampede a city, to lay a third of its population writhing in the fatal madness of hydrophobia; they must loot and pillage in the wake of their slaughtering hordes. As Wentworth watched, the doors of the bank swung wide and a dozen furred beasts rushed out to the attack. Some police, panic-stricken, turned to flee. Others loosed their guns upon the harbingers of horrid death. Bullets from the bank mowed the men down.

CHAPTER TWELVE
The Hordes Run Wild

FROM his vantage point, Wentworth had a full view of the battle, the brightly lighted street, the black alley behind it. Yellow illumination flung suddenly into the shadows of that alley, showed a half dozen vague figures plunging to its cover. Wentworth raised his gun, braced against the side of the house which concealed him, then stayed his hand.

Above the crackling reports of the pistols, he caught the roar of an automobile engine and saw an unlighted car dart from the alley and race directly toward him. When it was a half block from the bank, its headlights flared out. Wentworth, a distorted smile on his mouth, deliberately sent an entire clip of bullets clawing through the auto. It staggered like a beast, spun to the left and hurled the curb. It smacked nose-on into a house and bounced back like a crumpled toy. Not a man ran from the wreck.

Grimly Wentworth reloaded, speeding on. Nothing back there for the *Spider* to do. The police were too close for him to affix his warning seal, and he need not worry about the gangsters' fate. If the police did not kill the survivors outright, they would third-degree from them any information they might possess and strike with the full force of that knowledge. No, the *Spider* need not delay.

As he hurried on across Eatonville, skirting horror on every side, he worked swiftly on his disguise. He had no time, and no need, to alter his appearance much. The gray hat went into a trash can, the wig to another. A cap came from his pocket. Then, a slouching walk to replace that bold-shouldered swagger of Patrick O'Roone and he was altered enough to baffle the police.

At the airport, he avoided Patrick O'Roone's chartered plane, hired another and sped back to

Washington Courthouse where he sought some clue of Ram Singh. No one had seen him. The Hindu had vanished as completely as if the crocodiles of his native Ganges had trapped him in their maws. There was no help here.

He flew to Cologne, paid off the pilot and took a taxi to the city. It was nearly midnight. Once more he had been forced to abandon a disguise, and with it his hotel room and equipment. He went wearily to an all night restaurant to eat. A newspaper extra was scattered over a porcelain-topped table. Wentworth thrust aside the napkin holder and the mustard jar and spread the front page before him. As he read, his face set in a mold, like steel and his eyes became diamond-hard. The hordes had struck again!

The people of two cotton mill towns in North Carolina had fled before the onslaught of the Mad Hordes of Doom. Banks and jewelry stores had been looted. An entire district of western wheat country had been evacuated after men in the fields had been attacked by rabid coyotes. Two ships, upon the Pacific had been battling for forty-eight hours an invasion of mad rats which had attacked and infected four sailors and as many passengers.The *Atlantica*, speeding serum from L'Institut Pasteur, reported that the entire shipment had been destroyed!

But these were minor tragedies beside the news that three steel towns scattered over Ohio and Indiana had received notice that if they were not evacuated within twenty-four hours, the dread hordes would be loosed upon them. As a foretaste, the Horde Master had let six mad wolves run berserk through the streets, infecting scores before they were shot down. And on the forehead of each animal had been the burned brand of the Master's death's-head brand!

People were evacuating two of the towns at once, the paper reported. The third was preparing a defense, close mesh fences, machine guns, marksmen with stacks of ammunition. In advance they were wiping out the town's population of rats with hydrocyanic gas, dogs and cats were being executed by the hundreds.

WENTWORTH arose from the table. In a washroom he removed the last vestiges of disguise, became in fact Richard Wentworth, who carried the credentials and gold badge of the Federal Department of Justice.

In that identity, he took rooms at the Cologne-Vanderbilt and put through a series of calls. He ordered Jackson, the ex-sergeant of the A.E.F. who served as his chauffeur, to fly to Cologne with his slot-winged scarlet Northrup and its equipage of submachine guns. He phoned Washington and got authorization to act in Ohio on the hydrophobia murders as endangering the public health of the nation; he found that Professor Brownlee already was on the way West—that Nita had left hours before and should already have reached the Healy home.

It was too soon to go to the Healy home. He could enter the Castle easily as a federal investigator, but felt it would be better to seem simply a friend of Nita Van Sloan. Fatigue pressed upon him. Sitting bolt upright in a chair, assembling the jigsaw bits of the problem that had proved so far unsolvable, Wentworth felt an immense weariness, a sense of hopelessness such as had not oppressed him before in all the years of his ceaseless battling against the Underworld. He had struck a few painful blows, but he was as far this day from learning the headquarters of the gang and locating its leader as he had been when first that news item about the A.S.P.C.A. protest had caught his attention.

Wentworth retraced, step by step, his battle against the gang, the maniac attack which had led him to Healy's home, the death of the guard when Scarlet offered him a drink, the mad cats that attacked him, the loss of Ram Singh, the pursuit of the truck and the loosing of the first of the hordes on Eatonville. In all that chase, only two things presented themselves as tangible clues. The Dr. Brent against whom Rusk had gasped a dying warning was actually involved in the case, and the gang's headquarters in Eatonville had revealed a smear of greasepaint on a mirror.

Of all the baffling facts of this many sided case, that was the most puzzling.

Somehow, Wentworth felt, that greasepaint held the key to the entire affair of the Mad Hordes of Doom.

He arose wearily, checked his automatic and, placing it ready to his hand, threw himself down on the bed for the first sleep he had had in sixty hours of ceaseless struggle and death.

Less than an hour later, the continuous ringing of the telephone aroused him. He sprang instantly to his feet, automatic in hand, stared blankly at the phone. The heaviness of fatigue still clouded his brain. He jerked his head sharply, crossed to the instrument.

"Richard Wentworth speaking," he said quietly. The voice on the wire was that of his fiancée, Nita Van Sloan. "Dick," she said, "something horrible is threatening this house. I'm not quite sure yet where it will strike, but it's here and the blow may fall at any minute. No one is planning to sleep tonight."

"Definite information, darling," Wentworth asked her, "or just suspicions?"

Nita hesitated. "I have information, but nothing definite," she said finally. "Could you come at once? I told them I was going to call on a friend here who was an excellent shot."

"In half an hour," Wentworth promised.

IT was twenty-five minutes to the dot from the time he hung up till his taxi snubbed to a halt at the iron-barred gates of the Castle. At Wentworth's name, two guards opened the way and the taxi muttered up the winding road with its watching black trees, to the gray bulk of the Castle itself, ghostly in the white light of the moon. Despite the balmy warmth of the night, every window was tightly closed. Wentworth climbed broad stone steps to doors of studded iron that arched high above him. At his touch a dangling rope sounded a solemn bell note within. A butler opened the door, but Nita herself was there to greet him, her white hands outstretched to his, her red lips smiling a welcome that was shadowed by a fear which haunted her blue eyes. She was grace itself in a clinging gown of black.

She gave the faintest shake of her chestnut curls, clustering close about a poised head, and Wentworth, his face still formal, only bent above her hands.

"Nice of you to come so soon, Richard," Nita said, "I think I'll have need of your championship shooting before long."

Wentworth raised his smooth black brows, brows that arched to quirky points in which there lurked always a hint of raillery. "My good right eye is ever at thy service." His smile was gay.

Nita led him into the high ceilinged drawing room with its gaunt, draped walls of stone. The fireplace yawned like a black mouth. The occupants of the room were the same as on that other night when Wentworth had crashed through the French doors to warn them that a maniac was creeping on the house. They seemed more fearful now than they had at that first dread warning.

The two men and women were in a close group beneath a lamp that threw brittle white light upon the powdered shoulders of the women, upon the formal black and white of the men. Healy, his wife and daughter and Scarlet sat at cards about a low, square table.

At Wentworth's entrance, Healy threw his cards in a slithering heap upon the leather top. "You saved me from a terrific beating, Mr. Wentworth," he said, with an attempt at rough jocularity which fell strangely flat. "Four hearts, redoubled."

"Four hearts, redoubled." Wentworth glanced under amused brows at the four, at Healy and the dark, tragic warmth of Sybil Healy, to the glowing golden blonde of her daughter, Doris. Scarlet was standing, his shoulders so stooped that he seemed to lean, his small mouth puckered into a welcoming smile. Shadows were black all about them. In the doorway of the music room behind them, a butler stood like a sentinel.

"Which one of them do you want me to shoot, Nita?" Wentworth asked, smiling.

Scarlet's eyes jerked wide an instant, then the puckery smile widened. "Ah, I see. It's just a pleasantry."

Healy shook his head with its close cap of steel gray hair. "It wouldn't be much of a surprise if somebody did walk in and offer to shoot one of us," he said, heavily. There was an expression of keen interest on Wentworth's intensely vital face as Nita made introductions. Such was the force of his personality that his mere entrance into the room seemed to have relieved the tension. Doris Healy sat less rigidly in her chair, and Healy's square, unsmiling face seemed less drawn.

"I see I've been missing some fun," said Wentworth. "Will I really get a chance to do some shooting?"

A small door, half hidden in the shadow by the hearth, flung open and Doris jerked erect with a small cry choked in her throat. Sybil's hand flew to Scarlet's arm, then both women relaxed as the same curly-headed youth Wentworth had seen there before came striding into the room.

"Who is this man?" he demanded, pointing a dramatic arm at Wentworth.

Healy snorted breath out hard through his nose. Contempt was plain on his face. He deliberately turned square-set shoulders on the youth.

Nita walked before Wentworth. "Richard," she said, "this is Jack Collins, who has been very kind. Jack, this is Richard Wentworth, a friend of mine."

Wentworth bowed. Collins tossed a dangling lock of hair from his forehead, took two strides forward and clasped Wentworth's hand in a solid, brown grip.

"I'm glad to meet you, suh."

He said it seriously and looked as if he meant it. He turned then and crossed to Doris' chair, bent over her shoulder.

"Mighty sorry I startled you, Go'geous," he said. "The guards told me a strange man had come in and I thought I'd bettuh investigate."

The girl's smile up at him was completely forgiving. Her glance swept coldly past Nita.

"If you'll come into the library," said Healy, abruptly to Wentworth, "I'll tell you just what's been going on here. I'd like to have a sane man's view on it. Looks to me like we're all a little cracked here." He bowed to Nita jerkily. "If you'll pardon the liberty of my including you. You've been here long enough to get the poison into your mind, too."

IN the library, Wentworth saw that the high single

window had a new pane. Healy went over in detail the happenings of the hours since Wentworth, in his disguise as Sven Gustafsson, had cried a warning into the quiet house. There had been a series of attacks, especially at nights. Mad dogs had fairly rained on the place. A guard had been bitten, yet there had been no attempt to enter the Castle itself.

"Didn't this guard who died at your place," Wentworth asked, "mention some doctor named Brent?"

Healy nodded. "But police found no trace of him."

"Ever know a man named Brent who would have any reason to hate you?"

Healy stared fixedly at Wentworth.

"You're just a friend of Miss Van Sloan who can shoot straight?" There was a slight jeer in his voice.

"That was for your family and guests," said Wentworth. He laid a small gold badge on the arm of Healy's chair. The capitalist's eyes narrowed on it, raised swiftly to the vital strength of Wentworth's face.

"I see," he said slowly. "No, never knew a man named Brent."

Wentworth arose. "I don't think you need worry any more in the immediate future about attacks by animals," he said.

"Have you noticed, Mr. Healy, that though there have been a number of personal attacks on you, there has not been a single blow struck at one of your industrial towns, steel, or cotton, or wheat, or your ships— although against rival lines there have been repeated attacks?"

Healy stared fixedly up into Wentworth's eyes and rose slowly to face him.

"I'll ask you to explain that statement," he said heavily. There was menace in his bearing.

Wentworth shrugged. His face was a smiling mask that told Healy nothing.

"I just pointed out an obvious fact," he said. "I

see nothing to explain. I might add, however, that the attacks upon you have so far proved abortive."

Healy continued to stare into Wentworth's eyes. "Am I to consider myself under arrest?" he asked quietly.

Wentworth raised his brows. Their mockery was increased.

"Such a question, Mr. Healy! Shall we join the ladies?"

Their eyes locked. Healy hesitated, but presently moved toward the door. "I would rather," said Wentworth, "that you would not mention my identity. Be careful that no mad dogs bite you, Mr. Healy."

He strolled off toward where Nita stood idly turning the pages of a magazine. She raised her head of clustering curls and her eyes were questioning. Wentworth smiled, fingered the pages of the magazine as if he were interested in it.

"Darling, could you, without too much chicanery, make the charming Mr. Collins appear deeply—er—interested?"

Nita followed his lead, pointing to an advertisement and looking up at him with a laugh. "And if I can?"

"I will see if I cannot similarly beguile Mrs. Healy."

Nita straightened with a thoughtful air. "I don't see the maneuver very clearly. Of course, it places Doris and Scarlet together."

Wentworth smiled, turned to the others. "I have an entertainment to suggest," he said, raising his voice, "that I think will prove more exciting than bridge."

They all turned toward him, Sybil Healy twisting lithely in her chair, Doris turning a mildly puzzled glance. Young Collins frowned above his cards.

"Let's all take a walk," said Wentworth, "in the garden."

A rough exclamation jerked out of Healy. "But I've just told you that mad dogs and cats prowl the grounds. One man is dead. Another has been bitten."

Wentworth smiled at him. "I'm an excellent shot," he said, touching the lapel of his coat. He turned toward Sybil Healy. "And, may I have the honor?" he asked.

CHAPTER THIRTEEN
Death Waits in the Garden

FOR an instant the woman stared at Wentworth with eyes that widened slowly. Plainly she thought him mad. But as she met the challenge of his gaze, her face softened and she got slowly to her feet. She tossed her head.

"Why not?" she demanded.

"A walk in the garden!" Scarlet exclaimed. "That's an excellent idea!" There was eagerness in his voice.

Wentworth smiled at the thin, stoop shouldered man as he rose quickly. Despite his slightly unhealthy appearance, there was a certain attractiveness about him, an aspect of bored experience that would be irresistible to many women, to discontented wives, perhaps, or to very young girls.

"And you?" Wentworth turned to the scowling Collins.

"I think it's utter nonsense," Collins said vehemently. He got to his feet, taller than Wentworth by an inch and thick with the brawn that college football builds.

"Ooh," said Nita at Wentworth's side. "I choose him!"

She thrust out a finger in childish mimicry at Collins.

He stared at her in bewilderment.

"Why," cried Nita, artlessly, "aren't you going walking?"

He was too young to be proof against that, too young to turn angrily away as Healy was doing.

"If you're demented enough to go," snapped Healy, "you're going under full guard."

He jangled a loud bell violently, and a man popped in at the door. "Order four men with rifles to stand watch over these fools. They're going walking!"

"Really, my dear Healy," protested Scarlet, "you're taking all the fun out of the thing, you know."

Healy roared at him. "Have you gone mad, too? Remember it's my wife and daughter!"

"Both ably protected," Wentworth assured him.

He saw Nita laugh up at Collins, saw that young man reluctantly relax his scowl and grin back, saw them saunter toward the French doors that opened on a stone terrace and formal garden beyond. He offered his arm to Sybil Healy. She opened her slightly pouting lips, and her white teeth showed. The shimmering saffron of her gown revealed the quickened rise and fall of her breasts. She put her hand on Wentworth's arm. Scarlet offered his to Doris, and the six of them moved toward the double, glass-paned doors.

Nita lagged a little as she neared them, but Collins strode swing-shouldered forward and thrust the doors wide. The balmy softness of the night drifted in filled with the rasped chorus of insects. The moon was silver. Nita and Collins walked on, Nita with both hands on his arm, looking up intently into his face. Wentworth smiled secretly and turned to find his partner watching as Scarlet and her daughter moved off along a shrubbery-bordered path. Doris seemed nervous. She walked very close to Scarlet.

"Do you have any preference of direction?" Wentworth murmured, and Sybil Healy started, turned her head a shade too quickly away from the sauntering pair.

"Oh, no," she said, then waved her hand vaguely in the direction Scarlet and Doris had taken. Wentworth assented, but they did not move along the same path. He chose one parallel to it.

They had not taken fifty slow paces when a scream of torture rang out, punctuated by three swift shots!

WENTWORTH hurdled a low hedge, sprinted along a winding path and spun around a high clump of bushes to find Doris tight in Scarlet's arms. From his right hand dangled a pistol, and Wentworth stared beyond them where a huddled form was stretched on the earth. The ray of his flashlight revealed a dead wolf whose rear paw had been chained to a small tree. Upon the wolf's forehead was burned the death's-head of the Horde Master!

"You had all the luck," Wentworth said regretfully. "And you do shoot well. All three bullets dead center."

"Doris!" The rasp of Sybil Healy's voice startled Wentworth. He turned toward her. "Doris," she repeated. "Go to your room at once! You must rest. That beast must have given you a frightful scare.

"No—" Scarlet had started to help Doris toward the house. "I'll attend to her."

Collins panted up with Nita. He strode toward Doris, and her mother released her to him.

"What happened, Go'geous?" the boy asked solicitously.

Scarlet and Wentworth smiled at each other. Sybil Healy thrust between them.

"And as for you," she addressed Wentworth in a voice whose harshness belied the soft lines of her face. "You should have had more sense than to suggest any such fool adventure as this."

"Yes, Mrs. Healy," said Wentworth meekly. "Perhaps we'd better go in now."

He offered his arm to Nita and they moved off toward the house. A butler met them on the terrace. "A phone call, sir, long-distance for Mr. Wentworth."

Wentworth strode into the house. Healy glowered at him. "You may take the call in my library."

Wentworth nodded his thanks, walked into the book-lined room and casually closed the door behind him. He listened for moments with narrowed eyes, his face whitening.

"The time has come for desperate measures," he said. "Slow progress will no longer help. I'll go to Hurzon tonight. General Lansing, eh? Will you see that he knows I'm coming there and recognizes my power? Yes, I want it known publicly, too."

He laughed shortly. "You can do what you damned please. I'm playing a lone hand and I'm doing it my way. Very well then, I'll tender my resignation." He smiled with lips thinned as he said it. "I thought you'd see it my way," he said firmly, and looked up to find Nita standing inside the door.

"Washington," he said, as he hung up. "I think I'll send in my resignation anyway. The credentials help on occasion, but they can't seem to learn. I'll work in my own way, or not at all."

"What are your desperate measures, Dick?" she asked, quietly. "Can't I help?"

Wentworth crossed to her, folded her in his arms. "Darling, you can help me most by staying right here. Watch Healy."

"Watch Healy!"

Wentworth nodded. "I just received word that at Ashokan where they tried to fight off the hordes, mad bats*—they must be vampires obtained in some way from South America—flew over the fences and attacked men. The town was evacuated after that. The gangsters got more than half a million from the banks."

"Is that what's behind all this, Dick?"

Wentworth shook his head. "No dear. That's only part of it. The plot is industrial; and if it isn't checked soon, it's going to paralyze half the factories in the country. All rivals of a certain man are being wiped out so that his plants will become the greatest in the world, so that he will operate a virtual monopoly.

"Meanwhile, during the build-up, his plants aren't up to the demands. Work is being shut down all over the country for lack of the materials these plants should produce. It's creating another national crisis. And all so that one man can benefit."

"That man is Healy?" Nita's breath was quick. At Wentworth's assent, she began, "Then why not—"

"Why not arrest him?" Wentworth finished. "That would do no good at all, dear. You just leave that to me."

He swiftly made his excuses to the household—an unexpected business call would necessitate his departure—and borrowed a car in which he made a headlong race for Cologne. He made rapid arrangements there, found by phone that Professor Brownlee had set up a workshop and under heavy

* Carini of l'Institut Pasteur reported of a plague that destroyed about four thousand cattle and one thousand horses in Sao Paulo, Brazil, that he was convinced rabic vampire bats were responsible, viz. Ann. de l'Inst. Pasteur, Paris. Nov. XXV, II, p 785. —AUTHOR

guard was busy on some means of combating the Mad Hordes. Then Wentworth went to the airport, got out his scarlet Northrup and set it racing into the northwest.

Hurzon, second largest of the nation's steel towns, had been warned that all its workers must flee or the Mad Hordes would wipe them out. If the Horde Master won in this assault, there would be no stopping him! x

CHAPTER FOURTEEN
"Desperate Measures"

HURZON sprawled out on the prairies of Indiana like a vast black octopus, an army of huts about each plant that erupted from the soil.

Wentworth slanted through the smoky atmosphere, set down his speedy Northrup on the crossed concrete runways of the landing field and taxied up to the hangars labeled GUESTS with large black letters.

There was a squadron of Army planes on the line, and as Wentworth climbed out on the wing two soldiers marched up with bayoneted rifles.

The men's challenge was sharp, but at Wentworth's query for headquarters, they became more respectful and passed him through a series of lines to the offices of Brigadier General Francis Lansing.

The general sat behind a varnished yellow desk like a man at bay, grasping its edge with thin, nervous hands. At Wentworth's name he jerked to his feet and strode, spare and tall, to seize his hand.

"I don't generally welcome civilian advice." He snapped out his words like shots. "Not generally, but I'll be glad to cooperate with you, Wentworth. Anyone the President recommends..."

"Before we start," Wentworth told General Lansing, "there are certain arrangements I'd like to make. Will you have your oldest and weakest armored car segregated for my exclusive personal use? I'll drive it myself."

General Lansing studied him with calculating bright eyes and jabbed a punch bell on his desk violently. An orderly popped in, stiff as a rifle, received orders to call a car—the general gave its number.

"Don't worry about that," Wentworth told the general, "but if you can spare a man to follow me and report to you where I go, we may be able to trap the Master of the Hordes. Now then, this is what I have learned about the methods of these criminals."

When the conference was over, Wentworth went directly to the car, an awkward closed machine with straight sides of gray-painted steel and a narrow slit for vision which was covered with bulletproof glass. It was a model of 1929, Wentworth recognized, and nodded with satisfaction. There was a powerful motor beneath that slab-sided hood. He climbed in, kicked the starter and began a bumping, slow patrol of the lines.

Frequently he alighted and walked along the barricades that were being thrown about the town. A close-mesh inner fence had been completed and twenty paces from it another, supported by entanglements of wire with inch long barbs, was being erected. A few scattered houses outside had been deserted.

WENTWORTH climbed back into the car and trundled on. He moved alertly, though he had had less than an hour's rest in seventy-two hours of unending battle, seventy-two hours in which the nation had tasted of terror and death, of madness and wild panic. There were harsh lines about his compressed lips. His eyes were sunken but burned with a restless fire, and pounds seemed to have dropped from his body that was as lean as rawhide. Yet his fierce will, his sharp intelligence seemed to need no rest.

"You'll wear yourself out before the battle starts," General Lansing rumbled, studying him speculatively with his small bright eyes while Wentworth snatched dinner with him.

"My job's almost done," Wentworth said cheerfully. "They'll probably attack around midnight."

"I'd guess dawn," Lansing said.

Wentworth nodded. "Perfect, if you want troops worn out with waiting, but the Master of the Hordes wants men tense and nervous, so that panic will threaten."

At ten, Wentworth resumed his plodding patrol, bumping over lanes that had grown familiar now. At eleven-thirty, he alighted beside a machine gun embrasure and walked toward the men. One sat upon the tripod of a gun, his head sagging on his chest. He got sluggishly to his feet, breathing hard.

With a cold fear racing down his back, Wentworth heard the man's breath become hoarse in his throat so that he sighed noisily with each exhalation. He snatched out a flashlight and threw its beam into the man's eyes.

The soldier started back, leaned heavily against the gun shield, and Wentworth saw his throat muscles work. For an instant he sagged there inertly, then his face convulsed and he sprang for Wentworth; snatching for the bayonet at his side. His breath was like the barking of a dog. Wentworth knew those dread symptoms of hydrophobia. His fist flashed and he knocked the man flat. The three other soldiers sprang forward. "Attention!" Wentworth snapped. His voice crackled with authority. The men halted uncertainly and when the command was repeated they stiffened.

"That man knocked down is sick," Wentworth said curtly. "Bind his arms and take him to the hospital, you and you." He designated two of the men, saw them start their task and, springing to his car, sent it leaping over the ruts to headquarters. He slapped open the door, burst into the general's office where three officers were bowed over a map.

"I found a soldier suffering from hydrophobia," Wentworth bit out. "I think he's only one of many."

General Lansing jerked to his feet. "Everyone of the men was examined carefully," he said. "It's ridiculous—"

"I found one," Wentworth pointed out. "The rest is sheer guesswork, but it would be superb strategy on the part of our enemy to infect enough of the soldiers to demoralize the force. Remember, the Master of the Hordes has this virus developed to the point that it strikes within thirty-six hours. He may be able to time it just when he is ready to attack."

The other three officers were openly skeptical. General Lansing frowned, standing rigidly behind his desk, his jaw muscles knotting. The phone jangled and Lansing snatched it up.

"Yes," he said crisply. "Very well, take him to the hospital. Notify the sergeants that they are to shoot at once any man so stricken during action!"

He slapped up the receiver. "Another case," he said rapidly, caught up the phone again. "Colonel Roberts—Colonel, two cases of hydrophobia have been found among the men. Make an immediate inspection of all the troops and segregate any of which you are at all suspicious."

WENTWORTH waited for no more. He sped to his car, shot it back to the lines. Already doctors, each with an armed attendant, were hastening toward the troops.

It was ten minutes of twelve when Wentworth jerked to a halt again at the line. He stepped down. A shot cracked in the darkness twenty yards beyond the barbed wire where pickets stood watch. As if that had been a signal, another, softer sound made itself heard, a splashing of water. Wentworth whirled, flung the ray of a pocket flashlight toward the dilapidated huts behind him. The beam glinted on a hose nozzle, on a silvery stream of water that strengthened even as he watched it until it broke in a spray of glistening drops against the fence.

Choking back a shout, Wentworth darted to the hose and screwed the nozzle shut. He smashed against the door of the hut and plunged in, slashing the darkness with his light as with his word. The house was empty. Whoever had loosed the water had fled. Wentworth darted back outside. Still the soft splashing of water sounded and above it came other sounds, horrible with their senselessness, the screams of madmen!

TWO shots cut the night twenty feet away, and two men pitched screaming to the ground. An officer crouched over them with a smoking pistol. His sharp voice grew harsh in command. The crack of revolvers came from every side. Wentworth flung to his car, switched on its headlights. As far as their blue-white brilliance penetrated through the night, he saw glistening streams of water at intervals of fifty feet. Soldiers were choking them off, but their hellish errand had been fulfilled. Well Wentworth knew that the Master of the Hordes had bribed workmen within the fences to loose those streams of water—planning that the sight and sound of it should hurl into homicidal rages the soldiers he had injected with the virus of the mad death.

The scream of the stricken men, the crack of pistols still echoed over the brittlely tense battle line when Wentworth heard two ripping explosions, saw bunched spears of flame stab upward from the fences fifty yards to his right. Torn bodies were in that flame, and the screams of the wounded mingled with the cries of the madmen.

Like an echo of that first double blast, another and another tore out to left, to right, to the rear. All along the lines, the enemy had blasted the fences, making way for the Mad Hordes!

A reserve squad went past on the double to reinforce the dynamited troops. Two men were lagging. The sergeant spat an order at them. Without warning, one of the soldiers jerked up his rifle and shot down the officer. He whirled savagely on his companion, slashed at him with his bayonet. His face, illuminated by the white glare of a floating Very light, was twisted insanely. Wentworth shot him through the head. The second soldier whirled, throwing up his rifle, and Wentworth sped a second bullet.

The reserve jogged off to its task, but the men moved reluctantly with backward flung glances at the bodies on the ground. Would they stand firm when the Mad Hordes poured through the breaches?

Rifles popped like a string of firecrackers. The ground beyond the fences, white as day beneath luminance of floodlights, was strewn with the carcasses of slain dogs, but others and still others poured from the darkness.

They moved, with the stiff mechanical jerkiness of automatons, unswerving.

Drooling jaws agape, they loped toward the breaches in the fence, springing over the bodies of the dead. Soundless they were in attack or wounded. Struck once, they dragged onward until they were shot again or until they managed to penetrate the line. They snapped at each other, gashing the flanks of dogs that ran beside them, receiving bloody tears in their own hides. But they stopped for nothing.

They did not fight among themselves or with

men. A snap of their jaws and they were gone into the blackness of the night.

Wentworth threw his car across the breach and loosed a submachinegun in bursts upon those that got past the enfillading fire of the soldiers. Even above the crackling of guns, he could hear the fearful cries of men, struck from the rear by their own companions gone mad, or pulled down by the Hordes. He saw a great slinking cat leap upon a man's back and the two tumbled in a tangled mass that made it impossible to shoot. It might have been a war of the Beasts against Mankind.

FOR a few seconds, the waves of mad dogs ceased, then terribly from the night swept the most horrible of all those mad hundreds that had charged upon the beleaguered city—mad wolves whose foreheads bore the grinning brand of the Master of the Hordes, the death's-head! A dozen unnerved soldiers within Wentworth's range of vision whirled to flee, but were driven back by the flaming revolvers of their officers.

On rushed the wolves, slashing through the bright lights in a half dozen lightning bounds. They left some of their fellows dead upon the ground, but most of them charged even through Wentworth's deadly fire. The soldiers broke from all control, broke and ran backward, sweeping their officers with them. Upon their flanks ran the terribly silent wolves with their fearful brand of death. Their long white madness-laden fangs gashed into the men.

And, horror on top of horror, Wentworth saw a black-winged form flit through the light. An officer who had been knocked down by his retreating men reeled to his feet, stumbled to a machine gun to continue the vain battle. The black thing wheeled toward him and the man's face vanished in an embrace of leathern wings. The man's scream was high and cracked with fear. He tore the thing from his face, hurled it savagely to the ground and ground his heels upon it.

From the darkness, two more of the black forms wheeled, struck at his white and fear-ridden face. The officer whipped at them with flailing arms, turned and ran desperately.

The Master of the Hordes had released the bats, his plague of mad vampires!

What could guns and fences avail against these? The breach was unguarded by the dead and Wentworth's single gun. Cats still slunk among the dead and slipped through the opening or clawed over the fences. Scampering gray crawling things that were rats and mice poured past. Guns were useless against that horde. In the hovels of the town they would find ample concealment, and thousands of their fellows to spread the infection they brought.

Wentworth ceased his futile firing. Silence shut down about him, silence broken only by the groans of the wounded, the distant thin popping of guns where the defense still held for the moment—these, and the scampering, stealthy, murderous feet of the Hordes.

HIS mouth a grim, hard line, Wentworth started the car and turned it toward the breach. The battle had been fought and lost. It was time for his "desperate measures."

Wentworth pushed on, nosing along a street that was black as death. On the far eastern horizon, the moon crept into view like a lop-sided, bloodshot eye. Somewhere back here, Wentworth knew, were the leaders of this fearful attack, somewhere here the brain that had engineered this utter route of soldiers and machine guns, who had accomplished the doom of another town. Banks were being pillaged back in the city, jewelry stores looted of their wealth, the homes of the rich ransacked. The town was doomed.

Without warning, there was a smashing explosion behind Wentworth. He jerked his head about to find that a pit had been blasted in the road. Even as he stared the armored car jarred and trembled to a second ripping upheaval. He jammed on brakes, slid to a halt on the verge of another bomb-hole.

"Surrender," a voice called, "or the next bomb will be under the car. Be sensible, Wentworth."

Wentworth switched out his headlights, loosed his machine gun at the voice. He spun the steering wheel, jolted over a ditch and charged toward the sound. More bombs exploded around him.

A grim smile twitched Wentworth's mouth. He had half a drum of ammunition left for his machine gun, three clips of cartridges for his automatic. He loosed the half drum in a ripping roll of fire that rattled through the walls of the house before him. He wanted to be captured. He had made himself conspicuous in this armored car all day. He had pushed out beyond the last defenses for that sole purpose, but he didn't intend to yield too easily.

The machine gun emptied its last ripping blast and Wentworth dropped the overheated weapon. With his pistol he waited, and waiting, he felt a drowsiness stealing over him. He kicked open ventilators but the sleepiness increased.

He moved loggily toward the door and machine gun bullets racketed against its heavy steel. Wentworth knew he was being gassed. With his last gleam of consciousness, he raised his automatic and poured a stream of hot lead through the ignition switch, then he relaxed.

The *Spider* had employed his "desperate measures." If you can't find the enemy, let the enemy find you!

CHAPTER FIFTEEN
Human Guinea Pigs

THE blackness lifted slowly and became a cloudy gray. Semi-conscious, Wentworth was acutely aware of sensory stimuli. Points dug into the flesh of his back and legs, yet he was powerless to move. All about him he seemed to hear the slow-timed barking of dogs. A man was screaming hoarsely, without words, over and over again one high-pitched, cracked scream. A stench like the closed monkey house of a zoo was heavy.

Those points in his back were uncomfortable. Wentworth sought to move and relieve the stabbling pressure. His legs twitched and he heard a dry chuckle.

"I thought it was about time you came around, Mr. Wentworth," a voice as rasping as a rusty hinge creaked out. "I'll retire until you're able to chat."

Wentworth gathered his sleeping will to force himself back to consciousness. He moved a hand heavily and dropped it beside him. He felt a wooden floor and straw. Straw... was that what stabbed his back? His hand touched his side and felt bare flesh.

The breach was unguarded except for Wentworth's single gun.

Wentworth's eyes began to focus clearly and he saw black vertical bars. The barking sounds were clearer, the high, terrible screaming went on. He braced his hands, forced himself to a sitting position, and realized two things: he was stark naked and was seated upon the floor of a cell enclosed by close set iron bars!

"I would have awakened you sooner, but you

looked as if you needed sleep. And strong, rested men make the best virus," the voice said.

Wentworth echoed the words in his mind. Was this man, his captor, planning to make him work to produce hydrophobia germs? He shook his head heavily, braced hands and legs and reeled to his feet, stood staring as he swayed in the dazzling light. It was switched off abruptly and the monotonous screaming resumed.

"Can't you stop that noise?" he demanded in irritation.

The dry chuckle came to him again and now his eyes made out a small, stooped figure outside the cell, a bent little old man with stringy white hair that straggled thinly about a peaked head.

"In just a little while," the man promised. "You aren't half as impatient to stop that noise as the fellow that's making it. But it isn't time yet."

Behind the stooped figure of the little man he made out the bars of other cages. Men stood in all of them, mother naked, gripping the bars and staring. And with the suddenness of a stabbing pain Wentworth realized what that barking sound was. It was the breathing of these men! And men who breathed like that— Good Lord! *These men all had hydrophobia!*

SLOWLY, he turned his head to right and left. More cages. Fully thirty men imprisoned at the whim of this dry voiced torturer. The screams— Wentworth stared into the cage next to his own. The man was a giant Negro standing six feet three in his bare feet. His head was thrown back. His breath was a groan and with each panted exhalation he cried terribly. His knees were sagging, but he held himself erect with great fists gripping the bars.

"Perhaps you... are thirsty," came the dry voice of the stooped man, timing his words to fall between the screams. "The gas affects you... that way."

"In Heaven's name, no!" cried Wentworth, but only the dry laughter answered him and the man poured water from a gurgling bottle into a glass.

"Better drink... while you can," he said, and handed the glass to Wentworth.

A hell of screaming broke loose in the room. Men fell down and writhed on the floor, gripping their tormented throats. The giant rolled his great head from side to side in agony. His knees sagged more and more until he was holding himself erect by his hands alone. A man diagonally across from Wentworth shouted a scream of filthy curses. He demanded death for himself in a cry that could be heard even above the bedlam of pain and madness. He begged for it, though it was plain the madness did not grip him yet.

Wentworth turned from the torture and walked to the back of his cell. There in darkness he drank the glass of water. He was thirsty, yet he did not wish to torture those other poor unfortunates dying of hydrophobia. In the name of Heaven, what could be the purpose of all this torture?

"Why not shoot that poor Negro?" he asked. "His death is a matter of hours and there is no need for him to suffer."

The ugly, peaked head of the bent man shook from side to side. He hobbled from the room, being careful to keep clear of the hands outthrust to grab him between bars. He went out a small door at one end of the hall of the cages.

When he returned, the bedlam had died. He had with him two men who were thrusting ahead of them a third man.

The two men were clothed. The third was naked, his head was clipped and the corded muscles stood out like ropes on his brown body as he fought his captors. They thrust him up to the cage in which Wentworth stood, then held a gun on Wentworth while they unlocked the door and thrust him in.

"Greetings to thee, Ram Singh," Wentworth greeted the newcomer quietly. "I had thought thee dead."

"On thee the salaam," said the captive, bowing and touching a cupped hand to his forehead. He answered as Wentworth had spoken, in Hindustani. "Soon, *sahib*, we *will* be dead." On his upper right arm was a festering wound, a wound as if from human teeth!

Ram Singh bowed and touched his forehead. "It is a shame upon me, *sahib*, that I allowed this offal of a dog to capture me. *Wah!* If I but had my knife!"

"They tricked you, oh, Ram Singh?"

From without, the mad little man shouted abuse. They ignored him. The Hindu grinned like a wolf, lips thin against his fine white teeth. "Two of the dogs tasted my steel, *sahib*, before some vile vapor made my muscles like a woman's and three of them fell upon me. *Wah!* They were cowards! Five of them to seize me!" His voice grew harsh.

"May Allah deliver them to my knife!"

Wentworth shook his head slowly. "There is no disgrace when thy enemies bare thy head, oh, Ram Singh."

He told his faithful servant then how he had allowed himself to be captured so that he might learn where the headquarters of the gang were situated. The impatient snarling of the bent old man who was their captor broke in on them.

"May you have the joy of your reunion," the man rasped. "Shall I worry when my guinea pigs turn their backs upon me?"

His guinea pigs! Wentworth faced slowly about, walked to the bars. In Heaven's name, what could the fiend mean?

"Listen, old fool," he said curtly. "We must remain here for a little while, of course, but it behooves you to be civil while we are here."

The man giggled. He spat at Wentworth's face. "You think the soldier you had following you can give the alarm? I've got him in the other room. No, my dear Wentworth, you are beyond help!"

Wentworth smiled calmly into his sneering face. It stirred the man's anger. "I know! I know!" he screamed. "You are the man they call the *Spider*. When we captured your body servant, we traced him and found that out. But this once the *Spider* won't win. The *Spider* never before met Dern Bierkson." He tapped his hollow chest with a claw-like hand. "Shall I tell you what will happen to this mighty man who calls himself the *Spider*? Did you wonder at the swiftness with which the germs of hydrophobia struck? I did that, I"—once more he tapped his thin chest— "Even as old Pasteur built up his fixed virus by giving the disease to rabbits and using their spinal cords to infect other rabbits, I have built a stronger, more virulent form of rabies.

"I did it by using *human guinea pigs for rabbits*. And that's all you are, Mr. Wentworth, my fine bragging *Spider*, a human guinea pig. Sometime during the night, your man, Ram Singh, will have his first seizure. He will bite you and give you the disease, for that is part of the system I have evolved. The virus is stronger if communicated by the teeth instead of with the needle. And that is why I have stripped you, to make the biting easier."

THE man threw back his misshapen, ugly head and laughed his cracked shrill laughter. It was the mirth of a madman, no doubt of that, but a crafty madman. The man's hideous body and face, the dimly lighted room of cages with its suffering, dying prisoners, the cries of the maniac in the next cell combined to make a scene of incredible horror.

The madman's laughter mounted to a high-pitched note and broke. "So you do not like the idea of being the guinea pig of Dern Bierkson ? Well, others have not liked it, but it has done them no good. Shall a guinea pig challenge a scientist?"

Chuckling to himself, he walked toward the narrow exit door that squeezed in between two cages and there he lifted his voice, calling, "Jacques!" He shuffled with his queer bent gait back to Wentworth's cage. He could not seem to satiate himself with gloating over these new captives of his. Presently the narrow door opened and a man edged his broad shoulders sidewise through the door. He had a chest like a keg, this one, covered by a tight blue jersey and upon his head was a cocky cap of wool. A heavy pistol tapped against his thigh as he swaggered up behind Dern Bierkson.

Bierkson jabbed a bony hand at the cage of the Negro. "This guinea pig is ripe for the picking, Jacques," he said in his snarling, harsh voice. "Pick it up and bring in the new specimen."

The burly man in the blue jersey nodded his round head, shifted a cud of tobacco to the other cheek and spat an inches long stream.

The man stared at him, winked, and walked to the cage of the Negro. "Shoot me, too," begged the man diagonally across from Wentworth. He had a two-day growth of red beard upon his cheeks. His hands were gnarled. "Shoot me, you son of a pig and dry-uddered camel, you—" he lapsed into the French of the gutters, heaped filth upon the perverted old scientist and his man, but both ignored him. The pistol was thrust close to the bars. One shot blew the heart out of the Negro. His harsh breathing choked off and the gate clanged open. With a single heave, the blue jerseyed one hoisted the Negro giant's body to his shoulders.

"Remember," old Bierkson snarled after him, "bring in that other one at once!" He turned toward Wentworth, massaging his bony bands. "This is a little surprise I have for you. I hope you will appreciate it properly."

Wentworth felt tension grow in his chest, felt his pulse become hard and pounding. What new infamy had this madman committed? He clenched his fists at his side, then a curse tore from his lips and he snatched frantically through the bars for the bent old fiend. But the man dodged him with a surprising nimbleness and mocking, shrill laughter.

Wentworth gripped on the bars, gripped them and choked down the wrath that was strangling him with hot hands of hate. The thin white scar upon his right temple throbbed. He stared at the door that had swung open a little way to give him a glimpse of the new "human guinea pig" that stood beyond, and now flung wide to admit the swaggering, cocky executioner and his prisoner.

The prisoner was a woman whose clothing had been stripped from her except for a chemise of pale green satin that reached halfway down her round white thighs and upward to cover her breasts. Except for that single scanty garment she was naked. The men crowded against their bars. The woman hung her head.

"Bring her here! Bring her here!" snarled Bierkson. "I have a particular friend of hers for her to meet."

A friend! Wentworth had seen only that the new prisoner was a woman. But a friend! Good God in Heaven, could they have captured—

The girl was thrust before the cage. Slowly she raised her head of clustering chestnut curls. Her blue eyes met Wentworth's. He grasped the bars and fury sent the blood buzzing in his ears.

"Nita!" he cried hoarsely. "Oh, God!"

The leering high laughter of Bierkson mocked them.

"Nita indeed!" he sneered. "Do guinea pigs have names?"

CHAPTER SIXTEEN
For Humanity!

WHILE the mad scientist laughed in fiendish glee, while the barking breath of the doomed men sounded mournfully in their ears, Nita van Sloan lifted her head proudly, looked into Wentworth's eyes and smiled.

"Hello, Dick," she said quietly.

Wentworth fought down the horror that surged within him. If she did not know of the hell ahead, he would protect her from it as long as possible. He compelled his lips to smile.

"Delightful to see you again," he said cheerfully." These slumming parties make one appreciate one's advantages more, don't you think?"

Each carefully ignored the enforced nudeness of the other. Wentworth was thankful that the dim lighting of the place partly concealed Nita and himself. It stirred blind anger within him to see the brutal hands of Nita's captor gripping her soft white arms.

"I understand I'm to be a neighbor of yours for a while," Nita went on in her carefully casual voice.

"Next door," Wentworth nodded.

The man twitched Nita from before Wentworth's cage as if she had been a toy, thrust her through the door and slammed it shut with a dull ringing clang.

"A damned shame, Professor," he grunted, "to waste a pretty piece like her on your fool experiments. You might at least wait—"

"Out of here, vermin!" Bierkson spat. He struck at Jacques with a hand in which metal glinted and the man cried out in mortal fear and darted to the door in panic. The bent old man turned, stared at Nita.

"There is something in what Jacques says, at that," he cackled, "and if I were younger... Listen, my child, it is only tonight that you must sleep alone. Tomorrow I shall allow your lover to enter the cage with you. How much these others would give for the chance!" His voice turned gloating. "But you will not welcome your lover this time, my dear, for during this night his servant will go mad and bite him and when he comes to you the virus of hydrophobia will already be hot within his veins! You understand, my sweet one!

"I have been longing ever since this experiment started to try the virus on a woman. I have a theory that it will develop even more rapidly in a woman and strike even more swiftly when her—when yours, it is, my dear—spinal cord is cut out and used to spread the madness.

"But I hadn't told you, had I, sweet one, what your purpose is? You are just a guinea pig, just a guinea pig to spread the hydrophobia for Brent!"

WENTWORTH caught at that phrase. It was a confirmation of all that he had thought. Brent was behind this business. The mad old scientist was simply a pawn in the wild and terrible scheme. "It is a pity I could not have had you a few days sooner," Bierkson maundered on. "I would like to use your spinal cord for tonight's attack on Gary. It is the climax of Brent's plans. Would it not be an honor to participate, even if only vicariously?

"After last night, Brent will issue no more warnings, he will only attack. With such tactics, there is no reason why Brent can't master the whole country as he has a few towns, no reason why he can't take over Washington, the entire country. Then, what human guinea pigs I should have! All the world through all the ages would ring with my fame. I could solve the mystery of every disease!"

A man poked his head in at the narrow door across the room. "Professor, it's the chief calling about tonight."

Bierkson grumbled "All right," looked about him as if he regretted for a moment having to leave his guinea pigs, then shambled on across the room. Wentworth pressed against the bars of Nita's cell and whispered her name. Her hand touched his.

"Don't let what Bierkson said worry you," Wentworth whispered. "We can be out of here in five minutes any time we're left alone that long."

"I wasn't worried," said Nita calmly. "I knew you'd find a way out for us."

Wentworth laughed softly. "If only I had as much confidence in myself as you have in me!" he exclaimed. "Is it night or day, Nita?"

"It's late afternoon," she told him.

An exclamation escaped Wentworth. "And Gary is to be attacked tonight! Judging from what Bierkson said, the city won't be warned at all. Lord, it's a massacre! It is not ourselves alone we must save. It is an entire city!"

He bent over and from between the great toe of his left foot and the one next to it, he slipped a sliver of steel which had been secured there with flesh colored tape. In a stride he had reached the door and bent over the heavy lock. It was a simple fastening, but Wentworth's tool was not the most efficient, and working as he must by thrusting both arms through the bars and reaching at full length over the solid sheet of steel that protected the lock, it was slow work.

Twice he was forced to stop when he thought he heard footsteps, but finally the lock clicked back and he pushed open the gate of his cell. He sprang instantly to Nita's door and bent to the task. It was simpler now that he had opened one lock, now that he could manipulate without straining his arms in awkward positions. A moment later, her door also clicked open and Wentworth spun toward the exit from the room of the human guinea pigs, Nita and Ram Singh behind him.

A deep voice rasped out from the opposite cells. "Either you take me with you, or I'll yell a warning."

Wentworth jerked his head that way, but did not slow his swift stalking.

"I'm going to get the keys if I can," he rapidly told the man. "If I waited to pick all those locks; none of us could escape."

The man stared with narrowed eyes as the three stole on toward the door. "You're lying," he cried out hoarsely. "You're lying. Help!" he shouted. "They're getting away!"

Wentworth reached the door in a bound, knocked it open with his shoulder and dived to the floor beyond. Jacques was charging across the room with drawn gun. He snapped a shot but the swift dive confused him and he missed.

Before he could fire again, Wentworth sprang from a crouch, thudding into the man's middle with his shoulder, sending him reeling backward. His fingers locked about the man's gun wrist twisting shrewdly.

With an oath, Jacques dropped the weapon and wrapped arms like steel cable about Wentworth. No chance here to match science against brawn. Now it was muscle against muscle. Wentworth felt the arms close like the knives of the iron lady about him, bruising sinews, crunching joints. Peering over the man's shoulder, he saw a huddled bunch of other men burst into the room with daylight behind them. To their left a door flung open and the professor in a white surgical apron, a scalpel in his hand stood outlined in white glare from an operating lamp. They were trapped by an overwhelming force!

WENTWORTH had only seconds when he might escape. Now he battled a single man. Though that one was powerful as a Greek wrestler, his strength would be as nothing compared with the combined force of those others approaching warily even now from the doorway. He flung a glance about, seeking the soldier prisoner. He might help them. No soldier was in sight. No help but in himself. His chest laboring, Wentworth panted out a few clipped words in Hindustani— then a strange thing happened.

His breath became hoarse in his throat so that he seemed almost to bark with each exhalation, his jaws began to champ and snap, and his eyes glaring wide, he lunged for the throat of Jacques, baring his teeth like a dog. Horror and fright twisted the face of the man. Wentworth's teeth struck his throat, gouged into the flesh. Jacques screamed.

He snapped his arms from his prisoner and whirled to flee.

"La Rage!" he cried hoarsely. "He have hydrophobia!"

They scattered, screaming.

"Fools!" the bent old professor shouted from the doorway. "It is a trick! He hasn't got hydrophobia!"

He darted to rally his men, slashing wildly with the scalpel. Ram Singh plunged toward them now, teeth snapping as Wentworth's did. The professor lunged into his path, thrust the scalpel at him. A brown arm shot out and pinioned his old, stringy wrist, twisted the surgical knife free. A blow and Dern Bierkson slammed against the wall and collapsed.

Jacques, with Wentworth clinging to his back, smashed into the men. He went through it and out into the open, carrying two others with him. Ram Singh's cries of triumph were sharp, and at each cry a man groaned and collapsed with razor-sharp steel burning his vitals. A moment the huddle at the door lasted, then the battle was over. Ram Singh and Wentworth panted side by side, two naked men, one brown, one as bronzed as an Indian.

In Ram Singh's hand was a bloody scalpel. In Wentworth's was Jacques' heavy revolver. He raised it and fired once and Jacques, sprinting for a nearby house, stumbled. His feet hit the ground awkwardly, toes digging.

From the long low building toward which he had darted, other men darted out. Guns were in their hands. They spotted the naked men in the doorway and ran toward them.

Wentworth felt a touch on his shoulder, a soft hand, and jerked his head about. Nita stood just behind him.

"The hangar!" Wentworth panted. "The plane that brought you?"

"To your left," Nita said swiftly, and catching her hand, Wentworth darted that way. "Around this building," she directed. Ram Singh streaked beside them.

From the men behind, shouts rang out. The three fugitives whirled the corner, saw the hangar a hundred feet away.

"Ram Singh!" Wentworth shouted. "Start the plane, get Nita in. Come for me!" He released Nita's hand. "Run!"

THEY raced toward the hangar. Wentworth flung flat on the ground and waited with pistol leveled, a smile twisting his mouth corners.

A man slammed around the house corner and blazed away at the hangar. The man cursed and slapped his feet down hard in a pounding run and Wentworth knew Nita and Ram Singh had reached

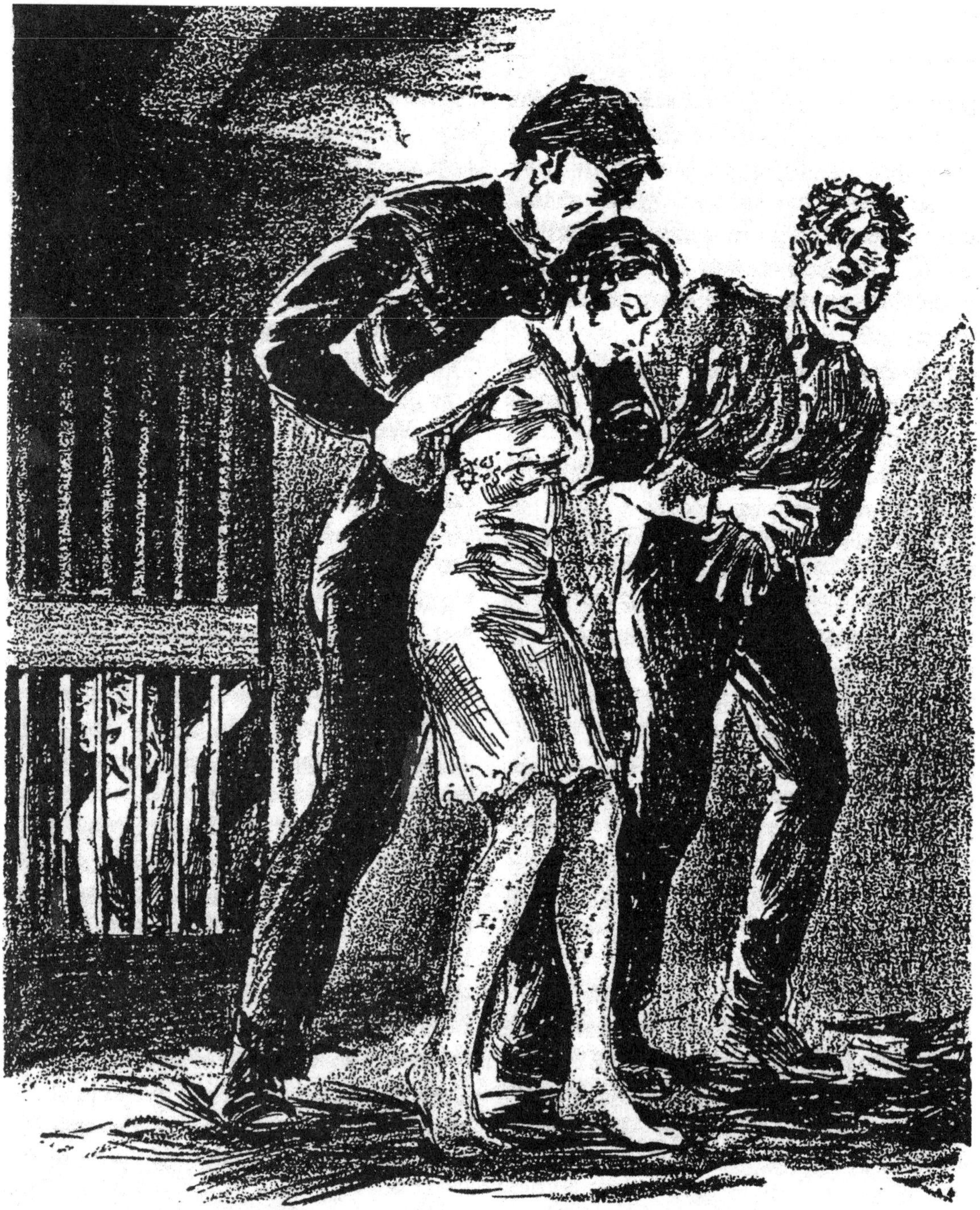

The girl was thrust before the cage, Wentworth grasped the bars and fury sent his brain spinning.

cover. He held his fire. In the dusk, the man overlooked the bronze body of the *Spider* stretched upon the ground. He saw him when he was within fifty feet and a frightened cry jerked from his lips. He threw up his gun. Three other men piled around the corner in a bunch.

Wentworth fired calmly. His first bullet drilled the forehead of the nearest man before he could shoot. At the flash of his pistol, the others loosed a wild fusillade. Lead whined high above him. One bullet spewed dirt into his face. Wentworth fired twice more carefully and two men were hurled into bloody death. The fourth fled. His cries, rallying other men, were shrill. Behind Wentworth the

plane roared.

Wentworth sprang up and raced toward his fallen foes, snatched up the pistol of the first man he had shot, dashed to the corner of the building where two more guns lay. He threw a swift glance over the quadrangle between the buildings. A dozen men were charging across it with guns glinting in their hands.

The sound of the plane behind him had steadied to an even, drumming bellow. The hollow note caused by the hangar was gone and he knew Ram Singh or Nita had taxied it out into the open. Wentworth loosed a telling burst of lead, slid to the cover of the building.

Swiftly, while his pursuers were slowed, he sprang to a window and scanned the laboratory's interior. He saw the dissecting table, cages of beasts, the door to the pen of madmen. But nowhere did he see the soldier he hoped to save. Had the professor been bluffing?

Wentworth frowned. He could wait no longer. He whirled, flung back his head and sprinted for the plane. As he neared, it wheeled, and he sprang to the right wing, seizing the edge of the forward cockpit. Instantly the roar of the motor deepened as it was given full throttle. It trundled out onto the field.

Wentworth turned his back to the hurricane of the slipstream, clinging with his right hand, a revolver in his left. A bunched rush of men swiveled the corner of the old professor's building. The flickering small flame of a machine gun danced in the deepening darkness. The plane seemed glued to the ground. It was intended to carry only two and the extra weight made it logy. There was no wind. It would take a long run to take off—and tall trees crowded close to the edge of the field.

Wentworth steadied his gun with a flexed arm to counteract the heavy jouncing of the ship as it rose slowly. The trees reared before them like a cliff. The propeller clawed the air with a thin scream, the engine labored. Death gibbered at them from those back trees.

WENTWORTH shot a glance downward. There was seventy-five feet of space beneath. Those trees, less than fifty feet ahead... Wentworth thrust his head toward the back cockpit, recognized Nita's white, tense face behind the controls. "Dive and bank!" Wentworth shouted.

The moan of wind through its wire stays mounted to a howl as Nita dove and whirled in a sharp right bank, dropping the wing on which Wentworth stood, so that his weight helped there, too. The breeze was light. It scarcely stirred the tops of the trees, their undercarriage almost touched.

Fighting slowly upward, they swung off in a wide arc southward. Wentworth, crouching on the wing, peered downward seeking landmarks, spotted an L-shaped lake a mile to the west where the faint last rays of the sun still lingered. He straightened then. The night air was sharp at this altitude, and Wentworth welcomed the flying suit that Ram Singh held out to him. He climbed into it before he squeezed into the cockpit.

He twisted and cupped his hands to shout to Nita, "Brownlee!" He saw her head nod and saw her arm, outlined black against the sky, pointing off to the southward and down. Wentworth peered where she pointed. Brilliant white lights from high lamps shone down upon an unpainted wooden house. As he watched, a wave of men rushed across a clearing toward the building. A few fell, but the rest charged on. They reached the house and a group of them began battering at the door.

Wentworth jerked his head about, and Nita nodded again. Good God in Heaven! That was Professor Brownlee's laboratory and it was being stormed by men! That could mean only one thing: The Master of the Hordes had located his workshop and was bent on thwarting his shrewd work. Wentworth felt a blow on his shoulder and, turning about, leaned far back to catch Nita's shouted words.

"Brownlee... finished... job."

Brownlee had finished. Wentworth clenched his fist and struck it upon the side of the cockpit. Professor Brownlee had found a way to stop the Hordes, Nita meant. And in the hour of his final triumph, in the hour when Wentworth had discovered the hiding place of the Hordes themselves, Professor Brownlee was being struck down!

CHAPTER SEVENTEEN
Brownlee's Job

DESPERATELY Wentworth fought to find a way out while the plane roared over the last few miles to Professor Brownlee's laboratory. The men still battered at the door. One fell writhing as he watched, shot from within. There were five of their number stretched on the ground now. They were not having too easy a conquest.

A sudden smile lighted Wentworth's face. He began to fumble through the pockets of the flying suit and found a piece of paper. Ram Singh's pockets yielded a stub of pencil. While the Hindu held a match in his cupped hands, Wentworth scribbled a dozen words.

He tied the paper to a wrench, signaled Nita to circle low and lower until they were flashing through the white glow of the floodlights from Professor Brownlee's place. Twice they swung through the light and Wentworth waved an arm to the men. Two darted out with rifles raised, then paused. Finally they waved a hesitant greeting back to him.

Then Wentworth threw the message to them.

Once more under Nita's hand the plane circled into the darkness, then swooped again. Wentworth waved again.

Three of the men were clustered over the note. They glanced up and as the ship flashed toward the night again, one waved his arm and nodded his head violently in assent. Nita shot the ship upward and they droned off straight away from the scene and, out of hearing of the men, circled for a half hour, then they returned and set the plane down in Professor Brownlee's front yard by the illumination of the floodlights.

The ship stopped with its propeller slicing the air

at the laboratory's doorstep. Wentworth sprang down, his hands high. He stood in the bright focus of the lights. There was a shout within, then the door hung wide and a short, erect little man bounced out onto the porch and clasped Wentworth in his arms.

"The papers said they had you!" he cried.

Wentworth grinned, turned back to the plane and helped Nita, barefooted but garbed as he was in a flying suit like white dungarees, to the ground. She threw her arms about the beaming little professor.

"I thought they had you sure," she said, "but Dick threw some sort of note down to them and they left in a hurry. I don't know what he could have written

Wentworth smiled wryly, striding toward the house. "I just wrote them to leave and protect Bierkson."

"But why should they obey you?"

"They recognized the plane as one of their own and the note was signed 'Brent'," he said, and was inside at the telephone.

Nita looked at Professor Brownlee. "There never was anyone like him, my dear," said the professor, and together they followed by the stern-faced Ram Singh, went into the white cottage.

Wentworth's sharp voice was ringing through the room. "Yes, General Lansing, there can be no doubt about it.

"They're attacking Gary tonight. In less than an hour, if you'll shoot my Northrup up here"—he gave him the location of Professor Brownlee's laboratory—"I'll be with you. Warn the Army men. I'll be flying the red Northrup."

WENTWORTH signaled the operator again, turned to the professor while he waited. "Nita said you had finished your job, Professor. Could you figure a gas such as I suggested?" The operator's answer interrupted and Wentworth said into the mouthpiece, "Saginal police, please. Yes, in a hurry," and turned back to the professor.

"Gas it is, Dick," Brownlee told him. "Your hunch was good, but I couldn't figure a gas that would kill the animals and not the men. However I have a narcotic gas that will keep so close to the ground—it's twice as heavy as air—that it should not affect men at all."

Wentworth nodded and turned to the phone. "The chief, please, and at once. It's important... That's good work, Professor. Better than my plan because it's safer.... Hello, Chief? Chief Gallet? This is Richard Wentworth, attached to the Department of Justice. Oh, I see. Well, I've escaped from the criminals and I know where their headquarters are." He described the L-shaped lake and the location of Dern Bierkson's gruesome laboratory. "Three hours! But Good Lord, can't you use planes? They'll all be gone before you get there if it takes three hours. Very well, do your best. And when you get there look out for mad beasts—and madmen!"

He slapped up the receiver. "Says there aren't any planes to be had. Government's taken them all." He strode to the middle of the low, crudely furnished room and stood on braced bare feet. His flying suit, open at the throat, showed the tight bunched muscles of his chest.

"Professor," he said crisply, "please have your men load a couple of carboys of your gas into the plane out front. When the Northrup comes through from Hurzon, have all it can carry put aboard." He nodded, and the professor hurried from the room. "Nita, any idea who engineered your capture?"

"I went for a walk in the garden and felt myself growing drowsy. Before I could cry out, it had me, I woke up in the plane."

Wentworth nodded, "Wait here until I come back with this plane, then you and Ram Singh fly back to Healy's home. Have Healy arrested at once. Ram Singh, on your life, guard the *missie sahib!"*

"Han, sahib!" Ram Singh bowed swiftly. "But, master, if the hydrophobia seizes me, I shall kill myself instantly so that the *missie sahib* need not fear."

Wentworth's forehead knotted in a frown. "Did you have a chance to burn the wound before you were captured?"

Ram Singh thrust forward his lean brown arm, showing a scabbed and clean wound on his forearm.

"I used the gun powder from two cartridges, and a match, *sahib*," he said, stony-faced. "And I gave myself the second injection as soon as you left."

"How many hours after you were captured was that other wound on your arm made?" Wentworth asked.

"It is now forty hours, *sahib."*

The incubation period of the Horde Master's virus was around forty hours! At any moment now the dread madness might seize upon Ram Singh, the faithful. There was a heaviness upon Wentworth. Many times in the years they had been together these two had braved death, had fought to save the other. Many times they had battled insuperable odds and won. But this was a thing that could not be fought. Unless the serum took hold before advanced symptoms set in, Ram Singh had absolutely no chance to recover.

Wentworth crossed, slow-footed to the table where stood a pitcher and a glass. His face was cut by sharp lines, and his eyes were stony.

"Drink a glass of water, Ram Singh."

Casual words! Yet if Ram Singh tried to do so

simple a thing as drink a glass of water and failed; if his effort brought his breath harshly from his mouth; if it closed his throat with paroxysmic spasms, there was only one thing for him to do—suicide, the knife!

RAM SINGH realized these things as well as Nita and Wentworth who watched him. He had seen what the mere sound of water did in that hell that Bierkson ruled, yet he walked with an utterly impassive face to the table. His hand reaching for the pitcher and glass were steady as a rock. Wentworth's eyes were fixed on Ram Singh's face, on his throat.

The margin of anti-rabic injection had been much less than prescribed, but the serum he had used was not one that had been widely experimented with. He was not sure what its effect would be. In addition to that, the serum was battling with germs of a more virulent type than ever before had been known to man, thanks to the intensification of the disease accomplished by Bierkson and his human guinea pigs. There was no way of telling what might happen.

Ram Singh had stood well the sight and the sound of water, but could he drink?

Slowly, Ram Singh raised the glass to his lips. His eyes were fixed upon it rigidly and despite his iron control, there was the dawn of horror in their depths. God above, was Ram Singh mad, or was it merely the uncertainty?

The glass touched his lips. He tilted back his head, opened his month. Slowly, smoothly he drank to the last drop!

Nita's pentup breath burst from her in a deep sigh. Wentworth realized that her nails had bitten into the flesh of his hand. He strode to where Ram Singh stood beside the table and seized his hand.

"Stout fella!" he said heartily. The serum he had given his man at the risk of his own life had taken hold, had immunized him against the dread rabies.

Professor Brownlee hustled back into the room. "The plane will be ready in two minutes," he said rapidly. "'I have the gas both in carboys and wax bombs. I put both in the plane."

"Fine!" Wentworth nodded. "Nita, when you get to Healy's home, be sure you order his arrest immediately. If you can't get it on any other grounds, swear that he assisted in your abduction. I'm going back to put my seal on the foreheads of those lads I killed at the laboratory," he said. "I didn't have my cigarette lighter before but the Professor always keeps a spare for me."

He received the lighter, a revolver and ammunition, canvas sneakers for his feet.

"If I'm not back in three quarters of an hour," he said, "do these things, Ram Singh, fly to Gary and use the gas the professor tells you. Nita, you'll have to use a car to Healy's home—if I don't come back!"

He grinned at them all from the doorway, strode out into the night.

CHAPTER EIGHTEEN
Madman's Justice

WENTWORTH'S plans for holding Bierkson and his men until police could reach the hidden laboratory were vague. Roaring through heavy night air on the short hop that separated Brownlee's place from that hell-hole of the mad scientist, he swiftly reviewed the battle ahead. If the police had got underway instantly at his call, they still would be fully two and a half hours from the spot when Wentworth reached there. And he could not tarry. Within an hour he must be speeding northward to Gary. Without him, the defense would crumple as it had at Hurzon before the assault of the Mad Hordes.

Eyes questing for the glint of water that would reveal the L-shaped lake which was his only landmark, Wentworth scanned the black earth below. It would be three o'clock before the moon rose tonight. The glimmer of the stars was faint and aloof. Fifteen minutes of swift flight and the distant black reflection of water gave him his location. Swinging in a wide circle, he spotted white buildings below.

He swooped a grenade in his hand. His mouth shut in a hard line. That bomb should blow to bits those vile laboratories below, spatter the henchmen of the Hordes over the landscape. He jerked his head in negative. Though he held little scruple about destroying these vermin who had loosed death and desolation upon the country, he still did not wish to kill those suffering men penned in Bierkson's prison of horrors. Doomed they might be, but they were innocent of wrongdoing and some might be saved. No, there must be another way.

He swung wide and hurled the bomb— into the woods. Circling again, he saw lights prick out in the buildings below. Searchlights swept the woods and swung upward to stripe the sky with light. Wentworth picked up his microphone.

"Turn off those searchlights or I'll blow every one of you to hell," he boomed through the loudspeaker.

Flame spat upward from rifles, flickered from machine guns.

"The *Spider* speaking," Wentworth thundered down at them. "Last warning. Turn off the lights or be blown up. Listen, fools, and obey. All your secrets are known. Brent had got all the wealth. He told your secrets and skipped. Brent has betrayed you. Brent didn't want you to share the gold. He has betrayed you."

Slanting downward in a propeller speeded dive, Wentworth hurled a grenade that blew the searchlight to bits.

The upward spitting flame of gunfire lessened, dwindled to a petty popping. Wentworth swung lower, saw the door of the laboratory and prison flung open, saw the bent old figure of the mad doctor of hydrophobia in a blazing oblong of white light. It poured out into the night and stretched his black shadow on the earth. He gesticulated like a medieval priest exorcising devils. Men trooped up to him and Wentworth saw their hands flying as they argued, magnified hugely, by their shadows.

A man stepped close to the professor and struck at him. The old madman reeled backward and the door slammed.

But it was shut only a moment, then it flung wide again, and the men fled from its light as from a physical blow. Their thin screams pierced even through the roar of the engine. Naked men stood in the light-flooded doorway. Wentworth knew them. They were Bierkson's human guinea pigs. Their jaws gnashed in the frenzy of hydrophobia!

THEY streamed from the brightly lighted doorway out into the blackness. A half dozen at first, then more and more until two score had poured out into the night, bounding crazily to the attack. Some fell from the scattering gunfire of the gangsters, but others survived to pursue. Behind them other hordes rushed, loosed by the enraged Bierkson; dogs and cats and scampering, vicious bats.

Wentworth swooped and smacked three bombs into the midst of the animals. The ripping grenades dug huge craters in the earth, blew the rush of hordes out of existence. No way to tell what was happening in the blackness below, how the gangsters' guns served them in their battle with the mad Frankensteins they had created. The hydrophobic men outnumbered their masters two to one. Many of the beasts, too, had escaped the bombs. They would strike naked men and gangsters alike.

Wentworth's bombs had not been out of mercy to the gang, but to avert the spread of the plague through wild animals and domestic cattle that these beasts could infect. He dropped one more grenade as a final scattering of the hordes shambled from the door.

Scarcely had the blast rumbled into silence when the hunched old figure of the insane experimenter threw its distorted shadow out upon the bomb-torn earth. He shook a scrawny fist at the night, stepped from the doorway. Suddenly he whirled.

As he spun, a naked white giant stepped from the blackness and flung upon him. He did not strike with his hands and feet, did not wield gun or knife. He seized the professor by his twisted shoulder. He pushed back his head with violent hand and sank his teeth into Bierkson's throat!

The old man's arms slowed. His hands beat feebly against the hunched shoulders of the giant, then one dropped and fumbled in his clothing. It jerked up, and steel glinted in its grasp. Bierkson slapped the steel against the side of the giant's neck!

Blood that glistened blackly spurted where the steel touched, but the naked madman gave no other sign of the wound. The professor's old hand reached straight up to Heaven, stiffened, and dropped. For moments longer the naked giant held his prey, then he dropped Bierkson to the ground like a broken toy. The man threw back his head. Good Lord! The man was laughing! For a long minute he stood like that, then his knees sagged. He dropped to them and slumped slowly down upon his face.

A shudder shivered over Wentworth. Never before had he seen death as horrible as that, death beneath the teeth of a madman! But it was just, just! The professor had died at the jaws of a man he had deliberately infected.

Once more Wentworth reached into the divided compartment before him and took out grenades. Sweeping upward and diving at top speed across the laboratory he sent two bombs smashing against the roof, raced and whanged two against the sleeping quarters of the gangsters.

Filled with the tense need for speed, for clean pure air to sweep the horror from his brain, Wentworth sent the plane roaring with throttle wide open back to the laboratory of Professor Brownlee.

Whatever happened at Gary, the fiend who had fathered the fearful hordes was dead. His henchmen were scattered into the night with raging madmen on their trails, with the shadows full of mad beasts whose teeth meant death with police racing to take them. These were destroyed, but Brent, the Master of the Hordes, survived.

But first must come Gary!

Gary. Thousands of lives were at stake there. And all depended on Professor Brownlee and his gas. The technique of battling the hordes had been improved, but Wentworth knew it would not suffice. God grant he could reach Gary in time!

Wentworth swung in a fast circle over the laboratory, spotted his scarlet Northrup in the edge of the shadows near the house and shot his ship down to a slam bang landing, side-slipping almost to a standstill, straightening out for a three pointer that did not roll a dozen feet. He sprang to the earth, darted toward the house, then abruptly he whirled and sprinted toward the Northrup.

A man with a gun crouched in the shadows of

the open door. Wentworth's grin was a fearful thing. That one man might doom Gary's thousands!

CHAPTER NINETEEN
On to Gary!

AS Wentworth swerved from his direct path to the house and spurted toward the safety of the night, the man sprang into view and blasted singing lead after him. Wentworth's grin was mocking, his eyes hard, and ugly. The man was a fool. But the first knowledge he had of his insanity was the *Spider*'s lead slamming like a trip-hammer into his chest, driving him back against the door jamb. That was as far as his sensations went. When he hit the floor he was dead.

A foot on the Northrup's wing, Wentworth vaulted to the cockpit. His feet struck something that yielded. A voiceless groan wheezed from it. Wentworth's hand leaped forward and seized hold of a man. The man's flesh was cold beneath his hand. The thick stickiness of blood oozed between his fingers. The man was dead. Wentworth's feet striking his chest had driven out his breath.

By the feeble light of the stars, Wentworth examined the body. The man was an Army pilot. A dozen bullets had torn through his head and chest.

Wentworth looked further and found he had contrived to wreck the throttle of the plane before he had died. Wentworth knew then the reason for this attack. These killers were men of the Hordes seeking to escape. They could not be those who had fled from the Camp of the Human Guinea Pigs. Perhaps these were some of that group he had tricked into abandoning the attack on Brownlee's place, some who had lingered behind and seen the plane they thought their own land Brownlee's friends.

Gently, Wentworth eased the corpse of the soldier from the cockpit, lowered it to the ground, then he reached for his submachine guns. Their compartment was well hidden and he did not think—ah, here was one. He drew it out, a compact instrument of sudden death, and, snapping on a drum of ammunition, he crept toward the house.

A pistol spat at him from a window and Wentworth ripped a burst of sizzling lead. The pistol was not discharged again. A shadow in the doorway. Wentworth jerked up the machinegun, then halted, cold horror trembling down his spine. The shadow in the doorway was Nita!

"Go ahead and shoot," a man's voice jeered, and Wentworth saw its owner crouched behind Nita. "Go ahead. You crack down just once more and I'm going to blow a hand off the girl. Just by way of warning."

Wentworth began to back slowly toward the darkness.

"Stand still!" the man snarled. "You stand right there until— Herb! Come out here and take this punk. He's got a typewriter, so watch him."

A man stepped boldly into sight, sidled along the house. Why were they taking so much trouble to capture him alive, Wentworth wondered. A single shot would put him out of the picture.

"Don't hurt him, Herb," the man behind Nita warned. "He's got to take us away from here!"

So that was it! They had no one with them who could fly a plane and did not know that Nita and Ram Singh were both excellent pilots. Wentworth held out the machine gun to the man called Herb and docilely allowed himself to be herded toward the laboratory.

It would not be difficult to overpower this man beside him, but escape without Brownlee's narcotic gas would be futile, the sacrifice of Nita that would be involved would be vain. No, he must allow himself to be taken an apparently willing captive, and trust to his keen brain. But delay meant the difference between life and death to thousands!

TREADING lightly with alert muscles and brain, Wentworth was taken up to the porch with a machine gun muzzle at his spine. Nita smiled at him wanly and he flung a swift glance about the room, saw Brownlee and Ram Singh tied and glimpsed the man behind Nita, a round-faced pallid man, with hairless eyelids like a snake's.

"I thought that would fix you up," he said in an oily voice.

Wentworth's glinting eyes fixed on his forehead. He seemed slightly amused. The man frowned.

"Listen, bozo," he snarled, "you're going to fly us away from here and do it quick."

Wentworth's eyes did not swerve.

"Get out of the way, Herb," the moon faced man snarled. "This baby is going to take a fall."

He took two strides forward and slashed sideways with the barrel of his gun at Wentworth's head. The head wasn't there. The man spat out a curse and stepped in close. Wentworth caught the wrist as the man struck and flung himself backward.

Wentworth, flopping on his back, dug both feet into the man's belly as he hit and heaved upward. The gunman crunched down on his head.

Wentworth rolled to his right, like a log, lunging down an incline. The machine gun bullets Herb loosed ploughed the floor so close behind him that Wentworth's flying suit jerked with the flicking tug of the lead. Herb yelled as Wentworth slammed against his legs. The machine gun bit off its chatter and Herb attempted to dance backward.

He hit the wall hard, kicked at Wentworth. Wentworth sprang up and smashed a right to the jaw. Herb went to sleep.

A knife from his pocket and Wentworth had freed the three prisoners.

"They got us when the Northrup landed," Brownlee explained shamefacedly. "We went out to meet the pilot."

"Where are your assistants?" Wentworth rapped out.

Brownlee's face grew bleak.

"Dead," he said briefly. "They tried to shoot it out with those four."

Wentworth jerked the last rope free, bound his prisoner. "And the gas, Professor?" he asked over his shoulder.

"About a third made," the Professor called as he ran to his laboratory.

Time, time! The fates seemed to conspire against Gary. For the professor must work alone on the gas since the assistants who knew the details of its manufacture were dead.

Wentworth finished binding the gangster. "Ram Singh!" he called. "The throttle of the Northrup is smashed. It must be fixed at once!"

The Hindu crossed the room in two bounds, plunged out the door.

"Nita, you'll have to take off alone," Wentworth told her swiftly. "It's more important than ever that you reach the Healy home and have him placed under arrest. I may fail at Gary. If I do—"

He broke off and ran to the laboratory to help Professor Brownlee, waving a hand as Nita also raced to the door.

Wentworth was still binding the strings of the rubber laboratory apron about him when the motor of the plane blasted into the night, steadied and hurtled off into the blackness. Nita was on the way! He turned to Professor Brownlee, already bent like a sorcerer above a steaming caldron from which brown acrid gas rose.

"Tell me what to do, Professor."

Through dragging hours, the two labored over mixtures that simmered from self-generated heat, over brews that steamed and smoked, over others that frosted the glass they touched.

A bit of dull gray metal dropped into a seething mess popped like a firecracker along its surface and Professor Brownlee raised a haggard face. The clock registered three minutes of eleven. "One more operation, Dick, and we'll pump it into the cylinders. I've got plenty of those, but damned few bombshells."

Wentworth nodded grimly, ran to the phone and called General Lansing at Gary.

The brigadier's voice crackled in his ear.

"I expected you here by now," he barked out. "We've been here only an hour. Oil trench is dug as you suggested. We're expecting the attack any moment."

Wentworth cut in.

"Please detail three planes to rush here at top speed," he asked. "And bring some chemists in them. The planes will have to be small. The landing field won't allow more than two hundred feet run. I can't carry much gas on my Northrup. Wait," he stopped Lansing's nervous interjection and went on. "I can bring all Professor Brownlee was able to manufacture in one batch. As soon as this is finished he'll start another.

"I'll take off in half an hour, be there in another hour. Any sign of attack yet?"

"No, none," Lansing said, then his voice cut off as over the wire came a rumbling vibration.

"What was that?" Wentworth cried.

"That," came General Lansing's grim voice, "was the attack." He slammed up the receiver.

Another half hour of racing work and the job was finished. Wentworth seized a carboy of gas. Hoisting it to his shoulder, he ran with long, even strides to the Northrup. Ram Singh straightened.

"All is ready now," he said.

"Start the motor and let it warm up," Wentworth snapped out. "Load this carboy in the baggage compartment."

As he whirled back to the house, sprinting, he heard the mounting whine of the compression starter, then the first coughing explosions of the motor. Six carboys they stored in the tail compartment. Two were lashed on each wing close against the fuselage. Ram Singh held another between his knees in the forward cockpit and he was no more than settled when Wentworth sprang in behind him, yanked open the throttle.

THE carboys were cast iron and though their contents were not heavy, they made a terrific load for the Northrup with its limited wing spread to lift on the short run that was possible on this restricted field. At Wentworth's signal, Professor Brownlee put chocks in front of the wheels and Wentworth, foot heavy on the brakes, let them remain until the engines were roaring full blast.

When he waved his arm and the chocks were jerked free, the Northrup sprang forward like a whippet behind a mechanical rabbit. Its dash was swift and violent and Wentworth muscled the ship off the ground with a zoom and a dive and a bounce from swiftly reversed controls.

Wentworth shot a glance at his radium gleaming wrist dial as he wheeled to the northwest. It lacked but twelve minutes of twelve. The attack had been underway twenty minutes, bombs blasting the fences, the Hordes pouring through the breaches, drooling jaws agape. And he was an hour away!

The Northrup, logy with its heavy load, trembled under the throb of its powerful engine, driven at peak speed. The black landscape seemed to crawl beneath them with leaden slowness, despite the better than two hundred mile gait.

Miles of defenses were flung about Gary. The Hordes might attack in a dozen places. A carboy could guard only one entrance for perhaps a half hour. The few wax bombs would take care of another. After that—

Professor Brownlee was already at work on another mixture and help was on the way—a series of black blots against the sky resolved itself into Army planes speeding to Brownlee's assistance and Wentworth rocked his wings in salute as he shot past—but at best it would be three hours before another load could start.

He strained his eyes into the northwest. Blue-white pencils of light wrote hieroglyphics across the northwestern sky, then as he watched all winked out but one whose beam cut off and on at space intervals. For a full minute that continued, then it began to flicker in dots and dashes.

Wentworth had requested certain information and advised against use of radio lest they be overheard. It was less likely the gangs would know Morse. The message was:

Seven o'clock wind. Worst breach three o'clock. Fires low.

That last phrase was ominous. The oil fires that alone supported that single fence were nearly out. When they flickered into darkness, the Hordes would pour into the city!

ALREADY Wentworth could make out the yellow rip of fire that girded the city. Minutes dragged past with a labored slowness that made the plane seem to stand still. At five miles distance, Wentworth threw the ship into a long dive, joyfully felt the vibration of his mounting speed. He swept toward the eastern flank of the city where the message had indicated the gravest danger.

"Ram Singh," Wentworth spoke into the headphone set that linked them, "get ready with that carboy. When I throw my right hand, open the valve and drop for the opening in the fence. Try to hit just to the south of it."

Lower Wentworth swept until the upturned faces of soldiers, caged in against the fierce forays of the vampire bats, showed plainly along the fence. Wentworth could not know, but as the scarlet plane streaked overhead, a faltering cheer arose. It gained volume and became a roar of hope. Those men, beleagued through hours of weird battling with tiny, fearful foes, saw salvation. They bent more vigilantly over their guns.

The breach in the fence jerked into view. Wentworth threw up his hand and a tumbling oblong of black, the carboy of gas, spun downward. It struck the hard earth with a fine accuracy that attested Wentworth's good eye and instantly the greasy dark gas began to coat the earth.

Would the gas operate as Professor Brownlee had promised? Would it bowl over those Hordes that swept terribly upon the city, or had his laboratory experiments been too hastily conducted? There had been no opportunity to make tests under identical conditions with these. Two blazing white Very lights burst upon the black night.

Across that patch of light-drenched earth loped the most horrible of all the Hordes, the wolves of the death-branded heads. They plunged into the greasy fog that hugged the earth like a black mobile snow. Wentworth focused his gaze on the gaunt horrible beast that led the pack. Once, twice he dipped into the gas and reared to leap onward. Three more such strides and he would be past the gas!

The third spring faltered. He bounded again, feebly, and his front legs collapsed under him. He kicked, rolled, and lay still. The gray killers behind him did not have his strength. They collapsed before they had twice dipped into the gas.

"Take the controls, Ram Singh, follow the fence!" he ordered and felt the Hindu's hand firm upon the stick. He climbed out on the wing. Black stretches blotted out the flames at intervals now along the fire trench. The oil was failing. Let it fail now!

At three more breaches in the fence, Wentworth dropped the carboys and did not wait to see the Hordes falter and wilt, did not wait to see the spiteful rifle flashes that finished them. With another huge bomb ready, he waited tensely as they raced near the next breach. But, almost on the point of releasing it, he checked. Not an animal was in sight!

CHAPTER TWENTY
The Human Horde

WENTWORTH checked the carboy on the verge of tumbling it to the earth. It yanked him off balance and he clung frantically to the fuselage with one hand, the other hanging on to the carboy that was incredibly precious. A hundred lives might well hinge on saving it—A hundred? A thousand. The plane hit rough air and tilted. The carboy slipped another inch. Wentworth's arm was nearly wrenched from its socket, still he fought to save the carboy through moment after moment of Herculean strain. He gasped out orders to Ram Singh, but the wind whipped the dim words from his lips. The motor drowned the sound. Abruptly the Hindu seemed to sense his master's peril. His lean hand seized Wentworth's. He deliberately rocked the ship to the right so that the carboy's own weight rolled it back on the wing.

Wentworth could not rest. There was no time. He

peered downward again. Each breach as he swept over it was brilliantly lighted by Very stars and at none of them did he spot the onrushing Hordes. Had the Master quit the battle so soon? Wentworth jerked his head in negative. That was ridiculous. No, there was some new strategy. His eyes narrowed. He spun to the cockpit where Ram Singh sat.

"Land there!" he shouted and pointed to a cleared space within the line of buildings as they slanted toward it.

Wentworth descried a park. With most planes of the Northrup's power, the landing would have been impossible, but Wentworth's Scarlet ship was equipped with wing slots which gave it a landing speed scarcely forty-five miles an hour. The field was illuminated only by nearby street lights but they knew the direction of the wind and Ram Singh boldly put the ship into a glide. It jounced once, then he snubbed the speeding ship to a halt. Wentworth sprang down and sprinted toward the street.

He spotted a garage, dashed to it and commandeered four cars with drivers. A phone call to General Lansing made, he hopped one of the cars and guided it back to the park, up over the curbing and across level lawns to the plane.

The carboys of gas were speedily loaded on the machines and, leaving Ram Singh to guard the plane, Wentworth raced to Lansing's headquarters. Other cars waited there and, loaded with one carboy each, they sped off into the night.

That accomplished, Wentworth strode into headquarters where General Lansing paced up and down a barren office in which were no chairs and only two tables. On one a map of the city was spread. On the other was a battery of telephones. They kept three men busy and they constantly ran back and forth between the phones and the map where a fourth man made notations and shifted colored pins.

Lansing grunted a greeting to Wentworth, but did not cease his pounding up and down with leather-heeled boots. His long skinny legs flexed at every step.

"You guessed his strategy exactly right. He waited until the plane had passed, then loosed his animals again. With a carboy placed at each breach, we can loose the gas whenever it is needed. Cover all points."

"I want hand bombs for my plane," said Wentworth briefly.

Lansing barked an order at the telephone men, and a man dashed excitedly to the table and removed yellow, red and blue pins and substituted white ones. He ran back to his phone. "The gas is turning the tide," Lansing jerked out. Muscles knotted along his jaw in his excitement. More white pins replaced other colors. An orderly saluted in the doorway.

"Bombs here, sir."

LANSING nodded and Wentworth stalked out, leaving the general bending over the map, barking occasional orders to the men at the phones. A motorcycle with a sidecar waited outside. Wentworth flung into the car and the driver jerked the machine forward. They passed the next corner at seventy miles an hour. In the floor of the sidecar bombs were wedged tightly. They jostled with the furious speed, almost jounced out as the cycle bounded over the curb.

The stutter of a machine gun ripped out on the quiet air. From the trees beyond the scarlet Northrup a ragged volley of rifle fire answered.

Wentworth knew what this attack meant. Forces of Hordes within the city! But it would be almost impossible to prevent such a thing. The animals themselves could be kept out, and had been, by the ceaseless patrol and inspection of buildings which most industrial towns had instituted on federal advice—inspired by Wentworth—almost from the first day of the plague. That was the reason it was necessary for the Hordes to make a frontal attack.

If Gary fell, there was an end of resistance to the Hordes. They would run wild over the land, and Brent would reign supreme.

These thoughts coursed through Wentworth's mind as the motorcycle eased up behind the plane. Ram Singh's machine gunfire was careful and accurate. Each flash of a pistol drew his swift lead like a magnet and many fell silent. Wentworth leaned down and with skillful fingers spun loose the wing bolts that held carriage and cycle together. The soldier twisted a surprised head.

"Stay here and load the bombs," Wentworth ordered calmly. He fastened two of the twelve pound bombs to the saddle, forked the motorcycle and sent it rocketing back toward the street. Bullets sped past. A hit on one of those bombs—

The motorcycle bounced into the street and Wentworth whirled toward the position of the enemy. For a moment the firing broke out with redoubled fury. It lasted for thirty seconds, then shut off entirely. Rounding the corner of the park, Wentworth saw a half dozen men dart to an automobile and race away. They continued to fire back at him. Gradually he allowed them to draw away, but never quite lost sight. He knew the tricks of dodge and pursuit too well. Doubling back, twisting and racing through streets all failed. He was always just in sight.

(Overleaf:) At the breaches in the fence Wentworth dropped the gas carboys—but did not wait to see the Hordes wilt.

After three-quarters of an hour of that, the auto ducked into a side street near the defense lines and Wentworth, whirling after them, found only a vacant thoroughfare. He halted and slowly surveyed the houses that fronted it. Not one showed a light. There were utterly no signs of occupancy. He propped up the back wheel of his cycle, wedged a bomb beneath his arm, and carried the other gun in his right hand, then he moved along.

Three quarters of the way down the block, Wentworth halted. Was his imagination playing him tricks or had something moved on that dark cellar stairway? He slipped into deeper shadow and waited, gun poised. For moments, nothing more happened. Then a man's head thrust out into the wan light of the moon; a man's head, then his naked torso, his entire body.

Behind him another man showed and, without warning, the first man whirled and struck at him viciously. The second snapped with his teeth, then others began to push past them out into the street and wander aimlessly toward the soldier's lines. The Horde Master's beasts had failed, so he was loosing human beasts upon the city!

Upon the breast of each man was a brand, the death's-head brand of the Master of the Hordes!

CHAPTER TWENTY-ONE
Death at the Castle

AS IF madness and death were not enough torture to inflict, the Master of the Hordes had submitted these doomed men to the torment of fire merely to satisfy his vanity. And now they were being forced to fight the battle of the Hordes, loosed upon soldiers to terrify them. A branded madman peered for a long moment more into the shadows where Wentworth crouched, then his head swung heavily about and he turned down the street behind the others.

They herded along like mad wolves, striking viciously at one another, never heeding the blows they gave and received. Wentworth trailed them, teeth clamped together, eyes bitter. These men must die, either by the guns of the soldiers or with the strangling torture of rabies gripping their throats.

They were pitiful, these men, and yet they constituted a formidable menace to the safety of the city. The gas would be useless against them. The terrifying threat of naked madmen with death's-head brands upon their chests might smash the lines and let the Hordes in—

The Human Horde, sixty strong, debauched from the street into the open behind the Army's lines and as they walked, flitting black shadows darted blackly across the face of the moon. The mad vampire bats! The Master was piling horror on horror! A gonged warning rang along the lines and men darted beneath wire covers, shields like huge hemispherical rat traps. Gas could not harm the vampires, but when that gonged warning rang out, men could take shelter from their piercing, death-laden teeth.

The naked madmen marched on like troops to battle. Bats struck at them and they tore them apart and flung them to the ground without interest. Wounds mean nothing to the victims of hydrophobia. A shrill shout of warning rang down the line. The soldiers had spotted this new flanking peril. White faces turned fearfully. A naked six-footer stumbled against a soldier's wire cage, snatched at it and hurled soldier and cage to the earth. Another man flung himself snarling upon the soldier, teeth gnashing.

Two men fired as one and the soldier who had fallen prey to the Human Horde sprang to his feet. Still screaming, he fled in panic from the Horde. Bats circled about him like huge lethal mosquitoes. His fear was contagious. Other men dashed in terror from the protection of their cages as the Human Horde rolled on. From beyond the fence, a black line rolled like a drowning wave toward the breach. It was such a force of mad beasts as never before had been loosed.

BENEATH the white, frightened moon, the charging beasts, the stumbling and murderous naked giants, the soldiers fleeing in panic made a nightmare scene. Cursing himself for his weakness, his moment of pity for these mad killers, Wentworth broke from cover, running heavily with the weight of the bombs upon him. He plunged toward the abandoned posts of the soldiers. In the wake of the bestial hordes he could make out now the vaulting leaps of the death's-head wolves, the slinking cats, the scamper of the rodents. On they swept, yet no hand loosed gas to stop them. The last soldier had fled from the horror of his own kind gone mad!

The sound of Wentworth's pounding feet caught the ear of a hulking hydrophobic maniac and he turned awkwardly, lowered his head and charged. Wentworth fired with his unfailing accuracy.

Wentworth ran on, saw others of the Horde turn toward him and shamble to the attack. His face set in a grim, forbidding mask. There was no help for it. These men were innocent tools of the Master, but it was their lives against those of the city's thousands.

Wentworth laid one bomb on the earth, seized the other by its finned tail with both hands and, whirling like a hammer thrower, tossed it a full hundred feet into the midst of the thickest group of the Human Horde. He flung himself flat with the momentum of his swing, felt concussion sweep over him like a black wave. Instantly he was up and racing toward the breach with the one remaining bomb. Bats darted at him, but the Human Horde was wiped out. He snatched up the overturned cage of a soldier who had fled, jerked it over his head, and raced on.

The first of that wave of beasts was almost at the opening of the fence. Wentworth hurled the cage from his shoulders, seized the other bomb and spun in a violent hammer throw. He fell and snatched at the cage again. A bat wheeled toward his throat. He struck it with the wire shield, knocked it aside and ducked beneath the cage. The tearing force of the explosion hurled him flat, wrenched at the wire protector. He clung to it desperately, yanked it over head and neck. A bat fastened its hooks into the shoulder of the thin flying suit. He rolled and ground it into the earth, jerked the cage into position and dashed on.

His bomb had torn a huge crater at the breach, had hurled back the first thick wave of the beasts, but they were closing up again like a tidal wave.

He reached the breach, stared about frantically. Where was the carboy? He searched desperately, finally saw a dull glint of metal half buried by the earth the blast had tossed up. He flung himself upon it, scooping earth backward with both hands like a dog after a bone. He cleared the head of the cylinder, twisted the valve, and the dark greasy waves of the gas spewed out in his face. He jerked upward, reeling, clung to the cage for support.

THROUGH eyes that were bleary from the narcotic gas, he saw the dark vapor spread over the earth, drift downward into the bomb-hole. The Hordes poured over the outer lip and collapsed in a writhing pile of bodies. The roar of a motor pulled Wentworth's heavy head upward and he saw his scarlet Northrup swish past. He had just consciousness enough left to drop flat before the bombs let go, blowing the unconscious Hordes to atoms. More bombs smashed down. He dragged himself upward with fingers gripping the wires.

Other planes droned through the air now and, his head clearing, staring into the night sky, Wentworth saw three ships in tight formation cross the face of the moon. Three planes! Three had gone to the laboratory of Professor Brownlee. Could they be back with the gas? Wentworth peered like a drunken man at the face of his watch. Three-thirty! It could be the same planes. They swung low and he saw a carboy tumble to the earth, saw black gas spread to reinforce that which he had loosed into the breach.

Wentworth lifted up the cage and staggered back from the lines, back up the long street that was silver on one side and black shadow on the other, back to his motorcycle and at long last to headquarters. General Lansing had three men busy on the telephones, giving out orders, distributing the new carboys of gas.

He took one minute to swing his long legs across to where Wentworth stood, clothing torn, face smeared with blood and earth. He wrung his hand.

"One more time, Wentworth, you have saved the city," he bit out. "That was glorious work there at No. 9 Breach. Got it all by phone. Going to recommend Congressional Medal, Distinguished Service Medal, Legion—but, hell, I forgot. You've already got those things."

He clasped Wentworth's hand once more and flung his long, energy-ridden body back to the phones, jerking out orders in monosyllables. Wentworth smiled faintly. Yes, the battle was over, the Hordes turned back. The city was saved, the threat to the nation was broken. But the leader of it all, the ruthless killer who had conceived this fantastic horror and loosed it upon the world remained free and unpunished. The faint smile became thin as a surgeon's scalpel. Work for the *Spider*!

Wentworth started to go, then turned back. "That soldier sent to follow me at Hurzon—ever hear from him—?"

Lansing nodded. "They found his nude body at the camp in the woods where you sent police."

Wentworth nodded and this time left headquarters, met Ram Singh face to face.

"Good work," Wentworth said curtly. "Tonight's deed will fill your cup with honor for many moons to come, oh, Ram Singh."

Ram Singh's body stiffened with pride, his eyes flashed.

"The glory is yours, *sahib!*"

WENTWORTH clapped him on the back and together they strode off into the darkness to mount the motorcycle again and speed to the airport and his scarlet Northrup. Minutes for refueling and they spurted into the air and winged swiftly off into the southeast. Immediately Wentworth was busy at his radio. At long last, he raised a Cologne amateur who got hold of the police for him.

"Has Healy been arrested?" he demanded. "Has Healy been arrested? Healy arrested?" The answer came back thinly, rasping. "No. Warrant refused. Warrant refused for Healy."

Wentworth's voice grew harsh and commanding, "I demand his immediate arrest. Unless you act, I shall see that Washington does. I'll appeal to Washington. Arrest Healy, or I'll call Washington."

"Call Washington and be damned to you," the police voice rasped back. "There is no evidence against Healy."

"But, it's absolutely necessary—"

Wentworth began. "Hello. Hello. Helloooo QZB2. Helloooo!"

"Sorry," came back the amateur's thin voice. "He got sore and left. He got sore and left. He got sore and went away. Sorry."

Wentworth called Washington and demanded and got official action after he had explained that all the attacks of the Hordes were for Healy's profit. "Well, get hold of them by phone. Get them by phone. Order arrest. We'll have Healy arrested!" Washington pledged.

Satisfied, Wentworth relaxed at the controls and let the plane fly itself with its full terrific speed back toward the Castle. He would have to land at Cologne and taxi to the Healy home. He might even snatch a moment to wash up before he went there, to wash and get some decent clothing. With Healy arrested, he could afford a moment of leisure.

He did those things and he took his moment of leisure, and when he reached the Castle, Berthold Healy was stretched upon the floor of his book-lined library with its high single window, his comfortable, homey library that was harsh now with unshaded electric bulbs. He lay on his back and there was a bullet wound in his right temple.

"He killed himself in here just after we came to arrest him," the sergeant of police said. "He came in here alone and shot himself. Geez, think of him being the brains of that mad dog gang all the time, and him the biggest man in the country and then some—"

CHAPTER TWENTY-TWO
The Master!

WENTWORTH went slowly from the room. Outside birds were twittering with the first thrill of the new day, a dawn blush was in the east. Nita met him with outstretched arms. Haggard circles were beneath her glorious eyes, tiny tight lines about her mouth corners. A loose blue negligee draped its heavy silken folds about her.

"I'm glad, Dick, that it ended this way," she said. "For once"—she glanced about her—"the seal of the *Spider* will not be necessary."

Wentworth smiled and kissed her tenderly. "Darling," he said. "I want you to do something for me when we have rested. After Mrs. Healy retires for the evening, go to her room and persuade her to spend the night in your room. Keep her there until I come."

Nita stared up into his face with eyes that once more were darkening with fear.

"Isn't it over, yet, Dick?" her breath caught in her throat.

Wentworth shook his head slowly. "Not yet, my darling. If Mrs. Healy demurs at doing what you wish, tell her it is a matter of life and death— her life and death. And remind her of the walk we all took in the garden."

"The walk in the garden?" Nita said it slowly, but Wentworth only smiled, squeezed the softness of her shoulders and sent her away to rest.

The household was late to retire that night after the naps of the day and Wentworth sat with them casually, his eyes burning with fatigue, but his smile never fading. At long last the women went up and Scarlet and Collins and Wentworth followed them after a drink around. Bidding the others good-night, Wentworth entered his room, but a moment later slipped out and angling across the hall listened a moment at another door that opened into the boudoir of Sybil Healy. He opened the door and went in.

An hour later he left the room and, going to Nita's, he returned with Sybil Healy beside him to her boudoir. She stared up in bewilderment at his taut, weary face. Once inside the room he left the lights out and secreted her and himself in the dark recesses of a closet whose door he left open. They could see her bed clearly by the dim rose lamp that, heavily shaded, threw a small cone of faint light there.

A woman seemed to be asleep in the bed, a woman with long black hair that streamed over the pillow.

"But I don't understand," Sybil Healy whispered for the twentieth time.

"Just keep thinking about the walk in the garden," Wentworth told her quietly. "Then when the person who is going to enter this room comes in, you will understand. But you must remain silent. Remember, it is yourself that lies in that bed so far as any other person in the world knows."

For long minutes, Sybil Healy continued to whisper in the fragrant darkness. All about them hung her clothing scented with lavender. If one moved, their silken rustle whispered in the air. Sybil leaned close to Wentworth. She laughed softly. "Is this a trick, sir, to get us alone?" Her shoulder pressed against his chest, her head was tilted up and back so that he looked down into the pale nearness of her face. Her lips were apart.

Wentworth spoke with weary disinterest. "There is a person coming here tonight to kill you. As long as that person remains alive and at large, your life will be in danger. If you don't remain quiet, the murderer will not come in." He put his hand on her shoulder, and startlingly his fingers touched not silk, but warm bare flesh. He merely pushed gently until she was standing straight instead of leaning against him. "If you don't mind, Mrs. Healy," he said, "I'm quite fatigued."

HER shoulder jerked away from his hand with a rustle of the silks that hung close about them, and for long moments more she stood stiffly.

"I'm growing tired of this," she said in a normal speaking tone, uglily.

Wentworth slapped a hand over her mouth. "Silent!" he hissed in her ear. "Look!"

He pointed across the room with a rigid arm that showed blackly against the rosy cone of light beside the bed. Beyond that cone was darkness that was impenetrable, but in that darkness something without form or character moved. Beneath his imprisoning hands, Wentworth felt the woman become rigid. He released her gently, taking her wrist, and she stood unmoving, her breath shallow and light. His hand felt the heavy pounding of the pulse in her arm.

Slowly the movement drew nearer the bed. Wentworth felt excitement mount in his own breast. He kept his eyes on the farthest dim edge of that cone of soft light. Into that peripheral where the rose merged with gray and black, where it laid an indefinite ray upon the soft rug, a foot showed. It wore a gleaming patent leather shoe and from it rose a black trouser leg. The other foot thrust forward softly and a man stood beside the bed.

The breath of the woman beside Wentworth grew so labored that he was forced to squeeze her wrist in warning. She silenced herself. Stealthily the man's hands slipped forward into the light. In the right hand, poised with thumb upon the plunger, he held a hypodermic needle. But the man's face was still in darkness. It was possible to see only that he was tall and thin. His hands began to ease aside the silken coverlets of the bed, the needle slid forward.

Wentworth pressed a flashlight into Sybil Healy's hand.

"I have a gun," he whispered, "go ahead!"

Her breath caught in her throat, eased out hissingly so that Wentworth knew her teeth were clamped tightly. She swayed forward from beside him. Light streamed from the torch. A man's face twisted up whitely above the bed, a man's face with a small puckery mouth, but handsome nevertheless, the face of Heinrich Scarlet!

"So nice of you, dear," Sybil's voice purred, "to pay me a visit. What is that dear little toy in your hand?"

She strolled toward the foot of the bed, entirely self-possessed. Wentworth saw her outlined against the glare of the hand torch, the svelte matured lines of her figure plainly visible through the scanty robes.

"Ah, darling," said Scarlet, straightening, wiping the moment's fright from his face. "I was just going to surprise you."

"Surprise me, hell!" Sybil Healy spat out.

"That needle holds hydrophobia germs!"

Scarlet's words jerked out, "Shut up, you fool!"

Sybil threw back her head and laughed wildly once. "Fool, is it!" Words poured out now. "Fool, is it! I've given up everything for you, helped you kill my husband, helped you fool the world into thinking Douglas Brent was a polished gentleman named Heinrich Scarlet, helped you to hide safely here while your mad dogs threw the wealth of the country into Bert's lap, so when he was dead and we were married—"

THE man sprang around the foot of the bed.

"Get back, or I'll shoot," Sybil bit out at him and there was no softness in her voice. Scarlet halted, but his voice was swift and urgent.

"Honest, darling," he said, "this needle had only narcotics in it. I've got to remove that fellow Wentworth tonight and I wanted you to have an unshakable alibi. Wentworth is suspicious somehow. That's why he's hanging around. His order to arrest Healy was a blind."

Sybil laughed again and it was a hateful sound. "I know how much you want to shield me, you coward. You wanted me to kill my own husband! I see now that you planned for me to be revealed as his murderer!"

"But, darling, all this is ridiculous," Scarlet cut in. "I couldn't possibly get any of the money unless I married you!"

Silence fell between them, silence and uncertainty. Sybil was wavering between what she wanted to believe and the evidence of her senses.

"Remember the walk in the garden," Wentworth spoke in to the silence calmly. Scarlet let out a small, startled cry.

"Stand still, Scarlet. My gun is pointed at your heart!" Wentworth snapped, went on with coldly precise syllables. "The walk in the garden, Mrs. Healy, when Scarlet killed a wolf he knew was there, when he comforted Doris in his arms. Wasn't Doris yours and Healy's sole heir, Mrs. Healy?"

Sybil gasped. "Doris! You planned to kill me and marry Doris! That was why you had me make a will in her favor.

"You said it would divert suspicion from me."

She took a quick stride forward and struck viciously at Scarlet's face with the flashlight. The glass smashed and they were in darkness. Scarlet let out a choked shout, hoarse and frightened, and reeled backward. Wentworth crossed toward him in a swift bound. A gun blasted. Wentworth felt the burning hammer blow of the bullet against his chest. He reeled against the bed and, bracing, yanked out his gun. Scarlet's silhouette raced toward the window.

Coolly Wentworth squeezed the trigger. Scarlet stumbled. Again and again Wentworth fired until he had emptied the last bullet into that sagging body.

Reeling, weak from the hot pain of the wound in his chest, Wentworth moved heavily forward until he stood over the thin man on the floor, the thin man flat on his back on the floor with six bullets in his vitals, with his hands flung wide and his bony face turned upward.

The *Spider* threw back his head and laughed a little wildly.

"Master of the Hordes!" he cried. "Who's master now?"

He laughed again and his knees gave way and he slumped unconscious to the ground.

CHAPTER TWENTY-THREE
Catharsis

THE world had to wait two weeks for the solution of the riddle of the Mad Hordes, two weeks while Wentworth tossed in pain upon a bed of fever from the wound of a poisoned bullet, two weeks in which Sybil Healy and Scarlet died in their cells of hydrophobia—Scarlet had pricked her with the needle during their struggle— two weeks in which Nita Van Sloan was ceaselessly beside him.

But finally the fever lifted and Wentworth, pale but strengthening daily, was able to give his story to the high Army officials and government dignitaries who waited upon him.

"Briefly, the answer is this," Wentworth told them. "When the crimes pointed toward Brent, I put a watch over every man in any way connected with Healy who could fit with the general description of Brent, which meant a thin, tall man and that was about all. I found greasepaint in a headquarters of the Hordes and that pointed to a disguise.

"Scarlet obviously was involved with Sybil Healy, perhaps with the daughter, the only means through which anyone could profit by the destruction of Healy's business and industrial rivals."

"But you insisted on Healy's arrest," a short, worried man with a perpetual frown broke in—one of the best criminal prosecutors in the government's many starred bureaus.

"Certainly," said Wentworth, "that was the only sure way I had to protect him from murder, and his murder was inevitable if these men were to profit. I was not sure of my criminal, I had no evidence against him. So I moved to defend the victim. The stubbornness of the police defeated me there."

He stared moodily at the white wall opposite, traced circles on the counterpane with a finger still brown and strong, though it seemed fragilely thin.

"As I said, I had no evidence that would stand up in court," he resumed. "I must trap the suspects. Mrs. Healy obviously had expected to marry Scarlet. From the course of events, he just as obviously expected to marry the daughter.

"You've got Scarlet's and Mrs. Healy's dialogue over the dictagraph I rigged there. It was a full confession."

The worried man still frowned. "But I don't understand your earlier reference to greasepaint as the clue."

Wentworth frowned. He was tired. Nita put an anxious hand on his head and felt the dry heat of fever. "I think, gentlemen, that you'd better postpone this," she said.

Wentworth shook his head slowly, smiling into her blue eyes.

"Just one minute more, darling," he said. He turned to the worried small man. "Healy knew Brent. I knew that. Hence greasepaint— and other makeup materials— were the key to the whole case." He smiled wearily at the men. "I bid you gentlemen good day, I've got a lot of sleep to catch up on."

THE END

IN THE NEXT ISSUE

A murder-master of the Underworld looses a loathsome weapon on America in—

THE CHOLERA KING

A soul-stirring account of the *Spider's* latest campaign against the Kings of Crime!

A black cross arching over the sky heralded a new and ghastly onslaught against mankind! Once more Richard Wentworth—whose fame as the *Spider* makes him feared wherever the lawless gather—found himself in a vortex of hazardous action and fatal intrigue! A ruthless criminal, clever in his madness, had spread deadly cholera germs—bringing death to every home and terror to every heart. And the only clues to the leader's identity were scrawled diagrams found on the breasts of the dead—a child's game, tit-tat-toe! . . . While horror holds high festival, while thousands die in writhing agony, the *Spider* fights to reach the mad monster who has caused this brutal massacre. Exhausted by the long battle, trapped by fiendish ingenuity, with Nita driving a shameful bargain with the murder-master for his life, Richard Wentworth must outwit and outfight his most savage foeman and conquer the despair which attacks the very stronghold of his courage!

Can the* Spider*, bearing the brunt of the madman's fury, save the helpless populace?

Victor in a thousand combats, can Richard Wentworth bring this new maniac killer to justice and death?

Will the Man in the Scarlet Robe succeed in his ambition to loot America and enslave her people?

NO CRIMINAL LEADER EVER CHALLENGED THE *SPIDER* SO SUCCESSFULLY BEFORE—OR CARRIED THE FIGHT TO HIM WITH SUCH PERSISTENT SAVAGERY! AN EXCITING NOVEL, FILLED WITH SWIFT ACTION AND DRAMATIC PUNCH, COMPLETE IN THE NEXT ISSUE OF—

THE SPIDER MASTER OF MEN!

10c

THE WEB by Will Murray

Once more we go back to the early years of *The Spider* magazine for our lead novel.

The Mad Horde appeared in the May 1934 issue of *The Spider.* This was the eighth *Spider* exploit, and Norvell Page's sixth entry in the storied pulp series. Still warming up from having taken over the characters from R.T.M. Scott, Page is already writing at full fever pitch.

For the second time that year, millionaire criminologist Richard Wentworth ventured outside of the Manhattan confines of the typical *Spider* novel, and blazed a bloody path through the Midwest—Ohio and Indiana, respectively.

This month's arch villain—who calls himself the Horde Master—wields hydrophobia as his principal instrument of terror. Rabid animals made for an extremely effective sequence of nail-biting incidents, resulting in another impressive *Spider* bloodbath.

The theme of pestilence and poison are ones that run like a bitter black thread through many *Spider* novels. Page's inaugural entry, *Wings of the Black Death*, employed bubonic plague. All through the series, there will rise again and again supercriminals intent on plunder and pillage, who think like medieval despots.

So, various plagues, diseases and other virulent strains of biological destruction are dispensed with wild abandon. By the time Page writes his final *Spider* novel ten years into the future, he will even have concocted a villain who inflicts leprosy on his victims.

It's difficult to know whether we can thank the Popular Publications editors, or Norvell W. Page himself, for these gruesome proceedings. By the time the series concluded in 1943, the newspaperman-turned-pulpster had probably absorbed more about deadly diseases than any other pulp writer of his era!

If one wanted to select an early *Spider* novel that is emblematic of the wildness of the entire series, *The Mad Horde* would be an excellent choice.

For our second story we leap ahead to the decade of the 1940s. The year 1940, to be exact.

In our previous volume, we told you about the introduction of Munro, the Man of a Thousand Faces, as a new type of supervillain introduced under departing editor Moran Tudury, in order to spice up the magazine, then in its sixth year. Loring

Norvell W. Page

"Dusty" Dowst took over the title late in 1939.

One could speculate endlessly why Page chose to create a new villain based on the oft-used Man of a Thousand Faces premise. Back in January of that year, the final issue of a different Man of a Thousand Faces, *Secret Agent X*, was published. Was

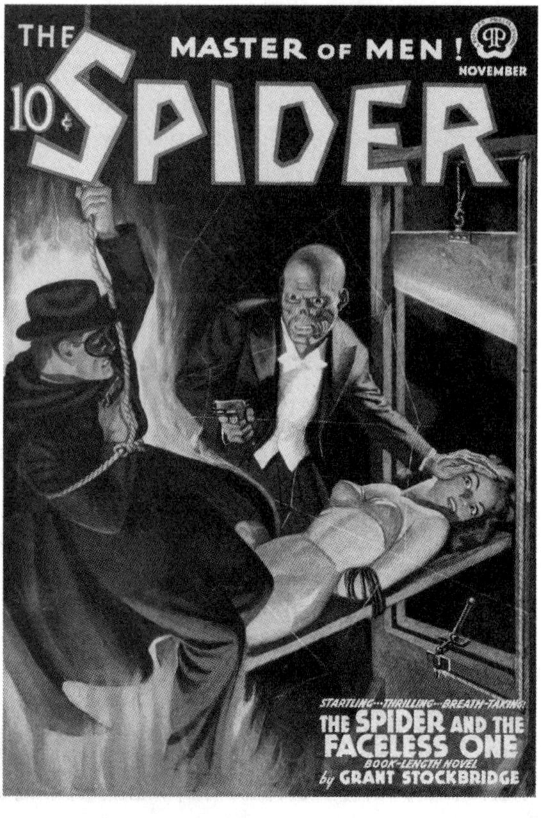

Munro a reaction to that? Or to the introduction of *The Avenger* that summer? He also bore that tag. Or was this simply a riff on the man originally so billed, celebrated Hollywod disguise master Lon Chaney?

Munro was introduced in *The Spider and the Faceless One*, which appeared in the November 1939 issue of *The Spider.* This sequel ran in the March 1940 issue. It was probably just enough time for the first lot of letters to inspire Page and his new editor into bringing Munro back from the dead. And when we say "back from the dead," we are not being figurative.

The monstrous master of disguise, whose unmasked face strangely resembled that of Lon Chaney in his classic silent screen role in *The Phantom of the Opera*, had been guillotined at the end of the previous outing.

How does Norvell Page explain—or for that matter Munro himself overcome—the handicap of being rendered headless?

You'll have to turn the page to see. But not yet. For there is more to this unusual issue than Mr. Munro. *Slaves of the Laughing Death* is not only the first *Spider* novel in many years to feature a returning foe, it also inaugurated a short-lived tradition in the magazine's colorful procession of covers.

***The Spider* cover artist Rafael DeSoto**

Rafael DeSoto had been painting the *Spider* covers for only six issues, and impelled by readers' letters, made a radical change in the covers.

It all started in the December 1939 issue, when a reader wrote into the Web column:

> And about your covers: Whoever paints them should be tossed a big "bokay." But why don't you show the *Spider* on the cover in full makeup, instead of merely a mask.Till the *Spider* dies, I remain
>
> Truly, Eugene Jackson

This was the first Web conducted by new editor Loring "Dusty" Dowst, who took over from Moran Tudury. Evidently, Dowst was open to new ideas. For in the January 1940 *Spider*, he wrote:

> You all remember Eugene Jackson's letter last month. He's the private detective from Sitka, Alaska, who asked why we didn't have the *Spider* depicted on the cover in complete costume, including facial disguise in addition to cloak, mask and hat.
>
> As for the *Spider*'s grotesque facial makeup appearing on the cover—well, we've run up against a stumbling block there—for the present, at least. We've checked through a vast file of readers' letters; again and again that cover question has come up, and if we abide by the majority of letters, we can't make any drastic changes in the *Spider*'s cover face quite yet. So many of you, it seems, have actually expressed a preference for the good-looking visage of Dick Wentworth on the cover, rather than the frightening countenance of the *Spider* in full war paint. We must admit that we favor Eugene Jackson's attitude, and as soon as a few more of you write that you agree, we'll go to bat again! Here's hoping, Gene—we're with you!

This didn't take long. In the following issue, Dowst reported:

> I have some special news for all of you who have been so earnestly crusading to have the *Spider* pictured on the cover in complete costume, facial makeup and all! Looks as if that detective up in Sitka, Alaska, has put something across the home plate. Congratulations, Eugene Jackson, and you other supporters of the cause.

The first such cover debuted in March 1940. Ironically, or perhaps with malice aforethought—it graced the issue featuring Munro's astonishing return.

That issue also printed a note from Paul Box of Kansas City, Missouri, who boasted that he had read all 76 *Spider* novels to date. Box weighed in with these comments:

> In the first place, there was this little matter about the covers. Personally, I would like to see the *Spider* on it in full makeup for a change. In the first few issues, before the *Spider* adopted his present costume, the mask was all right, but now I believe it is a bit old.
>
> Another point I would like to mention is the setting of the novel. Beyond a doubt, New York is a fine place to locate the *Spider*'s activities, but even New York can become stale—for reading. There have been seventy-six *Spider* novels published, of which *I have read every one!* Yet only a few have been situated outside of New York. Why not vary the stories by laying some plots in other parts of the country, or even in Europe?

To which "the Chief"—the name *Spider* editors usually signed "The Web"—replied:

> You folks who have been pioneering for the *Spider*'s appearance on the cover in full war paint have won a victory, as signified by the cover on this very issue! Now is a good opportunity for me to measure reader reaction. Let's have your views, friends!
>
> We all agree with you, Paul, on a change of locale. Of course, because of advance printing schedules, Grant is pretty far ahead of sales dates, but he's already got his smart brains dwelling on a new location. In the meantime, I welcome comments on this point.

By year's end, Dick Wentworth was battling in Colorado over the course of *The Spider and the Jewels of Hell*, and would go on to fight small-time crime in numerous fictitious hamlets throughout the United States.

Over much of early 1940, the controversy raged. The April 1940 issue saw this suggestion:

> In the Web, I notice that there seems to be quite a discussion about how the character on the cover should be portrayed. I am of the opinion that the *Spider* in action should be portrayed as written, although there seems to be a pro and con. The matter, to my mind, could be worked out very nicely both ways. Every so often in the story, the *Spider* is unmasked, unrobed—so why not show him in the clutches of his enemies once in a while without makeup? Otherwise, I think he should be in full costume. Simply let his attire match the action scene reproduced on the cover.
>
> George F. Edwards

Loring Dowst

Skimming "The Web," it appeared that Loring Dowst's changes met with positive reaction. One reader, James Anderson by name, approved of the new covers, and applauded Munro's return as well. As chronicled in the May issue:

> First, the covers you have now are a lot better than they used to be—so keep your present artist.... I think you should have your lead *Spider* novel at least eighty-six pages long, preferably one hundred.
>
> In your March novel, *Slaves of the Laughing Death*, the villain was Munro, the Faceless One. This is the second time in five months Munro has been the principal opposition to the *Spider*. What I mean is—I like it! You should bring back a lot of the criminals Dick has battled in the past. The two I want most to read about are: *The Emperor from Hell* (especially), published in July, 1938—and make it a long one! My next choice would be the Skull, who appeared in the May 1939 novel entitled *King of the Fleshless Legions*. I liked these because they seemed more sinisterly mysterious than most of Mr. Stockbridge's other criminal characters.

Dowst replied:

> You have indeed picked some "popular" villains. Munro receives more requests than any of Grant Stockbridge's crime kings. That is probably because the rascal provides Dick with such real and potent opposition. Conflict is the backbone of suspense, action and excitement.

The Chief went on to say that many readers preferred the newly emphasized mystery element, mentioning in particular reader Jimmy Hunt, "who votes for another Munro plot and tosses another bouquet at our artist...."

But not everyone was satisfied, as the July 1940 *Web* proved. F.H. Snyder, who claimed to have read every issue since the first one, noted:

> Your new covers are swell, but Grant Stockbridge has been doing something of which I feel entitled to complain. He brings criminals back from the past without ever explaining how they escaped from their first encounters with the *Spider*.

> Just a paragraph or two would suffice.
>
> Speaking of bringing back characters, how about having Professor Brownlee make some more scientific devices like the ones in "The Serpent of Destruction?" Let's also have more of Apollo, the Great Dane dog; and that most ruthless of the *Spider*'s enemies, the Fly.

Since those characters were long dead, no one was about to bring them back. Yet the suggestion seems to have birthed the 1940 novel, *The Council of Evil*, whereupon several past enemies teamed up to go after their nemesis.

The fanged, long-haired fright-faced countenance of the *Spider* continued to both fascinate and repel readers for seven consecutive issues. When DeSoto went back to the traditional domino mask, the experiment was over. It would not be repeated —although the readers who wanted to see Richard Wentworth on the cover soon got their wish when a top-hatted Wentworth appeared on the cover of *The Spider and the Scarlet Surgeon*, alongside his dreaded alter ego.

Publication of *Slaves of the Laughing Death* did not quell reader demand for more of Munro. Although it took a year and a half, the master of menace would return in *The Spider and the Deathless One.* It's scheduled for our next gripping *Spider* volume.

Now you can turn the page. But before you do, here is the appetite-stirring blurb for *Slaves of the Laughing Death*:

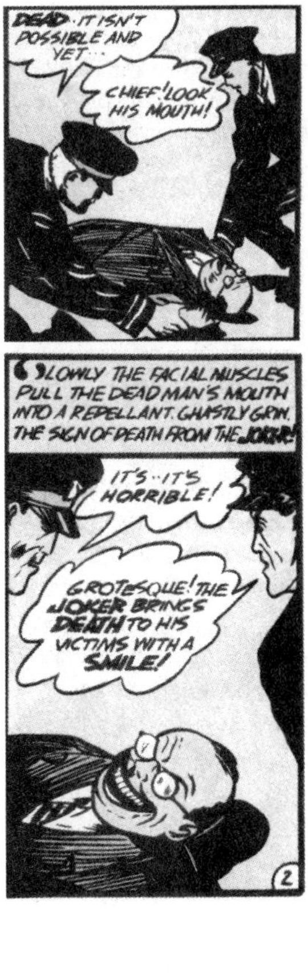

> An unseen weapon that drives men mad... A green gas which turns smiling faces into leering skulls... A master criminal who can assume at will any known identity.... Add to the separate menaces three big-game hunters sworn to destroy the *Spider*—and you have a situation in which the brilliance and courage of Dick Wentworth will thrill you as never before!

Now get ready to meet The Gotham Hounds! And watch to see if Munro's M.O. doesn't remind you of Batman's arch-foe, The Joker, who debuted three short months after this story broke into print. •

THE CHIEF SAYS:

THUMBS UP!

. . . for Grant Stockbridge's coming *SPIDER* novel

SLAVES OF THE LAUGHING DEATH

. . . in which Munro, the Faceless One, comes back with devices of evil more deadly, more sinister than anything from the Dark Ages. . . . The Man of a Thousand Faces might better be called: The Man with the Thousand Murder Methods. For now he has conceived a ghastly substance which, upon touching human beings, turns the flesh to cold-green flames . . . then eats it away, to leave in its place a grinning skeleton!

But this is not the only menace Dick Wentworth, in his courageous battle for humanity, must crush. . . . By a subtle, mysterious power, Munro has learned to control mass emotions at will! Think what this means—and ask your news dealer to save your March copy of The SPIDER—Master of Men!

THE SPIDER MASTER OF MEN! 10c

Slaves of the Laughing Death
Pulse-Stirring Book-Length Spider Novel
By Grant Stockbridge

Out of the dim recesses of the past came Munro, Man of a Thousand Faces, to corner America's gold with a sinister agency for devouring living flesh . . . and with a mysterious power to control mass emotions at will! Only one man was equipped to fight him—Richard Wentworth, alias the* Spider. *But the* Spider *was being stalked by three rich, fearless adventurers whose one aim was to destroy him as ruthlessly as in the past they had trapped and killed beasts in the jungle!

CHAPTER ONE
Death's Shining Face

THE man plunged headlong out of the drugstore, into the street. He blundered into a parked car, caromed into the traffic. Someone shouted a warning; taxis screamed to a halt, but the man ran on.

His right hand lifted upward, jerkily, but did not quite touch his face. Then he knotted the fist until the knuckles were bone white, and thumped it frenziedly against his skull. A whimpering sound squeezed out between his teeth.

His shoulder hit the door of the tall new apartment building on the corner and the glass jangled discordantly to the pavement. A uniformed attendant whirled indignantly to confront him, and the man's hands reached out and set upon the attendant's shoulders and shook him like a child.

"Wentworth's apartment!" he panted. "In God's name, Wentworth's apartment!"

The attendant stared into the man's face and the indignation was sponged from his own. His cheeks sucked in for a shout he did not utter, and grayness crept under the skin.

"That elevator!" he gasped. "That one, there! Top floor!"

The man freed the attendant and reeled into the elevator. He shot out an arm to the control panel, and as the door slid shut, his face peered back from the dimness of the cage—a face marked by pain, inhuman in its agony. And it glistened, as if the skin budded with little electric flames—small greenish flames that glowed coldly!

The door slammed and the attendant shuddered. He hurried toward a small corner counter, behind which sat the telephone girl.

"Quick!" he gasped. "Quick! Call Mr. Wentworth's apartment. Tell him... tell him there's a dead man coming up to see him!"

IN HIS apartment, Richard Wentworth confronted the three men grouped about his hearth. Behind a calm smile, his alert mind was wary. He was accustomed to traps. Life compelled him to walk as cautiously as a soldier in a forest sown with land mines. There was menace in these three men; that much he knew. How and when they would strike was less certain.

He said, deliberately, "So you wish me to join your organization, Hunter, and—"

"The Gotham Hounds!" Hunter boomed from where he posed dramatically before the stone fireplace. He uttered his hollow, professional laughter, and showed a great many teeth.

"—whose purpose, as I understand it," Wentworth continued quietly, "is to capture the *Spider*!"

"Or destroy him!" It was a second man, Carl Laird, who dropped these words coldly across Wentworth's speech. He was sitting rigidly in a stiff-backed chair, his feet carefully together, his squarish hands set solidly on his knees.

Wentworth threw a glance at him, looked deliberately at Hunter, then at Ralph Warring who rested his hands on the back of his neck in a deep chair with long legs thrust out before him. A leather-cased camera lifted and fell on Warring's chest with his breathing. His eyes were almost closed, unreadable.

Wentworth's smile deepened his mouth corners sardonically. "Professional adventurers and romanticists," he said tonelessly. "Embargoed in the United States by foreign wars, and seeking something spectacular to do—at home for a change."

Laird's face burned dully red, but Hunter's laughter boomed out and Warring dropped his words gently from scarcely stirring lips, scarcely veiling his hostility.

"Well put, Wentworth," he said, "and since we are in strange waters, we need a pilot. Will you lead our crusade?"

Wentworth shrugged slightly. "With appropriate publicity?"

"And pictures!" Warring drawled. He began to unsheathe his camera.

In the hallway, the phone bell whirred faintly, and the shadows by the portiered entrance stirred. From them, there stepped a tall bearded Sikh in a spotless white turban. He glided soundlessly from sight, and Hunter's head swung that way. He watched him out of sight with a slight narrowing of his eyes.

"Strangers are always watched here," Wentworth said casually. "There are others... Hunter, I'll give you your answer straight out. If you had another purpose than hunting the *Spider*, I might be tempted to join your Gotham Hounds; another more worthy purpose... such as supporting the *Spider*! You see, I happen to approve of his work, though not always of his methods. He fights... crime!"

Baird stood up. The flush lingered on his cheekbones. "He violates the law!" he snapped. "He himself is a criminal!"

Wentworth faced him directly, but did not lose sight of the other two men. "You make a general mistake, Laird," Wentworth said quietly. "You regard the law as an end in itself. Actually, the law was created by man to promote and safeguard justice. It is justice, not law, which we should serve. And where law obstructs justice, it should be violated!"

There was a flash of white in the darkened doorway of the hall, and Ram Singh bounded into sight. His dark eyes gleamed with excitement above his beard.

"Sahib!" His nasal voice was strong. "Sahib, the attendants below say a dead man is on his way to see you!"

Like a rasping overtone of his voice, the doorbell began to whir.

HUNTER and Laird stared toward the doorway in strained attitudes of amazement, but Laird's right hand moved with a deliberate speed and flipped a heavy-caliber revolver into sight. Warring, his lips smiling, had his camera ready. Wentworth saw this while his mind raced on. Was this the moment when the Gotham Hounds would strike? Wentworth's voice was easy, smooth.

"Open the door, Ram Singh," he said softly,

"and let us see this... dead man!"

In a movement of smooth speed, Ram Singh whipped open the outer door and the man with the glistening face flung himself, running, into the room. He stumbled to his knees before Wentworth. His voice lifted in a thin shriek.

"Oh, save me!" he gasped. "My face—save me, *Spider!*"

Wentworth stared down at the scarred face, shining with that cold glow of tiny, devouring flames. He was conscious of the tense men who flanked him; of the flare of a flashlight as Ralph Warring snapped the tableau with his camera. Was this part of the trap? Perhaps, since this kneeling man had called him the *Spider*. For a moment Wentworth hesitated; then a sharp oath rasped in his throat. The flesh of the man's face was dissolving!

"Ram Singh! Soap!" Wentworth snapped. *"Jackson!"*

From the dimness of the music room a broad-shouldered man in a chauffeur's uniform sprang into view.

"The laboratory!" Wentworth threw at him. "Ammonium phosphate!"

As Jackson spurted toward the hallway, Wentworth caught the shoulders of the kneeling man. "What happened?" he demanded.

The man struggled against Wentworth's grip. His hands became claws ripped toward his face. Wentworth seized his wrists.

"What happened?"

"A child... water pistol!" the man gasped. "It burned! The drugstore man said you'd help me. You... the *Spider!"*

His last word was a scream. Convulsively he ripped his wrists from Wentworth's grip, clawed in a frenzy at his own face. He groveled on the floor, ground his face against the hearth. His screams diminished. The flashlight flickered again, and before Ram Singh came back, the man on the hearth was still. Across the prostrate body beside which he knelt, Wentworth looked in turn at the three members of the Gotham Hounds. Hunter's smile was still on his mouth, strained a little; his eyes shone with excitement. Laird's long, serious face was stupid with shock. And Warring, carefully attending to his camera, still had his eyes half closed.

"Now we understand your reluctance, Wentworth," Warring said, amusedly. "Am I wrong, or did that man call you the *Spider?"*

"I am sure," Wentworth said coldly, "that you have been called other, less honorable names... and with perhaps more truthfulness, Warring. If you take another picture, I shall smash that camera."

He deliberately turned the dead man over on his back, and his face drew into harsh lines. The corpse's face no longer shone. It was gleaming white. The bones of the skull, which alone were left, were as clean as newly scrubbed marble.

Wentworth got to his feet. His fists were clenched at his sides. Were these three men involved in the death of this poor creature on the floor? He had thought the whole thing trickery at that first moment, until he had seen how the man suffered. The druggist on the corner had sent him, the man said. The druggist—

"I think I'll run along," Hunter said jerkily. "You will be busy for a while, and I'll phone you for your answer, Wentworth!" His voice came back from the hallway and an instant later, the door clapped shut, hollowly. Warring laughed, a faint, whispering sound.

"Hunter chose the name of hounds," he said. "I didn't know he meant the yellow kind. Well, Wentworth, what happens now?"

WENTWORTH'S hand flicked beneath the lapel of his coat, and reappeared with a heavy, black automatic in his fist. His fingers moved efficiently, checking the loading. He replaced it in its holster.

"I think," Wentworth said softly, "that I shall call on the druggist who sent this poor fellow here. It is just possible that the druggist knows more about the *Spider* than any of us."

Warring's eyes opened wide. His laughter was openly admiring. "Listen, Wentworth," he said. "Show me some excitement. I don't care whether the Gotham Hounds hunt *Spider*s or rabbits. You're pretty cool about being accused of being the *Spider*."

Wentworth was striding toward the door, Warring at his elbow. Carl Laird followed more deliberately. His long strides carried him swiftly in their wake.

"It is an old accusation," Wentworth said easily, "and one which honors me. Fortunately, or unfortunately, it is not susceptible of proof. Ram Singh, phone the police and tell them precisely what occurred here. They will find me at the corner drugstore... Jackson, I'll need the Daimler at once!"

The splintered glass of the apartment's front door was being swept into a neat pile, but the hands of the attendant were still shaking; his eyes had a strained and wild look. Wentworth thanked him briefly, while his keen gaze searched the street. There were parked cars nearby, but none of them was occupied. The drugstore across the street was brightly lighted, and empty of customers. Bob Hunter, leader of the Gotham Hounds, was nowhere in sight.

Wentworth was willing to swear that neither of the two men with him had had any part in the death of the man in his apartment; apparently Hunter had been panic-stricken. Yet in no other way could he account for the man coming to him with his dying strength. The druggist?... the idea was fantastic.

Still, did he represent some new threat of the venomous lords of the underworld? Some new threat directed at the humanity the *Spider* had sworn to protect from crime?

Wentworth was weaving a resolute way through the traffic toward the drugstore. His stride was long and purposeful. At his side, Warring began to chuckle. Wentworth's head whipped toward the man, and the chuckling grew louder. Even Carl Laird's long face wore a broad smile.

"What is so amusing?" Wentworth asked.

Warring laughed out loud. "Hunter was right green, he was so frightened," he said.

Wentworth frowned. The answer did not seem adequate, but the laughter seemed to have a curious effect of lightening the tension in his own breast. Everyone who passed seemed to wear a wide smile. A taxi driver, in a parked cab, apparently was shaken by uncontrollable hysterics. Wentworth stared at him, choked back an oath of amazement. The man's license badge, pinned to his coat, had an unmistakable, greenish glow!

Somewhere in the back of Wentworth's brain, there was a cold warning of danger, but it could not penetrate his consciousness. He was aware of something strangely confusing in the situation. He should be worried, be on the alert, and yet he smiled.

Warring chuckled, "Come on, let's call on this druggist friend of yours, Wentworth."

Wentworth nodded, and pushed open the door. It seemed to him, in passing, that the knob and fixtures had a slight greenish glow, but it was unimportant. The druggist, in white coat and spectacles behind the soda fountain, bobbed his head and smiled in a way that was familiar. Wentworth smiled back, strolled toward the man.

"You sent a man to my place," he said equably. "Poor chap with a shining face. I was wondering—"

Wentworth never finished the sentence.

As he smiled pleasantly into the face of the druggist, the man suddenly brought his right hand above the counter and revealed an automatic.

Still smiling, the druggist began to shoot at Wentworth!

CHAPTER TWO
Birth of Pear

DESPITE his lulled suspicions, Wentworth was in motion instantly. His leap to the left hurled Laird backward, arms wheeling wildly. In the same movement, Wentworth dived for the protection of the marble soda fountain behind which the druggist stood. It was the only bulletproof barrier in the room.

The druggist's first shot had punched through the spot where Wentworth first had stood. The explosion jarred against his eardrums; made a hundred stacked bottles rattle on their shelves; the crash of breaking glass was musical and thin. The second shot lifted a white dust from the edge of the counter—just above Wentworth's head. Fragments of shattered marble whined angrily, and Wentworth felt a stinging shock across one temple.

Wentworth's automatic flipped into his fist, and his gaze raked across the drugstore. Laird was flat on his back near the door. As Wentworth spotted him, he clawed out his gun, rolled over on his belly. Half behind a central counter of stacked cut-rate products, Ralph Warring was fighting to get his camera out of its case. His smile was wide, nervous... excited, more than frightened.

Wentworth's automatic rested lightly in his hand while he waited for Laird to get his gun clear. Out of the tail of his eye, he glanced into the glass cases across the store. They showed a distorted reflection of the druggist. He had a knee on the service portion of the fountain, was leaning forward with his gun to fire straight downward at Wentworth! And Laird's gun was free, was dropping into line!

"Don't shoot, Laird," Wentworth called quietly.

At the same instant, Wentworth sent a bullet scorching up past the edge of the marble counter. It notched out a small semicircle, left white dust in the air but on the upper side, it ripped loose a hundred tiny knife-like fragments. His showcase mirror showed him the stiffening figure of the druggist, an arm flung up across his face as he tottered backward. Wentworth was instantly on one knee. His second shot scored the top of the counter, shattered the mirror behind the fountain. A stack of oranges bounded with soft little thumps to the floor—and the druggist was no longer in sight. He had dropped to the floor!

Laird was scrambling to his feet, gun still in hand. There was an angry flush in his cheeks, but his eyes were not on Wentworth. They searched the top of the counter.

"I'll keep him down!" he snapped. "Cover the far end of the counter!"

It was not until that moment that Wentworth realized that he had expected Laird to open fire upon him! It had not been a conscious thought, but an expression of his subconscious distrust of the three members of the Gotham Hounds. But Laird had withheld his fire, now was charging to the attack—

Wentworth, bent double, sprinted for the opposite end of the soda fountain.

"I want the druggist alive," he called softly.

THE blast of a flashlight flung the whole store into momentary brilliance and Wentworth swore as he checked, gun in hand, to command the opening at his end of the soda fountain. He saw Laird bound to the top of the soda fountain. Laird's gun blasted in the same instant and he cursed violently.

"Trap door!" he shouted. "Behind the counter!"

Wentworth whipped around the counter's end, gained the yawning trap door, its steep steps slanting down into the basement. His hand flicked to an electric switch nearby, and lights blazed in the dark pit below. Over him towered Laird, eyeing the corpse that lay sprawled at the bottom of the stairs. Warring's flashlight flickered its mild lightning again.

Laird's voice came complacently. "How's that for shooting in the dark? I got the beggar right through the back of the skull!"

He jumped to the floor, started toward the steps, and Wentworth's rigidly outthrust hand stopped him in his tracks.

"Don't go down there!" he said. "Can't you see there's an orange on that man's back?"

Laird said, incredulously, "An orange! What of it?"

Wentworth shook his head impatiently. "My last shot spilled the oranges. Your shot came quite a while later. That man down there was already dead before the oranges fell. That man is not the one who was shooting at us!"

Laird swore. "But it looks like the same man. The same clothing. The same grey hair—"

Wentworth's face was becoming pale. He felt a cold fist closing on his heart. "Yes, it looks exactly the same. But now you can see that no blood flows from that wound, that it coagulated long ago. Now—" Wentworth snapped off the cellar lights—"in fifteen seconds, turn on the light again!"

He leaped down through the opening. His feet hit and he dived to the cover of barrels he had spotted from above. As he got his feet beneath him again, the lights flicked on. In all the cluttered basement, nothing moved, but a window that should have been bolted and barred with iron was hanging open. The bars had been sawed away.

Wentworth swore and sprinted across the basement, pulled himself up through the window. Outside was the pitch blackness of an alley. In it, nothing stirred.

There was not even the sound of a motor starting.

The killer had escaped.

Wentworth lowered himself slowly, returned to the dead man on the floor and rolled him to his back. Staring up at him was the same face he had seen a score of times, the same face that apparently had leered behind that powerful automatic a few minutes before. The gun lay beside his right hand now, a hand that was stained with chemicals. Wentworth frowned, remembering that the right hand that had held the gun had been stained like that, too. But there could be no contradicting the presence of that orange upon the man's back, or the fact that the blood had fully coagulated.

Wentworth cursed violently. He was not a man who gave way readily to his emotions, but this was no second-rate menace he was fighting. Once more that coldness swelled in his chest. When he climbed the steps, it was with a heavy tread.

He said, thickly, "We are fighting Munro!"

Carl Laird frowned at him curiously.

"A criminal you know?"

Wentworth laughed. "A criminal who has been reported dead a score of times! One of the most coldly vicious killers in all of crimedom! He has no scruples about mass murder, or any other delicate little horror that will help to line his pockets. God, I thought he was dead!"

Laird shook his head, "I never heard of him."

"You would know him probably," Wentworth said, more quietly, "as the Faceless One."*

Laird whistled softly, "Aye! I remember now! A devil in flesh! But how in hell can you be so sure?"

WENTWORTH nodded toward the dead man in the basement. "Munro's best safeguard is the fact that no one, actually, knows what he looks like. He has a thousand disguises, each one perfect. When he posed as this druggist in order to trap and kill me, he took the trouble even to stain his right hand with druggist's chemicals, as that poor devil below has done through years of work. Only Munro would have thought to attend even to that minute detail. God in Heaven! Now, a man can scarcely trust his closest friend, for it may be Munro!" His eyes narrowed. He said softly, "Where is... Hunter?"

Warring was perched on a stool, smiling across the soda fountain at them. "I've known Hunter quite a while," he said amiably. "I don't think he's Munro."

Wentworth smiled twistedly. "I don't think you get the point," he said. "How can you be sure that the man who called with you tonight really is Hunter? You two gentlemen I can exonerate. I saw both of you and the disguised Munro at the same time."

Warring shook his head, casually helping himself to a glass of soda water. "If Munro is as good as all that, couldn't he disguise one of his henchmen, also? No, my dear fellow Hound of Gotham, you can't be sure even of me!"

He set the glass down, and Wentworth took it by the rim, wrapped it in his handkerchief before he thrust it into his pocket. "Fingerprints can't lie," he said grimly. "When I get a set of Munro's prints, I'll compare them!"

Warring only smiled, with his eyes sleepy again, and Wentworth strode sharply from behind the counter, angled toward a telephone booth. He put through a call to police headquarters, and tried to reach Stanley Kirkpatrick, the Commissioner of Police. Kirkpatrick was his personal friend—though he was also, and bitterly, the enemy of the *Spider*!

But Kirkpatrick had left his office, so Wentworth rapidly reported the shooting to the desk sergeant, then put through another call.

There was a faint smile on his lips now as he listened to the distant whirring of the phone bell. As always, when a new battle loomed for the *Spider*, he must warn Nita van Sloan, the woman he loved. There was an especial danger this time, with Munro once more up to his demon tricks. The memory of the ghastly face of the dying man who had sought him out wiped the smile from Wentworth's lips, as he heard Nita's gay greeting.

"Listen, dearest," he said rapidly. "Munro is busy again. Yes, Munro! From now on, trust no one at all... least of all, anyone who seems to be me!"

Nita laughed, "But I never trust even you, Dick! So what am I to do now?"

Wentworth frowned, not at Nita's words, but at her gay humor. She, of all people, should realize the danger represented by Munro! She who so narrowly had escaped death under the merciless slash of his private guillotine!

"Nita," he said sharply. "This is deadly serious! Don't you understand? Munro—"

Nita's laughter rang again, and it had a thin, unnatural note. "Munro? Munro? Now, where have I heard that name before?"

Wentworth's fist whitened about the receiver as he listened to the silvery gaiety of Nita's laughter. He was remembering with a sudden fierce intensity the moment just before he himself had entered the drugstore. Laughter had been on his lips, a laughter which no man could account for by the sequence of events. A taxi driver had been almost hysterical over nothing at all, and on his lapel, the driver's badge had a greenish glow like the face of the man who had died!

Wentworth's lips tightened. He put hard emphasis into his voice. "Listen, Nita," he said firmly. "Try

* AUTHOR'S NOTE: Wentworth's last encounter with Munro was narrated in *The Spider and the Faceless One*, in which Munro loosed the horror of fire upon the city.

to listen seriously to me for one moment. On your mantelpiece is an old French clock of brass—"

"What a memory the man has!" Nita cried.

"Look at that clock, Nita!" Wentworth insisted harshly. "Are you looking at it? Good. Now, listen to me. Is there a greenish glow about that clock, as if it had been painted with radiolite paint? Is there, Nita?"

NITA laughed. She made no other answer at all, just that pointless laughter that went on and on. Wentworth fought for control of his voice.

"Please, Nita," Wentworth said quietly. "Are you laughing because the brass of the clock is green?"

Finally, Nita's voice, weak with laughter, came to him: "Dick, you must be clairvoyant. You should have told me before. Yes, the clock looks so funny, all shining green—"

Wentworth's voice rasped with sudden fierceness. "Nita, that green glow means that Munro is near you, threatening you! Do you understand? Oh, Nita, listen to me—don't open your door until I come there. Don't—don't wash your face, or touch any liquid, do you understand?"

Nita's fresh laughter vibrated in the phone. "Oh, Dick, I can't stand this! Please let me wash my face. It's very dirty. I've been making mud pie."

Wentworth struggled frantically to make her understand the peril that turned his heart cold with fear for her, but Nita refused to take him seriously. Finally, Wentworth hung up and left the booth. The pale tension of his face brought Laird sharply to his feet where he sat beside Warring.

"What now?" he snapped.

Wentworth strode swiftly toward the door. "Come with me, if you like, and I'll explain!" he snapped. "No time now!"

The big Daimler was at the curb. There was a police car across the street; plainly the uniformed men had gone to his apartment. A siren was dim in the distance, growing louder. But he could not wait now. He knew that in some unaccountable way, Munro was causing that wild, nonsensical laughter that poured from Nita's lips. He had used the same, unaccountable weapon to disarm his own suspicions just before he entered the drugstore. And in some way, that faint greenish glow he had noticed before was connected with the mad laughter. If only he could reach Nita in time.

Behind him, Laird called out in a tense voice, "I have my car here. I'll follow with Warring!"

Wentworth nodded, and stepped into the rear of the Daimler. It surged from the curb with lightning acceleration. Wentworth stared at the broad shoulders of the man in chauffeur's uniform behind the wheel, and his lips tightened grimly. He got out his gun.

"Jackson," he said softly. "What were the last words I spoke to you before I left the apartment?"

Wentworth caught the startled lift of Jackson's eyes to the rear vision mirror, the surprised line of his straight mouth. "You said, sir, 'Jackson, I'll need the Daimler at once.'"

"And before that?" Wentworth prompted softly.

Jackson frowned, weaving the car northward. Jackson—the laboratory. Ammonium phosphate." Jackson's voice sounded mechanical, woried.

Wentworth relaxed, thrust his gun back into his holster. "Good," he said. "Forgive my quizzing you Jackson, but we are fighting—Munro!"

Jackson uttered an oath. "Good God in Heaven! Forgive me, sir, but if you'll just tell me—what did you say to Mr. Warring just before you left the apartment?"

For an instant, Wentworth stared at Jackson without understanding, and then he laughed softly. It was justified. Jackson, too, was taking precautions against being tricked by the fabulous disguises of Munro!

Wentworth satisfied Jackson, told him their destination and the urgency of their purpose. The Daimler motor purred louder with mounting speed. A police whistle blew behind them, but Jackson ignored the summons and raced on. Wentworth's keen eyes flashed at the traffic about them. Munro had made a clean getaway from the drugstore, but even so he could not yet have reached Nita's Riverside Drive apartment. Therefore, he must have previously established whatever hellish device caused that mad laughter. It was entirely possible that Munro might be at this moment on Wentworth's trail! Hunter... what had happened to the Master of the Gotham Hounds, as that impetuous fellow styled himself?

Apparently, Hunter had fled in fright at view of the ghastly new death that Munro had devised; yet that did not fit with the man's reputation as a professional adventurer. Abruptly, Wentworth leaned forward and struck the window glass behind Jackson. The Daimler swerved to the curb, but Wentworth did not alight at once. He was staring toward two men in a dim side street that led toward Broadway. One of those men was a uniformed policeman; the other was—Robert Hunter.

As Wentworth stared, Hunter's fist struck the cop's jaw! Before the policeman had fallen, Hunter had ripped the man's revolver from its holster and was sprinting down the dark side street!

CHAPTER THREE
The Terror Strikes!

GRIMNESS settled about Wentworth's chiseled mouth. His hand moved to a button beneath the left cushion and the seat slid forward, revealing a secret compartment—the dressing room of the *Spider!* Wentworth shook his head. He could not yet be sure that Hunter was the man he sought!

Wentworth stepped to the pavement. "Keep the car close!" he ordered Jackson, and then sprinted after Hunter.

The man had hesitated just short of the lighted marquee of a theatre; the gun was no longer in sight. After that moment's hesitation, Hunter tugged down his hat—and went into the theatre.

Seconds later, Wentworth himself turned into the deserted lobby and crossed straight to the inner doors. Worry over Nita nagged at his mind, but he reassured himself that Munro could not possibly have reached Nita's home. And Hunter's strange behavior demanded immediate solution. He alone, of the Gotham Hounds, had no alibi!

Wentworth thrust open the door of the theatre, and from the darkness close at hand, he caught the muffled cry of a woman! He found himself staring into the white, terror-strained face of a girl usher. One fist was ground distortingly into her mouth to strangle her scream. Through a long moment, she stared at Wentworth and then she turned and fled frantically into the darkness!

Incredulously, Wentworth watched her go. There was no one else near, nothing that he could see to frighten the girl. He himself had only sauntered through the door. And yet, that girl had been half-mad with terror!

With cautious haste, Wentworth gazed into the dimness of the theatre. On the brightly lighted stage Charles Maurice, one of the world's great tragedians, was gesturing his way through Hamlet. Among the audience, there was no stirring at all; not even the muffled sound of a cough. Surely, a great tribute to Maurice! But was it?

Suddenly, uncontrollably, Wentworth glanced over his shoulder at the darkness behind him. Nothing... nobody there, but an oath sprang harshly, unbidden, to Wentworth's lips.

The brass doorknob gave off a pale, green glow!

On the instant, Wentworth was racing on silent feet across the rear of the theatre, speeding soundlessly down a side-aisle toward a door that would open backstage. At the drugstore, at Nita's home, brasswork had glowed like that. And uncontrollable laughter had gripped all who came near. Here, there was that same green light. But here, as the face of that usher had testified all too clearly, there was not laughter—but terror, scarcely held under control!

He knew past all doubt what held the audience spellbound. Not a great actor... but fear! Fear begotten in the same inexplicable, hellish way as that mad laughter. That terror was too horribly obvious in the stillness that gripped the audience. On the stage the actors faltered through their lines, were halting in what must have been a smoothly drilled play! Terror, or laughter, and that pale green glow— They could mean but one deadly thing.

Munro—who planned some fresh devil's business in this theatre!

Wentworth could not guess the nature of Munro's plot. He could not understand Munro's purpose in terrorizing an entire audience. How could the man gain revenue this way? There must be some ulterior motive of gigantic scope! Possible... no time now to ponder. Already he could feel the mounting tension of the audience like static electricity before a hurricane. He could feel its echo in himself, despite his foreknowledge, despite the power of his great will. The slightest untoward sound, the shock of a shot, and this cultured, civilized audience would become a stampede of fear-crazed animals, slaughtering each other to escape from... nothing!

A shot? Hunter had entered the theater with a pistol; had entered and disappeared!

AS CAUTIOUSLY as if he walked among sleeping dragons, Wentworth eased up to the backstage door. His plans were still unformed, but he knew that if this breeding terror were to be controlled, it must be from the stage. And those upon whom that task would normally devolve were equally besotted with fear!

Wentworth passed through the door and it seemed to him that fluttering wings of terror beat within his own breast—in the breast of the *Spider* who had never known fear! He stood stock-still and his face paled with the effort at control. It took all his mighty will to steel himself to the task ahead. He knew the method he must follow.

The *Spider* must tread the boards!

Wentworth's movements were deliberate as he resisted every impulse to be terror-stricken. A velvet drape, snatched from a box, furnished a long cape that swung about his heels. With stiff fingers, he fashioned his black hat into a slouch that pulled low over his brows. His shoulders hunched until, in the shadows, he became a menacing and sinister figure. The audience would recognize it instantly, and the sight would spread a fresh terror... but a *known* terror.

It was the only means he could contrive. Only one thing could govern now the mob that the audience had become. One thing—a greater, counteracting fear!

Wentworth's hands crossed on his breast and when they reappeared, they balanced twin automatics. His lips twisted thinly. Laird and Warring were following him closely. They would appear in time to see his parade in the robes of the *Spider*! Sardonic laughter pushed at Wentworth's throat. The *Spider* moved deliberately toward the wings!

At that moment, a woman screamed!

Bounding into the wings of the stage, Wentworth

sent his piercing gaze among the actors, seeking the cause of that cry. It was no part of the play. The girl who played Ophelia screamed again. She covered her face with her hands and whirled toward the wings, her draperies flying. Charles Maurice stood like a man knocked out on his feet. His face was uplifted, and its expression was dazed, incredulous. Across his forehead there was a faint tracery of blood. Then slowly, before Wentworth's eyes, Maurice's face took on a strange and ghastly hue.

It began to glow with small green flames!

A hoarse cry rose in the throat of the actor. He lifted his hands and his clawed fingers tore across his cheeks, and where they had dragged… the flesh came away like rotted cloth! Charles Maurice screamed then, terribly, and it was echoed by a hundred terror-laden screams from the audience.

With a long, fierce bound, Wentworth leaped upon the stage. The cape of the *Spider* swirled and whipped from his shoulders, and the massive guns in his fists caught sharp gleams of light. He leveled them at the audience, and his voice rang out with cold menace.

"Keep your seats!" he cried. "I'll kill the first man who moves!"

His eyes ranged the audience fiercely, saw the fear-stricken faces. But he had calculated correctly. Before this known menace, and under the threat of those leveled guns, the spectators froze in their places—all except one man!

Wentworth's gaze whipped to him, while the screams of the tortured actor rang out in his ears. He saw that one man streaking toward the rear of the balcony, and grim incredulity shook him. The man fleeing up the central aisle of the balcony was… the druggist whom Munro had killed!

There was that instant of shock, and then Wentworth's ready gun swung upward. Not the druggist, but Munro himself! Munro had loosed his horror-working chemical upon Maurice, and now was making his getaway!

Laughter surged to Wentworth's lips, and it was thin and metallic, the mocking flat laughter of the *Spider*! He leveled one automatic deliberately.

"You're finished, Munro!" he called.

MUNRO did two things with incredible speed. He wrenched a woman from her aisle seat, whipping her body across his own as a shield. In the same instant, a gun flashed in his hand, its thunder echoing into the theatre vault. A brilliant flash of blue-white light flared from behind the audience… a flashlight for a picture, a picture of Wentworth in the *Spider*'s robes!

Those two things snapped Wentworth's control over the audience. People surged to their feet. Seats splintered and crashed in the first panic of the stampede. Before the flare of the flashlight had died, the entire audience was streaming toward the doors! The screams of women, the hoarse, inhuman shouts of men drowned out every other sound. Wentworth saw a man crash his fist into a woman's face and step on her to escape. He saw a small man jerked bodily from the aisle and flung like a broken dummy over among the splintering seats. The doors were already jammed with men who struggled madly to escape their terror, and carried their terror with them in their own breasts.

In the balcony, Munro had disappeared in the swirl of scrambling, racing human beings!

For one instant, Wentworth poised there rigidly, shouting in his effort to regain control. He sent a bullet flying over the heads of the people, and it lent only speed to their flight. He whirled and plunged into the wings. Stagehands were fighting to crowd out of a narrow exit door and Wentworth was among them in an instant. His hard fists stung the men to fury, beat them into resistance. When they looked into his white, furious face, their terror seized them anew and they tried to flee. He seized two of them by the shoulders, pinned them back against the wall, and his will blazed at them from his eyes—the will of the *Spider*, who was justly called the Master of Men!

"Fools!" he shouted at them. "There is nothing there to harm you! Nothing… but there is death in my hands! Get that hose! Turn it on! Drench the audience with it! Batter sense into their fool heads! Understand me? Good! The hose—"

Under the lash of his command, the men moved stumblingly to obey him. They ran out upon the stage with the hose already struggling under water pressure like a great serpent. The white stream lashed out into the audience, tumbled men helpless to the floor, beating them from their mad slaughter of their fellows. Across the stage, Wentworth bounded again and caught two of the actors. Once more the fierce drive of the *Spider*'s will did its work and they leaped to drag down another hose and unleash it upon the audience.

Wentworth waited for no more. They would stay at the task he had set them, in very fear of the *Spider*!

Once more, he bounded upon the stage. Cape streaming from his shoulders, he stepped high upon the proscenium and launched himself out into space. His hands caught the edge of one of the boxes and he swung there a moment before he could muscle himself upward. Faintly, he heard the crack of a gun and, inches from his face, a bullet ploughed up the red velvet that wrapped the box's rail. Wentworth's lips tightened, but he did not glance toward the gunman. With a powerful swing, he had hurled himself over the railing and was plunging toward the dark aisle behind the boxes.

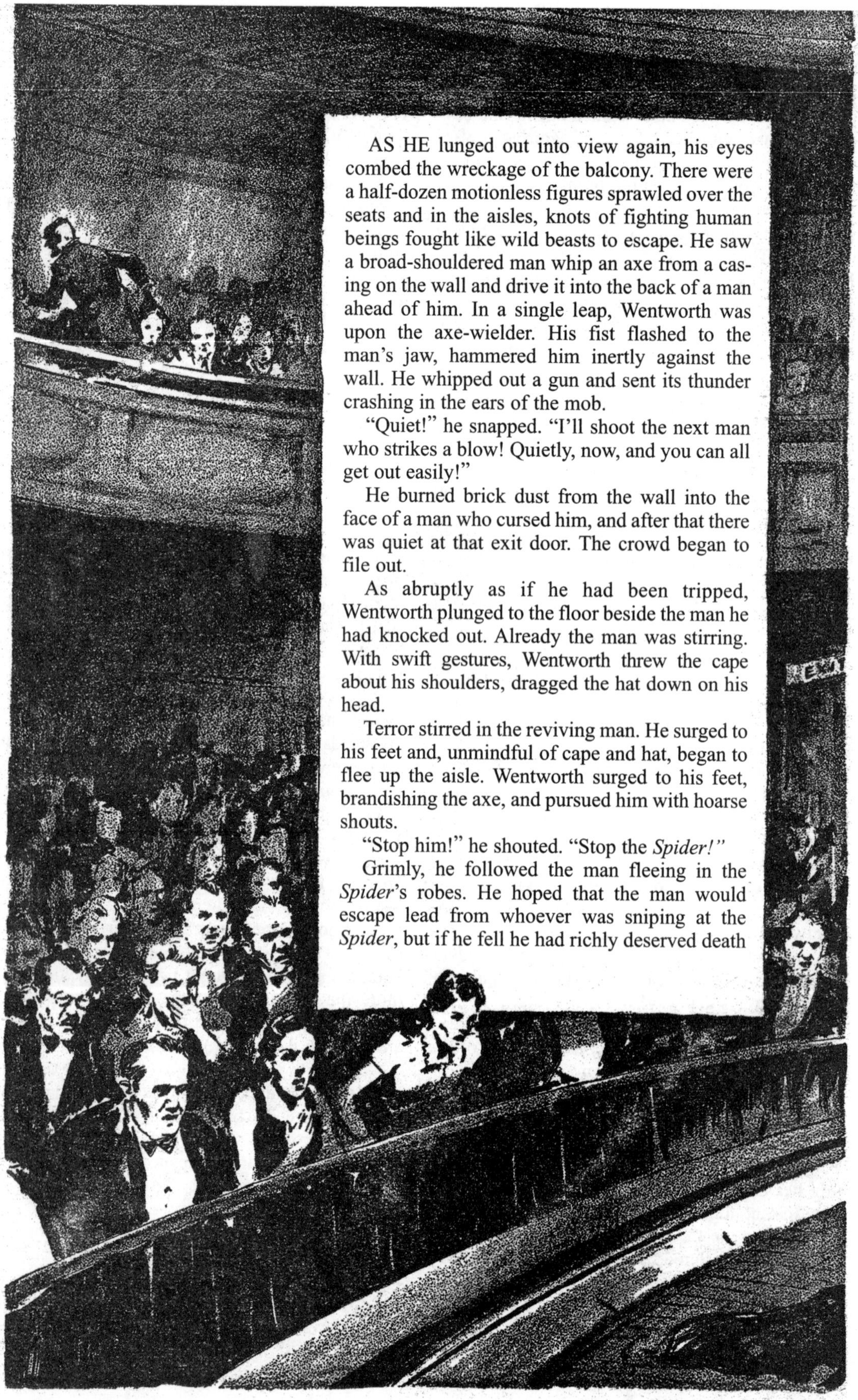

AS HE lunged out into view again, his eyes combed the wreckage of the balcony. There were a half-dozen motionless figures sprawled over the seats and in the aisles, knots of fighting human beings fought like wild beasts to escape. He saw a broad-shouldered man whip an axe from a casing on the wall and drive it into the back of a man ahead of him. In a single leap, Wentworth was upon the axe-wielder. His fist flashed to the man's jaw, hammered him inertly against the wall. He whipped out a gun and sent its thunder crashing in the ears of the mob.

"Quiet!" he snapped. "I'll shoot the next man who strikes a blow! Quietly, now, and you can all get out easily!"

He burned brick dust from the wall into the face of a man who cursed him, and after that there was quiet at that exit door. The crowd began to file out.

As abruptly as if he had been tripped, Wentworth plunged to the floor beside the man he had knocked out. Already the man was stirring. With swift gestures, Wentworth threw the cape about his shoulders, dragged the hat down on his head.

Terror stirred in the reviving man. He surged to his feet and, unmindful of cape and hat, began to flee up the aisle. Wentworth surged to his feet, brandishing the axe, and pursued him with hoarse shouts.

"Stop him!" he shouted. "Stop the *Spider!"*

Grimly, he followed the man fleeing in the *Spider*'s robes. He hoped that the man would escape lead from whoever was sniping at the *Spider*, but if he fell he had richly deserved death for that brutal axe work! He saw the man crash into the mob at the next door, and his momentum drove him through to the metal fire escape outside. The mob, separated by his charge, became more quiet; ceased its battling and scurried through to safety.

Wentworth peered around. The balcony was almost emptied, but suddenly, high up in the rearmost seats, he caught sight of a grey-headed man who sat quietly waiting for the panic to subside. As Wentworth spotted the man, he caught the flash of a gun in his fist, and dived to the floor just in time. And exultation burned in Wentworth's throat!

That man was Munro!

Wentworth whipped out a gun, lifted himself cautiously, and was just in time to see the man pop out of a window!

Wentworth whipped out a gun, lifted glass crashed there… too late! With a shout, he hurled

"Keep your seats!" he cried. "I'll kill the first man who moves!"

himself through the wreckage. He took two rows of seats at a high hurdle, stumbled into the central aisle and went up the steps three at a time. Ahead of him, and to the right, he saw Carl Laird pop out of an entrance.

"Munro!" Wentworth shouted. "He went out that window!"

Laird nodded and raced up the central aisle ahead of Wentworth, but in a half dozen strides, Wentworth passed him and reached the window first. He gazed down the sheer front of the building. No retreat there for Munro. He peered upward, and saw a man's legs disappear over the edge of the roof.

Laird was beside Wentworth, and his voice came coldly. "You got rid of your *Spider* robes pretty quickly, Wentworth. Or am I mistaken?"

Wentworth said harshly, "If you're tracking the *Spider*, he went out of that side exit over there. Personally, I think he did good work, stopped a worse casualty toll. I'm chasing Munro!"

Wentworth scrambled out of the window, set his hands in the narrow ledges formed by offset in the masonry that formed steps upward to the roof. If Munro peered over the edge now, a single shot would finish off the *Spider* forever! He was conscious that Laird was no longer beside him; he had gone to confirm Wentworth's story of the *Spider*'s escape, beyond a doubt! Wentworth's lips twisted bitterly. The police were like that, too; forgetting the pursuit of the real criminal in a frantic pursuit of the man who was their greatest ally against crime!

WENTWORTH climbed swiftly toward the roof. His hands were too busy for guns. His toes clung to the narrow ledges. Death might wait for him there on the roof, but equally he might destroy Munro! The man had just begun his operations, and already he had spread death and horror among scores of helpless human beings. In such a chase, the *Spider* would never falter!

The crash of a gunshot in the street whipped Wentworth's head about. He saw Laird poised on top of a taxi to which he had leaped and, almost at the corner, was the becaped figure of the axe-murderer! As Wentworth peered down, Laird fired again. The man in the *Spider*'s cape staggered… and disappeared around the corner. In an instant, Laird was racing after him.

Wentworth swore under his breath. There could be no mercy in his heart for the man who had committed that brutal axe-murder in the theatre, but it went against the grain that he should be hunted down in the *Spider*'s robes. No time for that now. He must climb on, capture Munro. Wentworth strained his arms outward and caught hold of the projecting roof ledge of the theatre, instantly let his body swing out into space. He hooked a knee over the verge, bellied the ledge… and a gun licked its powder flame at him from the roof balustrade!

Wentworth felt the bullet's wind brush past his ear. With a violent exertion of all the power of his mighty muscles, he heaved himself to the ledge and rolled flush against the brick balustrade. His gun was in his fist, his breath dry and brassy in his throat. For that single instant, he checked there. Then he drew his feet under him; his left hand crept to the balustrade. With an explosion of thigh muscles, he hurdled the brick rampart!

He had a glimpse of a white face, the glint of a gun, then his hurtling body crashed into that of the other man beyond the balustrade and they plunged together to the roof! The unexpected violence of the collision wrenched Wentworth's gun from his fist, sent it skittering across the graveled surface of the roof. With an acrobat's skill, Wentworth turned in the air, landed on hands and feet asprawl the body of the gunman!

Fierce and exultant laughter pumped into Wentworth's throat. There was no pause in the fierceness of his attack. His right hand clamped upon the man's throat, his left caught him by the thigh. A heave of his shoulders, and Wentworth lifted the man up out of the shadows of the roof, poised him high above the balustrade and sixty feet of empty space to the street below!

"Munro!" Wentworth panted. "Munro, this time, there will be no mistake! You die!"

He prepared to heave the man into space!

"No, no, Wentworth!" the man panted weakly. "In Heaven's name, no! I didn't know it was you! I thought it was Munro!"

Wentworth stared up then at the man he held on the brink of death, and a startled oath squeezed out of his throat.

He was gazing into the terror-stricken face of… *Robert Hunter!*

CHAPTER FOUR
Death Trap

RESTORED to his footing on the roof, Hunter leaned weakly against the balustrade and mopped his forehead.

His professional smile was sickly and forced.

"That was close," he said hoarsely. "Pretty close!"

Wentworth studied him silently. There was nothing in the man's build to contradict Wentworth's suspicions that he might be Munro; that he had, in the garb of the druggist, hurled death upon the actor on the stage. And he was positive he had seen Munro flee to this roof only moments before himself.

His eyes turned from Hunter and swept the roof carefully. He had not exonerated Hunter, but the *Spider* could not execute his justice upon a man whom he merely suspected. Yet the roof offered no hiding place. There was a slit of light from a stair kiosk door that swung half open, but aside from that entrance the roof offered no escape—none save another wall such as Wentworth had climbed.

"You came up the stairs?" he asked harshly.

Hunter nodded eagerly. "I was leaning out a window and saw the druggist start his climb up here. I rushed up the stairs, but the mob delayed me some. When I saw you swing over the edge, I thought you were the druggist who killed the actor, and I blazed away. God, that was close!"

"I don't know yet," Wentworth said softly, "just how you happened to come here... or why you knocked down the policeman and stole his gun!"

Hunter laughed, waved a hand airily. The hand didn't tremble much. His stance was heroic, legs braced, head lifted challengingly—a pose in which he had been photographed before the Taj Mahal; beside the Dalai Lama of Tibet.

"Oh, that!" Hunter chuckled. "I needed a gun, that was all. As soon as I heard that dying man's story in your apartment, I knew that something must be wrong in the drugstore. I darted over and kept watch. After you went in, and there was shooting, I saw this man in a druggist's white coat duck out of a basement window and so I followed him. He changed his coat in a car, and then came into this theatre. I thought I would need a gun to challenge him, and so I borrowed one!"

Wentworth said quietly, "Do you think you could point out the druggist's car from up here?"

Hunter shook his head, "I'm afraid not. You see, it was chauffeur-driven, and went on after the man got out. I'm afraid I didn't notice the license number either. Damned careless of me. But you see, in the places where I usually go, they don't have cars or license numbers. This detective business is new to me."

Wentworth said without emphasis, "Quite so. I think I'd like to have a look at the dead man on the stage. Poor Maurice."

He gestured Hunter toward the kiosk door, and Hunter walked before him with a deliberate swagger. "You're suspicious of me," he said, with a show of rankness, "and I can't say I blame you. But you're dead wrong, Wentworth. Dead wrong."

An uncanny silence lay over the theatre into which they descended. A woman lifted herself heavily from the aisle into which she had fallen and walked with the slow, steady movements of an automaton past them toward the exit doors. Her left arm hung limply, broken. The brilliant stage lighting still blazed down upon the fallen body of Charles Maurice, glinted on the whiteness of his fleshless skull. Into that silence, as Wentworth descended the last flight of stairs, lifted the burred voice of Carl Laird.

"Confound it, man, I don't care about your orders!" he was saying forcefully. "I tell you I pursued the *Spider* out of this theatre. He got away, and I have to rejoin my friends inside!"

Hunter started toward the door, told the policeman pompously, "It's quite all right, my man. Mr. Laird is known to me!"

BEHIND Wentworth, the two men walked toward the stage. The forced gaiety of Hunter's tones, repeating the story of his pursuit of the druggist, his encounter with Wentworth on the roof, was hollow in the dim auditorium. A fierce urgency was working in Wentworth's breast. He had to decide about Hunter. If the man were guilty, he must not be allowed to continue this work of slaughter and terrorization. At the same time, if he were guilty, Nita was safe so long as Wentworth kept Hunter under surveillance. If he were innocent—

Wentworth smothered a sharp oath as he stepped back stage. Ralph Warring's sprawled body lay just inside the door. He held a flashbulb gun in his fist, but the straps of his camera had been sliced, and the camera was gone! Under Wentworth's ministrations, Warring recovered. He surged to his feet, fists striking out fiercely.

"The Spider!" he said hoarsely. "Damn it, the *Spider* stole my camera!"

Laird thrust forward. "When?" he demanded harshly.

Warring rubbed his forehead with a heavy hand. "How the hell do I know?" he demanded irritably. "He jumped at me out of the shadows when I came backstage. I saw his cape swirling, got a glimpse of his face under the hat-brim. That was all."

"How long was that after you snapped a picture of the *Spider* in the balcony?" Wentworth asked quietly.

Warring shook his head, then snapped his fingers. "I remember now!" he said. "I saw you chasing the *Spider* with an axe in your hand! The *Spider* got out the door, and I ran back here, thinking I could get a shot of the whole theatre from the stage. He must have run down the fire escape, doubled back and... hell, I don't see how he could. It was too fast! But he did it; I swear I saw him!" Wentworth frowned at Warring, turned sharply toward the stage. Munro could not be the one who had snatched the camera, since Munro had been at that moment climbing through a window, or scrambling up the face of the building. Hunter, by his own story, was leaning out of another window at that moment. Laird had been beside Wentworth... Wentworth's lips tightened. Only one explanation was possible. Ralph Warring was lying! But, in the name of Heaven, why?

Wentworth stood staring down at the pitiful corpse

of one of the world's great actors. He stooped slowly and picked up the sword that lay beside Maurice's hand. It was a keen blade, scarcely the regulation stage sword, and Maurice had ripped it out at the last minute when he was attacked.

From the darkness at the theatre's back, a man called sharply, "All of you stand just like that! Don't move!"

Wentworth caught the glitter of police brass in the dimness, heard the heavy clump of feet as several men moved down the aisle toward him. Abruptly, Wentworth's eyes narrowed. By the heavens, Munro had overstepped himself this time! Maurice's death would end by trapping him! And Nita... Nita was in fearful and imminent danger!

Wentworth whirled, and the challenge of the police came to him again. He caught the glint of a leveled gun! Laird and Warring were moving toward him across the width of the stage.

"It's quite all right, officer," Wentworth said quietly. "We have no need to escape."

He flipped the sword into the air, caught it by the tip of the blade and held it, swaying for a moment. He laughed and sent it flashing off into the darkness of the wings. He saw Laird glance at him sharply as he moved forward to the lip of the stage. Warring moved forward with Laird, but Wentworth hung back a pace. He flung a sharp glance upward at the heavy asbestos curtain just behind the proscenium arch and slid a sidelong look off into the shadows. Yes, the sword had flown true. The rope that held the asbestos curtain had been sliced almost through, was rapidly unraveling.

Wentworth began to talk rapidly. "That audience was deliberately stampeded to distract attention from the murder of Maurice," he said. "He was killed by a fragile glass bomb thrown into his face from the balcony. The bomb contained a corrosive gas that, as you see, ate away the flesh from his face!"

A cop swore harshly. "Don't give me that stuff!" he said. "I suppose a bomb full of gas robbed the theatre safe, too!"

"A blind, purely a blind!" Wentworth said rapidly. "You see, by killing Maurice, the murderer gave me a valuable clue. Now, I know how to find... Munro!" And he knew something else, too. He knew Munro's purpose in this pointless seeming slaughter!

WARRING and Laird were staring at Wentworth. Hunter, strolling out of the wings, laughed loudly. "I told you we would do well to invite Wentworth to join the Gotham Hounds!" he cried.

It was at that moment the asbestos curtain's halyard snapped. Its sound was not loud, but the sudden downward rush of the curtain itself had the mounting whisper of a descending avalanche! Hunter cried out hoarsely, leaped out of its path, and the weighted bottom struck the stage just behind him. Wentworth was instantly alone, shut off from the theatre and all the others by the swift drop of the curtain.

On the instant, Wentworth had caught up the inert body of the dead actor and thrown it across his shoulder. With long bounds, he crossed the stage and reached the exit door on the narrow dark alley which ran beside the theatre. Behind him, he heard the crazy shouting of the police, the crash of a discharged gun, but he did not check his pace. They were still trying to get backstage, and he had, perhaps, a minute's start.

Ahead of him, a uniformed man sprang into the mouth of the alley, fumbled out his gun.

"Don't shoot, officer!" Wentworth cried. "I've got an injured man here! Quick, a car! An ambulance!"

He made his voice loud, and the alley funneled it ahead, sent it booming out into the street. As he blundered past the hesitant policeman, his Daimler rolled forward easily, and Jackson, ever alert for the slightest signal, leaped out to fling wide the door.

"You can use this car, sir!" Jackson cried. "What hospital?"

Wentworth leaped into the back, tossed Maurice's body to the cushions. "Roosevelt is near," he snapped, and turned toward the still uncertain policeman. "Tell them where I've gone," he said, and slammed the door.

Instantly, the car was racing down toward Broadway. The swirling crowd parted before the insistent demand of the horn, and Wentworth leaned forward to hurl swift instructions at Jackson.

"To Miss Nita's!" he said, with cold violence, "and let nothing delay you. Her life is in deadly peril!"

The hum of the motor deepened. Jackson's hands, bulging from their grip on the wheel, handled the heavy car like a toy. Traffic parted desperately at the urgency of the horn.

"As soon as we reach there," Wentworth said rapidly, "you will cut back to my house. Put this body under refrigeration at once. If police are there, you will have to circumvent them."

Jackson's voice came back in bursts because of his concentration on driving. "They know you got him, sir!"

"I'll see Kirkpatrick meantime!" Wentworth snapped. "Get on with your driving, man; we're barely crawling!"

The speedometer needle wavered up another ten miles to sixty. It would have been suicide, or murder, for any other driver than Jackson. Wentworth bent grimly over the ghastly body, set deliberately about fingerprinting it with equipment which he carried always in the car. Afterward, with a magnifying glass, he set about extracting their index.

"P—thirteen—nineteen—O, over twenty-three—seventeen—nineteen—twelve," he murmured.

Rapidly, he committed the index to memory. Wentworth had long ago learned that written records were less reliable than his memory. They might fall into the wrong hands. When he had finished his task, the Daimler was sliding to a halt before Riverside Towers, where Nita van Sloan lived. Wentworth sprang to the pavement, and instantly the Daimler was underway again.

THE dozen steps necessary to enter the building and reach the elevator required an endless time, and the sighing motion of the cage seemed laborious. Yet it was less than a dozen seconds before he was striding down the deep carpeted corridor of the twenty-first floor toward Nita's apartment. Hope and fear contested within him like warring armies, and it was fear that won when finally he rounded the angle of the corridor and could see Nita's door. An oath of despair lifted like a sob into his throat, and he hurled himself into a furious sprint over those last few yards.

In the dimness of the corridor, the brass knob of Nita's door glimmered with a pale and evil greenish light!

Wentworth wasted no time on the formality of ringing the bell. From a vertical pocket inside his vest, he slipped out a slim tool of surgical steel. It clashed against the lock and, seconds later, the door gave under his hand. He bounded through… and in the recesses of the apartment, Nita screamed!

The cry was high and tearing, mad with terror, and Wentworth called out reassuringly. The scream lifted again, and there was the slam of a closing door!

Wentworth plunged toward the sound and in his mind was a picture of the horror Munro's terror had wrought in the theatre. But what purpose could he serve by such tactics here? Wentworth shook his head against the futility of such questions, raced on.

"Nita!" he called again. "Nita, there's nothing to fear! It's only Dick!"

He rounded through the living room, brought up against the locked door of her boudoir. He leaned against it tensely, listening. Through the thin panels, he could hear her breathing, shallow and hurried with fear… and she would not answer.

"Nita, dear," he whispered softly. "Please open the door. It's Dick! Please, I want to help you!"

She did not answer, and Wentworth dropped to his knee, peered through the keyhole. At first, there was only darkness and then he saw the shifting lights on Nita's dress. She was moving backward. Her white, tense hands were thrust out toward the door, and horror twisted all the sweet lines of her face. Half across the room, she checked. She twisted her head about and stared behind her toward the open window!

A shout lifted to Wentworth's lips and died there. He could see electric tension run through Nita, could see a mad hope light her face. She turned and began to creep toward the window. And that window opened onto nothingness. Below it were twenty-one stories of empty space!

Frantically, Wentworth whipped out his lockpick again, and set it in the lock.

He must operate without any sound at all, lest he hurry Nita's approach to death! The lock was stubborn, and Wentworth saw that, for once, his hands were trembling. He brushed an arm across his forehead, forced himself to steadiness. And all the while, the cold fear that had no origin in fact but could drive men mad with fear, gnawed like a saw-toothed rat at his heart. What was happening beyond this door? He could not withdraw the pick to look again, and seconds were flying. Seconds… and it would take so pitifully few to destroy Nita!

At last the stubborn lock yielded. Instantly, Wentworth flung the door wide and leaped across the room. A shout of horror burned his throat. Nita was poised on the window sill, peering down into darkness with a fearful fascination upon her face. She took the time to cast one more look back at Wentworth, and in that split-second instant, Wentworth caught her about the waist. He snatched her from the brink of death.

BEFORE her feet struck the floor, Nita was fighting him. She was beating at him with her small white fists, drumming at him with her resolute heels. All Wentworth's pleading went unheeded. It required all his strength to wrestle her back from the gaping invitation of the window, toward which his own eyes swung with a fascinated fear.

It was while he stared, while he struggled with Nita, that he caught sight of something that flashed briefly in the outpouring light of the room; something that was hurtling forward out of the black obscurity of the night! Wentworth caught a single glimpse of the thing as it darted into the room, a glittering sphere in which something green and amorphous and horrible writhed like a living thing!

"Munro's bomb!" Wentworth gasped. He speared a hand toward the fragile sphere, and the wrench of Nita's unremitting struggle kept him from reaching it! The bomb sailed on across the room and smashed against the wall! Instantly, pale green tendrils were lifting into the air, reaching toward them! Wentworth swung Nita clear of the floor, started forward in a dash from the room—and another of the spheres flashed overhead to spatter its tinkling fragments on the wall!

A pattern of horror in green was *Spider*-webbed across the only exit!

With a choked curse, Wentworth wheeled back from the door. Only one exit remaining, and that was the one which Nita had fought to use… a window twenty-one stories above the street!

Wentworth reached the wall beside the window, he drew Nita toward him, and forced her wide-staring eyes to focus upon his. He stooped to her lips.

Through a long moment more, Nita fought him furiously with the madness that Munro had sent. Gradually, she quieted. She answered the kiss of the man she loved.

"Dick!" she whispered. "Oh, Dick, it's really you! I've gone almost mad. First, everything seemed so wonderful, so gay, and then suddenly, I was terrified."

"Later, dear, I'll tell you everything," Wentworth told her softly. "We have work to do. Munro is trying to kill us!"

"Munro!" Nita shuddered. She peered about the familiar safety of her room, and drew closer to Wentworth. "That gas!" she whispered. "I understand now who made that green gas!"

"Yes. It destroys human flesh," Wentworth said shortly. "We have to escape by the window. Munro will undoubtedly try to stop us, Nita." He snatched up a jar from Nita's dressing table and smashed the ceiling light. Darkness fell softly upon the room, but through the dark those green tendrils could creep, tendrils of death. Wentworth peered cautiously out the window. There was a narrow ledge, and the steel casements of the windows swung outward. Far below were the streaming lanes of Riverside Drive traffic, the black gleaming breast of the Hudson River. The sweet breath of the spring night drifted in. Wentworth fought down a shudder.

"Munro is above us," Wentworth said quietly. "He is in this same building!"

NITA was close beside him, and he began to unwind from about his waist a length of silken cord which the police knew as the *Spider*'s Web.

"In what disguise is Munro this time?" Nita asked. "I have my gun in my hand."

"I haven't seen him," Wentworth said quietly, as he knotted the silken cord beneath Nita's arms. "But he threw bombs in through this window. The only way that could be managed would be for Munro to whip them down from above with a length of cord. Here, Nita!"

They balanced there on the brink of death, and Wentworth peered cautiously upward along the sheer face of the building. He steadied himself against the out-swung casement, and coiled the silken line in his hand. Directly overhead, another casement window swung open, but Wentworth ignored that. If Munro were inside, waiting, even the *Spider* would stand no chance at all!

"I'll get a loop over the next window above and to the left," Wentworth whispered. "Our best chance is to get out through the apartment next to yours, and take Munro from behind!"

Wentworth's movements were swift despite his deliberation, and presently he had thrown a loop over the steel-framed, open window he had chosen: one floor up, second row over.

"Keep your gun ready," Wentworth whispered. "If all is clear, I'll toss the web back to you, then you swing over to me!"

Deftly, he twisted the silken line about his arm and, with no farther delay, swung off into space. His gaze was concentrated fiercely on the narrow sill where he must catch and hold until he could maneuver around the steel casement which stood open. Below him were two hundred feet and more of empty space. Men moved like ants on the pavement far below. But he could not think of them; dared not! Behind him, Nita screamed a warning, and her gun blasted punctuation to her scream!

"Munro!" she cried. "Above you, Dick! Munro!"

Wentworth kept his eyes on the narrow sill where he must balance, heard the gun slam out again, again. Fragments of glass rained down before him, catching tiny silver glints of light from the open casement. Wentworth strangled an oath. That glass could have but one meaning. Instead of being in the apartment directly over Nita's, Munro was lying in wait for him behind the window to which his rope was attached!

Even as the thought slashed across Wentworth's mind, he felt a shock in the strand to which he clung, and knew that something—probably a sharp blade—must have struck it. Nita's gun yammered hysterically behind him. Wentworth lifted his left leg high and reached out before him. If only he could get his knee hooked over that casement!

The rope slipped a fraction of an inch.

In the same instant, Wentworth realized that he was too low to get a leg over the casement. Frenziedly, he flung himself forward. It was the only chance. He released his hold on the silken rope and dived for the casement with both reaching hands!

As he plunged through the air, he saw the line of the silken rope writhing loosely before his face, severed by Munro! The next instant, Wentworth's hands clamped down on the top of the casement. His body swung violently forward, and the steel frame caught him across the belly, drove the wind from his lungs. Then Wentworth transferred the grip of his right hand to the inner edge of the casement, and hooked his other arm over the window sill. He accomplished that to the timing of Nita's gun, and even as his bent arm clamped home against the inner wall, he realized that she had emptied her gun! Until she took the time to reload, there was no threat to keep Munro from striking him down!

CLINGING there to the face of the wall, body and legs dangling in space, Wentworth did an incredible thing. He freed one hand and wrenched out his gun, and for the first time peered upward toward his ancient and terrible enemy!

Even as he stared, Munro was leaning out of the window. His head was encased in a huge metal helmet such as shallow-water divers use. Through the vision panel, his eyes glittered hostilely. His right hand was raised high above his head, and in that fist shimmered a greenish sphere—a gas bomb!

In the same instant that the man's hand swept downward, Wentworth fired. Munro's helmeted head was driven upward and back. The gas bomb arched outward into the night, spun past within inches of Wentworth's upturned face and Munro was no longer at the window. For an instant, his left hand gripped the casement there, but even as Wentworth loosed another bullet, the hand was jerked from sight. It seemed to Wentworth he heard a muffled curse, but he could not be sure.

Had he killed Munro? No time to speculate on that. He had to get into the apartment from whose window he swung, get to Munro's hideout. His left arm ached intolerably. It had been badly wrenched in that first violent swing against the window and, for long minutes now, it had supported his entire weight. Only the exertion of his powerful will compelled that arm to function.

Wentworth did not wait to holster his gun. He tossed it in through the window, clamped his right arm also over the window sill and heaved himself upward.

It was only then that he peered into the room beyond the casement. He swore incredulously, and checked his effort to drag himself inside. It was a woman's boudoir into which he looked. The woman was here, but she had been utterly silent throughout the whole battle.

The woman was seated before a dressing table, and there was a powderpuff in her hand, but the face that stared back from the mirrors had no eyes at all; nor any flesh. It was a skull only.

Wentworth's weakened arms almost lost their hold, and the realization dinned in upon his brain that he dared not enter this room. For here, the devouring gas of Munro lurked. In the apartment above, Munro himself was waiting. He clung, and turned his white face slowly toward Nita. For an instant, he stared blankly at the empty sill to which Nita had clung. Fear surged through him, then he heard her call.

"Here, Dick!" she cried. "I'm at the window below! I've fastened the web to my window for safety, but when I throw you the other end, tie it and slide down here!"

It was an incredible time that elapsed before Nita's third throw brought the silken line up to Wentworth. An eternity before his fatigued hands could arrange the loop as he wanted it. Then he slid down through the air, and but for the strong grip of Nita's arm, would have plunged on to his death.

The instant she had guided him through the window, he was running across the room. He heard the rapid tattoo of Nita's heels behind him as he wrenched open the door, sped along the hallway of this unfamiliar apartment. Munro… Munro was two stories above, and Wentworth still had a gun!

HE WAS sprinting when he reached the hallway, his feet soundless on the deep carpets. At the stairs, he flung back words to Nita.

"Hide behind this radiator. Reload your gun!" he said, but softly. "If he gets past me, and starts down… shoot! And don't stop shooting until your gun is empty!"

Nita dropped back as Wentworth spoke, and her eyes were wide and dark with apprehension. Not for herself, but for Dick, racing so valiantly into a battle while he still reeled from the fatigue of that struggle with death on the building's sheer side. She crouched behind the steam radiator, jacked a cartridge from the fresh clip into the chamber, and thumbed off the safety. Her hand was tense, but very steady. After a while, her forearm began to ache.

Wentworth burst out of the stairway well, and heard the door of the elevator open. A man in operator's uniform looked out, blinked stupidly at Wentworth.

"You ring, sir?" he asked.

Wentworth snapped, "Lock that control lever in place! Come with me!"

He had no gun in his hand, but the accent of command was in his voice. The man stared at him open-mouthed, but his hands were already moving to obey. He set the catch which held the door open, and moved awkwardly out into the hallway. Wentworth caught his arm and thrust him along the corridor as he hurried toward the entrance of Munro's hideout. The door swung open. The apartment was empty!

Wentworth swore under his breath and his eyes combed the open windows, the wreckage of glass that Nita's bullets had wrought. There was no sign of Munro. The helmet, then, had been bulletproof, although Wentworth had flung his lead against the vision window. He knew that it had sped true, for the shock had driven Munro back inside the window.

"All right," Wentworth said quietly. "We'll go down now."

Disappointment weighed heavily upon him. During those few swift moments while he had slid down the web to Nita, Munro had made good his escape.

He stopped the elevator two floors down and called to Nita, who came rapidly to meet him. The operator's head swung toward Nita. His eyes were admiring beneath the frosty sheen of white brows.

"He got away!" Nita said somberly.

Wentworth smiled slightly as the elevator sighed downward. "A master of disguise, like Munro, needs only a few minutes to disappear," he said. "I noticed that the police have been summoned. They undoubtedly have the building surrounded, and a close search will reveal whether there are any disguised persons in the building. Operator, I wish you'd come with me. You should know everyone in the building well enough to tell whether they're disguised."

The operator said, "Disguised?" He stopped the cage and slid open the door at the first floor. Three men were surging in through the main door, and Wentworth smiled grimly as he recognized them; saw a fourth man striding energetically forward behind them.

The Gotham Hounds had arrived, and brought Stanley Kirkpatrick, the commissioner of police, with them!

"Come along!" Wentworth said to the operator. "I'm sure you can penetrate any disguise we encounter."

Hunter flashed his wide, toothy smile. "We've got a clue to Munro!" he cried. "The Gotham Hounds will get him yet!"

Wentworth was still smiling, "An expert in disguises, such as you," he was saying to the elevator operator. "You did an excellent job, really, but you forgot that when bulletproof glass is fractured, such as the glass in Munro's helmet, it throws off a fine powder of glass—such as is caught in your eyebrows!

"Gentlemen!" Wentworth clamped a hand hard on the nape of the elevator operator's neck, jammed a gun into his side. "Gentlemen, allow me to present... *Munro!"*

CHAPTER FIVE
Cell for The *Spider*!

BLANK incredulity stared at Wentworth out of the faces of the four men who confronted him; and none of them seemed more stupid, more lacking in understanding, than the elevator operator whom Wentworth gripped by the neck. Nita had drawn her automatic as he spoke, leveled it at the man in the uniform of an apartment attendant. She backed away two yards, as Wentworth had taught her. When two captors were so separated, it was hard for a prisoner to shake both of them.

Kirkpatrick took a stiff stand before Wentworth, his carriage erect as a soldier, the spiked ends of his waxed mustache bristling. "Dick," he said coldly, "if this is some trickery, I warn you that you won't succeed in diverting my attention! You're going to pay for kidnapping that body from the theatre!"

Wentworth nodded, but did not glance toward his friend. He respected Kirkpatrick, and knew that this was no petty irritation that the commissioner expressed. Wentworth had violated a law; and all law was sacred to Stanley Kirkpatrick! Wentworth was looking at his captive with painful intensity, watching for any hostile move. The man made none. He cringed under Wentworth's grip.

"Aw, what's the matter with you, mister?" he whined. "I ain't done nothing."

"Only four murders within the last two hours," Wentworth said softly. "Plus God knows how many deaths at the theatre, and we won't even speak of your attempt to kill Miss van Sloan and myself! No, Kirkpatrick, this is no divertisement. I call your attention to the fact that, though this man apparently is an elevator operator, there are no callouses on his hand from throwing the lever. In fact, there is on his left hand, a smear of green pain put there by my bullet which just missed his hand as he gripped the steel frame of a casement window."

The operator writhed under Wentworth's grip. "You're nuts!" he said. "I'm a substitute, and I got that paint fixing a window for a lady on the twenty-first floor! I can prove it if you give me a chance."

Wentworth laughed shortly. "You're always a quick thinker, Munro. You'll say, no doubt, that it was in the apartment where now a woman is dead! Is that right?"

His prisoner lifted an appealing hand to Kirkpatrick. "Look, mister, you're a cop, I guess, from what you said. This guy ain't got no right to treat me like this. I ain't done nothing!"

Kirkpatrick's eyes shifted uncertainly from Wentworth to his prisoner. "There is powdered glass in your eyebrows," he said slowly. "Have you an explanation for that?"

The man started to speak, but Wentworth cut in on him softly. "Kirk, you'll admit that whatever else may be explained, there is no reason for an elevator operator to wear a disguise!" As he spoke, he reached out his hand with a lightning-deft movement... and clamped his thumb and forefinger on his prisoner's nose! The man yelled, wrenched away... and the tip of his nose came loose in Wentworth's grip!

"Putty!" Wentworth said, "and rather incompetently stuck on."

In the same moment, the man wrenched free of Wentworth's grip and darted toward the doors!

"My man!" Wentworth called easily. His hand flashed to the gun he had momentarily holstered, came free and the automatic lifted in steady rhythm. Wentworth's blue-gray eyes, which could be so kindly and humane, were implacable. The smile hardened on his lips, and the gun began its downward drop. The Gotham Hounds had scattered from the charge of the prisoner; Kirkpatrick was still fumbling for his gun... and, near the door, the man with the misshapen nose whipped about his head. He saw the gun falling into line, and he read his doom in Wentworth's eyes!

He faced Wentworth and flung both his hands high.

"I quit!" he cried. "I surrender! Don't shoot, Wentworth!"

WENTWORTH'S gun was in line at arm's length, and his eyes looked calmly along the barrel. There was regret in Wentworth's gaze.

The man, whose shoulders had been cringing, stood very stiffly. A faint smile stirred his mouth.

"You're a resolute man, Wentworth," he said. "You were going to kill me."

Wentworth said, flatly. "Of course. For four murders tonight. For a hundred in the past, Munro."

Kirkpatrick uttered a low, amazed oath. "It is Munro!" he cried. "I've heard that voice before! Wentworth—"

"Get handcuffs on Munro!" Wentworth interrupted. "He's not a man to take chances with. Handcuff him to me! I'll be responsible for him!"

Munro's voice was respectful. "I didn't know you were in command of the police, too, Wentworth!"

A slow flush touched Kirkpatrick's cheekbones. "Enough of that! *Sergeant Reams!"*

The bluff sergeant who was Kirkpatrick's aide thrust through the glass doors behind Munro. Two other uniformed men followed him.

"Reams, those two men will handcuff themselves to the prisoner," Kirkpatrick ordered sharply. "He is a dangerous murderer. I hold you personally responsible!"

"That's a mistake, Kirk," Wentworth said softly.

Kirkpatrick whirled toward Wentworth as the two policemen moved stolidly forward to obey, but Wentworth kept his eyes on Munro, and his gun, also. He did not move until the two men had each handcuffed a hand to Munro, and were ushering him out of the door.

"Nice work, Wentworth!" Munro called back, "I'll have to settle with you for this! My humble regards, Miss van Sloan!"

Wentworth said softly, to Kirkpatrick, "I'm going along!"

"You're staying here!" Kirkpatrick snapped. "Where is Maurice's body?"

Wentworth shook his head. "It isn't Maurice, Kirk. It was Maurice's understudy!"

Kirkpatrick said grimly, "Then he fooled the entire cast of Hamlet, as well as the audience. Stop evading me! Where is the body? I warn you, Dick, that you're under arrest on charges of interfering with the police in the performance of their duty! Also, tampering with evidence!"

Wentworth was only half listening. His acute attention was focused on the departing police, on Munro outside the building. He said, impatiently, "All right, Kirk. I accept the charges, and I'll plead guilty. But I'm still telling you it was not Maurice, but his understudy. If you know Maurice at all, you know that he never spoke to any member of the cast outside of strict business. He made a fetish of keeping to himself. Under those circumstances, and with the understudy's help, it would be easy for the other man to imitate Maurice. Here's a way to prove it. I can give you the fingerprint index of the corpse, and you can compare them with prints in Maurice's home! How about having that checked now?"

Kirkpatrick stared at Wentworth with narrowed eyes, nodded abruptly. "All right. I've rarely known you to be wrong, Dick. Sergeant Reams... check this fingerprint index with what you can find in Maurice's home. Relay the message to headquarters!"

The Gotham Hounds had been passive auditors of most of this, but now Hunter strolled forward. In the background, Laird wore a scowl on his dour face, and Warring's slitted eyes were amused as ever. Hunter was affably smiling.

"Look here, Wentworth, you're rather messing things up with this corpse-kidnapping," he said. "We've all had ourselves sworn in as special deputies to hunt the *Spider*. I'm afraid the commissioner won't do the same for you, now."

Wentworth smiled. "Quite all right," he said. "I'm afraid I'd find the badge hampering to... the *Spider*. I rather approve of the *Spider* these days!"

KIRKPATRICK said sharply, "In just what way, Dick, would your badge hamper the *Spider!"*

"My dear Stanley!" Wentworth cried. "It should be perfectly obvious! When once I have given my word, I invariably keep it! So the *Spider* might find

Two men—two horrors —were running toward them. Their faces were dissolving....

it inconvenient if I swore to apprehend him!"

Kirkpatrick checked an impatient oath, but his eyes continued their narrow regard of Wentworth. Laird said, sourly, "If you're suspicious of Wentworth, I can definitely prove to you that he's the *Spider*."

Wentworth kept a rigid smile on his lips, but it was difficult to keep the sudden apprehension out of his eyes. He felt Nita move closer to him, knew that she had the gun in her fist. Laird's face seemed angry.

"I chased the *Spider* in the theatre tonight," he said shortly, "and put a bullet through his shoulder. Now, if Wentworth has my bullet in his shoulder, he's guilty. Otherwise not! And I can't see any evidence of a wound!"

"And I," said Warring gently, "took some excellent pictures of the *Spider* tonight. Unfortunately, someone stole my pet camera, and I haven't been able to interest the police in finding it for me!"

Hunter laughed gaily, "In fact, Kirkpatrick, we have the *Spider* all sewed up in a sack, just as neatly as Wentworth here sewed up Munro. Signed, sealed, and delivered!"

Hunter's last word checked on his lips, a half-tittered sound, and his eyes glared wide in sudden fright. Every man in that lobby save Wentworth was transfixed. Perhaps he was more used to horror. For it was pure horror that split the night apart; the scream of a man in unbearable agony!

"I warned you, Kirk!" Wentworth snapped, and bounded toward the doors, gun already in his fist.

Kirkpatrick's voice rang out sharply. "Halt, Wentworth! My gun is on you!"

Wentworth said savagely, "Damn it, Kirk. Munro—"

The screams continued incredibly, and Kirkpatrick reached Wentworth's side with two long strides. A handcuff snapped its chill steel about his wrist, but Wentworth paid it no heed. He surged eagerly forward beside his friend, the commissioner of police, and they went out on the sidewalk together. Two men, two horrors, were running toward them. They wore police uniforms, and their wrists were handcuffed together, each to the other. Their faces… were dissolving!

Even as Wentworth saw them, the flesh streamed from their faces and he was gazing into the blank eye sockets of two skulls set upon living men! For just that second, the two inhuman things continued to stumble forward. Then they pitched to the sidewalk, and writhed out the last agony of their lives.

Munro had vanished.

Kirkpatrick stared down at the bodies of his officers. Wentworth knew that he felt those deaths with a personal pain, for he was father as well as commander to his men; and Wentworth had warned him! But Munro could not be far away!

Wentworth wrenched at the handcuff that bound him to Kirkpatrick, urged him into a pounding run toward the corner. The sound of swift traffic hummed from Riverside Drive. A few cars had swerved in toward the curb. Wentworth reached the corner, straining at the steel links that bound him to the reeling Kirkptrick, but the side street, too, was empty.

Abruptly, Kirkpatrick snapped from his lethargy. "My car, Dick!" he barked.

Two strides, and he was at the microphone of his two-way radio, hurling a general alarm out for Munro. Wentworth shook his head hopelessly. The description would not help at all. Just now, Munro was a mousy man in the uniform of an elevator operator, with sandy-gray hair, and cringing shoulders. Five minutes from now, he could be Kirkpatrick himself, or Wentworth… or the Mayor of the city! Once let that man get out of sight and he was as impalpable as a handful of smoke.

WENTWORTH'S lips closed bitterly. He, and he alone, was to blame for Munro's escape! He had allowed himself to be merciful for one moment; he had allowed himself to be swayed by the fact that the police were all about the building. That momentary weakness had already brought death in horrid form to those two officers; it might bring death to scores of others!

Sergeant Reams ran up heavily, gun in his fist, stared down in shocked amazement at the two dead men.

"My fault, sir!" he stammered presently. "But, God, he was handcuffed! We searched him!"

"Gas ducts along the backs of his arms, I imagine," Wentworth said slowly. "A reservoir within his trouser legs, perhaps. And some sort of protective substance on his hands… I know he left no prints on the lever of the elevator for I looked to see. I should have warned you, Reams. But talk of blame is foolish. We have to start over again! Kirk, get me to headquarters! I want to arrange bail on this charge of yours and get on with the fight!"

Reams shook his head heavily. "I was forgetting, Commissioner. They say down at headquarters they picked up Jackson. He had been batted over the head, and there wasn't any corpse in the car, nor in Mr. Wentworth's apartment, either."

Wentworth choked down a cry, and his lips straightened more grimly. "Will you believe me now, when I tell you it wasn't Maurice?" he said. "Let's get to headquarters!"

"Another report, sir," Reams broke in. "A screwy thing. The watchman at the Nation's Bank phoned up headquarters and asked for a special guard. It seems that when he went by the vault a while ago, he noticed the dial shining sort of funny, like it had radium paint on it. Green, you know."

Wentworth laughed sharply. "There's luck, Kirkpatrick! Let's get to that bank fast!"

Kirkpatrick turned his head heavily. "What do you mean, Dick?"

"That green glow means… that Munro is going to rob the bank! Come on, there's no time to be lost! Damn it, Kirk, I'll explain while we're on the way!" He saw a stubborn set come over Kirkpatrick's jaw and exploded angrily. "Damn your stubborn Scot's head! A few minutes ago I asked you to let me watch Munro, and you didn't listen to me!"

Kirkpatrick's face whitened, and anger touched his brilliant blue eyes darkly, but he nodded his head slowly. "That's just—" he said thickly. "All right, Wentworth, I'll listen this time. But you are going to jail!"

Kirkpatrick began to snap out orders, commanded a patrol wagon to meet him at the Nation's Bank to take charge of Wentworth; curtly refused to allow the Gotham Hounds or Nita to accompany him.

"You professional adventurers run along and bother the *Spider* for a while," he said shortly. "Nita, I'm sorry, but the safest thing you can do is to go home. And, I suppose, phone Dick's lawyer."

The commissioner's big limousine rolled from the curb, swung eastward and began to gather speed behind the mounting scream of its siren.

"Cut that thing off!" Kirkpatrick snapped. "Now, Dick, I want explanations, in detail. Why does a green glow on the bank vault's dial mean that Munro is going to rob it!"

Wentworth explained rapidly everything that he had found out, that he had guessed about Munro. "He has some device for generating either gaiety or fear. He may be able to build up any other sort of emotion. I don't know that, and I don't know the method. Since he uses a gas to destroy men, he may use a gas for this other. I only know that whenever this device is operating, brass or copper or its compounds begin to glow like radium! It almost sounds as if there were some electricity or a ray employed. But I don't think Munro will strike tonight, Kirk. Such a device as he uses obviously would be more potent against a crowd than individuals. My guess would be he'll strike either at the morning rush hour, or at lunch time. Place men high up in the surrounding buildings, Kirk, but do it secretly. I believe they should be above the level of this new device of Munro's."

KIRKPATRICK stared thoughtfully ahead. He shook his head sharply.

"Damn it, there must be some way to trap this man, Munro! If only we could hit on some means of identifying him. This business at the theatre has me stopped. I don't believe the murder had any significance. Just a trick to start the stampede as a cover for robbing the safe."

Wentworth was utterly relaxed against the cushions. The handcuff chafed his wrist a little, and there was iron in his soul. The *Spider* must be free when Munro struck!

"You can easily prove your theory on the theatre tragedy, Kirk," he said softly.

Kirkpatrick swore softly. "It's not a theory. Just a guess. I'll admit to you that I'm baffled!"

"Check the fingerprints!" Wentworth said. "They will prove that it was the understudy who died. Then you need only locate Maurice and ask him a few questions."

Kirkpatrick's head turned slowly. "Why don't you say what you mean, instead of hinting, Dick?" he demanded harshly.

Wentworth lifted a shoulder in a shrug. "I'm not sure what I mean!" he said shortly. "What about those fingerprints?"

Kirkpatrick leaned forward and picked up the microphone, asked headquarters for a report on the work in Maurice's apartment.

"Report is negative, sir," the announcer said. "Can't find any prints in that apartment to match with the index you gave us. And here's a report just came in, sir. The body kidnapped from the theatre has been found, in an abandoned car. Can't take fingerprints. Flesh is all gone from the hands, too!"

Kirkpatrick ripped out a harsh, strange oath. "That's torn it, Dick!" he cried. "That body was kidnapped from Jackson solely to destroy the fingerprints. Now we know who Munro is! Now, we have a means of identifying him!"

Wentworth frowned, shook his head slowly while Kirkpatrick switched on the microphone again and began barking out a general alarm for Charles Maurice.

"Get all possible pictures of him, get fingerprints from his apartment and broadcast them."

Wentworth leaned forward sharply. "Get all possible group photographs of Maurice, showing him with other members of the casts for years back! Particularly in England!"

Kirkpatrick stared at Wentworth, frowning, then repeated the order into the microphone. But he was still frowning when he turned back to Wentworth.

"Confound it, Dick!" he snapped. "What are you up to now? Today's development proves definitely that Munro and Maurice are one and the same man!"

"Munro is certainly a genius at makeup and disguise," Wentworth conceded carefully. "I'll grant that there is a close connection between Munro and Maurice!"

Kirkpatrick scowled, and his eyes were cold and speculative as they bored into Wentworth's. "No doubt," he said curtly. "The connection is close. As close as the connection between Richard Wentworth... and the *Spider*!"

Wentworth laughed lightly. "Why as to that, Kirk," he said. "We, the *Spider* and I, do have a great many things in common. Personally, I think Richard Wentworth the smarter man!"

THE patrol which Kirkpatrick had ordered was waiting at the corner beside the Nation's Bank, and Wentworth was turned over to the police with brief instructions to make sure he stayed behind bars until Kirkpatrick returned to headquarters.

Locked inside the patrol, Wentworth waved a hand airily, "There is plenty of time, Kirk," he said. "The robbery here won't take place until the streets are crowded... and it still lacks some several hours of dawn! I'll be looking forward to your visit!"

When the patrol rolled away, Kirkpatrick was still standing, an erect uncompromising figure, and his frown refused to lighten at Wentworth's quips.

He was Wentworth's closest friend, but he would brook no violation whatsoever of the law.

If he got the evidence he sought, to prove Wentworth and the *Spider* one man, he would prosecute with all the drive of which he was so resolutely capable!

The patrol had traveled ten blocks before Wentworth spotted the small coupé that was trailing. He watched it with narrowed eyes through a space of minutes, then saw another car whip around the corner and pass it. Wentworth started to his feet. There could be no doubt at all that a signal had passed between the occupants of those two cars, and now the new arrival was spurting toward the patrol with an added burst of speed.

There were three policemen on the patrol, two in the front seat and a third seated across from Wentworth, locked in with him. The third officer whipped up his gun.

"Sit down!" he snapped.

Wentworth pointed toward the pursuing car, now almost immediately behind the patrol. "The patrol is about to be attacked," he said flatly.

The policeman looked but the car was passing the patrol. At the same instant, a spurt of flame winked from the coupé Wentworth had first noticed. A tire on the patrol exploded. The police truck lurched and, forward, there was a crash of metal; the jangle of violently smashed glass!

Wentworth pitched to the floor. At the same instant, the policeman sprang toward him. Wentworth saw the raised blackjack, tried to dodge—and his head smacked against the wall. The blackjack jarred explosively against his skull.

Wentworth's dimming eyes stared up into the policeman's face. The devil! Was this some new trick of Munro's—His senses flicked out with that thought.

CHAPTER SIX
Terror at High Noon!

PAIN was Wentworth's first reminder that he still lived. He fought his way upward through tons of blackness that absorbed all his strength. Deliberately, at the end, he maintained a semblance of unconsciousness till he could gauge his surroundings. The attack on the patrol, even the policeman on guard, might well have been part of a Munro plot!

A footfall sounded lightly, close beside him, and Wentworth started to the touch of a soft hand on his forehead.

A voice called his name gently. "Dick! Can you hear me, Dick?"

Wentworth wrenched open his eyes and gazed into the face of—Nita!

He stared without comprehension for a moment. Was Nita a prisoner, also? He glanced rapidly over the room, caught the smiling sardonic gaze of Ralph Warring and recognized that he was in an apartment, in an ordinary bedroom.

"The Gotham Hounds, sir," said Warring, "have snatched you from durance vile! It involved us in a bit of a struggle, but though there were some broken police heads, and a bit of material damage to a patrol wagon, that was all. I may say, pridefully, that no one was killed!"

Before Warring had fairly started to speak, Wentworth realized the whole picture. His hand reached out to Nita's, and the clasp was hidden from Warring by Nita's body. He turned Nita's hand gently, looked at her wristwatch, and shock ran through him. Half-past eleven! And outside, the bright warm sunlight of the spring day streamed past the windows. That blow on the head had laid him out for hours, and in that time Munro might have struck at the bank! Morning rush hour, or noon—

Nita said, gently, "There has been no attack on the bank… yet!"

With a final, soft pressure of Nita's hand, he released his hold, thrust himself up from the pillow against which he rested.

"The bank?" he snapped. "To hell with the bank! Your confounded interference has got me in bad with the police! Who asked you to pull a fool stunt like that? Nita, if you helped them—"

Nita drew herself up proudly, but there was a smile in the depths of the eyes. "Why, Dick!" she exclaimed. "We were only trying to help you! To think you'd talk to me like this!"

Wentworth swore. He was dressed except for collar and shoes. He began to fumble for them while he fought down the agony of the concussion he had suffered.

"I've got enough trouble," Wentworth said petulantly, "without having to dodge the police all the time! You, Warring, and your damned meddling friends!"

Warring was watching with a wary smile on his lips, eyes almost closed. "What did you have in mind doing, Wentworth?" he asked softly.

"Doing?" Wentworth straightened, reached for his coat. "Doing? I'm going to surrender to the police! Oh, don't worry about my reporting you! I'll say that I haven't the least idea who it was rescued me. The policeman will be bound to admit that he knocked me out with his blackjack. I woke up in a hotel room."

WENTWORTH was watching Warring while he spoke, trying to guess whether the man would try to prevent his departure. There was so damned little time. Without any doubt at all, Munro would strike at the bank as soon as the lunch hour crowds were thick in the streets. Before that time, the *Spider* must be ready!

"So you don't appreciate our efforts?" Warring murmured.

"Asinine, stupid meddling!" Wentworth shouted, "No, I don't need your help! Nita, you at least should have known better!"

Nita's head was up, and her fists knotted at her sides. "You're an ungrateful wretch!" she said indignantly. "We help you, and then you behave this way! Go on back to the police—and I hope you get a year in prison!"

Wentworth made no response to that. He strode resolutely for the door and when his back was turned to Warring, he deliberately winked at Nita! There was no change in her face, but as usual she had caught his purpose clearly. She would be invaluable to him as a spy upon the movements of the Hounds—and if they thought she had quarreled with Wentworth, they would be more inclined to trust her. Wentworth was under no illusions as to why they had snatched him from the police.

"We crave your forgiveness, Wentworth," Warring said mockingly, "but you see, we considered it would be impossible to catch the *Spider* while you were locked up!"

"Don't try to mend matters by flattering me!" Wentworth flung back at him, though he fully understood the implication of Warring's words. Warring was telling him, clearly, that the Hounds were still convinced that Wentworth and the *Spider* were one and the same man!

"Nothing was farther from my mind," Warring answered, "but I insist upon driving you to police headquarters. You see, the Hounds have made me responsible for you."

"Very well, if you insist," Wentworth acknowledged quietly, "but it will have to be fast. And if the police capture me, in your company, before I have surrendered, it will be disastrous for you!"

There was no more conversation while they entered Warring's car and drove rapidly toward headquarters. Nita rode with them, but held herself coldly aloof.

Warring's lips were set in their perpetually mocking smile, and Wentworth was preoccupied. He stole a covert glance at clocks they passed. This was causing an endless delay, but it would have its value, also. Warring would be able to testify that he had brought Wentworth to police headquarters—and if he handled matters well, that fact might set up an alibi for the *Spider*!

At the curb before police headquarters, Wentworth sprang to the walk. Without a word to Nita, or to Warring, he ran up the steps and into the main hallway. He knew the geography of headquarters perfectly, and he angled swiftly for a rear exit, while he kept his head bowed as if in thought, altered his usually alert stride against recognition by officers he passed. Within fifteen minutes, a half hour at most, Munro would strike at the Nation's Bank—and the *Spider* must be there to greet him!

IT WAS at the same moment when Wentworth was hurrying through the halls of police headquarters that a limousine slid to the curb before the Nation's Bank and an oldish man alighted somewhat stiffly with the chauffeur's help. His shoulders, beneath the perfect fit of a cutaway, were stooped and his silver hair crisped out beneath the brim of his silk hat.

"Return about three, Francis," he said. "Oh, yes, bring that satchel into my office."

The chauffeur saluted, "Yes, Mr. Oldham."

The man called Mr. Oldham nodded slightly and stiffened his shoulders, used his cane as he crossed the walk toward the bank. The uniformed guard saluted energetically, swung the door wide. At the columned entrance, Mr. Oldham paused a moment. He looked slowly over the street. It was not yet crowded, for it lacked fifteen minutes of the noon hour. There were a number of loiterers leaning against the facade of the bank; in three cars parked nearby, there were a half dozen men.

The guard leaned forward respectfully. "Those are the extra police guards, sir," he whispered. "And there are lots more out of sight inside, too!"

Mr. Oldham nodded gravely, walked deliberately across the lobby. The door to the inner mysteries buzzed open at his approach, and an official hurried toward him.

"Oh, sir, you shouldn't have come down today!"

Mr. Oldham smiled. "Nonsense, man. Nonsense; there is no danger with all the police on guard! Set the satchel in my office, Francis, then you may go."

The eyes, keen behind rimless spectacles, watched narrowly as Francis swung the satchel to the floor. It jarred heavily, and Mr. Oldham stiffened, a little apprehensively. But nothing happened; Francis saluted once more, and marched out of the bank. Mr. Oldham strolled on into his office.

"I shan't want to be disturbed," he murmured back over his shoulder.

As the door swung shut, Mr. Odham swung about with an extraordinary alertness for so old a man. He sprang to the door, locked it and crossed the office to peer into the connected bathroom. No other door there. He nodded his head in approval, plucked up the heavy satchel and eased it down on top of the desk. Then he picked up a private direct phone on the desk and spun out a number with a stiffened forefinger. Presently, buzzing came over the wire. When it had sounded three times, and without waiting for an answer, he hung up.

He dialed another number. Six times, his head bent forward with every indication of alert youthfulness. He performed that task, and each time he hung up without waiting for an answer. Afterward, he sat rigidly, eyes fixed on a small bronze clock on the desk. Minutes ticked past slowly, and the hands stood at three before twelve when the man the staff greeted as "Mr. Oldham" began to smile. It was a slow smile, wolfish, cruel, and greedy.

The little bronze clock had begun to glow. It threw off a faint, cold, greenish light!

Mr. Oldham stood and opened his satchel. From it, he took a light metal diving helmet. Rapidly, he settled it over his shoulders. Then he dipped again into the satchel and, one by one, he took out six glass spheres. They were transparent, and within them green vapors swirled like filthy roiled waters. Mr. Oldham handled them very carefully and set them in a neat little row upon his desk. Afterward, he sat down and folded his hands. Through the vision window in the front of the helmet, his face showed dimly. That wolfish smile was widening on his lips.

The clock on the desk showed one minute of twelve. The green glow was vivid now. It quivered and sent out streamers of light.

Under the helmet, Mr. Oldham chuckled.

THE first eager rush of the luncheon crowd was streaming out into the street. The elevators were pumping out a rapid flow of humanity. The sound of their hurrying feet, of their lifting, liberated voices beat into the office where Mr. Oldham sat. His hand moved caressingly to the green globes.

The police guards in the cars, on the roofs, were conscious of a mounting tension. They had been at their posts throughout the morning. The blow had not fallen in the rush hour, and this was the second danger point according to their instructions. The sidewalks were getting jammed. Auto traffic was a crawling snake amid an ocean of people that overflowed into the streets.

In one of the watch cars, Mike Finnegan shifted restlessly. "Hell of a note," he grumbled to his partner, Al Haines. "How much longer we got to wait? My innards feel empty!"

Al laughed. "That ain't hunger. You're just plain scared!" he said. His laughter didn't seem quite natural and it cut off.

Mike looked at him. "Look," he said, "do you feel… scared, too?"

Al shifted in his seat. "Not exactly scared," he said, and then, looking at Mike, his eyes widened. "Hey, Mike! Lookit your shield!"

Mike pulled down his broad chin, and stared at his half-hidden shield under his lapel. His face lost its high color.

Al's voice was curious and flat. "Orders say: 'look for danger if your shield begins to glow with a green light!'"

Mike swore, thinly. "It's green, or I'm a Dutchman!"

Al tried to laugh. He felt cold and quivering inside. "You ain't no Dutchman, Mike!"

THE two girls were clattering along on their high heels, their voices high, a little shrill, but happy as they hesitated before a shop window.

"Come payday, Agnes, I'm buying me those!" One pointed to a froth of silken underwear.

Agnes shrugged. "They're pretty, but me, Lil, I'm holding onto my cash."

Lil twisted her blondined head around. "You! Holding onto cash! What are you scared of?"

Agnes didn't answer her at once. They stood and looked at each other without speaking. Agnes' shoulder shivered a little, and she looked behind her.

"I don't know," she said, in a muffled voice. "But I am… scared!"

Lil said, "Ah, don't be so silly!" She didn't sound happy, and she didn't look again at the silk underwear in the window. She was looking at Agnes, and her eyes had a strange light. "Funny," she said. "Your beads got a funny sort of green shine to them."

Agnes shivered again. "Look, let's go eat."

They started across the street toward the Nation's Bank corner. There was a street cleaner in a white suit with a wheeled cart and a long-handled brush, in their way, and they started around him. The man glanced at them, and his eyes were gray-blue and keen. His gaze drew to sharp focus on the beads that Agnes wore and his lips made a tight, straight line across his face.

"You girls better get off the street, quickly!" he told them quietly.

The two girls stared at him, and didn't answer, and hurried on toward the bank corner. The street cleaner swore under his breath. His long-handled brush clanged against the cart. On the sidewalk, a man started nervously at the sound.

"Damn you!" he rasped. "Do you have to do that?"

In Mr. Oldharn's office, the man in the helmet got to his feet and picked up two of the glass spheres.

THERE wasn't much laughing now in the street crowds. People moved hurriedly, with a jerky nervousness and quick over-shoulder glances. Voices were muted when anyone spoke at all, and the clatter and thud of swift heels was the dominant note. The narrow walls caught the sound and imprisoned it as if they, too, conspired with the terror that was breeding here. They would not let even the sound escape.

When people collided, they shied apart with paling faces, or quick, reasonless anger. Footsteps, suddenly behind a man, could make him whirl like an animal at bay. In their cars, the police were bolt upright, and their eyes held the trapped, despairing look of men at zero hour of a hopeless assault.

The street cleaner clutched his long brush and wheeled the cart toward the bank. His face was pallid; his hands made clenched white fists. His steps were deliberate and stiff, as if all his muscles were braced in titanic effort. His eyes quested everywhere, spotted a car loaded with men which forced its way through the flow of pedestrians to a halt before a small jewelry store. More police? Perhaps… still they might be killers!

He stared at them fixedly, saw how men darted in abrupt terror from their path. That was why he didn't see a window in the bank ease open. It opened only a few inches, perhaps six. The glass spheres were only three inches in diameter.

The window made a small creaking sound, and two girls on the sidewalk muffled their brief cries of fear and grabbed each other convulsively.

"Oh, Lil!" one sobbed. "Oh, look. Inside that window. A man in a… in a helmet!"

The two girls turned up white, terrified faces, and something flew through the air toward them from that partly opened window, something that glittered in a stream of warm sunlight: a dark, green sphere with a sheen like old bronze. Yes, very lovely in the sunlight.

The girls were frozen in their fear. Screams crowded up from their swelling throats, came out shrill and hoarse and terrible with fear; beat against the imprisoning walls of stone, and racketed up into the clear warmth of the day, fluttered in the ears of the crowd that terror rode.

That was before the sphere reached them.

Anges saw the sphere coming, lovely and glistening, floating toward her. She thrust out a wild, rigid hand to check it and it just brushed her fingers. It struck against her forehead. Not a hard blow; a drifting balloon would have been almost as heavy. It was enough to break the glass. Anges felt a minute burn as a fragile sliver bit into her forehead. Something green and greasy like coal smoke eddied down before her eyes. It laid its tendrils against her cheeks.

Beside her, Lil was screaming again and again as quickly as she could draw breath. She stood very still, and the tendrils were reaching for her, too. They seemed gentle and caressing; they had an especial affinity for warm young flesh. They twined and coiled against it.

There was just an instant when the screams stopped; when they burst out again, they were incredible. They were horror and terror, but they were more than that. They were sheer, animal agony!

IT HAD happened in a space of heartbeats, but when finally Agnes and Lil burst the bonds of their paralytic fear; when they turned to flee from the pain that they could not leave behind them, their hands thrust out blindly before them. They ran, and they struck against an automobile, and did not see it. They burst out into the street and other screams ran before them, men's and women's, as they stampeded like a herd of terror-maddened cattle. For Agnes and Lil were no longer human beings. Their faces were gleaming white, skeleton skulls!

In the car against which they crashed, two men sat rigidly, realizing that the thing they had been waiting for had struck. Al Haines twisted toward those awful skull faces, and beyond him, Mike Finnegan's lips burst apart in a strange mixture of curse and prayer. They were trembling with their fear, but they were policemen. They pulled out their guns, and leaped to the pavement. And another glass sphere sailed majestically through the air to greet them.

Afterward, there were two men also who ran screaming along that already panic-stricken street, beings with the bodies of men, but with faces that were the nightmare faces of Death!

More swiftly than ran those dying men and women, terror swept through the crowded street. Nameless fears had made them cold and empty within, and now in these screams that tore the air to shreds, they felt the fulfillment of their baseless apprehensions. But there was no tangible thought. An electric tension crackled over their heads, joined them fellow to fellow, in a thoughtless, emotion-ridden throng.

The street cleaner had whipped about with the first cry from the girls, and he saw the bursting of that first green sphere. Instantly, his white coat was torn open. His hands vanished to his armpits and when they reappeared, they glinted with the ominous black metal of guns. For the moment, there was no target. He could not have seen the source of that floating green sphere. He stood, feeling the terror that drained every soul about him, feeling it shake his brain and body. But he did not yield. Not even when the stampede burst… and he saw the source of the second bomb!

Instantly, the guns flamed in his fists! Two neat holes punched through the partly opened window of the bank; glass cascaded to the pavement. Behind it was only the emptiness of an office neatly paneled in wood. No one was in sight.

The man in white whirled toward the trash can, reached into its depths. When he straightened, a long black cape swirled from his shoulders, and low upon his brows was a broad-brimmed black hat. The black guns in his fists were ominous as death. No man who looked now could fail to recognize him.

The *Spider* raced into battle!

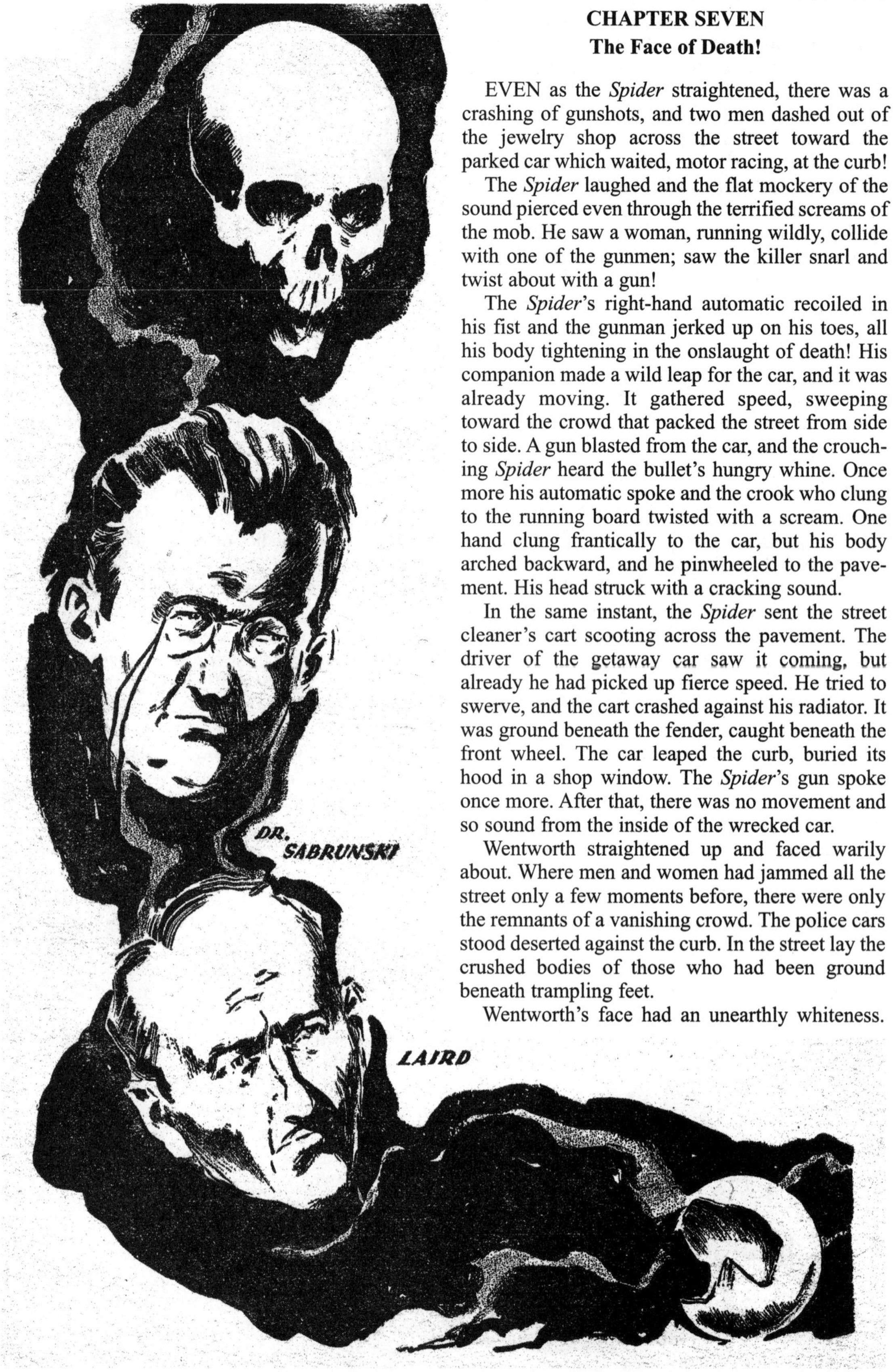

CHAPTER SEVEN
The Face of Death!

EVEN as the *Spider* straightened, there was a crashing of gunshots, and two men dashed out of the jewelry shop across the street toward the parked car which waited, motor racing, at the curb!

The *Spider* laughed and the flat mockery of the sound pierced even through the terrified screams of the mob. He saw a woman, running wildly, collide with one of the gunmen; saw the killer snarl and twist about with a gun!

The *Spider*'s right-hand automatic recoiled in his fist and the gunman jerked up on his toes, all his body tightening in the onslaught of death! His companion made a wild leap for the car, and it was already moving. It gathered speed, sweeping toward the crowd that packed the street from side to side. A gun blasted from the car, and the crouching *Spider* heard the bullet's hungry whine. Once more his automatic spoke and the crook who clung to the running board twisted with a scream. One hand clung frantically to the car, but his body arched backward, and he pinwheeled to the pavement. His head struck with a cracking sound.

In the same instant, the *Spider* sent the street cleaner's cart scooting across the pavement. The driver of the getaway car saw it coming, but already he had picked up fierce speed. He tried to swerve, and the cart crashed against his radiator. It was ground beneath the fender, caught beneath the front wheel. The car leaped the curb, buried its hood in a shop window. The *Spider*'s gun spoke once more. After that, there was no movement and so sound from the inside of the wrecked car.

Wentworth straightened up and faced warily about. Where men and women had jammed all the street only a few moments before, there were only the remnants of a vanishing crowd. The police cars stood deserted against the curb. In the street lay the crushed bodies of those who had been ground beneath trampling feet.

Wentworth's face had an unearthly whiteness.

The fists that gripped his guns were rigid as stone, and the line of his jaw was traced in white. He was riven by the fear he could not explain, that roweled him with as cruel spurs as had goaded these others into frantic flight. Only the mighty will of him who was known as the Master of Men gave him control against the wild urge to stampede with the others. That explained why he moved so slowly as he moved toward the doors of the Nation's Bank. He did not even trust himself to run, lest the terror gain control of his limbs over the domination of his mind!

A man and woman, both dead, lay upon the stone steps of the bank. The woman's face was… gone.

WENTWORTH'S eyes lifted fiercely toward the bank doors. He weighed the automatics in his fist. He plunged up the steps!

The black cape swirled out from his shoulders, and anger burned coldly in his eyes. His shoulder struck aside the swinging glass door, and he plunged into the bank!

For that first instant, just inside the portals, he stood motionless. Death was all about him. A bank guard and two civilians were sprawled upon the floor. There was no other human thing in sight; nothing that had been human. As he stood there a gun spoke!

Wentworth felt the shock of the lead in his left hand, and his right-hand gun blasted out its answer the same instant. He dived toward the cover of the marble counter from behind which the shot had come. There was a tingling numbness that ran from his left hand to his shoulder, but the arm answered the demand of his brain. It caught him as he struck on his chest, and rolled against the front of the counter.

He lay there, breathless through a long moment, waiting. He saw something that glittered toward him in a brilliant arc. And he knew the menace that promised! Munro and his devils were here. That was a gas bomb, such as would devour a man's face!

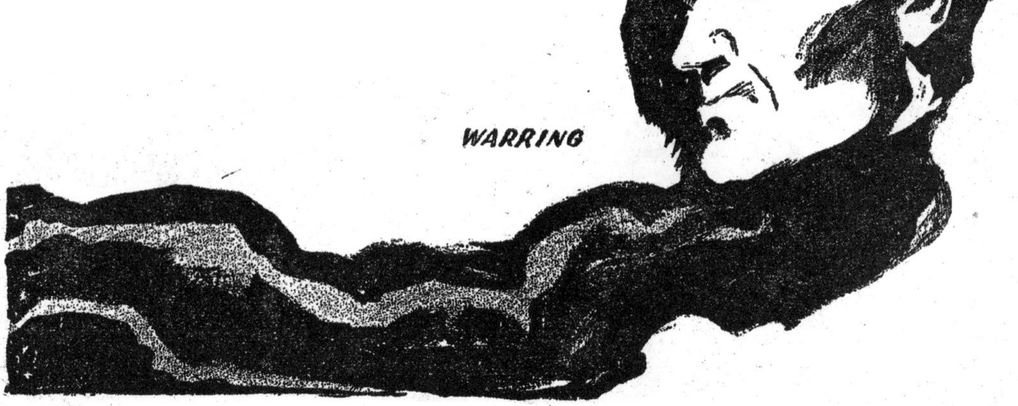

Wentworth's gun kicked in his fist and, half the length of the bank's concourse away, the glass globe met the bullet in mid-air. The green gas spread like a parachute in the air, settled in slow, coiling tentacles toward the floor. For the moment, Wentworth was safe. It would take several seconds for those tendrils to reach him. Before then, he must move. He slid like a snake toward the spot where the gas was settling.

It was the one thing that Munro would not expect, and Wentworth moved fast. It was not until now that he could glance toward his left hand; it was uninjured. By some trick of luck, Munro's bullet had only struck the gun from the *Spider*'s fist! But it had been his fully loaded automatic; only two bullets remained in the other, and there was no chance to reload as he raced to pass that slowly drifting gas before it should reach the floor!

Behind him, he heard the fragile spat of another bomb striking the floor. If he had retreated, he would have been defenseless, caught by the gas that devoured human flesh! But he was losing his race against the gas tentacles ahead! They were settling more rapidly! Wentworth got his feet beneath him, and once more plunged forward in a dive. His eyes strained upward to watch the green spirals of death. The eddy of his passage whirled them toward him, and he flung himself to his feet, sprinted!

A gun blasted again and again, hammering lead at him. He whirled and flung up his automatic. There was his enemy, crouched behind a desk. The man's revolver jumped as he pumped lead as fast as a finger could squeeze the trigger! Wentworth's mocking laughter rang out; he dropped his automatic into line.

Against the dazzle of a window, he could only make out the curved line of the head and the leveled gun; but it would be enough!

The *Spider* laughed… and squeezed off his last two shots!

Instantly, the gunfire was silenced. The hunched outline of the head was smacked down behind the desk!

"Munro!" Wentworth cried. "Munro, you're finished!"

With a shout, he bounded toward the desk. His gun was a club in his fist, and triumph was hot in his throat. With a long leap, Wentworth cleared the desk and a cry lifted in his throat. On the floor lay a helmet with a fractured vision glass; with a bullet dent upon the forehead. But of the man who had worn it, of Munro—there was no trace at all!

WENTWORTH stood, staring vacantly down at the helmet.

Through the windows of the bank, light streamed in and laid a sunny bar across the casque of steel. It was that sunlight which, for the moment, saved Wentworth's life. A shadow flickered across it, and Wentworth lunged straight forward a full ten feet! Behind him, he heard a gasped oath, heard the vicious crunch of wood yielding beneath a titan's blow.

The *Spider* whirled, and at a distance of a few yards, he was staring into the hate-maddened eyes of Munro! Munro still clutched the haft of a fire-axe which was driven deep into the desk beside which, a moment before, Wentworth had stood!

Through a long heartbeat of time, the two enemies regarded each other, Munro in the silvery wig, the formal garments of President Oldham of the Nation's Bank, shoulders arched with a power that belied the age of his makeup as he wrenched the axe free. Wentworth was upright, the cape graceful from his broad shoulders, triumph in the eager uplifting of his head. Face-to-face at last with Munro! It was a moment he had dreamed of, and he would not fail!

Wentworth's right hand whipped back, and he flung the empty gun at Munro's face! He leaped to the attack, his hands reaching out eagerly, fingers curled for a stranglehold upon the throat of this mass murderer of the innocent!

But Munro was ready for him. He made no attempt to dodge the gun, but interposed the haft of his axe. The heavy automatic glanced from the

wood, clattered futilely to the floor. Munro stood on braced legs, powerful shoulders taut as he heaved the axe high above his head with both arms. He was laughing, deep in his chest, and the happiness of this murder gleamed in his eyes. Then the axe flashed down!

Even in that desperate instant, Wentworth did not lose his head. He swayed out from under that axe like a boxer, thrust up a stiffened left arm toward the axe, as a fencer turns aside a powerful lunge.

The axe haft struck the back of his left wrist and Wentworth stiffened that arm in a frantic effort to make the axe glance aside. He might have succeeded completely, but in that crucial moment, his foot slipped. Down he went to one knee.

The haft glanced against Wentworth's skull. The blade, turned by Wentworth's swift thrust, struck flat across his shoulders and drove him to the floor. In that instant, as he fell, Wentworth reached up and set both hands upon the handle of the axe and… hung on.

The bank spun about him in a dizzy whirl, and there was a blackness inside his skull that made Munro's face appear in little flashes of green light. He dully felt the impact of Munro's kicks raining against his ribs, of fists hammering at his face. And he hung on to the axe.

Despite the murderous assault, his senses were beginning to clear, but all his muscles would not rouse to do his will. He realized that Munro's face had steadied above him, and that there was pain in his throat. Munro had given up the struggle for the axe. Munro was… strangling him!

WENTWORTH tried to drive his heavy body into action. It should be simple to break this hold, to roll Munro from his perch. But the grip of those murderous hands upon his throat swelled the agony within his skull. Munro's face floated above his own. The eyes burned down gloatingly, and the murder lust distorted even the careful disguise of old kind Oldham. The pressure of those deadly hands was increasing.

"Fool!" Munro panted. "Fool to think that you can destroy Munro! This is how I've always wanted to kill you, with my own hands! Slowly, as you deserve to die!"

Wentworth's brain seemed to take on a feverish clarity as his breath was pinched off. He had not the strength to throw off this murderer, but there still was a way… a possible way. If only, for a space of seconds, he could loosen one of these hands from his throat!

Wentworth's left hand was ground down into his side by the weight of Munro's body, but it was close to his vest pocket and that was what he wanted. If only… Ah! His fingers closed about the slim cigarette lighter that he always carried there, and somehow he wrenched it free of Munro's weight. His thumb clicked against the base, sprung it open. This was no sinister weapon, but there was a secret hidden in its base. Wentworth lifted it feebly, and set that base against the fist Munro clamped about his throat.

Then Wentworth heard Munro swear. Wentworth could not see it, but on the back of Munro's right hand, there glowed a crimson design… the seal of the *Spider*!

Munro swore, and the hand wrenched away from Wentworth's throat! It was the moment for which Wentworth had gambled. He jerked up on the axe, which lay upon his chest; and there was a cry of agony from Munro. He pitched to the floor, and Wentworth struggled to his feet. The axe seemed to weigh a ton in his hand as he attempted to raise it. But Munro, though he was bent double in pain, was scrambling away.

Wentworth tried to throw the axe, and it slipped from his hands. Munro was moving more rapidly now. He stopped and caught up a heavy satchel and darted along behind the marble counter toward the main doors! Wentworth tried to run after him, and his feet played him tricks. He stumbled and fell, caught at a desk with both hands. Munro was leaving!

Then Wentworth laughed drunkenly. He reached out with both hands and seized a telephone instrument and, as he reeled to his feet, he threw himself backward. The telephone pulled loose from its fastenings. He gripped the wires and swung the heavy handset around his head like a slingshot!

Munro reached the door, stooped for the gun that Wentworth had dropped. The wires of the phone were whistling over Wentworth's head. As Munro straightened, Wentworth let the phone fly.

The phone did not miss.

It struck Munro across the side of his skull and drove him to his knees. The gun skittered out from under his hand, the satchel dropped from his fingers. Then he pitched crashing forward on his face!

WENTWORTH felt a shout of triumph swell in his chest, but it came out weakly. He reeled away from the marble railing, started forward, still dazed. He could not take the most direct path, for the gas huddled in little green clots before him.

Wentworth was laughing, weakly, as he moved toward the door circuitously. He had won. He had downed Munro when he least expected it. If only he could reach him now before he recovered. The lighter was still in his left hand, and he laughed at it. That little thing! Munro had feared its symbolism, more than the seal itself; but he had feared, too, to have it printed upon his dead body. Now, as always, Munro wore a disguise. But the seal could never be eradicated. Fear of the *Spider* had beaten Munro in the end. It—

Wentworth came to an incredulous halt behind the teller's cages. He was staring toward where Munro had fallen. The gun lay there, and the satchel that plainly contained the loot of the bank. But of Munro, there was no trace at all!

A cry burst from Wentworth's lips. He reeled forward in a fumbling run. A trail of spattered blood drops led toward the front door!

Desperately, Wentworth snatched up his gun and drove his dragging body toward the broad portals of the bank. Munro could not escape him now! Dazed though Wentworth was, Munro must be equally injured after the savage impact of that telephone! If only he could overtake him, and—

Wentworth reeled out of the door. His cape swirled bravely behind him. His hat had been knocked off, and his hair sprawled across the high whiteness of his forehead. His eyes were fierce. He staggered to a halt on the steps, braced himself... and guns blasted at him from across the street—three different guns! Wentworth's own automatic jumped upward in his hand, ready, and then he rasped out an oath.

Munro was not in sight, but he knew the three men across the street. They were the Gotham Hounds!

Frantically, Wentworth hurled himself backward through the doors in the same instant the crash of bullets sent the glass of the panels cascading to the floor. Damn it, Munro must still be inside the bank—but no! There ran the trail of blood! Then, Munro was making good his escape while the Hounds covered his retreat by keeping the *Spider* prisoner in the bank!

Anger curled Wentworth's lips. Were the Gotham Hounds allies of Munro? He could not be sure. But Wentworth, the *Spider*, did not shoot men on suspicion! He must escape to find Munro!

Wentworth thrust himself out from the wall against which he leaned. His strength was flowing back through his limbs now, and he walked with more confidence. But, even as he neared a window, he heard the multiple shriek of sirens, saw blue-coated men spilling from squad cars to the pavement beneath the very window from which he sought to escape.

Wentworth dodged back into the obscurity of the bank's interior, and he cursed savagely. The Gotham Hounds had run the *Spider* to earth!

IT WAS only a few brief minutes later that the police charged in through the doorway. Behind them crept the three Hounds, guns in their fists.

"He's in here!" Hunter cried, in his deep booming voice. "We drove him back when he was trying to kill the president of the bank! And the place has been surrounded ever since!"

The police crept forward through the doorway, and swore as their eyes quested over the floor. Sprawled upon the white pavement were huge words.

"Beware green stuff! Poison gas!"

It was signed with the *Spider*'s seal! But of the *Spider* himself, there was no sign at all for that long first moment. Then one of the policemen spoke.

"There!" he cried. "There behind the desk!"

Bullets poured from his gun toward a hunched, becaped figure, wearing a helmet, that crouched behind a desk. There was a gun in the hand, but apparently the policeman's first bullets took effect, for he did not fire. The guns of the entire squad were spitting out their drumroll of death. A sub-machine gun added its mad chatter. They were all inside the bank, even the Hounds. Hunter held his post beside the door, but he did not notice the man dressed in white who sprawled face down where blood stained the white floor. He did not notice the man rise to his feet. The first warning he had was when the muzzle of a gun dug into his kidney!

"All right, Hunter," whispered the cold voice in his ear. "Back into this entry now! That's right! Now, stoop! You're going to carry me out of the bank and into an ambulance! Stoop, you yellow hound!"

Hunter shivered, bent his shoulders and the man in white threw his weight across them, as the gun continued to dig into Hunter's side.

"All right, Hunter," whispered the same voice. "Now, carry me to the ambulance! If you hesitate you're a dead man!"

A voice that sounded hoarsely like his own called out for an ambulance. The police opened a way for him, and Hunter scrambled into the ambulance with his burden. The ambulance got underway.

It was several hours before the protesting Hounds accompanied Kirkpatrick back to headquarters.

"Damn it," Hunter was insisting. "What could I do, with a gun in my back? As soon as we got inside the ambulance, he knocked me out. After that, I don't know what happened. And I don't know who it was! It might have been Munro, or it might have been the *Spider*! But I'm almost sure it was the *Spider*."

Kirkpatrick said grimly, "We'll take your statement down, Hunter."

Laird's voice was cold, "What I want to know is this: where has Wentworth been all this time?"

Kirkpatrick thrust open the door of his office, and a curse rasped from his lips. He strode across the threshold and then slowly, very slowly, he smiled.

"Apparently," he said, and nodded toward the man who slept, sprawled across Kirkpatrick's desk.

"Apparently, Wentworth has been catching a bit of rest in my private office!"

HE CROSSED softly to where Wentworth's head rested on folded arms and, carefully, touched a finger to the throat pulse. He nodded slowly. Wentworth was really very sound asleep. He shook Wentworth's shoulder.

"When did you get here?" he snapped. "Come on! Talk up! When did you get here?"

Wentworth's head snapped up and he started sharply to his feet. He shook off Kirkpatrick's hand irritably.

"That's a hell of a way to wake a man up," he said. "You keep lousy office hours. Kirk. I've been waiting for hours to surrender."

"Hours?" Kirkpatrick asked dryly.

Wentworth nodded sharply. "Exactly. I see it's dusk now, and it was broad daylight when I came here. Ask Warring, he saw me enter!"

Warring's smile was mocking, and he delayed speech while all eyes centered on his face. He nodded finally. "Quite so," he said, "and I did better than that. I took a picture of him going into the building, and there's a clock in the background. I think it may be accepted as evidence."

Kirkpatrick nodded gravely. "I'm taking no more chances with you, Dick," he said curtly. "You're going into a cell right now. I'll question you later about your escape from that patrol wagon."

Wentworth smiled and shrugged. "It won't help you, Kirk," he said. "If you question the officer who was inside with me, he'll tell you that he knocked me cold just when the crash occurred. He'll know more about it than I do!"

Kirkpatrick nodded, took his seat behind the desk. Wentworth studied his face impassively. The lines about the mouth were drawn and deep, and sitting wearily, Kirkpatrick dragged a knuckle across his pointed mustache. Wentworth knew his friend was deeply worried. His gesture as he indicated chairs for the three Hounds was infinitely tired. But Wentworth had no chance to hear what was said, or to learn the reason for the three men being brought to headquarters. Two police officers came and, with drawn guns, escorted him to a cell. The clanging of the door was sullen and heavy, and Wentworth dropped to the cot bed. He would be able to force arraignment and release on bail the next day. He thought that Munro would remain idle for this night at least. He had suffered a serious defeat, despite the early success of his plans. He had been forced to abandon the loot—important as evidence. Tomorrow, then. Wentworth forced rest upon his mind, blanking out the horror of the day's battling.

IN HIS office, Kirkpatrick rested his elbows on the desk, knotted his long fingers together as he bent his regard on the three men. Laird, as usual, was sitting bolt upright, while Warring lounged with a camera slung across his chest. Hunter, his head bandaged, had his knees crossed jauntily, his chin lifted in his perpetual challenge.

"This evidence concerning Wentworth," said Kirkpatrick slowly, "does not change your verdict, gentlemen?"

Laird shook his head crisply. "We can identify the *Spider*," he said, "if you will exhibit him to us in the same garments, under conditions similar to those at the theatre. We all had a good look at him then, and we have trained memories. Warring had pictures, also, but he was unfortunately knocked out and robbed of his camera."

"My favorite one, too," Warring sighed.

Kirkpatrick nodded crisply. "Very well," he said. "I will act upon your evidence. There is the possibility that the *Spider* is such a… gentleman as yourselves, but he is known to masquerade in the underworld, also." Kirkpatrick flipped a cam in the annunciator on his desk. "Sergeant Reams, request Captain Fillarty to assign me six of his best men; those who have the widest knowledge of underworld characters. I want them at once."

When the six men filed into his office, Kirkpatrick rose and faced them, outlined the prospects of identifying the *Spider*.

"Here is what I want," he ended crisply. "The *Spider* is known to appear periodically in the underworld in the guise of a crook. He would be a man well known to other criminals, under the masquerade, of course. He would be a man who made his appearance in New York usually at the time of some such series of crimes as confronts us now. His reputation is that he always works alone, and must pull some good jobs because he never lacks for money. He may, or may not, have a reputation as a skillful safe cracker. Can you name any crook who fits into that pattern?"

The six detectives looked at each other, concentrated frowningly on the picture. A few names were offered hesitantly. Bosco Smutts, a con man who was supposed to travel a lot; Flash Davis, who was suspected of staging bank robberies over a wide range of territory.

It was the big grizzled detective with a birth mark on his right cheek who snapped his fingers in sudden discovery.

"By the lord Harry, Commissioner," he said. "I've got the man who fits the bill all the way down to safe cracking, and the time of his appearance. Those other guys, I can't time them with your big crime waves, but this mug I can. He never seems to run out of money. I don't think he's smart enough to be the *Spider*. Otherwise, he fits all right."

Kirkpatrick nodded. "All right, Grogan. Who is he?"

Grogan hesitated, nodded. "Well he fits, all right. You may not know him. It's a half-blind peterman named Blinky McQuade!"

The door of Kirkpatrick's office was suddenly batted open, and Captain Fillarty of the detective bureau bounded into the room.

"Commissioner!" he rasped. "That damned Munro has struck again! He took a savings bank up town that has night banking hours. Had four guys with him! They threw those damned gas bombs, cleaned up about fifteen thousand bucks... and they killed eight people!"

Kirkpatrick rasped out a harsh oath.

"We'll get up there right away!" He swung toward the six detectives. "You understand your orders! Get those three men, and any others that fit into the pattern. And above all, get McQuade!"

CHAPTER EIGHT
The Trap for Blinky

COMMISSIONER Kirkpatrick's orders to the detectives were deliberately secret, so there was no possible way that Wentworth could have known about the search for Blinky McQuade, suspected of being the *Spider*.

That was one reason why Wentworth, as soon as he could arrange for release on bail, proceeded to disguise himself as Blinky McQuade!

It is doubtful that, even had Wentworth known of the dragnet search for Blinky, he would have chosen any other method. Through the masquerade as Blinky, he could gain entrance and hearing in the Underworld, where he had taken care to be well known. And he needed information fast!

So Wentworth raced to a certain private garage as soon as he could make sure he was not being followed. Over a secret cache beneath the floor, he knelt and undertook the rapid makeup of Blinky McQuade. He was even more careful than usual, because the man he must approach was a clever crook and, Wentworth suspected, a stool pigeon. There must never be any suspicion on the part of the police that Blinky McQuade was not just what he seemed!

Presently, Wentworth backed the battered old coupé with the secretly powerful motor beneath the hood out of the garage. It was not possible to recognize the dapper clubman in this grizzled oldster with the iron-gray hair, the sloppy, poorly cut clothing, whose eyes seemed weak behind thick, hooded spectacles. He drove rapidly northward through the city, only stopping once. He hobbled into a corner drugstore and put in a call for Nita's home.

Her voice came anxiously over the phone. "Oh, Dick!" she cried, "I hated not being there this morning when you were arraigned, but you seemed to want me to pretend a quarrel—"

"You did just right, dear," Wentworth assured her. "Those Gotham Hounds, as they call themselves, have some plan of campaign against me that I want to learn!"

Nita's laughter came to him trillingly over the phone and the taut lines of Wentworth's face relaxed. He felt the soothing release that Nita could always bring about.

"That Ralph Warring," Nita said, "fancies he has made a conquest. He's most anxious to impress me, and we're having tea this afternoon. He hinted at some special knowledge of the *Spider*! I know they're up to something!"

"Don't endanger yourself," Wentworth said quietly. "Dear, if you haven't heard from me by evening, I want you to go to Kirkpatrick with some information!"

"You're going into danger, Dick!" Nita interrupted.

Wentworth laughed softly. "Is that something new, Nita? No—don't interrupt. Listen. I'm convinced that Munro kidnapped the actor Maurice because he had need of more makeup skill than he himself possesses, or because he needed to train some additional men in such impersonations as he himself achieves. I think the latter. For this work, he would need to use crooks, and I'm sure the type he would use would be drawn from the more intelligent criminals, say confidence men, and he would necessarily choose the fancy dressers, since such men exhibit a certain dramatic art even in choosing clothing. These fancy-dressing con men would probably be absent from the city just now, and would have disappeared either just before, or just after, Maurice himself. I think Kirk would do well to check up on that theory. But hold it up until, say, six o'clock."

"I understand, Dick," Nita said quietly, "and it seems a sound deduction, but—oh, Dick, be careful!"

Wentworth's lips softened in a smile. "I'm always careful, dear!" he said. "I remember that you are waiting! Goodbye!"

Back in his car, Wentworth steered westward toward the apartment of Gabby Weissman. He was almost certain to find the small-time crook at home. He hoped that he would be alone.

WENTWORTH'S triumph over Munro the day before had given way today to despondency, since he had heard of Munro's raid on the small suburban bank. Yet, there was some consolation in the crime. It proved that Munro was desperate for money, since the fifteen thousand he had seized would ordinarily be unimportant to Munro. And since he had taken allies, he had left himself open to the methods that Wentworth would use to trace him! Very little happened in the Underworld that the grapevine did not soon carry—and Gabby was an excellent listener!

Wentworth was fortunate, for Gabby was alone when he rang at the crook's door. Gabby Weissman immediately held out a grubby hand.

"Well, well, well!" he caroled. "Where you been keeping youreslf, Blinky? Gee, I ain't heard of you in ages! What do you know?"

Blinky McQuade grunted sourly, and stumped across the threshold, picked out the softest chair and eased himself into it, with his stiff leg thrust out before him.

"What you asking for?" Wentworth asked in Blinky's harsh voice. "So you can tell the cops?"

Gabby drew himself up stiffly in the purple silk dressing robe he wore. He prepared to be angry, and then he saw by the sour smile on Blinky's face that this was supposed to be a joke. Gabby laughed, and slapped his thin leg.

"By God, Blinky," he gasped, "you had me fooled!"

Wentworth let the sour smile stay on Blinky McQuade's loose lips, but he seemed in no hurry to talk. In fact, there was some embarrassment in the way he fumbled his hands between his knees. Gabby Weissman watched him with bright, small eyes.

"What's up, Blinky?" he asked. "You ain't used to paying social calls on me."

McQuade snarled, "Any law against it? Now wait… wait a minute, Gabby. I got a favor to ask of you, only I'm paying for it, see?"

Gabby guffawed. "You paying for something, Blinky!"

McQuade hobbled to his feet. "Okay, okay, Gabby!"

But the small man was immediately placating. Gabby patted his hands against Wentworth's chest. "Now, just take it easy, Blinky," he said. "I didn't mean nothing by it, honest!"

"Saying I ain't got money!" Wentworth's tone sounded savage. "I got plenty!" He hauled out a packet of bills and waved it under Gabby's nose. "I got plenty, I have! Think I'm a punk?"

Gahby's eyes strained wide at sight of the thick roll. He licked his thin lips. "Geez, there must be ten grand in that roll!" he said. "What'd you do, Blinky? Knock over a bank?"

Wentworth let himself appear pacified. "That's my business," he said shortly. "Look here, Gabby. Here's the lay. Crowd I'm traveling with now is all nifty dressers, see. Now, you know I ain't never been much for duds."

Gabby giggled, thought better of it and drew a long face when Wentworth scowled at him suspiciously.

"But a slick lad like you, now," Wentworth went on stubbornly. "You know where I can get some flashy clothes without paying too much for them. And I'll make it worth your while. You can always use a new suit, can't you, Gabby?"

GABBY'S small dark eyes were snapping with curiosity. "Sure," he said. "Sure, I can always use another suit. Look, Blinky, who's this flashy crowd you're playing around with now, huh? They must be big time."

Wentworth let his lips grin sourly. "Well, they ain't small time," he admitted modestly. "Who you think?"

Gabby fairly danced with curiosity. "Well, ain't no jobs been pulled here would get you ten grand for your share. Some guy bungled the Nation's Bank here. Must of been out-of-town. Sure. Now, who's the flashy dressers ain't been around lately? Hummm. Now, there's Fancy Wade. There's Handsome Kelly. They're heist men."

Wentworth shook his head; behind his glasses, his eyes were keen. This was information he wanted. "Not heist men," he said. "Slicker lads than bank boosters."

"Got you!" Gabby snapped. "Slick Marshall was one of them! He's in the money, and he just got back in town. Put himself up at the Gotham Arms!"

Wentworth snarled, "That's enough funny business now! I ain't talking. Now listen, I'll be back by here in a couple of hours, and you be ready to help me pick some fancy duds, get me, Gabby? And if anything leaks, I'm going to pull you out from between your ears!"

Gabby grinned, winked wisely. "Hell, Blinky, you don't need to worry about me."

Wentworth stopped within a yard of Gabby Weissman, and looked at him very directly through the thick glasses of Blinky McQuade.

"I'm not worrying about you, Gabby," he said softly. "I'm not worrying about you at all!"

Gabby Weissman smiled weakly. He licked his thin lips, and didn't speak while Wentworth limped to the door, and closed it softly behind him. He darted across the room toward the telephone, and caught it up. He hesitated a moment, and there was a greenish cast to his face. But he finally dialed a number.

"Hello, Grogan," he said hoarsely. "This is… you know. I got a hot tip for you. Yeah. Blinky McQuade is back in town and he's flashing about ten grand around! Slick Marshall was in on the deal, and they're at the Gotham Arms… Yeah… yeah, I know Blinky usually works alone, but this time he teamed up, I'm telling you! That's worth fifty bucks, ain't it?"

WENTWORTH drove to the Gotham Arms by a roundabout route, and kept a keen eye on his back-trail. He didn't trust Gabby Weissman, but he didn't give the rat credit for much sense, either. Gabby might take it into his head to follow him.

The Gotham Arms was a flashy hotel, to which just such a confidence man as Slick Marshall would go when he was in the money. But no one would look askance at Blinky McQuade entering there either. The house dick would know him, of course.

Wentworth parked the coupé a half block away from the Gotham Arms, and there was a frown of concentration between his eyes. He had to work fast, for if Marshall really was tied up with Munro, it wasn't likely that Marshall would stay very long at the hotel. As he read Munro's plan, some big coup was underway which needed financing; the bank robberies which had cost a score of lives were mere preparation! Wentworth's lips twisted at the thought. Yes, the *Spider* had need to work fast, lest greater horror be loosed upon the people he loved!

Wentworth limped into the side entrance of the Gotham Arms and let his eyes slant over the lobby. He didn't see anyone who looked dangerous to him, and he slid into a booth and used a house phone.

"What number, Jack Marshall?" he asked hoarsely.

The operator gave it to him, and Wentworth clacked up the receiver and angled toward the elevator doors. He wasn't carrying a gun. He never did, as Blinky McQuade, unless there were real danger in the immediate future. It wasn't safe for a known crook to pack a gun, lest he be picked up by the police and sent up for a long term under the Sullivan Law. But he didn't think he would need a gun to take care of Marshall. The con man wasn't a gun carrier, either.

Wentworth was within a yard of the elevator when he saw a broad-shouldered figure moving toward him, and glanced around quickly to see a big man with a birth mark on his face stepping up behind him.

"Hello, Blinky," the man said easily. "It's been a long time since you paid us a visit!"

Sharp apprehension stabbed Wentworth. He knew Detective Grogan well enough, and his appearance here at this time was a little too fortuitous to be coincidence. But Blinky McQuade had committed no crimes.

"Shove off, Grogan," Wentworth snarled in Blinky's cantankerous way. "I don't like the smell of cops!"

Grogan's smile was easy on his mouth, though his eyes had a hard and wary light. "Now, that's no way to talk to a friend, Blinky," he said. "I can't understand the commissioner's choice of talking mates, but he said he'd like a little chat with you!"

Wentworth swore harshly and with feeling. "Listen, Grogan, you got nothing on me! Just because I did time once—"

Grogan stepped close, and abruptly pulled Wentworth's body hard against his for a rapid search. Wentworth's muscles jerked taut. It would have been easy to knock out Grogan then, and take to his heels, but it was damnably important now that there should be no general alarm out for him as Blinky. Also, he couldn't afford to spend the time to be taken to headquarters. There was no telling what Kirkpatrick wanted. He might even suspect that Blinky McQuade was the *Spider*! But there was no proof. He had committed no crime.

"Look, Grogan," he whispered hoarsely. "I'll go along all right, but —"

"I'll say you will!" Grogan growled.

"Look," Wentworth put a whine in his voice. "Look, I got a cache in the room upstairs, and I ain't trusting nobody in this dump. You know how it is."

"A cache, huh?" Grogan's eyes were sharp and interested.

Wentworth nodded his head rapidly. He said, bitterly, "I don't trust the cops at headquarters no more than I do the punks here, but look... there's ten grand in this roll I got cached. I don't care if you take care of it, you should peel off a grand. That's fair, ain't it? Only, I don't dare leave it in this dump, see?"

Grogan shot a glance around. "Ten grand, huh?"

Wentworth nodded. "That's right. Look, you don't need to be afraid I'll skip. There ain't nothing but empty space under the window, and it's on the twenty-second floor!"

Grogan knotted a fist into his collar, shoved him into the elevator. "Okay, punk," he said. "Twenty-second floor!"

THE operator threw the lever, turned around once to look without particular interest at Wentworth and Grogan, and after that kept his eyes on the wall sliding down past the cage door. Wentworth was thinking swiftly. He had to keep Grogan out of Marshall's room, while he made sure Marshall would wait until Blinky McQuade was released. Wentworth didn't think it would be hard for him to persuade Marshall!

He twisted against the grip on his collar. "Look, Grogan," he whispered. "You don't have to go in, do you? Look, I use this room a lot, and I got this cache—"

Grogan shook him into silence until they were on the twenty-second floor, then he let him go and Wentworth slid a hand inside his vest to the lock-pick in a vertical pocket there. He held the slim hook of surgical steel palmed in his hand.

"Look, Grogan," he said hoarsely. "I can't get away, see? Why not give me a break? Look, you can peel off a grand and a half!"

Grogan grunted, "Listen, Blinky, do I look like I ain't growed up yet?"

Blinky checked before the door, and his voice was still a whisper. Looking back at Grogan over his shoulder, he manipulated the lock pick without a sound.

"Be a sport, Grogan," he whispered. "Hell, I can't get away, can I? On the twenty-second floor?"

There was doubt in Grogan's face, but he was a full yard behind Wentworth, and the latter now felt the lock yield under the pick. Without waiting for more, he pushed open the door, jumped inside and in a lightning-like movement, slammed and bolted the door! On the bed, a man reared up. His hand snaked under the pillow, but Wentworth wheeled toward him, motioned silence.

"Look, it's worth a grand to me," he whispered, and snaked out his roll of bills, "to have you phone my mouthpiece, Marshall!"

Marshall swore softly, "What the hell, Blinky?" he demanded.

"Cop outside there!" Wentworth whispered.

Grogan was knocking on the door persistently, but he wasn't making much noise about it. Wentworth was within a yard of the bed now.

"Cop picked me up in the lobby," he said rapidly, "and I told him this was my room. Knew you were here, and—"

"You had a nerve, you lousy rat!" Marshall snarled, but his hand came out from under the pillow.

Wentworth leaped, and his fist crashed savagely against Marshall's jaw. The man's legs kicked, and he flopped backward on the bed, cold. In a single swift heave, Wentworth had Marshall off the bed and was dragging him toward the closet.

"Just a minute, Grogan!" he called over his shoulder, placatingly.

In the closet, he rapidly bound Marshall's hands and feet, wedged a gag between his teeth. He crouched and made a rapid search of the man's clothing. There was nothing betraying in the clothes, except for nearly a thousand dollars in bills. From the breast pocket of the man's coat, Wentworth fingered out a long strip of paper. He frowned down at a railroad ticket of the type handed out by the conductor when a cash fare is paid on the train. It was punched for Ozone Springs station, and the date was for the day before.

WENTWORTH frowned over it, but there was no time to delay. He thrust the ticket back into Marshall's pocket, tossed his gun into the closet beside him, and sprang toward the dresser, shoved it askew from the wall, then raced to the door. He unbolted it, and the drive of Grogan's shoulder sent him reeling against the bed. Deliberately, Wentworth loosened his grip on the money, and the bills fluttered to the floor.

Grogan's questioning gaze fastened on the money greedily, and Wentworth began to talk rapidly, wheedlingly. "See, I didn't try to run out on you, Grogan. I just didn't want to give away my cache."

Grogan glanced at the dresser, grinned slyly with his fat lips. "Okay, punk. Get your money, and come on," he ordered. "But that little trick is going to cost you two grand, instead of one."

Wentworth whined out a curse, but he didn't protest. And he submitted to the handcuffs Grogan held out. This was a bad break, but thanks to Grogan's cupidity, it need not be disastrous. Marshall would stay put until Wentworth came for him. It had never occurred to Grogan to suspect a timorous, cantankerous crook like Blinky McQuade would be committing assault behind that locked door!

At police headquarters, Grogan found that Kirkpatrick was busy and wouldn't see Blinky McQuade until the other suspects had been picked up, so Wentworth was thrust into a cell to wait. The hours dragged past; no word came to him, nor was there any hint of the purpose for which he had been taken. It took the full exertion of his mighty will to force himself to remain carelessly inactive in the cell. No man save Wentworth could, under these circumstances, have forced himself to relax in sleep!

It was the middle of the night when finally the police came to the cell where Wentworth, his sleeping long finished, lay waiting upon his cot. Grogan was out of sorts, snarling, and he thrust Wentworth roughly before him along the cell-lined alley.

Other detectives were hazing along men Wentworth knew, and his bewilderment deepened. Con men, racketeers, a yegg who worked usually out of Chicago, were being thrust along the corridors with a half dozen others whom Wentworth did not recognize. But in a few minutes, Wentworth knew where they were heading—it was toward the lineup room!

The brightly lighted stage, the dim blur of faces beyond the bright lights that focused there, were all familiar to Wentworth. It was Kirkpatrick's voice that called from the darkness.

"We'll take Blinky McQuade first!"

Grogan grunted with satisfaction, and thrust Wentworth forward. He reached to a chair set beside the stage, picked up a dark bundle.

"Here," he ordered roughtly. "Put these on, and then get up on the stage."

Wentworth took the bundle, and the clothing

drooped from his hands. He stared at it, and felt coldness race along his spine. They had given him… the cape and black hat of the *Spider*!

CHAPTER NINE
McQuade—For Murder!

IN A SINGLE instant, the background of the entire affair flashed before Wentworth's keen brain. The Gotham Hounds were out there before the light, waiting to identify the *Spider.* For what reason he and the others had been chosen as suspects, Wentworth did not know. But the comparison would be deadly to himself!

His disguise as Blinky McQuade was sound, but the personality had been deliberately designed so that, with the least possible change, he would become the *Spider*. Blinky McQuade walked with a limp, with hunched shoulders, even as the *Spider* did. If he altered his walk, the detectives would know it. If he failed to, he would be identified!

Wentworth whipped the garments high into the air and whirled toward the other men in the line. "You see it, don't you?" he howled. "They're going to frame one of us as the *Spider*. He's one of their pals, and they got to clear him, so we take the rap! You won't frame me, damn you! You won't frame me for the *Spider*!"

He flung the cloak and hat of the *Spider* out into the darkness, made a wild break. He wasn't actually trying to escape. That would be too suspicious, but if he could stir the others to revolt—

The shouts that broke out from the file of men behind him was all that he could have hoped for. In a space of seconds, the entire line of captives was rioting.

"You ain't going to frame us into the *Spider*'s rap!" they cried.

Grogan was after Wentworth in the darkness. A blackjack swung from his wrist, and his face was hot and angry. Wentworth whirled to confront him, dove in under the blackjack and set his arms about Grogan's body, ground his head under the man's chin.

"You slug me, Grogan," he whispered, "and so help me God, I'll swear you took a bribe. You still got my two grand on you."

Grogan swore angrily, but he stopped trying to use the blackjack. "You can't get away with this, Blinky!" he gasped. "Starting a riot!"

Wentworth broke away from him and sprang up on the stage in the spotlight. He shook his fists at the darkness.

"You're out there, Kirkpatrick!" he howled hoarsely. "I heard you! You ain't going to frame us for no *Spider* rap! You want to see the *Spider*, you get your pal Wentworth up here on the stage."

Kirkpatrick's voice came crisply out of the darkness. "That will do, McQuade! You men, cut the fighting, or I'll send you up for a year! Understand? There won't be any parade. There doesn't need to be. We've got the man we want! Grogan, bring McQuade to my office! The rest can be released!"

On the stage, Wentworth's manner changed abruptly. He was no longer belligerent and challenging. His shoulders cringed, and his voice became a whine. "Hell, now, Commissioner," he said, "you ain't going to frame me for no rap like that! Look, I ain't done nothing, have I, except stand up for my rights? You ain't got no—"

Grogan came striding out onto the stage. "Shut up, Blinky!" he snarled. "And come along!"

Wentworth winced at the big detective's approach, shivering. His mind combed frantically over what he had done, over the things he had said. There was nothing in any of it to give him away. Blinky had been built up as a pretty smart crook; smart enough to scent a frame-up in an attempt to make him parade in the *Spider*'s clothing. But if he were wrong, he would have to make a break for it. He had wanted desperately to preserve the identity of Blinky McQuade. It was essential to him in his present course of action against Munro. And if Blinky McQuade became identified as the *Spider*—

His cringing accomplished its purpose. Grogan made no attempt to handcuff him, but knotted his fist into Wentworth's collar and shoved him along toward Kirkpatrick's office. He was belligerent, and took every chance to grind his knuckles into Wentworth's neck, to kick his ankles and administer other petty penalties.

"Threaten me, will you!" he growled. "You low-down rat!"

HE FAIRLY hurled Wentworth into Kirkpatrick's office, where the commissioner sat behind his desk; where Laird and Warring and Hunter sat in characteristic poses against the wall. All their eyes centered on him, but Wentworth felt reasonably secure in his disguise.

"Take off those glasses!" Kirkpatrick ordered.

Wentworth fumbled them off slowly, and managed to poke his finger into his eyes when he did it. Kirkpatrick was shrewd. He knew that the eyes were hardest of all to disguise; that such glasses as he wore would mask them completely. Uncovered, thanks to the minor injury he inflicted, Wentworth's eyes were watery and red. He blinked, squinting against the light, cringing.

"I ain't the *Spider*, Commissioner," he whined. "Gees, he's a flashy guy. You ain't thinking—"

"Shut up," Kirkpatrick said grimly. "Walk over to the right and back again."

Warring drawled from where he rested on his spine

in an arm chair, "His eyes are watering because he stuck his finger in them, taking off his glasses. I've got a pretty good ear, and I'd say his voice tones were pretty close to those of the *Spider*, especially when he's shouting. It's hard to alter tones in a shout."

Wentworth made no answer, but grimly he chalked up a mark for Warring. The man was smarter than he had credited. He would have to be clever indeed to escape without identification.

"Say, mister," he whined at Warring. "What are you picking on me for? I ain't never done anything to you, have I? I'm an ex-con, sure, but that ain't no reason to push me around. I want my mouthpiece!"

He was over near the printer machines which brought to Kirkpatrick news of all the precincts. On all of them simultaneously, a bell began to ring. Kirkpartick jerked to his feet.

"Munro again!" he rasped, and strode past Wentworth toward the machine.

"Maybe not," Laird said crisply. "It's more likely they've found something in this roundup that Wentworth's friend, Miss van Sloan, recommended. It sounded very shrewd to me."

Wentworth was peering furtively toward the machine. "What's it say?" he whined. "Me cheaters… look, can I put my glasses on?"

No one heeded him, but Grogan's eyes-were focused on him watchfully. Wentworth could read the message easily. It started:

"HOMICIDE…"

A sudden premonition raced through him. Nita had followed his orders and had reported his deductions concerning Munro's next move; they would be searching for flashy dressers, for smooth confidence men like Slick Marshall! But he had not killed Marshall, of course. He was probably all wrong.

The bell was still clanging, while the flying keys punched out the message in deliberate rhythm. The words came out slowly, with a maddening patience.

"Man, bound and gagged, murdered in Gotham Arms."

Wentworth smothered an oath. There was no longer any doubt that it was Marshall who had been murdered; and another doubt was resolved. If Marshall had been killed, it was because he was an assistant to Munro! Nothing else made any sense. Munro had come for Marshall, found him bound and gagged. That meant, of course, that Marshall had been suspected, and Munro kept himself safe by never taking chances on a thing like that.

Munro, and no one else, had killed Marshall!

Wentworth thought swiftly. His eyes searched the room under his false brows. Kirkpatrick exclaimed something about the Gotham Arms, and Grogan moved closer to the machines. His eyes were bright and hard on Wentworth, but Wentworth scarcely heeded him. This murder meant more than that. Marshall would have told Munro who had bound him up—and henceforth Munro would know that Blinky McQuade was not what he seemed; might even come to suspect that he was the *Spider*!

THAT would have to wait. There was a more immediate danger. Within a matter of moments, the room number would come over the wire, and when it was stated, Grogan would know past any doubt that Wentworth had tricked him; he would be in a position to accuse Wentworth of murder! Either way, the value of the Blinky McQuade masquerade was finished for all time!

With that thought, Wentworth was in action!

A lithe spring put Kirkpatrick between himself and Grogan, and his hands clamped solidly on Kirkpatrick's neck. As he whipped the commissioner across the room, he snaked out the long-barreled thirty-eight that Kirkpatrick carried in a shoulder holster, and leaped for the door!

So swift had his attack been that Kirkpatrick was still reeling across the room when Wentworth reached the door and pivoted with the long-barreled revolver swaying like a snake's head in his fist.

"Everybody stand just like that," he ordered, with cold venom, "or I'll burn holes through your guts! Grogan, I'd like a chance to drop you! Don't tempt me!"

The three Hounds were grouped against the machines, and Kirkpatrick was against the outer wall of the building. Grogan was nearest to Wentworth, his face drained of color. Menace was cold in Wentworth's voice.

"Grogan will tell you," Wentworth said, "that he arrested me coming out of the room where Slick Marshall was found murdered. That's true, but I didn't bump off Marshall. Only, it ain't convenient I should stick around just now! And I ain't being framed for no *Spider* rap, either. Get me? *Kirkpatrick, I warned you not to move!"*

Kirkpatrick had pulled his shoulders loose from the wall. There was a cold fire in his blue eyes, and his mouth corners were pulled down.

"You won't shoot, Blinky," Kirkpatrick said calmly, and took a step forward. "I know you now. You're the *Spider*, and the *Spider* doesn't shoot the police! You don't stand a chance, Blinky! Give yourself up! If you shoot, the whole force will be on your neck!"

Wentworth's gun was centered on Kirkpatrick and a smile tugged at his mouth corners. In that moment, he loved Kirkpatrick more than ever before. The man had the indomitable courage of a veteran soldier.

Deliberately, he squeezed the trigger of the long-barreled revolver, and Kirkpatrick's coat jerked under his left arm. Grogan started forward, and the barrel of the gun swung toward him. He checked.

"You see, Commissioner," Wentworth whispered, still in Blinky's harsh voice. "I mean business! I'll tell you one thing, and then I'm going out of here, and nobody follows... or he dies! Marshall was mixed up in that bank knockover downtown today. Better check up on where he's been spending his time the last few days."

Alarm bells were jangling in the corridors. Wentworth could hear the shouts of running men. Kirkpatrick was smiling grimly, and he took another slow step forward.

"You've just confirmed my guess, *Spider,*" he said. "Grogan, take him!"

At same instant he spoke, Kirkpatrick hurled himself forward. The habit of years of obedience made Grogan start forward to the attack at the same moment. Wentworth saw Laird snake a hand to an armpit gun.

Wentworth seemed to move almost lazily. The long-barreled gun sailed through the air from his right to his left hand. His right hand flicked out at the same moment and caught the wrist of Grogan as he reached out to hit. The next instant, thrown across Wentworth's out-thrust hip, Grogan sailed through the air and collided with Kirkpatrick as he lunged across the room! They went down together and the door clapped shut behind the *Spider* as Laird's gun crashed out.

The frosted glass panel of the door shivered into fragments and Laird's dipped, cold voice rang out. "I'll take him!" he shouted.

He reached the door, thrust his gun hand through the opening—and the next instant, was yanked bodily into the outer office.

IT was split-seconds later that the outer floor of the office opened and a wedge of bluecoats poured through. Laird stood rigidly beside the door, his hand pointing toward Kirkpatrick's shattered door.

"In there!" a voice rasped. "They're fighting!"

The police charged across the room, and Wentworth, who had been holding Laird erect from behind, lowered him gently to the floor. Then Blinky McQuade faded out through the door as the charging police collided with the rush of men headed by Kirkpatrick, trying to get out of the inner office. When that mess had straightened out, Wentworth was already in the street, fading into the darkness!

Wentworth climbed into a taxi and ordered the driver to head north. The man twisted in his seat.

"Let's see the oughday?" he demanded. Wentworth realized with a shock that he was without any money at all. They had taken it from him at police headquarters! But he had to get away, and fast.

He said, "Certainly!" He reached beneath his coat and presented the long-barreled revolver. "Is that adequate?" he asked softly.

The driver whipped to his wheel. "Excuse me, boss!" he gasped, and the cab surged forward.

"As a matter of fact," Wentworth said softly. "I don't have any money. But I will take your name and number from your card and send it to you presently. You may depend on that."

The driver said, frantically, "Hell, skip it!"

The cab bored northward and Wentworth flicked on the radio while his brain ranged ahead. Marshall's murder proved conclusively that he was allied with Munro, and that made the railway ticket he had carried of paramount importance. Ozone Springs was a small suburban center in Westchester, and not a place to which a man of Slick Marshall's stamp would go by choice. Therefore, it must be on business connected with Munro. And—

Wentworth chuckled softly. He had just remembered that there was a sanitorium near Ozone Springs, run by a Dr. Sabrunski, who specialized in building up overworked businessmen. More an athletic camp than a real sanitorium... and perfect as a hideout for Munro! But there would be more to it than a mere hideout. It could provide the headquarters where Munro could work the plan for which he had kidnapped Maurice; for which he had enlisted the services of men like Marshall!

Now the radio whined a police call and Wentworth recognized Kirkpatrick's own voice!

"All cars, attention!" he said crisply. "This order will take precedence over all others! Pick up Blinky McQuade for murder! McQuade has been identified as a disguise of the *Spider*, so use maximum precautions in taking him. Also, pick up Richard Wentworth. His bail has been cancelled. All cab drivers are warned to be on the lookout for him. He is armed, without funds, and in desperate haste—"

Wentworth saw the cab driver start to turn his head, then face front rigidly. The back of his neck showed taut cords, but he spoke over his shoulder.

"You don't need to get tough with me, if you're the *Spider*," he said. "I like the way that guy works! Saved my bacon once. My kids, that is, that was caught in a fire!"

A slow smile twisted Wentworth's lips. His heart warmed to the man's words, but Kirkpatrick's voice was still describing Blinky McQuade. Munro would know now that Blinky McQuade and the *Spider* were one. Yes, this masquerade was finished... and his work of catching Munro was made a dozen times more difficult. If only the police could work with him! But there were few people who thought of the *Spider* as other than a clever crook; a few like this taxi driver who had been helped personally.

He spoke softly, "Yes, I am the *Spider*," he said. "And you won't lose by helping me. Straight north, and then west to Central Park West. I have a car parked up there."

No question as to what he must do now. He must visit Dr. Sabrunski's sanitorium at Ozone Springe, and somehow fathom the next plan of Munro and, in the meantime, dodge eighteen thousand police!

THE mid-morning sun was burning down hotly on the scattered white cottages of the Oak Crest sanitorium when Wentworth tooled the old and battered coupé over the last hilltop and could look down on the fenced grounds of the place. New York City had been alive with police, and it had been only after a series of narrow escapes that he had succeeded in getting out into the country. The lack of money had not simplified matters. A small loan from the friendly cabby enabled him to purchase a used suit, get hold of fresh cartridges for Kirkpatrick's gun, and assume an inconspicuous disguise.

Tennis courts were busy behind the main building; a swimming pool had its quota of pot-bellied bathers and, on the green lawn, a troup of men tossed a medicine ball disinterestedly. Wentworth nodded with a frown. Nothing there to contradict his suspicions. Munro would make sure that the externals were natural. An artist in makeup would not neglect such matters.

Wentworth swung the coupé from the road, took a pair of powerful binoculars from a compartment, and made a careful scrutiny of the grounds. Finally, he thought he had found what he sought. Remote among the trees behind the sanitorium were two cottages. A smaller fence cut them off from the balance of the grounds and there was a gray-uniformed guard at the gate! That would be the place… the ward for "mental breakdown" cases, in the polite medical vernacular; actually, alcoholics would normally be cared for there. And any outcries would be attributed to the delirium of the patients!

Wentworth smiled thinly, tooled the coupé back to the main road and sped on to take the sanitorium from behind. It would be doubly difficult to invade the grounds by daylight, but he could not delay. He did not know how long he could continue to evade the police—nor how soon Munro would strike again!

He succeeded in working the coupé along a wood lane to within a half mile of the sanitorium grounds; made the rest of the way rapidly on foot. The high metal fence cut through a lane of fifty feet, where trees had been cleared away. Wentworth studied the barrier through a long minute from the undergrowth, then nodded and made up his mind. The fence might very well be wired to alarms, but there was no other way to cross unless he wanted to waste a good deal of time. He would risk the alarms!

His mind made up, Wentworth sprinted across the clearing, leaped high on the fence and, with a quick swing of his body, vaulted clear! Seconds later, he was making his way swiftly toward the guarded cabins.

So far, he heard no evidence of an alarm.

The search came sooner than even he could have expected. He was still a hundred yards from the cottage which was his goal when he spotted movement in the underbrush ahead, and crouched into the shelter of dense shrubbery. Moments later, the movement revealed itself as a gray-clad guard, with a drawn automatic in his fist!

Wentworth smiled thinly and waited in his concealment. This, he thought, was luck!

The guard came on steadily, sharp eyes stabbing about him. When he was thirty feet away, Wentworth slipped from the covert. His feet made no sound, and the man's back was turned. It was only when Wentworth was sailing through the air in his final leap that the man sensed his danger and started to whirl. He did not complete the movement…

Five minutes later, in the uniform of the guard, Wentworth stepped casually out of the woods and marched toward the cottage!

WENTWORTH'S eyes were wary and alert. He had identified the guard as a gunman once prominent in New York rackets, and it helped to confirm his suspicions that Munro had his headquarters here! He stepped boldly up to the cottage and tried the door. It resisted his thrust, and he experimented with the guard's keys until he found the right one.

Wentworth bounded inside, gun in his fist—and six men looked up apathetically from their seats about the living room. They looked at his gun, and then their heads sagged again. Despair was potent in the air, and Wentworth cursed under his breath, for he recognized everyone of these men! Each was a prominent broker from Wall Street—and the president of the stock exchange, Harvey Williston, was one of the men! Yet, the morning papers had told of a stock exchange dinner the night before, which all of these men had attended.

"Williston!" Wentworth snapped. "How long have you been here?"

Williston's head lifted heavily, and his eyes were puzzled and afraid. "How long?" he asked thickly. "You ought to know, really. I mean—"

Wentworth took a stride forward. "How long?" he snapped.

The man shook his head slowly. "A week. Five

days, maybe. An age!"

Through a long minute, Wentworth stood staring at the six men grouped so apathetically about the room; remembered the guards and the extra precaution of the fence. And this despair... Wentworth could feel depression eating at his spirit, and he swore softly. No question what that meant! Munro was directing upon these captives the device by which he could control emotions.

"By God!" Wentworth cried softly. "That's it! That's Munro's plan!"

He wheeled from the room, locked the door behind him. He had to get word to New York! He strode rapidly down the path toward the gate, toward the main building of the sanitorium! The guard there looked up sharply, but recognized the uniform and looked back to the magazine he was reading. Wentworth's gaze probed toward the main building. He would have to knock out this guard, and there were a dozen windows overlooking the man.

"Hey!" he called, hoarsely. "Get up here, quick! Something damned funny!"

He turned and hurried back toward the cottage, ducked inside. The guard at the gate hesitated, then toiled after him up the slight grade. Wentworth waited for him just inside the door. His punch was clean and hard to the jaw! Afterward, he hurried again toward the sanitorium. His mind raced quickly. He couldn't afford to go through the main exchange of the building, nor could he delay to find Munro. The office of Dr. Sabrunski would probably have a direct wire at least to the village of Ozone Springs.

He passed the group of medicine ball tossers at a distance of fifty feet, but no attention was paid to him in the gray guard's uniform. He strode in through the main entrance, saw a male nurse in a white jacket and turned the other way. His feet echoed along the hallway, and his eyes ranged ahead, picked out the door of Sabrunski's office. But he sought a private exit.

He turned the corner of the hallway and found it. He crouched over the lock, and his fingers were sly with the lock pick he was never without. The bolt yielded silently, and he eased open the door a slight crack. It was Sabrunski's office all right, and it was empty!

Wentworth waited only to lock the door again, then he bounded to the two telephones set upon the desk, snatched up the one that showed a number placard on its face.

"Commissioner Kirkpatrick. New York City police!" he snapped "This is an emergency call!"

THE connection went through swiftly and Wentworth, waiting, drew Kirkpatrick's long revolver from his waistband and put it under his hand on the desk. His eyes were narrow on the door of the outer office, and grimness traced his jaw in knotted muscles.

"Wentworth speaking," he said curtly, when he heard Kirkpatrick speak over the wire. "Quiet for a moment, Kirk. This is overwhelmingly important! I've fathomed Munro's new plan. He has kidnapped six members of the stock exchange, including the president! They're prisoners at the Oak Crest sanitorium, Ozone Springs. Listen! Munro is going to rig the stock market through his emotion machine. He'll probably concentrate on the floor of the exchange and drive them crazy with fear so that prices tumble to the bottom. For God's sake, get down there and stop it before what little prosperity that there is—is destroyed!

"Yes, I'll give you the names of the six men. Williston, the president...What? Good God in Heaven, then it's already started? Get down there fast, Kirk. Yes, the others are—"

The door of the office opened without warning, and a quick-moving, stoop-shouldered man with a mane of fiery red hair came striding into the room. Instantly, Wentworth snatched up the gun, and leveled it.

"Close the door and come in," Wentworth ordered quietly. *"This is the end, Munro!"*

The man stiffened. "Put down that phone, fool!" he snapped. "Don't you recognize me? I am Dr. Sabrunski!"

Wentworth smiled thinly, and his gun hand did not waver. He spoke softly into the telephone, "Hello, Kirk, I have Munro a prisoner here!"

The phone had no vibration in it, and Wentworth's eyes contracted. He spoke into the instrument again, set it slowly into its cradle. It was not that the connection had been broken; the instrument itself was dead! Somebody, without moving after he had entered the room, Dr. Sabrunski-Munro had contrived that!

The man was smiling slowly, with a deep movement of full lips. Behind gold-rimmed spectacles, his eyes seemed benevolent, but there was nothing kindly in his voice.

"Ah, now I know you!" he said softly.

"You are the *Spider*. It is you who created this little disturbance in the isolated cottage!"

Facing the man, Wentworth felt cold anger flow through him. This was the fiendishly clever, utterly ruthless devil who had murdered by torture so that he might line his pockets! He had him under his gun muzzle now, and there could be only one fate for him.

Monro shook his head. "No, you dare not shoot me, Wentworth, or *Spider*, or whatever you call yourself," he said. "You told Kirkpatrick you, as Wentworth, held me prisoner! If now, the *Spider* kills me… you see? You are afraid!"

Wentworth swore softly, and realized that he was afraid! There was nothing physical in the fear that ran through his breast. He knew that, once more without seeming to move, Munro had contrived to focus a fear-creating machine upon him! But that knowledge did not allay the rising tide of dread and apprehension that crept through him. He brought his powerful will to bear to combat the terror. His mouth became a compressed slit.

"Yes, I am afraid," he said slowly, "through your damnable machine. But it will not save your life!"

Wentworth slowly lifted the heavy revolver, and resolution was as iron in his soul! Nothing mattered now, save the destruction of Munro! He lifted the revolver and saw, with unutterable dismay, that his hand was shaking! The hand of the *Spider* that never trembled under any assault of horror or despair, was shaking like the hand of a foolish child!

Munro's smile had become sardonic. "You are terror-stricken!" he said amiably. "No matter how hard you try, you cannot even pull the trigger of that gun!"

SLOWLY, Wentworth eased himself down into the chair behind the desk. He braced his forearm on the desk, and deliberately set about Munro's execution! In spite of the support of the desk, Wentworth's hand still shook badly. He could not be sure of his aim, even at this short range of twenty feet!

"You cannot even pull the trigger!" Munro whispered.

Wentworth strained at the trigger and could not budge it! The perspiration sprung out on his forehead. Deliberately, Wentworth contracted all the muscles of his body! He started with his right leg, and drew the tension up through his thigh, along his side and into his shoulder. His hand was shaking erratically, but Munro dared not move toward him, lest the slightest movement shake the power he and his machine exerted. The contraction crept along Wentworth's right arm, as the will of the Master of Men drove it on, slowly.

He knew that his first shot would miss. It could not help but miss with his hand shaking so wildly. But he thought the shot would snap the paralysis through sheer shock, and after that—

Wentworth felt the tension slide into his hand, saw the cording of his tendons in titanic effort. Ah! His trigger finger—

The blast of the gun was like a cannon, and Munro went backward, reeling. His hand slashed out against the wall, even as Wentworth ripped the muzzle of the gun around… and the floor went out from beneath Wentworth!

His fall was as sudden as death, but there was no jar. The chair merely slid down a steep, smooth incline and rocketed out across another room below Munro's office. It brought to a halt against an overstuffed davenport, and Wentworth was instantly out of the chair, leaping for the incline. He knew that Munro, in desperation, had dropped him down an escape chute that had been intended for Munro himself in extremity.

Wentworth was scrambling up the slide, gun ready in his fist, when the trap door in the floor slapped shut! In the same instant, alarm bells began to clang throughout the building!

Wentworth wasted no more time in futile efforts to burst through the trap door. Munro was already in full flight, but there was one thing he would contrive to do before he fled. He would kill those six captives!

Wentworth knew that without thought. It was Munro's technique, to leave no one who might be a witness against him! Wentworth hurled himself at the door of the room, whipped it open and savage gunfire blazed at him from the darkness of the outer corridor, in which every light had been extinguished. Wentworth's gun bucked in his fist and he lunged aside into the protection of the darkness. But the *Spider* did not fire blindly. He never did. His keen eyes had spotted each spot that blossomed fire, and one of his slugs sped toward each flame!

Wentworth fired three shots, and through the rolling echoes of his blasting, silence fell suddenly upon the corridor.

One man was running away, but the other two made no sounds at all.

Grimly, Wentworth flung himself forward in a headlong sprint in the wake of the man who fled. He was in a central basement corridor of the building, but he was speeding in the direction he wished to go—toward the cottages on the slope of the hill! The screams of the fleeing man cut off behind the closing of a door, and Wentworth raced past it, on toward the end of the corridor. There was another door there, and Wentworth fired twice as he darted toward it, took off in a leap that drove his entire weight, shoulder-first, against the barrier.

It crashed open, and Wentworth plunged through, reeling. A window—

Wentworth scooped up a chair and sent it hurtling before him. The glass exploded outward and, before the fragments had shivered to the earth, which was level with the sill, Wentworth was through the opening.

AHEAD of him lay the graceful slope of the sanitorium lawn, the fence and the cottage. A man was going through that gate this very instant, a man with a mane of fiery red hair. Wentworth flung up the revolver, realized that Munro was out of range and began once more to sprint. He could feel the hard pounding of his heart, keeping pace to the thud of his feet on the soft turf. A clear exultation was in his soul. This was victory!

He darted through the gate, and the door of the cottage was closed! Wentworth's eyes stabbed beyond, but the woods yielded no trace of Munro... and then, within the cottage, a man screamed!

A shout rose to Wentworth's throat and he took the slope in two-yard leaps. The glass in the door shivered as the whole barrier crashed in under the drive of his shoulder. He staggered through the opening, and there was a muffled blast in the adjoining room! From the fireplace, tongues of flame starred out into the room, driving before them coiling, greasy green spirals and puffs of Munro's torture gas!

Wentworth's gun vibrated in his fist and the glass smashed out of the windows in the room.

"Out the windows!" he shouted at the stunned men. "Out the windows, before I kill you!"

He sent a bullet slapping into the back of the davenport beside Williston's shoulder, and the man yelped and leaped to his feet. He plunged out the window and Wentworth hung more lead close to the others, jarred them into motion.

In the nick of time, Wentworth sprang backward out of the doorway. The greedy tentacles of the green gas crawled after him, and he leaped on to the ground. Five of the men were picking themselves up from the earth, but the sixth had begun to scream. He was clawing at his face with futile, frantic hands! Even as Wentworth raced forward in a hopeless effort to help him, the man reeled to his feet and began to run. His face was a fleshless skull!

Wentworth sprang toward the other five men. "Get up the hill!" he ordered. "Toward the fence! And hurry!"

The roaring blast of a motor startled him, and he whipped about. From a shadow that seemed only a fold in the hill, but obviously hid the mouth to an underground garage, a powerful car leaped out. As it rolled down the slope, a machine gun began to spit from its window. The slugs tore up the earth under Wentworth's feet, glanced whining into the air. They rattled among the tree branches and another of the fleeing men screamed, and fell threshing to the earth. He continued to scream with every breath.

Wentworth flung prone and whipped up the revolver, but he knew, subconsciously, that he had only one shot left though he had reloaded in that swift pursuit across the lawn of the sanitorium. Desperately, he squeezed off the shot, saw the car lurch as the bullet took effect on a tire. It lurched, reeled, and dashed on!

Wentworth staggered to his feet, but the car was sweeping about to bring the machine gun into line again. Wentworth turned and dashed on toward the four men who remained on their feet. They still stared stupidly at the trees about them, at the man who kept screaming. They were still dazed from their long captivity under the dominance of Munro's emotion-machine! Wentworth hurled curses at them, drove them into the shelter of the trees. He fumbled more cartridges from his pockets, stuffed the chambers of his revolver... suddenly realized that the drone of the automobile motor was diminishing.

HE WHIRLED about, peered through the trees, and saw the car whip around behind the sanitorium. Moments later, there was the roar of another powerful engine. An airplane! It ripped into sight from behind the building, skated into the air with only yards to spare above the fence, soared toward the sky. Then it whirled back toward the woods!

Wentworth swore in despair. Against the machine gunning of an airplane, he was helpless, though the trees would furnish some cover. He herded the five men together and drove them away from the fence, through the woods to eastward. The airplane motor whined up to high pitch, and slugs began to rip through the trees behind them. But this once Munro had miscalculated. He had thought Wentworth would make straight for the fence.

Presently, the plane roared off in a bee-line for New York City, and Wentworth could get the weary men over the fence and race toward his coupé. He dragged Williston into the machine, told the others how to reach the main road, and jammed on the gas. The remaining four men would be safe enough now. Munro was the leader, and without him, the killers would think only of flight. Yes, they would be safe, but the stock market in New York was going crazy! Men were being stripped of their fortunes through the machinations of Munro!

Wentworth bore the accelerator to the floor and the powerful engine beneath that battered hood hummed its song of might. Wentworth was racing not alone to save the fortunes of the men on the exchange, though the crash of the market might bring the renewing prosperity of America tumbling about the ears of the multitudes. But Munro would be there. No doubt as to where he was headed. And Munro must be destroyed, lest scores, and hundreds more die under the torture of that awful gas, under the torment of the machine that could drive men mad with terror!

At the first town, Wentworth dragged his racing car to a halt, and bolted into a store to find a telephone. He slammed through another call to Kirkpatrick. It was possible that, by intercepting the plane, the police could seize Munro before he could do any further harm!

His phone call went through swiftly, but it was not Kirkpatrick who answered the phone. It was Captain Fillarty.

"The Commissioner went down to the exchange an hour ago," Fillarty said, and worry was in his voice. "Haven't had any orders from him that make sense, but a little while ago, he had me send a cop over to his safety deposit box to bring him all his securities! He sounded scared as hell—or just plain crazy!"

CHAPTER TEN
Rule of Terror!

WENTWORTH pressed down the despair that rose to his throat.

He needed no more than that to know that Kirkpatrick had succumbed to the virus of terror that Munro had loosed upon the exchange. But Wentworth could not blame him. He himself had been so terrified he could not shoot straight!

He threw his information at Fillarty, gave the license number of the plane, and rapidly put through another call for Nita. In swift words, he told her what had happened to Kirkpatrick.

"This is what you must do," he said. "Fasten a strip of some kind of metal about your head, pressing it down behind the ears. Fasten wires to that strip, and group them in plates upon the heels of your shoes. Go to the exchange then and see if you can get Kirkpatrick outside, and insulate him the same way. You'll be safe then from the terror!"

Nita agreed without question, but threw words at him quickly before he could hang up. "Dick, Warring wasn't robbed of that camera with which he took pictures of the *Spider*! He hid it, to prevent it being stolen, or seized by the police! He bragged about it to me yesterday. And he'll be here in a few minutes to take me down and help him recover it! I'm going to get those pictures, Dick!"

Wentworth said, violently, "There's no time, Nita! Get to the exchange, and let the pictures wait! Nita—"

It was no use. She was gone… and he knew that she would delay help at the exchange to recover those pictures. Nor would telephoning again help matters at all. He flung back behind the wheel of the coupé and sent it racing out through the city streets, boring into the long miles to New York.

Beside him, Williston, the president of the stock exchange, was beginning to recover a little. He asked slow questions and Wentworth flung information at him. Anger began to burn in Williston's face.

"I'll fix that!" he snapped. "Just get me to a telephone!"

Wentworth shook his head. "You don't understand, Williston. You're on the stock exchange right now. That is, a man who looks and talks and behaves exactly like you, is on the stock exchange. Everyone of those other five who were with you is being perfectly impersonated, also! Through those five men, and your own double, Munro—you know him as Dr. Sabrunski—will be cashing in heavily on this panic. When it is over, he will cash in the other way, by buying at the bottom of the market! Our only chance is to get there in person, and face down the impostors!"

Long before Wentworth had reached the outskirts of the city, the radio he had switched on brought him the news that an airplane had crashed in Bowling Green, but without any pilot in the cockpit. Wentworth's lips drew bitterly thin. Munro had jumped out by parachute, obviously, and would be even now making his way to the stock exchange to thwart any effort to uncover his operations! Munro was on his way there and Nita, despite her delay, should be already on the scene!

Those last miles of ripping down the West Side highway, the last half of the way with police sirens screaming in pursuit, seemed endless to Wentworth. Williston sat stiffly forward, hands braced against the cowling, and did not seem to notice that the speedometer needle wavered above a hundred miles an hour most of the way. The wind was a solid wall that yielded reluctantly, whining about the coupé. Other cars skittered frantically from their path.

The sweep down the final ramp was like a land-

ing in a racing plane. The tires screamed as Wentworth whipped the coupé over, and sent it scuttling through the narrow canyons of the financial district toward the stock exchange. As Williston batted open the door, Wentworth leaped to the pavement. He caught sight of Nita in the corridors before the broad doors of the Floor itself, and leaning against the wall beside her was Kirkpatrick! A strip of metal bound his temples, and wires dangled to the floor. He looked about him with the dazed incredulity of a man awaking from a nightmare.

WENTWORTH bolted past him, dragging Williston with him, and even so soon, Wentworth could begin to feel the crawling fear that gripped the entire building.

"Blow out the electric system!" Wentworth shouted back over his shoulder. "Pull the main switch, and be quick about it!"

Kirkpatrick shivered under the lash of his words, and Nita was running toward Wentworth.

"I got them, Dick!" she called, and shook her purse.

Wentworth nodded. "Keep off the Floor, Nita. There will be danger!"

Williston plunged through the doorway, with Wentworth a stride behind him. The Floor was a shambles. Men were going mad with fright, and it shone from their eyes. Their clothing was torn, and their voices harsh from shouting. Wentworth took a single glance at the big board with its electric lights that flashed the prices and consternation stopped him in his tracks. Even in his wildest imaginings, he had not expected such prices as these! The bottom had fallen out with a vengeance!

Williston was charging across the floor toward a man who was, in every way, a replica of himself. About this man was none of the wild disorder that marked the others. He faced about coolly as Williston dashed up. His eyes widened in surprise. Then he whirled and called sharply to the guards.

"Arrest this man!" he shouted. "He is an impostor!"

Wentworth flashed past Williston and seized the poser by the neck. His fingers tore at the flesh, found the thing he sought… two fine wires that ran down from beneath the wig that covered his head. Wentworth yanked at them savagely, and they broke.

"Now, fool!" Wentworth panted. "Now, Munro's fear machine is working on you! You are terrified! You will confess, for you are discovered!"

The man looked into Wentworth's stern face, and his own countenance turned pale. Wentworth's whole body was braced against the fear that was consuming him, but he would not yield. He could not. He was the Master of Men! He shook the fake Williston violently by the neck.

"Confess, fool!" he cried. "Where is Munro?"

The man's lips sagged open, and from the gallery of the Floor, a shot crashed out raggedly! The jar of the bullet, striking into his prisoner's body, jerked the man from Wentworth's grasp, tumbled him to the floor, dead. Wentworth flopped flat behind him, raked out his revolver… and saw only the swinging doors of the gallery through which the killer already had disappeared.

But Wentworth needed no second guess to know the man's identity. It was Munro!

Instantly he was on his feet and running. As he took off in a vaulting leap for the balcony railing, he heard a gong clang out peremptorily, and Williston's sharp voice cry out:

"The exchange is closed!"

So that peril was averted for the moment. By tomorrow, the explanations would be out, and confidence should be restored. The thought was a flash across his brain as his upreaching hands snagged the railing of the gallery. He swung himself up, yanked the gun from his trouser band, and plunged in pursuit of Munro.

Yes, the exchange would be equable tomorrow, but the people had no protection against Munro. There could be only one protection, and that was Munro's death!

Wentworth flung himself out into the corridor behind the balcony, and the way was empty. The steps! Wentworth reached them in a half dozen bounds, circled downward. It was just as he skated out into the first floor hallway that he heard a woman scream—Nita!

He raced for the outer doors and a motor roared into violent life out there. He plummeted out into the street, gun lifted in his fist. It was his own coupé that was roaring around the corner! He had just a brief glimpse of Nita's slumped body, of Munro hunched over the wheel. Before even the *Spider*'s lightning speed could squeeze off a single shot, the car had ripped around the corner out of sight, and was gone!

WENTWORTH'S eyes quested desperately over the street for a car. There were one or two, but they would stand no chance at all of overtaking hisown powerful coupé. If Kirkpatrick's car were near now! Wentworth ran for the corner, and a long, sleek limousine rolled out of the side street. The bearded Sikh behind the wheel leaned out to throw the door wide.

"I came with the *missie sahib, sahib!"* cried Ram Singh.

Wentworth sprang gratefully into the rear of his own limousine, flung a hand out to point.

"Down that side street!" he gasped. "Munro has kidnapped the *missie sahib."*

The mighty engine of the Daimler began to roar, and the limousine surged across Broadway with a smooth burst of power, hurtled downgrade toward the Hudson. West Street was empty of any sign of the fugitive coupé with its precious burden, and when the Daimler charged up the ramp of the elevated speed highway, that, too, was deserted. Wentworth was sitting tensely forward in the rear, and his keen eyes combed the way in vain. The Daimler arrowed along the drive at mounting speed, but still there was no trace of the car they sought.

Cursing, Wentworth ordered the Sikh back to street level, as it became clear that Munro had doubled on his trail to elude them, but it was too late. Emptiness everywhere; and Munro had made good his escape!

Wentworth beat his temples with his fists. "Munro can't escape," he said thickly. "He can't. There must be a way to trace him. Ah, Maurice!"

Wentworth sat bolt upright. "That's it," he muttered. "Maurice! He is being hunted by the police in the belief that he and Munro are the same man. Yes, he would make sure that Maurice was found, dead, before he finally vanished! Now, I need only to find Maurice!"

Wentworth caught wild laughter surging into his throat, forced himself to calmness. He need only do, in a few brief hours—but probably only minutes remained!—what eighteen thousand police had been attempting for days! But perhaps Nita would find some way of signaling him? There was a two-way radio in the coupé in which she was fleeing. There was a slim chance—

Dispiritedly, Wentworth switched on the radio of the car, and words stashed out at him immediately, words in the mocking tones of Munro!

"I hope you are listening, Wentworth!" Munro said. "I am keeping Nita with me for a while. Also the things that she carries. I am sure you will understand!

"Presently, I will have orders for you, Wentworth, and it would be wise if you obey! Otherwise, I'm afraid you will never see Nita alive again, even briefly!"

Wentworth was working the direction finder of the car rapidly, but he had barely begun when the radio went dead! Still, it definitely pointed uptown. Uptown, in Manhattan? But how to find one man and one woman—

Slowly, the firm line of his lips began to curve. He whipped forward. "Get me to a telephone, Ram Singh!"

Minutes later, he was bounding into a cigar store, into a phone booth. He put through a call to the Cornell Medical Center, asked for the staff physician of the psychiatric department by name.

"This is Richard Wentworth," he said rapidly. "I need some information vitally. There is in New York City somewhere, I remember having read, a small hospital which has experimented extensively in the control of mental cases with music. Can you tell me the name and address of that hospital? Yes, that's it! The Durward Memorial! Off Riverside Drive!"

WENTWORTH clashed up the receiver, and put through a call to police headquarters. "Fillarty? Wentworth.... Munro will be found at the Durward Memorial Hospital. He has prisoners there he will murder if you storm the place. Order a quiet encirclement, and try to catch him coming out! Yes! No, I'm not issuing orders to you, Fillarty, but if it's learned you had this information and didn't act on it, then Heaven help the entire police force."

Wentworth slammed up the receiver and vaulted across the walk into the Daimler, sent it hurtling northward again. His hand dropped to the left side of the cushion, pressed a hidden button there, and the seat slid slowly forward, revolved to reveal the secret wardrobe in its back. Wentworth bent tensely over the makeup tray and the lighted mirror racked there. Long before the giant Daimler swung off the elevated highway and circled toward the hospital, Wentworth was ready. His face had changed incredibly; a beaked predatory nose, lipless mouth, the long, lank hair were those of the *Spider*.

The Daimler slid to a halt before the doors of the Durward Memorial, and Wentworth leaped out. "Wait around the corner!" he snapped at Ram Singh. "If Munro attempts an escape, stop him!"

In the entrance hall of the small, private hospital, Wentworth checked. He threw back his head and sent the eerie, mocking laughter pealing through the corridors!

A nurse screamed, looked into the corridor from a doorway, and then began to run up the stairs, still crying out in a hoarse, frenzied way. An elevator door popped open, and a man peered out. For an instant, the eyes of the two men met, and then Wentworth uttered a shout and whipped out his automatic! He bounded toward the door, but the man had ducked inside. The door slammed shut, and the elevator was dropping toward the basement! Wentworth darted at the steel door above which a red light burned, and the door was rigidly locked.

His gun kicked against his fist, slamming lead into the lock, but still the door resisted. Screams burst out over the buildings, and there was the sound of men running in the corridor behind him. Above the clatter, Wentworth heard the roar of an automobile engine starting up!

Wentworth whirled and raced toward the front exit again. Hospital attendants scattered before his charge like leaves before the wind. As he hit the sidewalk, there was a grinding crash of metal around the corner, a hoarse cry.

Wentworth flashed out past the corner of the building, and skated to a halt. The Daimler was a piled wreck in the middle of the street and, on the walk, Ram Singh lay motionless! His right hand gripped his knife, and there was blood spreading from beneath that arm.

Dwindling up the broad reach of Riverside Drive was a heavy, closed truck as large as a moving van!

Even as Wentworth watched, Ram Singh staggered to his feet. His right arm swung limply at his side, but curses of pure rage poured from his lips. Wentworth bolted back around the corner, his eyes seeking desperately for a car he could use... and a limousine swung to the curb. From the front seat beside the driver, a man leaped to the pavement with a gun in his fist.

"All right, *Spider*!" he shouted. "We've got you this time!"

Wentworth was staring into the cold, courageous eyes of Carl Laird!

THE *Spider* laughed... and the gun in his right fist streaked out flame! The gun was wrenched from Laird's hand as if by a mighty fist, and a moment later Wentworth was upon him.

"Back into the car!" the *Spider*'s voice rasped. "Back, I say, or I'll blow you apart!"

Laird stumbled into the back of the car, and Wentworth flung himself into the front seat while Warring and Hunter were groping for their guns.

"Roll this car!" Wentworth rasped at Hunter, behind the wheel. "Roll it! Munro is escaping!"

Hunter stepped down on the gas, and the car lurched forward, made a screaming turn into Riverside Drive. Wentworth swayed easily to the rocking of the machine, and his two guns were restless. One rested against Hunter's side, and the other covered the two men in the rear seat. Warring, he saw, was smiling as usual.

"Laird," Wentworth ordered softly, "you will reach over with your left hand and take the gun from Warring's coat pocket. You will throw it out the door!"

Laird obeyed with stiff movements. His right hand hung limply at his side, and there was a trace of blood on the fingers from lead that had spattered from Wentworth's bullet. At Wentworth's further orders, he picked up two pairs of handcuffs from the floor, fastened his left wrist to Warring's right, with the link over the coatrail that ran across the back of the front seat. Wentworth turned his attention then to Hunter, disarmed him, and handcuffed him to the wheel.

"I regret these inconveniences, gentlemen," Wentworth said mockingly, in the *Spider*'s flat voice, "but certain injustices are sometimes necessary in the pursuit of justice outside the law! I take it you were at police headquarters when Wentworth phoned in that report? Yes, I'm afraid we'll find the poor devil is in that truck ahead, with Nita and a peculiarly vicious killer named Munro. You are going to overtake him, Hunter!"

Hunter nodded stiffly. His, face was very pale, but his hands were firm on the steering wheel, and his foot bore heavily on the accelerator.

Laird said gravely, "I underestimated you, *Spider*!"

Wentworth did not answer him. His eyes were boring ahead on the truck. It heeled heavily and swung into the ramp that stretched up toward the George Washington Bridge!

Wentworth's eyes leaped ahead to the magnificent stretch at the bridge, two hundred feet above the river, and his lips were pale. In God's name, what did Munro plan? A quiver ran through his body, and he felt the sudden slowing of the car. He whipped toward Hunter, and the man's face was completely drained of color, his eyes wide in… in *terror!*

Wentworth swore and jammed his foot down on top of Hunter's, bearing the accelerator to the floor.

"Steer, damn you!" Wentworth rasped, "or you'll be killed!"

A whimpering moan came to Hunter's lips, but he clung desperately to the steering wheel. Wentworth twisted about, and even Laird showed fear upon his face.

"Don't be fools!" Wentworth said, and his voice was strained. "You understand what's happening, don't you? That devil, Munro, has got his fear-generating apparatus in that truck ahead. It's working on us now. That's all it is!"

Hunter gasped, "I'm afraid!"

Wentworth had to force out words against the shaking of his whole body. "There's nothing to be afraid of," he said hoarsely. "Listen, I'll tell you how Munro generates fear, and then you'll understand that there's nothing to fear."

THERE were cars in the other lane of the driveway, heading downhill in the opposite direction. Things seemed to go wrong in that line of traffic as the great racing truck blundered past. Men lost their nerve, and with it the control of the cars. Horns blared wildly, as if the autos themselves were screaming. There was a frantic scream, and a car wrenched broadside in the stream of traffic. In a second, four other cars had smashed into it. They veered together toward the stone balustrade, and it did not hold them.

"Nothing to be afraid of," Wentworth repeated hoarsely. "In that hospital, they experimented with the control of mental cases through musical rhythms. With the use of that great, evil mind of his, Munro found out what those rhythms were. He analyzed the rhythms that are accidents in music, bringing a little lightness of heart, sometimes at others, grief, or even fear. By winnowing out those basic rhythms and emphasizing them to the exclusion of everything else, he found out how to play upon the emotions of men, especially men in the mass where the mob spirit can take hold of them!"

Laird was trying fiercely to concentrate. "I have heard nothing!" he said harshly. "I can hear nothing now!"

Wentworth shook his head. "That's the hellish part of it," he said. "If people understood, they might fear less. He has converted those sounds into electric impulses which play directly upon the brain itself! That is all it is. That's what makes us afraid now, the beating of unseen waves upon our brains. The rhythms of music. Is that a thing to fear?"

Laird said, "No, but I'm afraid!"

Wentworth laughed wildly. "I'm not afraid!" he cried. "We cannot be afraid. We must not be afraid!"

The car was screaming into the last wild turn toward the bridge. Hunter was clinging desperately to the wheel. His foot struggled to be free from the grip of Wentworth's, on the accelerator, but could not.

But the truck was rolling again, gathering momentum and speed. Wentworth struck the glass of the window beside him and drove it out. He leaned his body out of the window, and began to shoot. His automatic rose and fell as steadily as on the target range. Two shots and the two tires on the right rear of the truck went out with a hissing blast.

The truck veered wildly, rocking and swaying… but losing speed! It swung crazily to the right, toward the guard rail.

Desperately, Wentworth squeezed off two more shots and the two left rear tires of the truck exploded under the impact of his lead. The truck straightened out, but the tires began to dance and wobble crazily. The truck was barely crawling, but it was squarely in the middle of the roadway, so wide that it could not be passed. Abruptly, the truck jerked to a halt!

With a great cry, Wentworth wrenched on the handbrake of the car, and ripped the ignition key from the lock.

"You'll stay as witnesses!" he cried back over his shoulder, as he raced toward the truck. He saw the cab door bounce open, and flung two bullets against it as he bounded forward at top speed. The door slammed shut, and Wentworth heard a scream; heard Nita scream! At the same moment, he realized the truck was rolling backward!

A hoarse cry lifted into Wentworth's throat. He saw legs on the other side of the truck. Munro had leaped to the ground with Nita... but the truck was rolling backward! And the car, with the three Gotham Hounds helpless prisoners within it, was fairly in the truck's path!

Wentworth's guns lifted. He heard Nita cry out again, in pain. He had no target. With a despairing cry, Wentworth whirled and began to race down the gradient toward the stationary car. He could see Laird and the rest fighting desperately against the handcuffs, but that was futile.

Back there, Nita was being carried off by Munro, but Wentworth could not condemn these three men to the horrible death that was rolling toward them.

THE screams of the three men came to him now, even above the pound of his feet, above the rumble of the truck. He dared a glance over his shoulder. He was twenty-five feet ahead of the juggernaut, but now it was rolling almost as swiftly as he could run! There would be no time to use keys on those handcuffs.

Wentworth hit the running board beside Hunter in a flying leap. He reached through the window with both hands and seized the steering wheel. With all the power of his mighty muscles, the incredible concentration of his force and will together, he heaved on that steering wheel... and it snapped! It came free from its crossbars, and Wentworth tumbled to the roadway. He was up in an instant, and Hunter was fumbling his way out of the door. Wentworth had his gun in his hand and, as he flung toward the car again, he began shooting.

Twice more, as he leaped toward the car, Wentworth flung his bullets and they slashed into the upholstery at one end of the bar to which the two men were cuffed.

"Pull!" Wentworth shouted.

Laird and Warring looked at him, and their lips moved with words that Wentworth could not hear; could not even listen to. He reached in through the window once more, set his mighty shoulders.

Wentworth hit the pavement on his shoulders, and Warring catapulted out on top of him, dragging Laird by the handcuffs on their wrists. Instantly, Wentworth was rolling, thrusting them away from himself toward the side of the roadway. Hunter was out there, screaming, jumping up and down. The rumble of the truck was overbearing, was on top of them.

Frantically, Wentworth thrust Laird and Warring before him, heard the roar of the truck on top of him, and felt crushing weight on his shoulders. It increased intolerably. Cloth tore. Wentworth's eyes, straining upward, saw the body of the truck towering above him... then the strain released. With a final desperate lunge, he hurled his body against those of Laird and Warring, driving them inches to safety.

Wentworth staggered to his feet, reeling backward from the concussion that beat upon him. The truck and the limousine had met and the limousine was no more!

Wentworth looked down at himself, and saw that the tire of the truck had squeezed past his shoulder with the fraction of an inch to spare. It had been the pinching of the pressure on his clothes that had compressed him. He staggered when he stooped to catch up his gun. He was reeling when he began to run once more along the bridge toward where he had last seen Nita and Munro. His eyes quested wildly over an empty roadway, swept to the sidewalk and a cry that was almost a scream mounted into his throat!

Nita was fighting desperately, but Munro held her helpless from behind, and even as Wentworth watched, Munro mounted to the railing of the bridge!

For the first time, Wentworth became aware of the other people on the bridge. They were stampeding in wild terror, in the madness that Munro's damnable machine brought on. Munro clung to the cable with the hand that gripped his gun, and the other arm was wrapped about Nita. He began to shoot.

WENTWORTH was sprinting desperately. He was no more than fifty feet away, but he might as well have been fifty miles. He stood no chance at all to save Nita and Munro! He could not even shoot at the author of all this horror!

But Wentworth's lips were set in a rock-firm line and his swift brain was working. As he ran, he thrust

(Overleaf:) The truck and the limousine had met and the limousine was no more.

32
AMERICAN
FORWARDING

his guns back into their holsters, and snaked out the silken web! No time to uncoil it. Wentworth grasped an end, and threw the coil from him violently, threw it high toward an overhead cable that arched down from the sky. He was running, and the coil sailed high. It crossed the cable and swung back toward him. Wentworth was already in the air.

Munro's face was twisted into a mask of hatred and fury. As Wentworth swept toward him, he struck at Nita's hand with the butt of the gun, and pushed her body away from him, tried to plunge her to death in the waters far below!

Wentworth had ripped his gun from its holster now. Too late to thrust it back. Too late to do anything at all, except to pray speed into the swing toward the railing where Nita's sweet body was toppling toward death. He was only ten feet away and traveling with the speed of the wind, and he seemed to float tantalizingly. The flapping of the cape, stiffened straight out from his shoulders, was a brake upon his movement. His left hand, twisted and knotted into the rope, was aching with the grip. He… swung out over the rail!

Sweeping downward with his free arm, Wentworth flung it around Nita's body just below the shoulders, scooped her up against his chest. The strain on his left hand lifted a cry of sheer agony to his throat. Bones were breaking there, but it was knotted too tightly to let go. He was sweeping out, out over space. Far below were the steely waters.

Wentworth twisted his head about, uttered a cry of horror and despair. Munro was still poised on the railing, but he had discarded the revolver. Instead, he grasped in his hand something that glinted evilly in the rays of the slanting sun, evil and green glistening; a bomb of the flesh-eating gas!

It was only then that Wentworth remembered he had his automatic in the fist that was knotted under Nita's arm. But he could not point it. He could not free Nita to point the gun. He strained Nita closer against his breast while he twirled there at the end of the rope.

The jar of the gun in his knotted fist almost shook loose his grip upon Nita. He shut his jaw hard and shot again, again. Munro's mocking laughter came to him; mocking and triumphant. Fiercely, Wentworth jerked up his arm, bringing Nita with it, lifting her face to his and once more pulled the trigger.

The gun tore loose from his fingers. A cry lifted to his throat and, for that first instant, he thought that it was he who had screamed. But no such cry as that ever came from the *Spider*'s lips. Why… why, good God, it was Munro!

THEY swung past the railing of the bridge again, and Munro was there. His outthrust right hand was alive with the burning cold green fires of the gas, and he was screaming as he leaned out from the railing. He was pitching out into space. His scream came up, up, for an incredible while, faded out finally into nothingness.

Wentworth was aware then that hands were holding him, helping him down from the precarious grip upon the rope; aware that Nita had been taken from his arms. He turned his head heavily, and looked into the grim, icy eyes of Laird. Only those eyes did not seem so cold now.

"Yon was a bonny sight," Laird said dourly. "A bonny trick, and a bonny way for a man like Munro to die!"

And Wentworth shook his head. From his pocket, he pulled out the slim platinum cigarette lighter and thumbed open its base. He pressed it down upon the railing where, a moment before, Munro had stood; afterward, there blazed there the seal of the *Spider*! Bravado? Perhaps.

Laird had a gun in his fist, but as Wentworth watched, Laird turned that gun toward Warring and Hunter!

"Best you be going now, *Spider*," he said grimly. "The police will be here in a matter of moments. I'll hold these two hounds on the leash if they get too excited over the chase!"

Warring cursed Laird harshly and Hunter turned a heavy head. It was Hunter who spoke. "Don't be a damned fool, Laird," he said. "The *Spider* can burn down the city and I won't lift a hand to help catch him. By God, *Spider*, you're all man!"

Wentworth straightened and managed a very formal bow.

"Gentlemen, I thank you!" he said.

It was all he could contrive. He staggered off down the bridge.

IT was not surprising that Richard Wentworth, when they found him in the battered truck that Munro had abandoned, should be pretty badly used up; or that his left hand had been fractured. But battered as he was, he insisted on going straight to Kirkpatrick when he heard of Munro's plunge, so that he could demand that the river be dragged.

"You can't be sure of that man's death!" he said flatly. "It's possible to hit the water right from that height, and survive!"

Kirkpatrick agreed, and Wentworth spent a week in the hospital before he could be arraigned in court.

Wentworth was his old dapper self when he appeared, and there was a contrite expression on his face.

"Your Honor," he said slowly. "I want to plead guilty… to charges of obstructing justice!"

The Judge glared down at him through a long minute. "I've very little patience with you high-living sybarites who should know better! Going around committing crimes for a thrill! You're a disgrace to your class!"

Wentworth said, meekly, "Yes, sir!"

"Have you had enough of this playing at being a detective?" the Judge demanded, leaning forward to peer over his spectacles, "or do you think a prison term would help to teach you to quit meddling with the sure processes of the law? The law always wins, young man! Justice will always prevail!"

Wentworth said, meekly, "Yes, sir!" The Judge grunted, leaned back.

"The sentence of this court," he said grumpily, "is that you shall—"

The door at the back of the court slapped open and Kirkpatrick entered.

"I wish to beg the court's pardon," he said, "for the Intrusion. Dick, we found Munro's body in the river, and I was right. He was Maurice!"

Wentworth jerked about. "Are you sure? When I was his prisoner in the truck, I saw his right hand, and he had the seal of the *Spider* on its back!"

Kirkpatrick shook his head. "That's no good," he said. "This man had no right hand! There were some negatives—completely ruined!"

Wentworth shook his head. No, there was no proof yet that Munro was dead.

The Judge leaned forward. "Mr. Commissioner," he said. "Do you want to be fined for contempt?"

Kirkpatrick apologized hurriedly and withdrew, and the judge glowered down at Wentworth. "So they caught the man, in spite of your obstruction, young man! The court wishes to be lenient! The sentence is one year!"

Nita rose to her feet in protest.

The Judge glared at her. "Another interruption? Have you anything to say, young woman?"

"Plenty!" Nita snapped.

Wentworth said quietly, "It's all right, dear. After all I did obstruct justice!"

The Judge smiled suddenly. "I like your spirit, young lady, if not your good judgment. A year in prison, prisoner at the bar… suspended!" He chuckled. "But don't think it's going to be easy! In bed by ten o'clock every night. No drinking and no carousing. No moving without permission. No leaving the jurisdiction of this court. You can't marry, and your companions will be rigorously supervised. If you associate with criminals, you serve the full term!"

Wentworth said meekly, once more. "Yes, sir. It serves me right… for obstructing justice!"

THE END